THE DEEP GREEN

THE DEEP GREEN

A Novel

JOHN LYMAN

This book is a work of fiction. People, places, events, and situations are the product of the author's imagination. Any resemblance to actual persons, living or dead, or historical events, is purely coincidental.

ISBN – 13: 978-1511471411
ISBN – 10: 1511471417

john@johnlymanauthor.com

Cover art by Travis Schmidt

ebook design by Zebra Sun Design

For Susan, Chris, Tony, and Greg

ACKNOWLEDGEMENTS

I would like thank retroviral scientist, Anna McCulley, PhD, for her brilliant assistance in making sure I got the science right when I began wading into the deep waters of biotechnology and genetic engineering. I am extremely grateful to her for keeping me on track while she juggled work and family around my constant questions.

I also owe a huge debt of gratitude to my wonderful wife, Leigh Jane Lyman, for her unwavering support and assistance. Without her help I'd still be trapped in front of my word processor.

And finally, a special 'thank you' to my dear friends, Peter and Jay Kuys, for their unending support in all my literary endeavors.

"Everything is everywhere, but the environment selects."
Lourens Baas Becking

THE DEEP GREEN

PROLOGUE

The Congo – Present Day

The old DC 3 slogged through the wet sky, giving the man seated in the back only fleeting glimpses of the Congo River and the fog-shrouded jungle below as the pilots dipped a wing and aimed for the red dirt runway straight ahead. It was May—the rainy season in Yangambi, and the young woman waiting for the man beneath the shelter of a rusty hangar could barely hear the engines above the drumming rain when the plane emerged from the gloom and taxied to a stop.

Two days earlier the phone connection had been poor when she had called the research ship docked in the port city of *Matadi*, making it unclear if the man she was waiting for would even be on this flight. She squinted at the figure walking toward her. Dr. Peter Dinning smiled back through the rain dripping from the ends of his short-brimmed hat.

"Hello, Peter!" Allison Lynch shouted through the downpour. "We weren't sure you would make it."

"I almost didn't," he huffed. "But your call sounded important."

"It was. I think we've found something."

"In the river?"

"No... in the old Belgian research station ... on the second floor of the library. Musa found it."

"The library?" Dinning frowned. "You do know that most of the research papers in that place are over fifty years old."

"This isn't a research paper. That's what makes it so interesting."

"What then … a specimen of some kind?"

"I wish. Unfortunately, most of the specimens in the old library are long gone, but there's a picture. From what I could tell, it was obviously blind and covered in gas bubbles. If I had to make a guess, I'd say it died from a case of the bends."

Dinning stopped. His wet khaki shirt clung to his chest as he removed his hat and ran a calloused hand through a short crop of salt and pepper hair. "What do you expect me to do with a picture? We came here to collect DNA samples."

"I know. That's why I called. There has to be more of them down there."

"There probably are, but the expedition is wrapping up and the ship is returning to the states in two weeks … hardly enough time to retrieve a specimen from a species that may not even exist anymore." Dinning's voice echoed in the sudden silence when the rain stopped just as quickly as it had begun, leaving only the rhythmic plop of dripping water.

"Come on, Professor. The jeep's parked out front. You should probably change into some dry clothes back at the station. You'll never dry out in this humidity."

Hefting his backpack over his shoulder, Dinning followed the freckle-faced biologist outside, dodging a smiling boy pedaling a bicycle bending under the weight of a load of young banana plants. Returning the boy's smile, the two scientists climbed into a mud-splattered jeep and splashed away through water-filled potholes on a road that had been hacked from the jungle in another era.

A mile from the airport the jungle closed in overhead, wrapping them in a cocoon of darkness until they passed into an area of open grassland that fell away to the river below. All around them, rising like gravestones in the wheat-colored grass, Dinning could see the ghostly shells of elegant villas that had once housed the families of expatriate Belgian scientists before Congolese independence had sent them scurrying back to Europe in the mid-1960's.

They were driving through a post-apocalyptic-like vision of a once-thriving settlement that was slowly being reclaimed by the green tendrils of an advancing jungle, and Dinning knew the history of this place well.

Once the center for all major biological and agricultural research in the Congo between the 1930's and 1960's, the Belgian government had created a small city here. The massive complex stretched from the banks of the Congo River inland for almost 30 kilometers, and most of it was still visible. Roofless offices and vine-covered laboratories bordered disappeared streets, where the ruins of hundreds of residential homes spread outward from the old station's Art Deco club house—the center for all social activity that had once included a restaurant, a swimming pool, and even a bowling alley.

But now, fifty years later in a post-colonial world of decay, the voices of over 750 scientists and a thousand Belgian families had become nothing more than whispers on the wind. Dinning was looking at a ghost town, and it was startlingly evident that Nature had retained her crown as the preeminent force over the land. Like a slow-healing wound, the jungle was erasing the chaotic stamp of man.

Topping a rise in the road, Dinning's eyes were automatically drawn to the wide river below. Once known as the Zaire River, the Congo was the deepest river in the world. Not only was it the deepest, but it was also one of the fastest, and it flowed through a hot zone known for spawning some of the most lethal diseases the world had ever seen.

After all, this was the birthplace of HIV—the dreaded virus that had jumped from a jungle creature into an isolated group of humans before it jumped again, spreading outward in a ring of viral wildfire that had eventually engulfed the entire planet. But there were other things out there in the deep green that were even more terrifying—microscopic things—things like Ebola Zaire. The deadly hemorrhagic virus had evolved sometime in the past and continued to raise its virulent head from time to time, leaving its victims swimming in pools of their own blood before burning itself out and retreating back into its deep green hiding place until another unsuspecting victim pulled some invisible biological trigger.

But none of this was why Dinning and a dozen other scientists had traveled across the Atlantic aboard the research ship *Searcher* to one of the hottest hot zones in the world. They weren't looking for a cause or a cure, because disease was not the reason they had spent almost half a year in one of the most dangerous regions on Earth. They were looking for something else.

Driving through the ruins to the river's edge, Allison brought the jeep to a halt in front of one of the few buildings that remained intact—the still-impressive Yangambi Research Library.

"I thought you would want to stop here first, Professor. Musa's probably still inside airing out old books or cataloging something."

"Is this where you're staying?"

"No. We didn't want them to think we were trying to take over. The team set up camp in one of the old residence houses. There's no electricity or running water, but we make do."

"Peter!"

Dinning turned to see the widening grin on the creased face of an old African man walking toward the jeep with a pronounced limp.

"Musa!" Dinning jumped from the jeep and the two old friends embraced. "I see you're still working in the library. Are they paying you yet?"

"I'm afraid the government has higher priorities right now, Professor. The check we received from you last month helped. Thank you."

"My pleasure. I hear you've found something interesting."

The old man's eyes seemed to glow brighter. "Follow me."

For the past fifty years, ever since the Belgians had fled Africa when he was still a teenager, Musa Longolo had lived with his family near the abandoned buildings of the old research station. His father had worked as a laborer there, and Musa had attended one of the three schools built for the children of native workers—until the Belgians left and his world of associated privilege fell apart just like the buildings they had left behind.

Like most third-world children who viewed education as a saving grace, the departure of Musa's European teachers had left a giant void in his life. But the seed of learning had been planted. His eyes had been opened to the outside world, so he had begun rising before sunrise to walk for miles along a jungle road from his little mud house to a mission school in the nearby town of Yangambi. He began learning again, until fate placed him in the path of a speeding truck on his way home from school, leaving him with a fractured pelvis and a permanent limp.

Separated from his school by a long walk that had now become impossible for him, Musa looked for other ways to expand his mind. He began spending long nights in the abandoned library, reading old research papers written in French under the glow of a single candle. In a way his accident had been a saving grace, for over the years he had become a respected, self-taught biologist, and his expert knowledge of

xiv

the river and the deep green that lay beyond had placed him in a position of great demand by every scientific expedition that passed through the area on a regular basis.

Now, following his limping friend through the entrance of the old library, Dinning was dismayed to see that none of the broken window panes had been repaired, leaving the books and papers inside exposed to the dampness that seeped from the jungle. Without electricity and air conditioning, the deterioration of the library's collection had been accelerated by the elements, but every day Musa and his small band of unpaid colleagues showed up to do whatever they could to halt Nature's advance. The people of the deep green still prided themselves in keeping their library intact, and without them, thousands of books and carefully catalogued research manuscripts would have surrendered to decay long ago—lost forever on the banks of one of the greatest rivers in the world.

Inhaling thick moist air tinged with the aroma of mildew, Dinning and Allison followed the old man up a winding staircase that circled an open, wood-paneled atrium topped by a stained glass skylight. On the second floor, Musa beckoned them on with a wave. He led them down a darkened hallway, past glass cases that contained bottles stained with the residue of whatever they had once held, until finally they came to a high-ceilinged room. A wall of tall windows faced the river, illuminating shelves filled with yellowed manuscripts.

Reaching over his head, Musa teetered on his good leg until he found the manila envelope he was looking for and tossed it onto a worn table in the center of the room. As soon as he opened it, a photograph fell out. Gathering around, they all peered down at the image of an ugly, mole-like fish about the size of an adult hand.

The fish had lost all pigmentation, and a thin layer of pale skin covered two dark spots—ancestral remnants of tissue that had once been eyes, making it obvious that they were looking at a species that had evolved in complete darkness. To Dinning, it looked almost prehistoric. It was exactly the kind of creature he was looking for, but to be of any use, he needed a specimen.

Allison pointed to the bubbles covering the fish's body. They were looking at one of the hallmarks of rapid decompression syndrome; proof that the poor creature had been alive when something had rooted it from its dark world and sent it streaking for the surface.

"Has anyone else seen any of these fish around here?" Dinning asked Musa.

"No. We believe it came from somewhere farther upriver."

"That's true," Allison added. "It probably drifted from somewhere upstream after it surfaced. The water in this section of the river is almost 700 feet deep, and we've measured the flow at 1.25 million cubic feet per second ... enough to fill 13 Olympic-sized swimming pools every second. Finding a specific species of fish here could take months, if not longer."

Dinning nodded, suddenly overcome by a rush of sadness. It was abundantly clear that this fish and others like it had chosen a life of darkness over light out of a sense of fear—fear of the predatory creatures that lived closer to the surface. It had become a bottom feeder, settling for a dark existence at the depths of a muddy river to ensure the survival of its species, even if it meant going blind.

"The Belgians discovered almost 300 previously unknown species of fish in the river between here and Kinshasa, Professor," Musa said. "They believed most of them evolved in isolated pockets on opposite sides of the river without ever coming into contact with one another because of the strong current in the middle."

"I know. I've seen most of them, but not one like this. This is the most promising thing we've seen to date." Dinning laid the photo gently on the table and walked to a window overlooking the river. The latte-colored water held one of the highest concentrations of freshwater fish that existed nowhere else in the world, making it seem especially cruel that he might have been jilted at the altar of discovery once again because the very thing that could hold the answers to their questions had chosen to remain hidden. Like a mother protecting her young, Nature was guarding her secrets—and time had run out.

The freezers on the research ship *Searcher* were already overflowing with DNA samples collected from the jungle, and everyone on board was tired. They were tired of almost everything. They were tired of the constant heat. They were tired of the flies and mosquitoes. They were tired of collecting specimens from the mulch of a steamy jungle and the pleas for money or food that came from the ragged throngs of people who gathered on the dock next to the ship every day. But most of all they were tired of the monotony of living in an oppressive backwater, where life seemed to hang by a tenuous thread for those who eked out a barely sustainable existence along the banks of an ancient river. Even the simple act of dropping a fishing line into its murky water was an exercise in probability. Over the years the river had become a dumping ground for the generational detritus of a war-ravaged land ruled by a seemingly endless parade of violent warlords that flourished in the jungle just as prolifically as the verdant fauna that crept to the water's edge. Discarded land mines and other unexploded ordinance had been carelessly tossed into the river by their rag-tag armies, and more than one fisherman had discovered death instead of life entangled in his net.

At least the area around the old research station had been spared, but why the warlords had avoided it was anyone's guess. Some said it was the isolation of an area with no strategic value, while those prone to more colorful explanations said it was because of a large tree that grew in the center of the complex. Known as the *Tree of Authenticity*, many of the locals claimed it possessed the special power to grant long life to anyone who ate its bark, while others said it hosted evil spirits—a more likely reason the old station had never been raided by the superstitious warlords.

Despite the dangers, Dinning loved it here. Turning away from the window, he returned to the table. "Mind if I keep this picture?" he asked Musa.

"Of course not, Peter. Take it. Do you want the bones too?"

Dinning traded looks with Allison. "Bones?"

"Yes. I believe the bones of that fish are in a box around here somewhere." Musa began rummaging around some low shelves. "Let's see … I think …"

"DNA!" Allison exclaimed. "We assumed all the specimens were long gone."

"People still bring strange things to the library," Musa said, moving some boxes aside. "Ah, here it is. Still sealed."

With the same expectation felt by a father reaching out to hold his newborn child for the first time, Dinning took the small wooden box and gingerly broke the seal before opening the top. The aroma was fishy, and there were dried pieces of organic matter still clinging to the brittle bones. Closing the box, he carefully slipped it into his backpack along with the photo before they made their way back down to the front steps of the library.

Looking out at a line of dark clouds crowding the horizon, Dinning turned to Allison. "I'm afraid there's another reason for my visit. I'm taking you and your team back to the ship today."

"What?" Allison's face squished into a puzzled mask. "But I thought we weren't leaving for two more weeks! I assumed you'd be staying here with us tonight, and the last flight out of Yangambi is long gone by now."

"The plane I arrived on is a charter. They're waiting for us."

"But we still have specimens to tag, Peter! This place is a biological gold mine. Even if we stayed here another six months we'd barely be scratching the surface of one of the richest areas of biodiversity any of us has ever seen."

"I know ... I'm sorry, but this has been an especially bad rainy season, and the airport here is prone to flooding. Things have changed aboard the ship. People are tired. They aren't the same happy group they were when we first arrived. I'd have a mutiny on my hands if our departure was delayed because I left a team stranded in the jungle."

Allison's shoulders drooped. The reluctant look in her eyes told Dinning that she had grown to love the deep green and the people who lived there almost as much as he did.

"Fine," she huffed. "I'll go see if the others are back at the residence and tell them to start packing."

"The sooner the better. I'll wait here and catch up on the local gossip with Musa while you round them up."

"Not much gossip to share." Musa grinned. "Unless you want to hear about some missing chickens."

Alison moaned as she jumped into the jeep. "Very funny, Musa. Be back with the others as soon as I can find them."

After watching her drive away, Dinning's eyes narrowed at Musa. "Chickens?"

"It's an ongoing joke, Professor. The first night your team was here we surprised them with a chicken dinner, but Allison couldn't resist telling the others that they were eating monkey meat."

"I'll bet they freaked."

"Yes, but they tried to conceal their alarm like all westerners do by pretending to take the news in stride. Allison almost fell off her chair laughing when they said it tasted just like chicken. I don't think they've forgiven her for that one yet. Care for some tea?"

"Earl Grey?"

Musa winked and disappeared inside. A few minutes later the two old friends were sipping English tea on the front steps of the library, enjoying the stillness in the fading afternoon light. Unlike the chatter-filled meetings between friends back in the states, the only sounds were those of birds chirping in the canopy of the jungle, and as Dinning peered at the river below through the glistening blades of wet grass across the road, he thought of the fish bones in his backpack and the reason he had traveled across an ocean to be here.

Dr. Peter Dinning had begun his academic career in the study of ethology—a little-known branch of zoology. The term ethology is derived from the Greek word *ethos*, meaning *character*, and ethologists utilized a combination of field and laboratory work to study the behavioral process of a number of unrelated species instead of a particular animal group.

In other words, they looked for patterns—measureable patterns, and as time went on, Dinning began to see patterns of aggression within the animal kingdom that varied by a large degree from one species to another. His interest piqued, he decided to look at the differences between human aggression and the kinds of aggression he had observed in the animal kingdom. The results stunned him.

After years of comparative analysis, it quickly became apparent to him that the human species was almost overwhelmed by aggression. We were saturated with it. But it was a different kind of aggression from that he had observed in the wild. Where most animals resorted to aggression as a means to obtain food and fend off predators, the tendency toward aggression in humans extended far beyond the need to eat or defend themselves.

Humans seemed to use aggression almost like a tool. There was evidence that it even fed the pleasure centers of their brains, like a drug. But unlike the rest of the animal world, where the levels of aggression usually followed the same instinctual baseline for survival, the capacity for aggressive behavior in humans varied wildly from one individual to the next. And there was another observation that jolted him even more.

Humans were the only species that killed for sport.

At one end of the spectrum, there were those he labeled as being hyper-aggressive. These were the people who seemed unable to control their aggressive impulses; the ones who had been born into the world primed to pounce on anyone or anything that crossed their path. Yet at the opposite end of the spectrum, there were those who viewed the world around them in a more cerebral context. For them, the tendency toward aggression lay buried deep within their psyche—a dormant force that rarely expressed itself in violence, even when provoked.

The bully and the bullied.

For Dinning, the comparison between aggressive and non-aggressive humans was almost like looking at two similar but very different kinds of creatures, but any attempt to look at his own developing theories through the lens of those who would inevitably call them into question one day only brought more questions.

After all, everyone had their moments. We all got mad at times. Anyone who had ever watched a sporting event with any kind of emotion had felt the occasional tug of focused aggression, and a certain amount of aggressiveness was even necessary for the survival of a species—especially for a species that had become as dominant as the human race. But aggression linked to such a high level of intelligence, along with the fact that some possessed the trait to a far greater degree than others, was alarming.

Ever since he had been a child, Peter Dinning had always wondered why some people were just naturally nice, while others seemed to have been born mean. Like everyone else, he saw evidence of the less appealing nature of our species everywhere he looked. There were the usual murderers and crazies he saw on television every night, shuffling into prison in chains because they had just committed an act so violent they had to be segregated from the rest of society.

But then there were the ones we passed on the street every day—the ones who displayed all the warning signs but hadn't acted on their aggressive impulses yet. They were waiting for their turn, and we were all blissfully unaware that we might be in the predatory crosshairs of a person who possessed all the empathy of a crocodile, sunning itself as it watched us go about our daily lives.

They had a hollow, vacant look that telegraphed an invisible message. Stay away. And there was a collective instinct within the rest of the human herd that they were looking at a creature that more closely resembled something else—a loosed predator—and you could tell just by looking in their eyes that there was a pocket of meanness in them.

For most people, their first encounter with one of these individuals usually came in the form of the schoolyard bully. These developing little bundles of joy seemed especially adept at picking out the more vulnerable among us as they scanned the playground with lifeless, half-closed eyes. And their parents, who were usually just as bad or worse, would always whine when they were called to the school in the wake of yet another unprovoked attack by their tainted offspring against a weaker classmate.

I don't know what to do with him! That boy's always had a mean streak in him. What can ya do? He was born that way. Ya gonna lock 'em up? Why ... he's just a kid! He'll grow out of it one day!

But for the most part they didn't grow out of it. They went on to become the sadists and rapists and muggers and arsonists we saw being led into prison. And there were others who had even more troubling natures. Like the ones who began torturing small animals as soon as they were old enough to recognize an innocent victim—probably the biggest red flag of all in predicting the future behavior of a serial killer.

What was it that made these people so different?

The question rolled over and over in Dinning's mind. Were we living with the descendents of those who had branched off the human evolutionary path sometime in the past? Were we looking at a different kind of human who had lost the genetic roll of the dice to become something else?

In the absence of mental illness, there were several schools of thought as to why humans behaved the way they did. The behaviorists believed it was our environment that shaped the way we interacted with the world around us, while others saw us only as intelligent, biochemical organisms that responded to outside stimuli according to a unique genetic blueprint no matter what environment we came from. And then there was the theory that we were a hybrid mixture of both, which basically left us rolling our eyes with the knowledge that all we really knew about ourselves was the fact that we were a highly intelligent but unpredictable species with a tendency toward violence, no matter what color or sex we were.

To some extent Dinning favored the hybrid theory, because unfortunately he had seen both ends of the behavioral spectrum within his own family, and it had totally mystified him. Why had his father always been so pleasant and kind-hearted, while his mother had alienated almost everyone around her with her surly moods and angry outbursts?

Even their neighbors had shied away from her, going so far as to cross the street when they saw her in the yard outside.

He had also seen it in his older brother, Milo. While Peter was more like his father, enjoying interactions with friends, making models, or just lounging on the front porch with a good book on a warm summer afternoon, his brother had followed his mother in both temperament and action. He was always picking on the smaller children and getting into trouble at school before eventually dropping out. A year later he was in prison for committing a series of brutal assaults against homeless people.

What made people behave like that?

In the animal kingdom, a species was either aggressive or non-aggressive. There wasn't any such thing as a gentle rattlesnake. A rattlesnake was a rattlesnake, and they all behaved in a pretty predictable way when it came to being aggressive. Why weren't people like that?

Were we nice rattlesnakes or mean rattlesnakes?

Dinning had to know. After years of seemingly endless observation, he had finally come to the conclusion that the root source of problematic human behavior lay at the molecular level of our genes, so he did what any reasonable and driven scientist would do. He abandoned his comparative animal studies and returned to school, where he obtained a PhD in molecular biology.

For Dinning, the decision had made perfect sense. Just because something was big didn't mean it was more aggressive than something much smaller … even something microscopically small. Microscopic things had been killing humans ever since our species had risen from the great morass of wriggling, fertile life to step from the jungle as forward-looking, meat-eating, hunter-killer apes. But unlike John Speke, the explorer who tramped through Africa in 1858 looking for the source of the Nile, Dinning knew the source of the thing he was looking for would most likely be found under the beam of an electron microscope.

Somewhere out there in the deep green, lurking farther down the evolutionary chain that flowed through the Dark Continent, the answer to his question was waiting for him. It was waiting in a strand of DNA from one of the tiny, insignificant creatures that moved through the jungle, and if the source for aggression was still present in its undiluted, molecular form somewhere on the planet, then Africa was where he would find it.

In a way it was like looking for a disease. And just like a disease, the thing he was looking for had the potential to extinguish everyone and everything he held dear just as surely as any lethal fever that had suddenly jumped from the deep green into our twenty-four-hour world of fast food and jet air travel.

It was actually a very simple and reasoned premise, and the more he thought about it, the more convinced Dinning had become that our aggressive tendencies would one day tear us all apart unless we found the cause and stamped it out just like we would a disease. In other words, Dr. Peter Dinning was searching for a way to save us from ourselves.

Turning his gaze from the hypnotic lure of the river, Dinning saw the jeep approaching with the other two members of the team. Finishing his tea, he said his goodbyes to Musa and the others who had come to see him off before joining the sulking group of researchers for the trip back to the airport.

The overnight flight to *Matadi* was long, and the bumpy ride from the airport through the frenzied, third-world traffic to the harbor the next morning was slow. As soon as they were back aboard the research ship, Dinning made his way down some steep metal stairs into a world far removed from the one outside. Stretching along both sides of a narrow passageway, a dozen stainless steel doors opened into large freezers, where literally thousands of DNA samples collected over the past six months were kept at a constant temperature of minus 20 degrees.

Continuing past the freezers, he entered his air-conditioned lab and collapsed in a sweaty heap at his desk. In the relative silence, he could feel the muted drone from the ship's generator vibrating the steel deck below his feet as he leaned back in his chair and let the cool air from the vents above pass through the moist fabric of his shirt. After reclining for several minutes with his eyes closed, he pulled the small wooden box from his backpack and stared at the bones inside.

He wanted this specimen analyzed before they left Africa, but without a DNA sequencing machine on board, he would have to express-mail a sample of the poor creature's bones back to the university and hope the results were back before they sailed away from the deep green.

John Lyman

TWO WEEKS LATER - THE DAY OF DEPARTURE

The early morning breeze carried excited voices across the deck as Dinning exited the galley after breakfast. The ship's crew was making last-minute preparations for their trip back across the Atlantic, and with thoughts of home on their minds, no one needed any prodding. Peering up at an orange glob of sun, he continued across the deck and wandered down to the ship's lab.

As soon as he entered, a flashing blue symbol on his computer screen alerted him to the fact that an email from the university had just landed in his inbox. The message was from Dana Wilkins, a young research assistant and promising PhD candidate who worked in his lab at the University of Texas in Austin. In her early twenties, with oversized brown eyes, a sallow complexion, and spiky black hair, she was so pale and thin that Dinning had initially thought she might be battling anorexia or possibly even drug addiction. But after observing her working in the lab, he found that she was just one of those people who became so focused on the research that she simply forgot to eat; a problem he quickly corrected by holding morning briefing sessions in the college cafeteria to make sure everyone ate breakfast before they started work.

Dana had impressed him from the beginning with her enthusiasm for rummaging through the minutiae of long strings of unrelated data in marathon research sessions. The work of science was more like a game to her, and watching her enter the lab in the morning was akin to watching a track star settle into the starting blocks before a race.

Minus the tattoos and body piercings that adorned most of his other students, she was quiet and reserved and seemed to have a hard time relating to others on a social level. Her work was her life, and she was always the last to leave the lab late at night for the solitary walk to her spartan apartment.

But even after she had left the lab their research continued throughout the night, because most of it was done by machine. Specifically, it was a refrigerator-sized, three-hundred-thousand-dollar DNA sequencing machine known as a *Prism*, and Dana treated it like a baby. She even cooed to it when she walked by, much to the amusement of Dinning and the other members of the team.

Unlike the heavily-funded National Institutes of Health, with their seemingly unlimited computer access, or the biotechnology companies, with their vast financial resources, Dinning's team had only the one sequencing machine, and they were forced to compete with other researchers vying for time on the university's mainframe computer when they needed to run long strings of data. But that was okay. Dinning and his young group of researchers were just happy that the university had sprung for the single *Prism*, because unlike the gargantuan Human Genome Project, they were looking for something much more specific.

As Dinning had explained to the university higher-ups who occasionally stopped by his lab to see what he was up to, the human genome contained at least 3.2 billion letters of genetic code, but only three percent of human code consisted of genes that held the recipes for life. That meant that the rest of the genome apparently contained nothing more than random sequences of seemingly meaningless letters.

But were they really meaningless?

For lack of a better term, these small bits of DNA that floated in a coded sea along with billions of other seemingly unrelated bits had been referred to as junk DNA by the genetic explorers who had first opened the *Book of Life* fifty years earlier. But was it really just junk—or did the first researchers who discovered it fail to understand its true function? As Dinning liked to quote Einstein, "God didn't play dice with the universe," and the scientific community had recently begun to take a second look at it.

Within every living organism on the planet there is a code within its cells that determines its fate. In other words, the world is run on code, and why not? Computers run on code, and aren't we, after all, nothing more than highly advanced biochemical computers, albeit with a soul? As a religious man, Dinning believed that everything God had given us had been given to us for a reason. He had even read in a scientific journal recently that a group of Israeli mathematicians had discovered a code embedded within the Old Testament. To a man like Peter Dinning it was a no-brainer. We were surrounded by code, which meant that the Rosetta Stone for aggression was probably still embedded in the DNA of a seemingly insignificant life form that had evolved long ago and was still crawling in the moist earth at the base of a jungle tree or at the bottom of the world's deepest river.

Returning his gaze to the computer screen, Dinning noticed that Dana's only other concession to the serious way she approached her work was strangely absent. The line of dancing happy faces and exclamation marks that usually graced her emails was missing.

She must be tired.

Dinning rubbed his temples and frowned. A vision of her working in the lab formed in his mind's eye. He could see her long, thin fingers adjusting the focus of the electron microscope or typing away at her computer as she geared up for another all-nighter by gulping coffee and downing donuts while the bed in her little apartment grew cold. He was going to have to have another fatherly talk with her as soon as he got back, but for now he had to see what had kept her awake all night.

From: dana.wilkins@UTbioresearch.gov
To: peter.dinning@UToverseasresearch.gov
Sent: 04:38 AM, Tuesday, June 5, 2015
Subject: Imaging results

Peter,

Apparently, having to deal with all the flies and sweat may have paid off. Unfortunately, our sequencing machine is down now while some new upgrades are being installed, but I was able to obtain some images of a very interesting-looking segment of genetic material I isolated from the last sample of DNA you sent.

This is nothing like I imagined we would see when we first began looking for the biological markers of aggression. This is something completely new and different. I've attached the file with the images, but because our machine is down, I'm afraid I won't be able to sequence it before you leave Africa.

At first I thought I was seeing things, but as you can tell from the pictures, this is something brand new. None of us here knows exactly what we're looking at. I'm hoping your experienced eyes can tell us what it is.

As per our standard operating protocol, I've encrypted everything and logged it into our database here before sending it to our offsite backup computer. I'm running a check on the images one more time before I head out the door, but I don't think the results will be any different. Hurry back! I can't wait to find out what this thing is.

Dana

Against the sound of the ship's air-conditioning droning in the background, Dinning opened the encrypted data file and placed his cursor over the image icon just as the first gunshots rang out. Instantly he was on his feet. For a second he just stood there, frozen, trying to process what he was hearing as the adrenalin coursed through his system. Bolting from the lab, he ran up the stairs to the main deck. Through the smoky haze of gunfire, he saw people running and screaming in every direction.

A few feet away, a young crewmember was lying motionless in a pool of blood, his vacant eyes staring up into a cloudless sky, and to Dinning's left, men wearing camouflage uniforms were climbing over the sides, spraying the deck with automatic rifle fire as they advanced. They seemed to be coming from every direction at once, organized with a definite mission in mind.

"I want all the data from their computers!" a voice shouted through the drifting smoke. "Then we'll blow it."

Bullets were pinging all around as Dinning dove back inside and closed the steel door before scrambling down the ship's narrow stairs. Missing the last three steps, his ankle folded with a snap, but he kept going, hobbling down the passageway to his lab with the sound of screams and gunfire fading behind him.

A series of small explosions rocked the ship.

They were inside! They were blowing the doors!

Dinning worked to slow his rising panic. He tried to think. Something about the attackers seemed out of place.

More gunfire now, in the hallway outside the lab.

They were white! The men attacking his ship were white!

This was no local uprising or rebel attack on an American vessel. From what he had just seen, these guys were too methodical, too expert in the way they moved and communicated, making it obvious this wasn't some random terrorist event.

Who the hell were they ... and why was one of them shouting about their computer data?

This was just a scientific expedition, and they had only been collecting DNA samples from jungle ... unless.

Unless they had accidently stumbled onto something ... something worth killing for.

Whatever it was, it would take months to sort through all the data they had on the shipboard computers, and …

The data! Dinning ran to his computer terminal.

If that's what they were after, they weren't getting it!

With time running out, he hit reply to Dana's message. He knew he had only a few seconds before the door to the lab exploded off its hinges. With shaking hands he began typing, measuring his words.

Dana – Our ship is being attacked. The lab in Austin may also be in danger. Erase all research data from the university's mainframe and get out of the lab! Don't go home and don't contact the authorities until you hear from me. This is no joke. Ditch your cell phone and run! Now! Sorry …

Seconds later a blast sent the lab's steel door flying inward and a group of armed men swarmed inside. The lab was empty. Walking over to the desk, a tall, blond-haired officer with striking green eyes noticed a blue bar slowly moving across the bottom of the computer screen. Beneath the bar, he saw a message flashing in red.

ERASING ALL DATA!

"Stop it!" the officer shouted. A short civilian who was following behind him stared at the screen and shrugged his shoulders. "I can't."

"What do you mean, you can't? Just take the hard drive!"

"This is only a terminal, and it's locked. The mainframe is probably in a secure location somewhere else on the ship. It's being wiped clean as we speak."

"Find Dinning! We need that hard drive!"

A muscular sergeant stepped forward. "None of the bodies outside match his description, sir. Maybe he jumped over the side."

"What part of alive don't you understand, Sergeant? Our mission profile called for bringing him back alive. He's down here somewhere. Keep looking!"

The sergeant held his hand to his earpiece. "We're out of time, sir. The lookouts are reporting that government troops are headed this way."

"Damn it to hell! Did you set the charges?"

"No time, sir. We've been searching the ship like you told us to do."

"Fine. Leave it. We can't risk an international incident by getting tangled up in a firefight with the locals. Grab anything that looks important and let's get the hell out of here!"

CHAPTER 1

Port Aransas, Texas – One month later

Samantha Adams could already feel the hum in the air. Like an electric charge, the distant, muted buzz seemed to come from nowhere and everywhere at the same time, and the feeling was especially strong today. But no matter how many times she had tried to describe it to the lifelong residents of the tiny seaside community, they never seemed to notice the invisible hum that came from the ocean. Maybe it was just her. Maybe she was the only one who felt it because she hadn't been born on the island and the locals were somehow immune to its presence because they had never known life without it.

Rubbing the sleep from her eyes, she sat on the edge of the bed and slipped on a white, spaghetti-strap top and a pair of pale green shorts before walking barefoot into the kitchen and turning on her coffee maker. Blinking in the morning sunlight, she tied her blond-streaked hair into a ponytail and squinted through the window over the sink at the salty haze drifting over the dunes.

It was July, and the puffy white clouds of summer had long since erased the gray skies of winter. It was now high season in the beach town of Port Aransas, Texas, and hordes of tourists had begun to descend on the northern end of Mustang Island.

After pouring coffee into a thick mug, she walked out onto the front porch of her little clapboard house and looked down the stairs into the yard below. Like most of the homes on the island, hers was also built high above the floodplain on thick wooden pilings.

Settling into a wicker loveseat her mother had purchased the year before she died, Sam propped her feet against the glass top of a wrought-iron coffee table and peered through the tendrils of hanging plants suspended under the eaves. Everywhere she looked she was surrounded by memories of her mother. Practically everything in their house had come from garage sales, including the plants. But despite their humble origins, the eclectic blend of furnishings and artwork she had assembled over the years had given the house the sort of rustic charm professional decorators everywhere tried to emulate for well-heeled clients who paid twenty times the price to achieve the same look.

"Morning, Sam," Bee Hastings called up from the side yard of the house next door.

"Morning, Mrs. Hastings," Sam returned. "Your roses look beautiful this year."

"Thank you, honey. I see you're running on island time today."

"I overslept."

"You're working too hard, girl." The woman tugged on a twisted water hose. "How old are you now? Twenty ... twenty-one?"

"Twenty-two, and I know what you're going to say. I should be in college. I tried that ... remember?"

"Well, you need to try again, sweetie. You can't keep sellin' bait to those old coots out on that pier all your life."

"It's good money," Sam replied. "My little bait business pays the bills, and I just made the last payment on my sailboat. Right now that's all that matters."

"All that's fine when you're still young, hon, but remember what your mother said. She would have wanted you to finish school."

Samantha set her coffee mug on the glass tabletop ringed from sweating beer bottles the night before and slipped on a pair of worn flip-flops. "I'll keep it in mind, Mrs. Hastings, but first I have to make sure those old coots out on the pier don't run out of bait today."

"My old coot left before the sun came up," Bee said. "I think they're fishin' for trout behind Saint Joe's island."

"Hope he catches some. No one fries up fish the way you do."

"I'll save you some, Samantha."

"I can't wait." Sam waved and bounced down the steps. She could already feel the sand sticking to her toes as she crossed her patchy front yard and pushed through the squeaky gate in the picket fence before jumping on her dirt bike. She had a car. Well, not really a car. It was a rusty old VW bus she used to carry her nets and deliver freshly caught bait to her customers around town. But for now the bike would do. She was only making a quick run to the pier to check on the bait boxes.

With a staccato-like burst from the two stroke engine, she spun the tires and leaned into a corner at the end of the street, fishtailing in the fine sand that gathered in pockets on every road on the island. Twisting the hand throttle, she picked up speed, waving to a familiar face as she passed a surf shop and turned up a paved road that twisted through the dunes to the long white beach holding back the blue infinity of the ocean.

Driving out onto the sand, she parked her bike at the bottom of the stairs leading up to a quarter-mile-long concrete pier that extended out over the warm water of the Gulf of Mexico. More fish had been reeled up onto its stained wooden decking than on any other pier in the Gulf, including a 13 foot tiger shark that had been winched up from the depths back in the 1960's.

At the top of the stairs, Sam paused for a moment to watch a pair of surfers paddling furiously to catch a small three-footer before she entered a briny-smelling bait shop. Already she could tell there was trouble.

"I was just getting ready to call you," Mable Sanders called out from behind the aged, plywood counter.

"Why ... what's wrong?"

"The pumps on the live bait tanks stopped working last night. Half the bait died, and with all the tourists here now I'm afraid we'll run out before the end of the day."

"Let me check them for you, Mable." Sam walked past an ice machine and a glass cooler filled with beer and sandwiches to a row of fiberglass-coated wooden tanks foaming with circulating sea water. Peering down into the largest tank, she saw hundreds of small, silvery fish darting back and forth in the bubbling salt water, while in the next tank, shrimp crackled as they propelled themselves through the briny froth. "These tanks look fine to me, Mable."

"They are now. Bob just fixed the pumps. I already threw all the dead bait over the side."

Sam laughed. "I'll bet the surfers loved that."

"Yeah, you should have seen 'em scatter when I threw all those fish over the railing this morning. I don't know what the big deal is anyway. They all know they're swimmin' with sharks out there, but every time a drop of fish blood hits the water they think it's gonna drive a big ole shark right up their little white butts."

"Well, you know what they say, Mable. As soon as you go into the water you become part of the food chain."

"Yeah, but everyone knows these little sand sharks around here don't bother no one. This here pier is a lot more dangerous than any ol' shark. Why only last week one of them surfers was ridin' a wave right through the pilings and got snagged by a hook. Thank God Doc Roberts was out here fishin' that day. He pulled that damn hook outta that boy's shoulder lickety split. Never saw a man get a hook out that fast. He told the boy to stay out of the water until it healed, but the kid was back surfin' the next day anyway. Those kids don't listen to no one."

Samantha smiled as she peered back into the tanks. "You've got enough fish to make it through the day, but you'll run out when the night fishing crowd shows up. Tell you what, Mable. I've got to get some mullet for the sport fishing guys. I'll net some extra bait fish for you while I'm at it."

"Thanks, Sam. I knew I could count on you, hon."

Pushing through the screen door into the sunshine, Sam strolled down the length of the pier to see what the locals were catching. Most of the people she saw along the railings were regulars who seemed more interested in drinking beer than catching fish, but every now and then one of them would reel in a good-sized speckled trout, squealing in delight like a kid who had just caught their first fish.

She could already feel the heat radiating from the bleached wooden planks as she watched the way the sun's rays angled down through the clear blue water—liquid searchlights illuminating the depths below. She loved watching the way the color of the water changed closer to shore. From the sapphire-like blue of the deeper water, the color of the sea turned a frothy green when the two worlds of water and land collided on the underwater sandbars before finally crashing up onto the crystalline beach.

In a metaphor that mimicked life, the sea was constantly changing. Samantha wished she could just stay out there all day, looking out over the water and feeling the sun on her back as the waves crashed between the pilings below, enveloping the pier in a salty mist. Sometimes she would hold her finger in the air for a few seconds and then lick it so she could taste the sea, and no matter what kind of day she was having, just being near the water seemed to make all her troubles disappear.

Turning away from the railing, the warmth on Samantha's shoulders reminded her that she had forgotten her sun block again as she began to make her way back to the beach. A man everyone referred to as *Old Hank* was walking toward her, his sack lunch and beer cooler in one hand and a fistful of ancient fishing rods in the other.

"Hello, Hank," Sam said. "Whatcha fishin' for today?"

The grizzled old man pushed a faded red baseball cap back over a mass of thick white hair and smiled back through a pair of missing front teeth. "Maybe a great white. A shrimper saw one last week between here and Brownsville."

"Must have been some other kind of shark, Hank," Sam said. "Water temperature here is around eighty degrees ... great for swimming but too warm for those big boys."

"Tell that to the men who caught one right here off the coast back in 1943. Big as a pickup truck."

"I heard that story too, Hank. Personally, I think it's just bar talk."

"Nope, I remember. Saw it myself. I was just a kid then, but I'll never forget that monster. Everyone told me it was dead but it scared the hell outta me. Once you look into those black eyes you never forget 'em."

Old Hank's gaze drifted out over the water, giving Samantha a chance to study his leathery skin. The creases were so deep that the skin inside the folds probably hadn't seen daylight in years. It was safe to say that the old man had never worn sunscreen a day in his life, and when you looked into his gray eyes, it was almost as if you were looking at the sea on a stormy day.

"Well, good luck on your shark hunt." Samantha grinned. "Just don't let yourself get pulled off the pier when it hits your line."

Hank winked and headed off. His fishing rods were almost as old as he was, and Sam wondered how he ever managed to land anything without them snapping. Even if he did ever happen to snag the thousand-pound monster he was so intent on catching, his rods would snap like dry twigs on the first pull.

Mounting her dirt bike, Samantha looked skyward. The sun was already high, meaning she would have to step up her pace if she was going to catch all the bait she had promised her customers. Speeding back home, she traded the bike for the VW bus and headed south on the coastal highway. Three miles outside of town she turned off on a side road made from crushed sea shells. The dazzling white road twisted through a reedy marshland filled with birds until it ended on the bay side of the island.

Known in geological terms as a barrier island for its proximity to the mainland, the little split of land she called home was barely two miles wide and less than twenty miles long. With the Gulf of Mexico running along the east side of the island, and Corpus Christi Bay lapping at its western shore, Mustang Island was centered in a chain of barrier islands that ran along the Texas coast from Galveston past Corpus Christi and the famed King Ranch all the way down to the Mexican border.

At the southern end of the island, a series of bridges provided a link with the mainland. But for the residents of Port Aransas at the northern end, their closest link was by ferry boat across the fast-moving water of a deep ship channel. It was this single watery barrier that had thankfully kept the island-like feel of the place intact.

Jumping down from the driver's seat of her beloved VW, Sam paused to watch the water splash against a distant promontory point on the mainland before kicking off her flip-flops and pulling a fishy-smelling throw net from the back of her little bus. With the nylon net hanging from her shoulder, she waded out into the clear, shallow water, feeling the soft sea grass between her toes as she stood and waited for the tell-tale circular pattern of motion moving across the water—a sure sign that a darting school of silvery fish was swimming just below the surface.

Turning her head, she watched the current and tried to differentiate between the normal wave action and the shadows cast by passing clouds against the white sand bottom, until finally she saw the ripples of a dark circle moving straight toward her. In the blink of an eye she threw her net in a practiced arc over the moving shape and yanked on the line. Hundreds of tiny fish thrashed in a panicked attempt to flee as she dragged the net through the water and returned to the bus, where she released the wriggling mass into one of two fiberglass tanks filled with fresh sea water.

Working through the morning, she repeated the process, moving down the shoreline and looking for the larger schools of mullet so prized by the sport fishing crowd. Every morning their high-speed fishing boats would leave the marina and head out into the Gulf—their brilliant white hulls flanked by long outrigger poles that extended out over the water, making it look like they were about to take flight as they leapt over the waves on their way to the offshore fishing grounds in search of marlin or sailfish.

The captains of the sport fishing boats were a world unto themselves. Masters of their universe, they were a picky bunch when it came to choosing those who supplied their bait. Their reputations as skippers depended on their ability to find and catch some of the biggest fish in the world for those willing to pay the price, and the bait they used was a big part of their success.

For years, ever since Samantha had been a kid, she had hung around the docks. Catching bait for extra money had been a natural progression, and once the captains noticed that she could be depended upon to deliver fresh bait on a regular basis, she suddenly found herself making the rounds of the docks twice a day to ensure that the freezers on all the boats were well-stocked with mullet and ribbon fish for the next day's hunt.

With the tanks in her bus now filled with thrashing life, Samantha sat in the open door and sunned herself, thinking back to the day when her mother had first brought them to this isolated strip of land surrounded by the sea. Sam had been only five years old the day they arrived on the island, and her mother's strength was still seared in her mind. With almost no money, she had taken her daughter and fled from an abusive husband and a house in Houston filled with nothing but bad memories.

Gazing out across the marshlands, Sam couldn't resist looking at the ruins of the first place they had lived. What little remained of the old Seaside Inn was still visible between two high rise condominiums facing the beach. Once the crown jewel among the old beach resorts scattered up and down the Texas coast in the 1960's, the well-dressed guests of the day had been greeted by the sight of a cantilevered roofline that swooped over a multi-level brick building designed by a protégé of the late Frank Lloyd Wright.

Nestled in the dunes between the highway and the Gulf, the building flowed with the land like most Wright-inspired structures. The bright patterns of the sun-bleached world outside mixed with the dark wood tones of the elegant space inside, where flickering candlelight highlighted diner's faces as they leaned on white tablecloths and gazed out through

7

floor-to-ceiling glass at the same water their seafood dinner had been swimming in only hours before.

Wright's handprint could even be seen in the way the hotel's rustic bungalows stair-stepped down to the beach away from the main building. The design coaxed the guests to walk outside, where they inhaled the salty air and felt the sea breeze in their hair as they made their way in formal dinner attire along a wooden boardwalk toward the sound of soft Brazilian jazz playing in the lounge.

Unlike the line of uninspired condominiums that now dotted the coast, the ambiance of the place had been magical, drawing big name sport fishermen from all over the country when they descended on the island for the big fishing tournament every year. But big name fishermen weren't the only ones drawn by its allure. The elegant little inn had also been a beacon of hope for Samantha and her mother the day they had arrived on the island—penniless and with a broken-down old car that had actually broken down on the beach road right in front of the hotel.

For almost an hour they had sat in the broiling sun with steam drifting from the open hood of the old Chevy, until the two men who owned the inn noticed their plight and walked down to the road to see if they could help. But the old car was obviously on its last leg. Like an aged horse that had finally found greener pastures, it refused to move, leaving the men with only one option. They would have to take the woman and child in and give them a place to stay for the night.

But that one night had stretched into years after the men noticed Sam's mother sweeping sand from the front steps and offered her a job as a housekeeper. The job had included a small cottage, where Sam and her mother had lived until they were finally able to buy the little clapboard house in town.

Samantha had naturally captured the two men's hearts, and as time went on, they became like surrogate fathers to her. They had reveled in taking turns teaching her to play the grand piano that faced the sea and making sure she knew how to swim in the hotel's pool. And like a family, they had taken her on outings to the pier, where she had learned how to fish and clean her catch for the inn's picky chef.

Now, looking across the highway at the bleached remains sticking up through the sand, Sam knew she was looking at the first place she had ever really called home. But just like all the other structures on the beach from a bygone era, it too had become nothing more than another nameless ruin.

Like the inn, the two men were also now gone—victims of too many alcohol-fueled nights that included men from out of town who gathered around the circular pool late at night far from prying eyes. Their fiery lifestyle had naturally given the locals something to gossip about through the years, but despite the rumors, nothing could erase the love Sam and her mother had felt for the two men who had rescued them from the side of the highway.

Even the locals, as hard-nosed and crusty as they tried to appear, had embraced the two men as their own. They had always been tolerant of those with differing lifestyles as long as they didn't flaunt it. Their enlightened worldview had brought an eclectic taste of culture to the small fishing village long before it had evolved into a condominium-encrusted party town more famous for spring break than the grand fishing tournaments that had even attracted such luminaries as Franklin D. Roosevelt. The president had traveled there to fish for the giant tarpon back in the 1930's, and his signature on a tarpon scale was still on display in the lobby of the famed Tarpon Inn.

The high-pitched scream of a racing motorcycle jolted Sam from her reverie when she saw a bright red bike turn off the pavement, leaving a cloud of white dust in its wake as it sped along the shell road and slid to a stop behind her bus. Leaning the bike on its kickstand, the grinning rider removed his helmet and wiped the sweat from his shaved head before grabbing Samantha around the waist and kissing her on the lips. It was Brian Slater, her boyfriend.

"I thought you were on duty today," Samantha said, gazing into his mischievous blue eyes.

"I switched shifts with Alan. He had a family emergency … so guess who's on flight call tonight."

"Tonight!" Sam threw her nets into the back of the bus and sat in the open doorway. "But we had plans … remember? Dinner for two at the Tarpon Inn. We've had reservations for a month, and this is the height of tourist season. It's probably the only time all year I'll get to wear a dress and put on makeup."

Brian gave her his best puppy dog look. "I'm sorry, Sam, but the Coast Guard doesn't care about my plans. I'm a rescue swimmer … that's what I do … it's what I've always wanted to do. When they say I'm

9

on call, then I'm on call. My year-long probationary period is almost over, and if I start whining about missing a date with my beautiful girlfriend, it probably wouldn't go over too well. Maybe we can get a reservation for tomorrow night."

Samantha looked down and brushed the sand off her shorts in a failed attempt to hide her disappointment. "You know that's impossible. The waiting list is a month long this time of year."

"I'm sorry, honey … really. I was looking forward to it just as much as you were. I'll make it up to you … I promise. I have a leave coming up in a few months. Maybe we can take that skiing trip you're always talking about."

"A skiing vacation would be nice." Samantha had never seen snow … or even a mountain for that matter. "It's okay … really. I knew what I was getting into when I started dating a *coastie*. All the other wives and girlfriends told me I could expect this kind of thing when we started going out. Anyway, Mable's pump at the bait shop broke down again, and I've got a ton of bait to deliver this afternoon. Maybe I'll take my sailboat out for a little sail before the sun goes down."

Brian's eyes instantly came alive with the familiar flash of protection so often seen on the faces of men who risked it all to save the lives of others at sea. "You know you shouldn't be sailing out in the Gulf all alone. Little mistakes have a way of turning into big tragedies out there."

"I'll be fine, babe. I just checked the batteries in my EPIRB like you told me. Maybe I'll set it off just so you can come rescue me."

Brian rolled his eyes. "Yeah, that's a great way to win friends in the Coast Guard."

"You know I'm just kidding, but at least now you know you can find me just in case. I'm probably the only girl who's ever received an emergency position-indicating radio beacon for Christmas. Not to mention the new life jackets and the big red fire extinguisher you bought me for my birthday."

"You had to have those things, Sam, and I didn't have any money left over for anything else."

"I'm teasing you, Brian. Those were the best presents you could have given me. I guess you've noticed by now that I'm not much of a jewelry kind of girl. I'd much rather have what you gave me than some fancy fluff designed to make me weep with joy and jump into your arms. Maybe that's why I love you so much."

10

"I just want you to be safe out there." Brian paused to look at some dark clouds in the distance. "Maybe you could do a radio check with the station every now and then so I know you're alright."

Samantha touched his forehead with hers and crinkled her nose. "Really, Brian, I'll be fine. Besides, I know how you hate it when the other guys hear you say '*I love you Sam*' on the radio."

Brian laughed. "Yeah … one of the new guys almost peed himself when he heard me say that the other day."

Samantha grinned, but her grin quickly faded when she glanced down at her black divers watch. "Holy cow! I'm really running late now. I'll call you tonight when I get back from my sail. Maybe I can drop by the station with some dinner for you and the guys."

"Sounds great." Brian lifted her off her feet and kissed her again before pulling his helmet on and mounting his bike. As soon as he turned out onto the highway, she could hear him going through the gears as the sound of his motorcycle faded in the distance.

Climbing back into her bus, Sam started the engine and drove to the pier. After filling all of Mabel's bait tanks she headed for the marina, where she began checking the bait freezers on all the sport fishing boats that had just returned. Stepping onto the deck of a sleek new boat with the name *Just in Time* painted across the stern in gold script, Sam looked up to see the young captain climbing down from the flying bridge. Reaching into a cooler, Randy Monroe pulled out a beer and popped it open. "Want a beer, Sam?"

"It's a little early for me, Randy, but thanks anyway."

Wearing a white T-shirt and tan shorts, he walked barefoot to the stern and sat in a large padded chair bolted to the deck. Pushing an expensive-looking pair of blue-tinted sunglasses up into his sun-bleached hair, he scratched the stubble on his chin and watched her retrieve some fat mullet from her wheeled bait box.

"How's Brian?" Randy asked.

"He's on duty tonight."

"I thought you guys were going out on the town. Julie loves those family-style feasts they put on over at the inn on Saturday nights."

"You can have our reservations. In fact, I'll call them as soon as I'm through with your bait."

"Really? That would be great. I think my wife needs a break from the kids."

11

"You guys have five now, right?"

"Uh, yeah, I think so," Randy laughed.

"You do know what causes that, don't you?"

"Very funny, Samantha. By the way, Julie has given me a mission. She wants me to find out when you and Brian are going to tie the knot."

Sam opened the boat's freezer box without missing a beat and began stuffing it with bait. "We've talked about it, but you know what it's like being married to someone in the military. He could be transferred any time, and I'm never leaving the island. Port Aransas is my home."

Shrugging his wide shoulders, Randy leaned over to help her lift a bag of ribbon fish just as a couple of men with beers in their hands walked by on the dock behind them.

"Hi there, sweet cheeks," one of the men shouted out. "What do you local girls like to do for fun around here on a Saturday night?"

Before Samantha could reply, Randy was on the dock, along with several other captains who had heard the man's remark.

"She usually enjoys watching people who call her *sweet cheeks* get the shit kicked out of them," Randy said, jerking the sunglasses off the top of his head. "So unless you want to be her entertainment for the afternoon, you two might want to keep right on walking and watch the way you talk to the ladies around here."

The two men looked around to see that they were quickly becoming surrounded by other beefy-looking sea captains, and some were holding gaff hooks in their hands.

"Uh, we meant no disrespect," one of the men said quickly, backing away from the fire in Randy's eyes.

"Yeah, too much beer and sun," the other man chimed in. "Sorry, miss. We'll just be on our way. No hard feelings … huh?"

Against a wall of silent glares, the two drunken tourists squeezed through the circle of grizzled fishermen and staggered up the dock toward the restaurant.

Randy pushed his sunglasses back on his head and grinned. "Well, what are you going to do tonight, sweet cheeks?"

"I'm going to drill holes in the bottom of your million-dollar boat." Sam laughed as she looked around at all the captains grinning back at her. She loved the fact that she lived on an island surrounded by a bunch of big brothers who were always looking out for her. Now that her mother was gone, they were her family, and she could never see herself leaving this little fishing village she called home.

"Actually, Randy," Sam continued, "I'm taking my boat out for a little sail before it gets dark. Hank says there's a great white out there. Maybe I can spot him for you."

Randy rolled his eyes. "I think Hank's been drinking too much of the cheap stuff lately."

"I heard the same story, Randy," said a short, heavyset captain. "Bob White told me he saw something big and dark cross under his boat yesterday. Said he didn't know what it was … and Bob can always tell you what's swimmin' under his boat."

"Now see what you've gone and done, Sam?" Randy frowned. "You've got the most superstitious bunch of guys in the world all stirred up over some fish story Old Hank told you. Next thing you know they'll be seein' sea monsters out there."

"Sorry, guys. I was just repeating what I was told. Consider the source. Anyway, I've got to get a move on before I lose all my daylight."

"Okay, but you be safe out there, Sam. There's a storm front moving in from the north, but it shouldn't hit until after dark."

"Thanks. I'll keep my eyes open."

"You do that, and you can double my bait order for next week."

"Yeah," another captain chimed in. "Same for me, and that probably goes for the rest of us."

Samantha looked back at the men for a moment until it finally dawned on her. "Oh, right … the big fishing tournament. Looks like this might be my last free time for awhile."

Sam started to leave but turned back. "Oh, and thanks for coming to my rescue, guys. I do appreciate it."

"No problem, sweet cheeks," Randy said, laughing, then ducking when Sam threw a ripe mullet over his head before walking off the dock.

Pulling her wheeled bait box behind her, she rolled it up a little ramp into her bus and drove around to the side of the marina where the smaller boats were tied up. Stepping out, she looked down the dock at her new pride and joy—a twenty-four-foot sailboat with a small cabin. It wasn't much, but at least it had enough room for a couple of bunks, a tiny head with a shower, and a small sink next to a double propane burner. She had bought it used and repainted it herself—a brilliant white with a thin red, white, and blue stripe running the length of the boat. She

13

had named it the *Miss Nancy*, after her mother, and she had received a lot of smiles and waves from the locals on her first sail.

Circling overhead, a few of the ever-present seagulls cried out to her as she climbed down into the boat and unlocked the door to the cabin. Switching on the marine radio, she called the Coast Guard station to let Brian know she would be back before dark.

"Where will you be sailing?" he asked.

"Just off the coast … south of the pier. Shouldn't be long. Just enough to get my sailing fix for the day."

"OK, babe … be careful, and don't forget to wear your life jacket. There's a front moving in."

"I know … Randy told me. Anything else, Mr. Worry Wart?"

Samantha could hear the pause, which meant that some of Brian's Coast Guard buddies were probably standing right behind him.

"That's okay," she said. "I'll say it for you. I love you. See you later … over and out."

CHAPTER 2

Stepping back out onto the textured deck of her little sailboat, Sam cast a quick glance at a line of clouds in the distance as she began removing the blue mainsail cover. The boat was sloop-rigged, which meant she had only two sails to deal with. There was the large mainsail that ran up a single mast in the center of the boat and the smaller jib sail attached to the bow, forming the familiar white triangle that marked the passage of a sailboat across the horizon.

The little boat had been in less than pristine condition when she had purchased it the year before, so in addition to repainting the hull, she had taken advantage of the gray days of winter to replace the original aluminum mast with one of the new carbon fiber ones usually found on more expensive boats. At first she had balked at having to dish out the last of her savings, but the new mast was lighter and ten times stronger than steel, giving her a little extra peace of mind in case she encountered strong winds or heavy seas offshore.

But the old motor was dead, and with no money left for a new one, Sam had become very proficient in maneuvering around the docks on wind power alone—something most sailors would never attempt within the tight confines of a marina next to yachts that cost millions of dollars.

That's the way they had done it in the old days, Sam had told herself. And she was all about the old days. There were times when she was sailing alone that she felt like she had been born in the wrong century. The stack of books on her bedside table revealed a love of history, and when she read about the lives of those who had lived and died long ago, their stories seemed almost comforting in an age dominated by computers and smart phones—things she had never felt a need for the way others of her generation did.

Raising the mainsail, Sam let it flap in the breeze while she used an oar to push away from the dock. As soon as she was clear, she grabbed the curved wooden tiller and quickly pulled in the main sheet. The sail instantly ballooned with air, driving the boat forward past a forest of towering aluminum masts that tinkled in the wind, turning the marina into a gigantic wind chime.

Watching the wake recede behind her, she made the turn into the ship channel. She could feel the stiffening wind on her face as the boat began to pitch in the rougher water, reminding her to strap on her life jacket. Approaching the marker at the end of the channel's protective rock jetty, she was forced to compete for space with a fully-laden oil tanker and altered her course, passing as close to the jagged rocks as she dared. Holding a straight line, she watched the gigantic tanker slide by, marveling that something that massive could actually float.

With the tanker behind her, she entered open water and tied off the tiller so she could run barefoot over the cabin to raise the jib before winching in the main sheet, increasing her speed. The word *sheet* was a confusing nautical term to non-sailors. In the sailing world, the word sheet referred to a rope or a line, and when sailors gathered at a bar to talk about things like main sheets or jib sheets or mizzen sheets, the people around them usually assumed they were talking about the sails instead of the lines.

By now the breeze was picking up, and already it was evident that this would be a short sail. But short sail or long it didn't matter. Like a pilot who frolicked among the clouds, she was free from any earth-bound problems, left only to the variances of the wind and the watery hiss of the ocean as her little boat sliced through the clear blue water.

Pulling the tiller in close, the boat leaned as she headed south along the shoreline past the end of the pier. Aside from a few dolphins swimming next to her boat, the sea was relatively empty as she changed course and sailed into deeper water. The horizon contained only a few greasy-looking oil rigs and a shrimp boat that appeared to be heading for Mexican waters. It was one of those hot summer days that made Sam feel glad to be out on the water with the sun warming her face and the comforting sound of the hull cleaving through the swells while the sails snapped in the changing wind.

Peering over the bow, she used a distant oil platform for a reference point. Judging by the wind and the angle of the sun, she calculated she would have just enough time to circle the platform and make it back to port before the weather worsened. With the land now fading from view, she would have to rely on her compass and the Port Aransas water tower to guide her home. The old blue water tower was the last thing fishermen saw when they headed out to sea and the first thing that greeted them home on their return.

After adjusting her sails, Sam looked down to see that her dolphin escort had grown. They played in her wake and swam closer, peeking up at her with one eye above the surface as the sea around them turned gray when a dark cloud passed overhead. Glancing up, she saw the curved line of the approaching front. It seemed much closer. The sky was darker, and a misty haze had formed over the water, obliterating her reference points. Rising over the top of a swell, she looked for the oil rig. It was gone, and the sea had suddenly become peaked with whitecaps.

It was time to turn around.

In the building seas, her little boat pitched and rolled as she tried to come about. She had heard of sudden squalls that preceded storm fronts, but this was the first time she had ever experienced one first hand. The misty haze was all around her now, and the compass was swinging wildly as she tried to decide which way to point her boat in a confused ocean.

Securing the tiller again, she climbed down into the cabin and switched the radio on to give Brian a quick update on her position and the fast-moving storm front. Dialing in the non-emergency frequency for the Coast Guard, all she got was static. Her radio had been working perfectly before she left the dock, so she tried again.

More static.

Quickly she changed to the emergency frequency. This time there was nothing—not even static.

That had never happened before.

She called a few more times before checking the wires to the antenna. A green light indicated the radio was still getting power, so she dialed in the NOAA weather frequency broadcasting on a never-ending loop—a sure-fire way to see if her radio was receiving. Like a sulking child, the radio stared back at her in silence. She would have to use her cell phone to call Brian on the way back in.

Climbing back out on deck, Sam could see that the sky had grown even darker, and the gray mist over the water had turned into a dense fog. She grabbed the tiller and turned into the wind, keeping the tension in the mainsail to power up the side of a thick wave. At the top she shoved the tiller all the way over. The boom snapped to the side as the bow swung around to the west. She was only half-way through her turn when she saw it.

Like a ghostly apparition, the rust-streaked bow of a large white ship emerged from the fog. It was almost like watching something happen in slow motion. Time seemed to stop for a moment as the horror of what was about to happen next hit Samantha with all the subtlety of a sledge hammer. A millisecond later, the ship's steel bow sliced through her boat with a grinding screech.

The force of the collision was more like an explosion. Sam went flying through the air and over the stern railing, but something was preventing her from swimming away. Dangling from the twisted steel, she felt herself being pulled underwater by the very thing meant to save her life. Her life jacket had become tangled in the crushed railing, and as the stern was pulled under the hull of the massive ship, she was being dragged down with it.

She could feel the pressure in her ears as she worked to release the jacket. It seemed like it was taking forever, and she could see the bottom of the ship moving above her by the time she freed herself. Kicking away from the tangled wreckage, she swam for the surface.

As soon as Sam felt the brush of air against her face, she took in a deep breath and opened her eyes. The stained waterline of the ship was rushing by only a few feet away, and she could already feel the pull from the giant props as she slid along the side with pieces of crushed fiberglass and torn sails. With time running out, she began swimming away as hard as she could in a desperate attempt to escape the suction created by a heavy steel ship displacing tons of water.

And then it was over.

Left behind in a vortex of swirling debris, she looked up just in time to see the name *Searcher* painted across the stern of the ship before it was swallowed up by the fog.

Treading water, Sam felt a sharp pain in her left shoulder as she drifted with the current in a widening debris field. Her mind began to race, and she could feel the first disorienting flash of panic as she looked around. The collision had been so sudden, so brutal, she wondered if her emergency locator beacon had even been activated. In theory, it was supposed to activate automatically after being released by hydrostatic pressure from its exterior mounting bracket, but if it failed to release or was run over by the ship, there would be no distress signal marking her position.

A large wave lifted her up and she slid down the backside. She was already beginning to shiver, and with the wind picking up, she knew that any remaining pieces of floating wreckage would soon be scattered over hundreds of square miles of ocean. Judging from her last position, she guessed she was about five miles from shore. But without a life jacket, in a storm-tossed sea with an unpredictable current that could carry her away from shore just as easily as it could push her toward it, she wondered if swimming toward the beach was really her best option.

A picture of the ship's bow bearing down on her boat flashed before her eyes. An unexpected sob escaped her lips, coming more from a place of anger than fear. Another wave struck her from behind and drove her underwater. Like an athlete prodded by an unrelenting coach, she pushed her way back to the surface with memories of the game she had played in the hotel swimming pool—when her surrogate fathers had made bets with her as to how long she could hold her breath. With practice, along with a child's zeal to earn a few quarters tossed into the deep end, she learned to hold her breath longer than all the other kids her age, eventually humiliating even the local high school jocks who found themselves unable to match her ability, no matter how hard they tried.

Five miles. *She could make it!*

The memory of a child's game now became a tool for survival. The increasing wind was already beginning to dissipate the gauze-like veil of misty fog that had hidden the sails of her boat from the approaching ship. But with the passage of the front the sea had grown even darker, and the tops of the waves were whipping into foamy caps that made it harder for her to see as she rose and fell in the building swells. Pulling the wet hair from her eyes, she squinted through the lifting fog at the disappearing sun as it began its downward plunge in the west. The night was coming, and soon total blackness would cover the sea. Samantha started swimming.

John Lyman

CHAPTER 3

The emergency locator beacon had blared to life for only a few seconds before growing silent when it had been sucked into the ship's prop. But those few seconds had been enough to trigger an alarm in the Coast Guard station. The distress signal sent Brian and the other members of the rescue crew racing across the hangar floor to their orange and white chopper.

The storm front had obviously arrived ahead of schedule, and even though launching in bad weather was nothing out of the ordinary for the men and women who patrolled the seas, the approaching darkness would make finding the source of the signal even harder. Especially now that it had grown silent.

Crowding into the back of the chopper, Brian and his partner, Larry Wilson, pulled on their helmets and began strapping in while the helicopter was towed from the hangar. Brian shouted into his headset against the sound of the blades spinning over their heads. "Did they get a lock on the signal before it died?"

"Uh, yeah," Larry said, avoiding eye contact. "Looks like about five miles from the beach."

"What about an ID code?"

Larry looked up and the two men locked eyes. "It's Sam's boat, Brian."

Pulling on his gloves, Brian worked to maintain a neutral expression. "Any radio contact?"

"No. But you know as well as I do that most of these calls are false alarms."

"It could also mean she didn't have time to use the radio."

Both men grabbed for the handles and closed the sliding door as the chopper leapt into the air.

"Don't worry, buddy," Larry said. "She's probably headed back to port with a broken antenna, but if she's still out there, we'll find her."

* * *

With the sun's surrender below the western horizon, the sky began to merge with the sea as Samantha swam toward a line of lights that marked the distant shoreline. By now the rain had stopped and the sea had begun to flatten, and behind her, she could see the flashing red and white strobe lights of the Coast Guard helicopter crisscrossing the area where her boat had sunk. The current had carried her at least three miles to the south, but the shore looked a little closer.

With nothing to signal her position in the darkness, she had already accepted the fact that her best chance of making it out of this alive was to keep on swimming toward the island. Over the years a number of shrimpers had fallen overboard in the Gulf, and many had survived by swimming to shore in its warm water.

If they could do it ... then so could she!

Like a mantra, the words rolled over and over in her mind as she swam. By now she had been in the water for almost four hours, and her arms and legs were growing heavy. She rolled over on her back and floated. For awhile she just drifted, looking toward the beach and the tiny red light blinking from the top of the water tower. With the current running to the south, the light was getting farther away. *Not good.* Reluctantly, she rolled back over and started swimming again.

Five miles! Maybe less now. *She could do this!*

People had swum across the English Channel, and thousands of triathletes had covered at least half that distance before biking a hundred miles and running a marathon. It would probably take her all night if the current wasn't too bad, but she was a strong swimmer. She just had to pace herself.

Looking back out into the inky blackness covering the Gulf, she saw that another set of flashing strobe lights had joined the search.

Brian's words echoed in her mind.

I'm a rescue swimmer ... it's what I do.

22

If she didn't make it to shore he would never be able to forgive himself. His words kept repeating over and over again in her head. But she would make it. No matter what it took, she was determined to make it, and the story of her nighttime swim through shark-infested waters would make Brian and the other rescue swimmers in the Coast Guard green with envy.

Sharks! She hadn't even thought of them. In reality, she knew she was probably still in shock from the collision, and the thought of sharks had never entered her mind—until now.

Bob White saw something big and dark swim beneath his boat yesterday.

Great! Why did she have to hear that fish story today? It suddenly felt as if the sea around her was full of predators, just waiting for the right time to take a bite while she was treading water. Once again she could feel the panic welling up inside. It was the last thing she needed right now.

She had to stay focused, and the only way she could do that was to keep her eyes fixed on the distant lights and swim.

John Lyman.

CHAPTER 4

The pictures lining the hallway leading to the Special Ops briefing room was a rogue's gallery. There were pictures of Army Rangers and Green Berets, Navy SEALs and Marine Corps snipers, plus some new additions from the ranks of the Air Force's Special Operations Command— all legends within the tight-knit community of warriors who passed through the hallways of America's Joint Special Warfare Operations Center. They were all there, hanging in plain sight for anyone to see—if they happened to have the security clearance necessary to enter one of the most secret and secure facilities in the world.

Steve Brooks had always made a habit of looking at all the faces staring back at him when he made his way down the long corridor before punching in his code and opening the soundproof door to the darkened briefing room. Inside, gathered around a long, polished table, a group of very seasoned-looking Special Forces operators were listening to Admiral Nathan Bourdon as he pointed to the large, flat-screen display on the wall behind him.

"Ah, Commander Brooks," Bourdon said, interrupting himself. "Glad to see you could make it."

"My apologies, Admiral. I was mowing my lawn and didn't hear my beeper go off."

The admiral cast one of his famous sardonic smiles in Brooks' direction. "You're the second man to use that excuse today. If I was a terrorist, I'd be out looking for half-mowed lawns right now so I'd know where all the special ops guys live."

Muffled laughter filled the room as Brooks leaned against the wall and grinned back at the admiral.

"We were just discussing the ship that ran aground in Texas, Commander. It's beginning to look like someone made contact with it five miles offshore. The satellite images we just received show that a small sailboat was headed straight for the ship around 16:30 local time. After that the image was lost due to the storm. Thirty minutes later the ship was on the beach."

"The beach, sir?"

"That's what I said, Commander. She drove right up on the beach in Port Aransas under full power." Bourdon paused to scan the room. "There's more. When the local authorities boarded her, they discovered that no one was on board ... at least no one alive."

Brooks felt the hair on the back of his neck rise.

"Apparently, it was a research ship," the admiral continued. "And the freezers on board had been stuffed with bodies wrapped in plastic next to boxes that contained some kind of biological specimens. Cause of death appeared to be gunshot wounds."

The men exchanged looks around the table—their only display of emotion.

"At least we can rule out pirates," said an Army Ranger. "They would have thrown the bodies overboard. What about the sailboat, sir?"

"Disappeared. Probably half-way to Mexico by now with Dinning on board."

The commander looked confused. "Excuse me, sir. I must have missed something. Why are we being briefed on this ... and who's Dinning?"

The admiral exhaled. "Last month the ship disappeared from a port in Africa after some kind of incident, and no one's seen it since ... until today. Professor Peter Dinning was the man in charge. He's a molecular biologist, and he and his team had been in the Congo for almost half a year collecting samples from the jungle."

"But someone had to bring the ship back across the Atlantic."

"We ran the coordinates and did the math and came up with a recent satellite photo of the ship crossing the Gulf of Mexico. Dr. Dinning was standing out on deck two days ago. That puts him at the top of the list of people we want to talk to. But right now we're more worried about what's inside those specimen containers. We could be looking at some kind of major biological event on our own shores."

"So you think this Dinning is some kind of bad guy, sir?"

"We don't know at this point, but something weird is going on. I'm putting him on our most wanted list until we find out what it is, and I want to be the first person to talk to him if he's found. As far as the sailboat is concerned, we're still looking into who owned it. The rendezvous with the ship was obviously planned. The satellite images clearly showed it heading straight for the ship after it left the marina in Port Aransas. Evidently, whoever was on the sailboat activated their EPIRB briefly to make it look like they were in distress."

"Looks like they timed it perfectly," Brooks added. "Now the Coast Guard is on a wild goose chase while the sailboat slips away."

"Exactly," Bourdon responded. "Not to mention the added confusion of having to deal with a large ship full of dead people that just ran aground on their beach. Whoever's behind this has everyone running around in circles down there."

Brooks scratched at his short beard and stared at the screen. "But we're talking about a sailboat here, sir. Has anyone called the Naval Air Station in Corpus Christi to see if they're tracking it on radar? I mean, an aluminum mast would give them a big glowing target to follow."

The admiral stared at the screen. "All of the targets in that section of the Gulf have been verified. For all practical purposes, the sailboat has vanished."

"What about radio transmissions in the area?"

"Nothing but a bunch of Cajun shrimpers talking to each other."

The door to the room opened and a young soldier handed a computer printout to Bourdon. After reading the message, his face paled.

"Shit!" The admiral slammed the printout on the table. "This is from the Coast Guard station in Port Aransas. A local woman and her sailboat were just reported overdue back in port. Apparently, she's the girlfriend of one of the Coast Guard men stationed there."

"Did they include a description of her boat?"

Bourdon looked back down at the printout. "Yeah, here it is. I've actually sailed one of these. It's a low profile sloop, but it's not exactly the kind of boat I would have picked to make a getaway in. A boat that small …"

The men watched the admiral's eyes grow wide.

"What is it, sir?"

"According to this, the girl's boat just had a new carbon fiber mast installed."

"I guess that explains why it's not showing up on radar," Brooks responded. "It probably has the radar signature the size of a seagull now.

These people really knew what they were doing. Do we have any history on this girl yet?"

Bourdon stood. "We're working on that. Let's grab our gear and head for the airfield. I want all of our assets on the ground in Port Aransas before the sun comes up."

CHAPTER 5

It was past midnight and Samantha Adams was still swimming. To the north, she could see the flashing strobes of a helicopter circling a Coast Guard Cutter, and several smaller boats were shining their lights over the water in the same area. They looked closer.

Maybe they're adjusting their search area to match the current, she thought.

Rising up on a swell, she caught a quick glimpse of some flashing red lights on the beach before she slid back down into the trough.

Were they looking for her?

She wondered briefly if they were checking the incoming tide for debris … or a body. Turning on her back, she floated for a moment, staring up into a starless sky while she tried to relax, but a breaking wave washed over her face and filled her mouth and nose with seawater. Wracked by fits of coughing, she waited for the burn in her nose to subside.

If only she could just sleep for a few minutes!

Even in the warm Gulf water her teeth had begun to chatter whenever she stopped swimming, making it obvious that the first effects of hypothermia were beginning to set in. Holding her breath, she ducked beneath a breaking wave and drifted beneath the surface in the womb-like embrace of the sea. It would be so easy to just give up. She had heard stories of people who had almost surrendered to their exhaustion in the dark water because the peace beneath the waves was so dream-like.

Is this what they had felt … the urge to finally let go for that long sleep from which they would never awake?

She could feel her mother's presence—floating beside her, urging her on. Like a fighter that had just taken a shot to the head, Sam shook away the lure of the depths. Her eyes were startled open, and the call of death that had come cloaked behind the promise of a restful sleep was silenced when she saw the world of blackness around her and kicked her way back to the surface. She would do whatever it took to reach land again—to see Brian and sit on her porch and drink coffee while she smelled Bee's roses.

Taking long, even strokes, Sam tried to focus on the future—but only visions from the past accompanied her on her long night's swim. She could see her mother's face, but it was a younger face. It was the face she had seen on the day when her mother had lifted her up and carried her from that house in Houston seventeen years ago. They had left in the middle of summer, and she could still remember the sweltering Texas heat that made life almost unbearable for those without air conditioning.

The images were still deeply imprinted on her mind with a mixture of clarity and fantasy that were the hallmarks of a divided childhood. She remembered the limp curtains that hung in her airless upstairs bedroom and her small, metal-framed bed with the ragged quilt and bare mattress that had been squeezed into a corner under the angled roof. She could almost feel her tiny, five-year-old feet running across the wooden floor to a bare cardboard box—a box that held the few precious toys her mother had bought at the dollar store with money she had taken from her husband's pockets after he had passed out in front of the TV among a forest of empty beer bottles.

Other details began to return. Like the splintery wooden chair she had stood on in front of an old pink dresser with a cracked mirror, where she could watch herself brushing her thin blonde hair before jumping down and running to the window to look outside.

From her gabled perch overlooking the sloping porch roof, she would gaze across the green shingles at the fat leafy trees that lined her neighborhood street. She remembered wishing they had a green lawn like the other houses on the block instead of a few patches of grass that had somehow managed to claw their way through the hard-packed dirt whenever it rained, and how her rusty tricycle had laid on its side all summer with a broken wheel—a wounded reminder to the outside world that a child lived inside.

Sometimes, in the afternoon, she would sit on the sagging couch on the front porch, fantasizing that the white flecks of peeling paint that drifted dandruff-like from the neglected exterior of the house was really snow.

And then there was the big oak tree. It was the only thing she could remember that seemed unaffected by neglect. From her upstairs window,

Samantha had spent countless hours watching the way the light filtered through the tree's quivering leaves, projecting flickering patterns of light across the walls of her room that lulled her to sleep every afternoon after her mother had put her down for her nap.

On the day they had left, a large butterfly had fluttered down from its branches and landed next to her window. With no wind to disturb it, the insect just sat there, moving its large wings up and down while Samantha marveled at the beautiful colors.

"Whatcha doin', honey?" The sweet sound of her mother's voice came rushing back to her, as did the memory of the purple bruise at the corner of her eye.

"Oh, mama, did you hurt yourself?"

"Mama fell down, honey. I'll be good as new in a few days."

Samantha remembered kissing her mother's swollen eye. "That will make it all better. I have magic kisses … like you, mama."

"It feels better already, baby. What you been lookin' at out that window?"

"A big butterfly. He lives in the tree. I think he wants to talk to me."

"He does? What's his name?"

"I don't know. We didn't talk yet. Come look at him."

Together they both peered outside. The butterfly was still there, slowly moving its wings up and down, seemingly oblivious to their presence.

"You and me are going on a little trip today, baby."

"A trip … like to the store, mama?"

"No, honey. A long trip … like when we used to go to grandma's house in the country."

Samantha bounced up and down on the window sill. "Is daddy coming too?"

"Not this time, sweetie. Daddy is staying here. It's just you and me."

Samantha had giggled when she heard that just the two of them were going, but her mother's voice had taken on a hard edge. "You have to be very quiet, Samantha. We don't want to wake your father up. He's very tired."

Aided by the rhythm of her swimming, the memories came rushing back to her at an exponentially faster rate. In her mind's eye she could see her mother leading her from her room into the upstairs hallway, where they had crept by the closed door to her parent's bedroom. She could hear her father snoring inside, but when the wooden floor had creaked loudly, the snoring had stopped.

"Nancy?" Her husband's voice echoed from the other side of the door.

"I'm just going down to the kitchen, Carl. I'll be right back."

Looking down at Sam, her mother had held a finger to her lips until the snoring started up again. Seconds later Sam was in her mother's arms and she was running. She ran down the stairs and out the back door, crashing into a metal trash can full of empty beer bottles before they reached the car parked next to the house.

Her mother's eyes had remained focused on the house when she lowered Sam onto the front seat of the big black Chevy and climbed behind the wheel. With shaking hands, she started the engine and looked through the windshield. "Buckle your seatbelt, Samantha!"

"I can't do it by myself, mama. What's wrong? Your hands are shaking."

"It's okay, honey. Mama's just in a hurry."

And then, just as she was reaching over to buckle Sam's seatbelt, her mother froze when she saw her husband's hulking figure jump from the front porch, landing on the driveway between the car and the street. Wearing only a faded pair of jeans, her father's chest was covered in jailhouse tattoos, and his bulging eyes had made his rage-filled expression look even more menacing. Like a bull chasing a red cape, he had lunged for the car.

Samantha would never forget the look in her mother's eyes when she stepped on the gas. The car hurtled straight toward her surprised father, forcing him to throw himself against the side of the house just as the big Chevy brushed past. It missed him by inches before bouncing across the sidewalk and into the street in a shower of sparks.

Through the back window, she had seen her father running behind them—waving his fists in the air and shouting, but when she looked back inside the car, her mother was smiling. "Samantha, you're going to have to learn how to put your seatbelt on by yourself, honey. You're a big girl now, and mama doesn't have time to stop."

With the sound of her mother's voice still in her ears, Sam found herself drifting again.

How long since she had stopped swimming?

She could feel herself getting colder, and the lights along the shoreline seemed to be moving sideways. Right away she knew she had been caught up in one of the riptides that paralleled the coast , and the only thing a swimmer could do at that point was to go with the flow until they were out of it.

Locked in the current's grip, Sam felt herself shaking, then sobbing. She was only twenty-two years old—too young to die without a fight. So she drifted, until finally she felt the current slacken. She began swimming again. She swam for all she was worth. She swam without thinking of the time, and when she finally had the courage to look up, the lights along the shoreline seemed closer again. What had seemed impossible now seemed possible, but victory would only come one stroke at a time.

In a way her swim was a lot like the journey she and her mother had made to Port Aransas seventeen years ago, wondering if the old Chevy would make it another mile as they sped over the interstate's cracked concrete and looked out at old wooden structures that lay collapsing in the thick underbrush. The thought made her long for the feel of land— any kind of land—even creepy land filled with ghostly abandoned buildings.

A sudden rush of fear coursed through her body. Her growing exhaustion and the reality of her situation was hitting her full force now. She was alone out at sea—much farther out than the end of the pier. The thought gave her chills, and to top it off, she was swimming at night in dark water with creatures that had already sensed her presence in their watery world.

Her mind reeled, and for some reason she thought of the woman who had lived next door to them in Houston. "You've got to get away from him, honey!" the woman had told her mother over a cup of coffee. "A man like that who's been in prison ... no tellin' what he's liable to do next."

"But where would I go ... what would I do?" Sam's mother had asked. "I've got Samantha to think of."

"That's exactly right, honey. You've got your little girl to think of. It's only a matter of time before he starts beatin' on her too. In a way you're lucky. Right now you're young and you've still got your looks and your health. Why hell, girl, you've got your whole life ahead of you. You need to head on down to that island place you're always talkin' about and get yourself a job waitressin'. I made a good livin' at it before I met up

33

with my husband. They got lots of seafood restaurants and resorts and stuff like that down on that part of the coast. Why, a good lookin' girl like you will find a job in no time. You'll be fine."

And they had been fine.

As soon as they topped the bridge over the Intracoastal Waterway and looked out over the water-filled world ahead, they knew they had just arrived in a place that was vastly different from the land-locked one they had just left behind. Water was everywhere. It stretched as far as the eye could see, and it had been Samantha's world ever since.

Looking up, another wave slapped Sam in the face. She coughed and pulled a string of wet hair from her eyes, trying to catch a glimpse of the shoreline again. She was getting closer, and all she could think about was dry land and water she could drink. Sam's arms and legs were colder now. She could barely feel her hands and feet as another swell lifted her up. The lights on shore looked dimmer for some reason.

She had to rest again. Reluctantly, she let her body go into drift mode. With her ears now underwater, she could hear all the little pops and crackles from a mass of shrimp moving across the white sand bottom, and when she opened her eyes, she saw a glimmer of light on the water around her.

It must be the dawn!

The light was growing brighter, and as she floated with her hair spreading on the water like some painted vision of an ancient mermaid, she closed her eyes again and waited for the warmth of the sun. But there was a bothersome noise, and it was growing louder with a sound that beat the air and disturbed her solitude.

Go away!

By now she had stopped caring. Her grip on reality was beginning to slip away, and all she wanted to do was drift with the current, abandoning her fate to the whims of the sea. The sound was getting louder, and when she tried to open her eyes, she was blinded by a bright light. And then something had her in its grip!

Maybe it was a sea monster, she thought. A delirious half-smile crossed her lips as she thought of the dark shape that had swum beneath Bob White's boat.

And then she heard the monster's voice.

It was Brian, and he was holding her in his arms, talking sweetly into her ear. "I've got you, babe … I've got you. Just hold on … I've got you."

Squinting up, she could see tears in his eyes as he cradled her in his arms and floated her into the yellow stretcher before she was hoisted up into the orange and white helicopter hovering above.

* * *

On the beach, two men with binoculars were watching the rescue a few hundred yards offshore. Samantha had almost made it to the beach. Without speaking, one of the men reached for his smart phone and punched in a pre-programmed number.

"Yes?" a gravelly voice answered.

"They found her, sir. Looks like she's still alive."

A pause. "Well, then, let's try to find out what she knows." The line went dead.

CHAPTER 6

There was an antiseptic smell in the room when Sam opened her eyes and saw Brian sitting next to her bed. He was watching baseball on TV, but she could tell by the way he kept looking out the window that he wasn't really following the game.

"Who's winning?"

He switched off the TV and gave her a lazy smile. "Well, someone's had a nice long nap."

"How long have I been asleep?"

"Since yesterday morning. You were kind of out of it from the hypothermia."

Sam scanned the pale green walls and the sink next to the door. "Hospital?"

"Yeah. We flew you into Corpus Christi. The nurse told me your core temp returned to normal during the night. The only thing you need now is rest." Brian hesitated. "What happened out there, Sam?"

"You mean the part where a big ship cut my sailboat in half?"

"So that's what happened." Brian reached out and squeezed her hand. "We kind of figured something catastrophic occurred when your emergency signal went silent all of a sudden. Was the ship white?"

Sam's eyes widened. "Yeah ... with rust streaks. Did you guys find it?"

"It was kind of hard to miss. The damned thing drove itself right up on the beach."

"Drove itself?" Sam inched herself up in the bed. "We're not talking about a whale here, Brian. Ships don't just drive themselves up on the beach."

"Well apparently this one did. Some of our guys were the first ones on the scene and no one was at the helm." Brian paused. "All they found were some freezers full of bodies wrapped in plastic."

37

"Bodies?"

"It was a research ship, and they were all squeezed in with a bunch of lab specimens … and it gets weirder. The last time anyone saw it was a month ago … in Africa."

"Africa!" Sam blinked back at him. "That's impossible. A ship under power like that didn't cross the Atlantic and thread its way through the Caribbean without someone alive on board to steer it."

"That's what the FBI guys said."

"FBI guys?"

Brian cast a nervous glance at the closed door. "A lot of government people have been flying in from Washington. I just talked to one of the new men back at the station who was guarding the ship last night before the Special Forces soldiers took over."

"Special Forces soldiers!"

"Yeah. They arrived before the sun came up, and they didn't come alone. There were a few CIA types with them along with a bunch of people from the CDC."

"CDC?" Sam pulled the sheet up to her chin. "What the hell is going on, Brian?"

"I'm not sure, but the bodies probably had something to do with it … not to mention whatever else is on board that thing."

"My God … those poor people." Sam peered over her covers at Brian. "This might sound weird, but when I saw it disappear into the fog I had a feeling I was looking at a ghost ship."

Brian frowned. "That's what the FBI guys are calling it. They want to talk to you."

"Me? What for?"

"Probably routine. Sounded like they just want to know if you remember anything about the collision."

A light rap on the door signaled the return of the nurse. "Ah, I see you're awake," he said. "How do you feel?"

"Like I just ran a marathon. When can I go home?"

"Your doctor is at the nurse's station now. You've got some pretty significant bruising in your shoulder, and she's still waiting on some lab results. If everything looks good she'll probably discharge you today, but you'll have to take it easy for awhile." The RN stood awkwardly at the end of the bed before he continued. "The two FBI agents that were here earlier are back. They seem pretty anxious to talk to you."

Sam sat up and ran her hands through a mass of tangled hair. "Do I have to talk to them now?"

"No. I can be your guard dog a little while longer. They just went for coffee, but as soon as you're discharged I have a feeling they'll be waiting at the entrance."

"Which entrance?"

"Tell you what." The RN grinned back at her. "As soon as the doctor lets you go, I'll grab a wheelchair and take you out through the employee entrance. That should give you some breathing room for awhile, but the way these guys are acting I'm pretty sure they'll be showing up at your house as soon as they find out you've left the hospital."

* * *

The seagulls circling overhead seemed to be welcoming Samantha back to her little island home as Brian drove his dark blue '68 Camaro onto the ferry for the short hop across the channel. Sam couldn't wait to take a hot shower and relax on her front porch with a cup of freshly-ground coffee, but as soon as she rolled her window down and caught a briny whiff of the sea, she was jarred with a sudden realization.

"The bait!"

"What about it?" Brian asked.

"Where have my customers been getting their bait while I was on my little sea cruise?"

"It's being taken care of."

"What do you mean … it's being taken care of?"

Brian swiveled in his seat. "I gave Old Hank the keys to your VW bus while you were in the hospital. He said he'd take care of the bait until you got back on your feet."

"You gave Hank the keys to my bus?"

"He had to have a way to get the bait to your customers, didn't he? Randy told me he used to catch most of the bait fish on the island until he got tired of it." Brian paused to watch the way the ferry captain powered the boat against the current. "Seems odd that a person who used to catch fish for a living retired so he could spend the rest of his days fishing."

"You don't know these guys like I do, Brian. Sometimes I think they were born with a fishing pole in their hands."

"I've heard some of them die that way too," Brian quipped. "One of the guys at the station told me they found a dead guy sitting at the end of the pier with a fishing pole in his hand a few years back."

"I heard that story too." Samantha giggled. "It's not true, but it might as well be."

The deck beneath the car shuddered when the captain threw the engines into reverse and guided the ferry into the angled dock. As soon as the deckhand waved them off, they headed for the center of town.

"You know, you might want to think about taking on a partner or hiring someone to help you," Brian continued. "You just got run over by a ship, and all you can think about is getting back to work. No one can work seven days a week without a break, Samantha. If you don't take a day off every now and then you'll end up looking like Old Hank."

"I can think of worse ways to end up." The memory of her long night all alone on a dark ocean was still fresh in her mind as she squinted in the sun's reflection bouncing off the wind-sculptured dunes bordering the road to her house. "Let's go see the ship!"

"Now?"

"Yeah. Why not? Besides, I want to find out who owns it. Somebody owes me a sailboat."

"You're supposed to be taking it easy, remember? Trust me, that ship will still be there tomorrow, and I can already tell you who owns it. It's registered to a company in Massachusetts that leased it out to the University of Texas."

"University of Texas?"

"I know … weird."

"It's more than weird, Brian. It sounds like someone was trying to get home."

Brian peered back from beneath a pair of furrowed eyebrows. "I'm not supposed to discuss this with anyone, but since you're already involved I think you should know. When one of our officers entered the ship's bridge after it ran aground, he noticed that someone had programmed a set of GPS coordinates into the auto pilot a few hours before it hit the beach. Someone on that ghost ship was still alive, and they knew exactly where they wanted it to go before they got off."

"Got off? That means they either jumped overboard or were picked up by another boat after they entered the coordinates."

"Believe me, Sam, there's all kinds of wild rumors circulating the island. People are starting to lock their doors. I mean, you never know. Maybe someone on that ship went crazy and killed everyone else on board. Or maybe there's some kind of virus on the loose. Who knows? We'd like to find out what happened out there as much as anyone else, but ever since all the government people showed up, no one else has been allowed near that ship ... not even the Coast Guard. We've been ordered to keep searching the area off the coast. But other than a few pieces of your boat, the only other thing we've found floating around out there is you."

Brian slowed when they came to her street, but Sam grabbed his arm. "Please, Brian. I have to see it."

With a sigh indicating he had lost this particular battle, Brian sped up and headed for the beach. As soon as they turned onto the access road they were greeted by the flashing lights of several local and state police cars blocking the way ahead. Pulling up behind a line of cars and trucks, they noticed that only military vehicles were being waved through.

"Sorry, babe." Brian started to turn. "Doesn't look like anyone's going to the beach today."

"Keep going," Sam said, pressing her face close to the windshield. "I need to find out if the pier is closed too."

In full surrender mode, Brian inched the car up toward the roadblock. The scene was chaotic. Cars trying to turn around were spinning their tires in the soft sand along the road, and a group of angry fishermen were shouting out questions to a line of silent police officers. A State Trooper was already walking toward them but was waved off by Melvin Bolt, a local Port Aransas cop. Bending down, he grinned into the car. "Hey, Brian."

"Hey, Melvin."

The cop pushed his sunglasses down on his nose to see Samantha glaring back at him from the passenger seat. "Oh ... hi there, Sam. Glad to see you're okay."

"Have they told you anything about that ship yet?"

"Not really. The military people don't seem to be in a very talkative mood, but I can tell you right now they're not letting anyone near that thing."

"What about the pier?" Sam asked.

"Closed for now. The entire beach from the jetty all the way to the second access road has been blocked off."

Sam looked past the roadblock at a cluster of military vehicles parked on the hard-packed sand where the road ended in front of the pier. "Did they say when the roads will be open again?"

"Not a clue. One of the PR people from Homeland Security was up here a while ago talking to the press. He said the ship and the area around it has been quarantined. You're gonna have to turn ..."

The cop's voice was drowned out when a large gray helicopter flew directly overhead and the driver of a pickup truck behind them laid on the horn.

"Let's go," Sam said. "Melvin's got his hands full, and it's obvious we aren't going any farther. Thanks for trying."

Brian gave her one of his *I told you so* looks. Five minutes later they were pulling up in front of her little house. All Sam could do was stare at it. The sight had jerked her thoughts back to her long night all alone on a dark sea when she thought she'd never see it again. It was like waking up from a bad dream. Looking back at Brian, she saw that he still had his hands on the wheel and the car was still running.

"Aren't you coming in?" she asked.

"Can't. I'm due back at the station in twenty minutes. They've called in the navy and expanded the search area, so it looks like we won't be getting much time off for the next few days. You gonna be alright?"

"Yeah, I'm fine. My skin still feels a little itchy. I guess I'll take a hot shower and sit out on the front porch for awhile."

"Sounds like a good idea. I'll call you later. Try to get some rest."

Sam kissed him on the cheek and stepped out onto the warm sand to watch him drive away. Looking back at her house, a feeling of emptiness had already settled in when she pushed the gate open and climbed the familiar wooden steps to the porch. She had never really minded being alone before. In fact, she usually enjoyed her moments of solitude. But after the gut-wrenching loneliness she had experienced on her terrifying swim, she found herself longing for the sound of a welcoming voice.

The house smelled like home when she entered. It made Sam smile, because it always reminded her of her mother. With the late afternoon sun streaming through the west-facing windows, the bright morning kitchen was now locked in shadow as Sam grabbed a glass of water and walked through her bedroom into the tiny, green-paneled bathroom. For the first time since she had left the hospital, she noticed that she was still wearing the scrubs the nurse had given her. Dropping them to the floor, she stepped into the shower and let the hot water massage her sore shoulder.

With the itchiness of the sea washed away, she slipped on a T-shirt and shorts and grabbed a Lone Star from the fridge on her way out the door to the wicker loveseat on the porch. By now the sun was starting to set with shades of pink radiating across a darkening blue sky, but instead of leaning back and enjoying the sight, she was jolted by the memory of the terror she had felt when she had watched the sun setting over a storm-tossed sea that would surely swallow her up before she would ever see another day again.

What was wrong with her! Was this some kind of delayed stress response to her ordeal—a form of PTSD?

For a lingering moment she focused on her little dirt bike leaning against the railing at the bottom of the stairs and waited for the feeling to subside.

Where was Old Hank and her VW bus?

Someone had obviously moved her motorcycle into the yard to keep it safe while she was in the hospital. She would have to give Hank a call and let him know she was home, but she had no idea if he even had a phone.

Her phone!

She had taken it with her the day she went sailing, meaning it was now lying on the bottom of the sea with the crushed remains of her boat. She wondered if it still worked underwater. The thought made her smile at the mental picture of a few crabs sitting around listening to her ringtone of Joe Cocker belting out his rendition of "Feeling Alright" the next time Brian tried to call.

Uncurling her legs, she lifted herself from the padded loveseat and walked to the railing to look out at the dark sky beyond the dunes while she sipped her beer. She could hear the invisible hum in the air that no one else seemed to hear, and for some strange reason, she felt drawn to the water—as if seeing it again would somehow reassure her that she was really back on solid ground and that all of this wasn't just a cruel dream before she slipped beneath the waves one final time.

Her thoughts drifted back to the ship. It had come out of the gloom at her so suddenly, so violently, that when the bow loomed overhead and sliced through her little boat, time slowed. Somehow, in that split second before it hit, her mind had detached. It was like watching it happen to someone else. Frozen in time, a collision that only took a few seconds had seemed like an eternity. She could still hear the rending sound of sails ripping and fiberglass crushing before she had been pushed underwater, and the image of the stern disappearing in the fog kept playing over and over like a song stuck in her head.

Searcher.

The name painted across the stern was etched in her brain, and right then she knew she had to see the ship again—no matter how many soldiers were guarding it. But how?

She would go through the dunes!

Of course. Why not? Ever since she had been a little girl she had loved running through the dunes as much as she enjoyed splashing in the surf. She had called them sandy mountains, and she would roll down their steep, rippled sides—land-swimming between waves of shimmering white silica—until her body was coated in sand and she was forced to run back across the beach to the water. The sandy mountains between her house and the beach had been her playground for years, and no one knew them better than she did.

Leaving her empty beer bottle on the porch railing, she opened the screen door and walked back through the house into the bedroom. Trading her shorts and flip-flops for jeans and running shoes, she glanced at the flashlight she kept on the night table.

Leave it.

A beam of light moving over the dunes would only give her away, and the glare of the moonlight against the white sand would provide more than enough light for her to find her way to the beach. She would take only the K-bar knife Brian had given her for protection when she was fishing the back bay.

Brian. She hadn't thought of him. Hopefully he would think she was just sleeping if he called to check on her. Besides, it wasn't that far to the beach through the dunes—maybe a quarter-mile at most. She just wanted

44

to sit in the sand while it was still warm and sip a beer while she looked at the ship.

Squeezing another cold long neck into the back pocket of her jeans, she locked the front door and bounced down the porch steps before making her way around to the back of the house and out into the dunes. She loved going out there at night—the way the white sand glowed blue in the moonlight as she followed a hard-packed trail that wove through the land waves rising all around her.

With the sound of the surf crashing against the beach in the distance, she decided to climb a tall dune on her right to check her progress. She was almost to the top when she heard the cough. Sam froze.

Someone else was out here with her!

Taking in a deep breath, she let her body slide back down the steep face of the glowing dune into the shadows around the base. She hadn't really given much thought to the fact that there might be soldiers out here too. She figured they would all be on the beach guarding the ship or blocking the roads, but Brian had mentioned something about Special Forces soldiers, and those guys covered all their bases. They were probably watching her right now, laughing as they looked through their night vision goggles at the girl with a beer in her pocket who had just slid down the back of a dune.

For awhile she just laid there and waited for something to happen, but nothing did. Depending on the direction of the wind, voices drifting off the beach could be heard for hundreds of yards. Maybe the person who coughed hadn't been as close as she first thought. Rising to her feet, she brushed herself off and continued on. After all, what could they do to her for taking a nighttime stroll through the dunes?

She had just taken her first step toward the next dune in line when a thin hand reached from the darkness behind her and tapped her on the shoulder. Samantha fought the urge to scream as she swirled around and moved crab-like away from whatever had touched her. Like the ghostly bow of a crewless ship emerging from the fog, a pale face floated from the darkness and held a finger to its red lips before pointing to a spot halfway down a moonlit dune twenty yards off to their right. There, in the moonlight, Sam could see the shadowy figure of a man projected against the shining dune behind him.

45

"It's just a shadow," a soft voice whispered. "That means we can see him, but he can't see us."

Gripping the knife on her belt, Sam squinted in the darkness at a thin girl with spiky black hair peering back at her. For a moment the two just stared at one another. In the faint light, Sam could see that the girl's thin arms hung loosely at her sides, and she wasn't holding anything.

"Whoa! You scared the crap out of me!" Sam took in a deep breath and tried to slow her racing heart. "What are you doing out here ... who are you?"

"I could ask you the same questions," the girl replied. "But first I think we should move around to the other side of this dune before that shadow hears us."

Without waiting for a reply, the girl turned and walked away. For a moment Sam hesitated, but as the girl's silhouette began to fade, Sam followed her into the shadows on the dark side of the dune behind them.

"You're her," the girl said, staring back at Sam. She had a pair of dark eyes that were so large they seemed almost out of proportion to the rest of her face. "You're the one who was rescued by the Coast Guard. That ship on the beach hit your sailboat."

Sam took a step back. "How do you know about that?"

"Haven't you been watching TV? You're all over the news." The girl continued looking at Sam with a detached gaze—as if she was thinking of two things at once. "You want to see that ship again, don't you?"

Sam's eyes narrowed at the ghostly wisp of a girl who had just read her mind. "You seem to know a lot about me."

"Just a guess." The girl shrugged with a pair of shoulders so thin that the movement seemed amplified beneath her black T-shirt. "I know I'd want to see it again if it sank my boat... if for no other reason than to get some kind of closure."

Sam could feel her body begin to sag from the events of the past few days. "Yeah, I guess you're right. That's exactly why I'm out here. Now it's your turn. Who are you, and what are you doing stumbling around out here in the dunes?"

"My name is Dana ... Dana Wilkins. I'm a research assistant. My boss was on that ship. Before it disappeared from Africa last month, I received an email from him telling me to run."

CHAPTER 7

R un?" Sam blinked back at her. "Why would he tell you to run? Run from what?"

"I wish I knew," Dana whispered.

"You mean he just emailed you and told you to run … and you haven't heard from him since?"

"That's about the size of it. It's a long story, but I believe it has something to do with our research. Peter was …"

"Who's Peter?"

"My boss … Dr. Peter Dinning … head of the molecular biology department at the University of Texas in Austin. Or at least he was. Something happened in Africa that totally freaked him out. He told me not to go home and to ditch my cell phone."

"Don't go home?"

"I know … freaky, right? Anyway, a few days later I heard on the news that the ship had vanished, so I went back to our lab to see if anyone else had heard from him. There was a big closed sign on the door, and some guys in suits were going through everything. I didn't know who they were or why I was supposed to be hiding. Peter was definitely worried about my safety for some reason, so I turned around and walked out of the building."

"Where have you been staying all this time?"

"A cheap hotel in San Antonio. I kept thinking I should go to the police even though he told me not to. Then I heard about the ship … and the bodies. I took a bus to Aransas Pass and hitchhiked here yesterday morning. As soon as I saw all the roadblocks I started to feel even more paranoid. There's something they're not telling us, and I think Peter knew what it was."

Sam's mind was clicking with all kinds of scenarios, and Dana's frail appearance was starting to alarm her. "Was he studying diseases? Maybe that's why ..."

"Our research didn't involve disease. The team in Africa was just collecting DNA samples."

The two grew silent as they continued to size each other up.

"How long have you been out here?" Sam finally asked.

"Since last night."

"Did you bring any water?"

"I bought a few bottles from the store in town, but it ran out this afternoon along with the beef jerky."

"Beef jerky?" Sam frowned. "You look a little dehydrated. Why don't we go back ..."

"I'm not leaving until I see that ship."

"You sure?"

"Positive."

"Good, because I have to see it too. You watch my back and I'll watch yours. Fair enough?"

Dana nodded. After making a quick scan of the area, they crept past a small marshy area filled with stagnant water that buzzed and clicked with nocturnal life. Together they wove through the shadows, stopping every now and then to listen before moving on to the last row of dunes facing the beach. An enormous dune towered over their heads.

Checking their backs, they waited. Both girls knew that as soon as they left the dune's shadowed base their dark silhouettes would be highlighted against the stark whiteness when they began to climb. Making a final check of the area behind them, they scrambled to the top and peered down at the scene on the beach below. What they saw took their breath away.

The bow of the massive ship lay wrapped in an island of light a hundred yards directly in front of them. Tilted to one side, the first half of the vessel rested in a V-shaped trench carved by the bow, while the stern section floundered in the surf, hopelessly trapped by the suction of wet sand.

Soldiers were everywhere. It looked like a small military camp had sprung up on the beach. Several military Humvees were patrolling the area, and next to the pier, a line of unmarked government cars were parked between a row of inflatable tents and a black motorhome.

Turning her attention back to the ship, Sam witnessed a scene of frenzied activity as faceless men in yellow bio-hazard suits flowed up and down a steel ramp carrying small red containers to a waiting line of four-wheel-drive military trucks. It reminded her of a lifeless beetle being picked clean by ants.

"Wow!" Dana exclaimed. "It looks like D-Day down there!"

Sam nodded without answering, her eyes drawn to the ship's bow. She didn't want to look at it, but she couldn't turn away either. The scrape marks where it had sliced through her beautiful little boat were still visible. The shriek of tearing fiberglass came rushing back.

How had she survived being run over by that?

Closing her eyes, she could feel the tiny beads of sweat forming on her upper lip and forehead.

"Are you okay?"

The voice sounded distant to Sam. Opening her eyes, she saw Dana staring back at her.

"Yeah ... sorry. I didn't know seeing that thing again would have this effect on me."

"I think being run over by a ship at sea would affect anyone. Maybe we should go."

Sam shook her head. "No ... not yet. I want to see what these guys are up to." Using her forearms, she inched closer to the sloping edge of the dune. "Do you know what's in all those red containers?"

"Probably DNA samples," Dana replied. "They look like the containers Peter designed to keep the samples from becoming contaminated. Some of the more interesting samples were shipped back to our lab in Austin, but the bulk of the collection was still in the freezers on board."

Sam squinted against the harsh glare from the lights. "Are you sure they were only collecting DNA samples? I mean, those guys aren't wearing those yellow protective suits for fun. It's pretty obvious they're afraid of something."

"Our protocol called for all of the samples to be screened for known pathogens before any DNA was extracted. My guess is they're just being cautious because they don't know what they're dealing with yet."

"What about unknown pathogens?"

"Anything's possible when you're dealing with specimens gathered from a rainforest ... especially the one in the Congo. There's still a lot we

49

don't know about that part of the world, and some pretty nasty things have come from there." Dana tried to wet her cracked lips with her tongue.

"You need to drink something," Sam said, pulling the beer from her back pocket. "Here ... I hope you like Lone Star."

"Anything liquid is fine. Thanks." Dana quickly downed half the contents and wiped her mouth with the back of her hand before offering the rest to Sam.

"Keep it. Beer probably isn't the best thing to give someone who's dehydrated, but at least it's got electrolytes. I've got a gallon jug of cold water in the fridge back at my house."

"Your house?"

"Yeah. I think we've seen enough for now."

Dana took another swig of beer. "You don't even know me."

"I know you're tired and thirsty ... and you don't look too dangerous to me right now."

For the first time since they had met, Dana smiled. "Let me guess. You're a student at the marine lab."

"No, but I catch all of their bait fish for them."

"Bait?"

"Yeah, it's how I make my living. I catch bait for fishermen."

A sudden flash made them squint as a bright light swept the dunes. Both girls flattened against the sand. "Better go," Sam said. "Now!"

"Do you think they saw us?"

"I don't know, but I'm not hanging around to find out. Coming?"

Both girls moved away from the edge and slid down the backside into the shadows. They stood perfectly still, looking and listening. Satisfied they were still alone, they took off at a sprint, swatting mosquitoes as they ran in the moonlight past the tall reeds of the marshy area. They were now in full view of anyone watching from the tops of the dunes, but they kept running through the gritty maze, trying to stay in the shadows as much as possible until they finally stumbled from the ocean of sand into Sam's back yard.

Looking back at the glowing white mounds, Sam motioned for Dana to follow her beneath the pilings supporting her house and jogged up the front stairs. They were still breathing hard from their run when they entered the living room and Dana collapsed on the sofa. Sam filled a glass with cold water from the fridge and handed it to her. "Drink all of it and I'll get you another. Believe me ... I know what it feels like to be thirsty. It's even worse when you're floating all night in salt water and you know you can't drink it. When's the last time you peed?"

"Maybe this morning," Dana said, gulping down the last drop with shaking hands. "I really don't remember."

Returning to the kitchen, Sam thought she heard a car pull up out front and stop while she was refilling Dana's empty glass.

Maybe it was Brian come to check on her. Crossing the room, she handed the water to Dana and stood behind the screen door to look out at the street. Parked in front was a plain black sedan with two men sitting inside.

"Looks like one of the cars we saw parked on the beach," Dana breathed, peering through the bamboo shades covering the front window. "You think they're looking for us?"

"They're looking for me. Typical Fed car. Probably the FBI guys."

Dana's eyes grew wide. "FBI!"

"Yeah. They wanted to talk to me earlier at the hospital, but I didn't feel like talking to them then. I kind of figured they'd show up here eventually. I just didn't know it would be tonight."

"Great." Dana stood and jerked her head around like a cornered animal. "Do you have a back door?"

"They just want to ask a few questions about my run-in with the ship. You can wait in my bedroom while I go outside and answer their stupid questions. I really don't have much to tell them, so it shouldn't take long. Might as well get this over with."

A pair of car doors slammed, sending Dana streaking into the bedroom as Sam stepped out onto the front porch. Two men wearing dark blue windbreakers were standing at the front gate.

"Hi there," said a man who was obviously older than his partner. "Are you Miss Adams ... Samantha Adams?"

"Yes. You the two FBI guys who wanted to talk to me at the hospital?"

The two men exchanged glances. "May we come in?" the older man asked. The younger man remained silent, looking up and down the street.

"Sure. I was just coming out on the porch. It's a little cooler out here than it is inside."

The two men walked through the gate and mounted the steps.

"Grab a seat," Sam said. "Those wicker chairs are stronger than they look. You guys have badges or something?"

The older man smiled and pulled out his ID. "My name is Preston ... Gil Preston, and this is agent Redding. We're not actually FBI. We're DIA."

Sam fought to maintain a neutral expression. "DIA?"

"Yes, ma'am. Defense Intelligence Agency. We're from the Pentagon."

"The Pentagon! Is this about the ship?"

"Yes it is," Preston replied. "We just want to know what happened out there."

"Wow! Must be pretty important. The FBI wanted to talk to me too ... at the hospital."

"That was us," the younger man said. "That was a pretty sneaky exit you made."

"I didn't feel up to answering any questions then," Sam shot back. "Besides, the only thing I saw was the bow of a big white ship before it cut my boat in half."

The two men traded looks again. "You've been through quite an ordeal," Preston said, adopting the look of a concerned father. "Is there anything else you remember ... anything at all?"

"Like what?"

Redding swatted at something buzzing around his head. "Did you happen to see anyone on the deck of the ship?"

"Are you kidding?" Sam laughed. "I was dragged underwater when it hit my boat. All I remember is that big white bow coming straight at me."

"You think it hit you on purpose?"

"No. It was getting real foggy. I don't think they ever saw me."

Preston's eyes narrowed. "What were you doing out there, Miss Adams?"

"Sailing."

"Were there any other boats in the area?"

"I saw an older shrimp boat heading south before the storm front moved in. Other than that I was pretty much alone until that ship appeared." Sam paused, thinking. "Oh, I did see the name of the ship before it disappeared in the fog. *Searcher.* But you guys already know that, don't you. I mean, it's lying out there like a beached whale right now. How come the Pentagon is so interested in it?"

Redding straightened in his chair. "I'm afraid that's classified."

"Classified! Is there something dangerous on that ship you're not telling us about? Because if there is, you need to let us know about it so we can get off this island."

"Classified doesn't mean there's something dangerous on board," Preston responded, leaning forward. "It just means we aren't allowed to talk about it." Reaching under his windbreaker, he pulled out a photograph and handed it to Sam. "We were wondering if you had seen this woman around the island recently."

Sam blinked hard when she saw Dana's large brown eyes staring back at the camera in an unflattering, university ID picture. "Uh, no ... can't say that I have. What did she do?"

Preston's eyes drifted to the large plate glass window behind Sam. "We just want to talk to her. She disappeared around the same time the ship did." Slapping his hands on his knees, he stood and motioned to the younger man, who was still busy swatting at something buzzing around his head.

"Thank you for your time, Miss Adams. You've been very helpful." Preston took the picture and handed her his card. "Just in case you happen to remember anything else, my direct number is on the back."

The two men were halfway down the steps when Preston stopped and looked back at Sam. "Oh...there is one more thing. I'm afraid I'll have to ask you to keep our little visit here a secret for now."

"A secret?"

"Yes." The man's fatherly smile was back. "I wish I could tell you more, but if word got out that we were here on the island it could hamper our investigation."

Sam smiled politely. "I understand. My boyfriend's in the military. Coast Guard."

Still swatting at the air around his head, the younger agent finally abandoned all pretense of trying to look official and jumped into the car, closing the door behind him.

"Those mosquitoes really seem to like your partner," Sam observed. "They're usually not this bad, but we had a pretty rainy spring and there's not much wind out tonight."

53

Looking back at the darkened windows of the car, Preston frowned. "He'll be okay. Poor guy just got back from Africa. He saw a lot of people dying from malaria. Mosquitoes and fleas are at the top of my list of things I'd love to see become extinct."

"Extinct? That's a pretty heavy word to use around here. The big tarpons almost vanished from these waters from overfishing a few years back, but I hear they're starting to make a comeback. Oh, and you might let your partner know we don't have malaria in Port Aransas. Maybe that will ease his mind a little while you guys are here. Any idea how long that will be?"

Preston smiled back without answering.

"Oh right." Sam's eyes narrowed. "Classified."

"Smart girl," he called out, descending the stairs to his car. "Don't worry, Miss Adams. Things will be back to normal soon enough."

As soon as they drove away, Sam entered the house and called out to Dana.

"I'm in here."

Sam turned to see her sitting on the couch. "You should have stayed in the bedroom."

"I know, but I wanted to hear what they said."

"Then you know they're looking for you, and they're not FBI."

"I heard. Military intelligence. That's even scarier."

"Why's that?"

"The DIA is like the CIA. The only difference is they fall under the umbrella of military instead of civilian authority."

Pulling a beer from the fridge, Sam turned on a lamp in the living room before curling up on the opposite end of the couch. "Military, huh? I wonder why they're questioning a civilian."

"I don't think they're supposed to," Dana continued, "but things have changed over the past few years. Ever since 9/11 the military has taken over a lot of what the old CIA used to do."

"Old CIA?"

"Yeah. Apparently, the U.S. intelligence community has evolved into a federation of seventeen separate agencies. Supposedly they all work together now, although I have a feeling that's not always the case."

"Seventeen agencies! How do you know all this?"

"I Googled it one night on the hotel computer when I was at the height of my paranoia. The fact that the military was just at your door instead of the FBI is sending up all kinds of red flags to me. At least with the FBI you have a better chance of knowing who you're dealing with, but with an intelligence service nothing is black and white. They exist in a world of gray, where things aren't always what they appear to be."

"I guess that's why they call them spooks." Sam smiled.

"That's a good word for them. I mean, don't you find it a little odd they asked you to keep their visit a secret? And why did Peter send that cryptic email telling me to run ... not to trust anyone. You didn't know him like I did. He wasn't one of those people who indulged in drama. Now his ship is lying on a beach an ocean away from where it was last seen ... and your sleepy little island is starting to look like Iwo Jima. Hello! Something's going on here, and someone is trying really hard to keep it a secret for some reason." By now Dana was holding her knees to her chest and rocking back and forth.

"How many glasses of water have you had?" Sam asked.

"Four."

"Your color looks better. How about a beer?"

"Sounds great. I'll get it, and you don't have to lie about my color. People are always telling me I look like death warmed over."

Sam grinned as she watched Dana walk into the kitchen and retrieve a beer before returning to her spot on the couch. She was starting to like this girl. In a way, she did look like death warmed over. With ghostly pale skin covering an anorexic frame, her spiky black hair and Goth-like eye makeup made her oversized eyes look almost cartoonish. But once she opened her mouth it was obvious she was no dummy, and she didn't try to hide the fact that she wasn't too fond of authority figures.

It had been years since Samantha had taken the time to just sit with another girl her own age, enjoying a cold beer and talking against the sound of crickets on the front porch. Most of the girls she had gone to high school with had moved away from the island, and those who had stayed were either busy raising children or had their own hectic careers—careers that had eventually confined their socializing to a closed circle of work-related friends.

She had Brian of course—and that was great. Even though she always winced when she heard the expression *soul mate*, she knew that's what he was becoming to her. She really couldn't imagine life without him. But every now and then a girl just had to hang with the girls, and it felt good to be sitting there with the taste of cold beer in her mouth, talking to another female. It was a welcome departure from the reality of a life more devoted to work than to play.

Sam leaned her head against a big red pillow on her end of the sofa. "What exactly do you do in that Austin lab, Dana?"

"We do a lot of stuff. I'm a PhD candidate in the molecular biology department. The university frowns on doctoral candidates working, but Professor Dinning hired me anyway to help with all the DNA sequencing and photography in his lab. I guess you could say I'm a glorified lab assistant."

"Sounds like fascinating work."

"It was until all of this happened. Now I'm homeless and out of a job … and I don't even know why. I keep wishing I'd wake up in my apartment with only a vague memory of a bad nightmare."

"I know the feeling. What about the other people in your lab, Dana? Why didn't he tell them to run?"

"I was wondering about that too until I realized they were working on other projects and I was the only direct link with the African expedition. I called to check. They're all back at work."

Sam peered through a crack in the bamboo shades at the darkened street outside. "Are you sure your boss wasn't working on anything for the military?"

"Not that I'm aware of. All of our research was pretty much out in the open, and I never saw any military types visiting the lab."

"*Pretty much* in the open?"

"What?"

"You said your research was *pretty much* out in the open. Does that mean you were doing things that weren't out in the open?"

"Dana uncurled her legs and set her beer on the coffee table. "It's not like we were working on anything secret. Most of the scientific concepts we were dealing with have been around for years, but you have to realize that no one in the academic world wants to release the results of their research until they're sure of the validity of their findings. The people funding us are looking for results with real-world applications, and if it looks like we're just spinning our wheels on some far out theory, our credibility takes a major hit. It's an incredibly competitive environment, and the scientific community is all about credibility. The more cred you have, the more funding you get."

"I thought the university funded all of your research."

"Only partially. In the world of molecular biology a lot of the money for research comes from pharmaceutical and genetic-based biotechnology companies, but Peter was the one who dealt with those kinds of things. I never asked where the money was coming from."

Sam leaned her head back and stared at the ceiling. "Maybe this would be a good time to find out. Think about it for a minute. The people footing the bill for your research have the biggest stake in this game, and from what we just saw on the beach, it's obvious the military is pretty interested in that ship for some reason. Look who just showed up on my doorstep."

"Good point." Dana sank back down into the couch. "Sorry you got mixed up in all of this."

"I got mixed up the minute that ship ran over my boat," Sam replied, "and from the way that DIA man was talking, it didn't sound like they thought it was an accident. These people really are spooky, and you're staying here tonight."

"Thanks, Samantha … really, but I can't."

"Yes you can. I'm not trying to freak you out or anything, but you should have seen the look in that man's eyes when he showed me your picture. Until we find out why they're really so interested in finding you, it's not safe for you to leave this house. You can sleep in my mother's old room."

"Your mother's room?"

"She died two years ago … cancer."

"Oh … sorry, Samantha."

"You can call me Sam. Everyone else around here does." Sam tossed the pillow aside and heaved herself off the couch. "I'll grab some towels. There's a shower in the connecting bath between the two bedrooms. I'm guessing you're pretty anxious for one after being in the dunes for two days. I'll make us something to eat while you're in there."

Dana ran her hands through her short hair. "A shower sounds great. Thanks. Need any help with supper?"

"I'm just gonna heat up some leftover beans and wieners. Nothing fancy … but I've got ice cream."

Walking past the kitchen window, Sam froze. There was something glinting in the dunes behind her house. Leaning over the sink, she switched off the light. In the glowing moonlight, she could just make out a line of dark shapes sliding down the backsides of the dunes—and they were moving toward her house!

CHAPTER 8

B acking away from the window, Sam crossed the living room. "Turn off that lamp!"

Dana's large eyes grew even larger. "What did you see?"

"Soldiers … in the dunes … and they're coming this way."

Dana jumped from the couch and stood next to Sam behind the front screen door. Peering down the street, they saw the black sedan parked in the shadows away from the street light at the end of the block.

"Those DIA guys are back too," Sam said.

Dana's voice started to tremble. "You think they know I'm here?"

"If they do it means they were probably watching us in the dunes. Those DIA men showed up right after we got back to the house, and the older one kept trying to look through the front windows. We've got to get out of here … now!"

"But how?" Dana shrank back. "We can't outrun them."

"Ever been on a motorcycle before?"

"No."

"Well you're about to check it off your bucket list, because you're riding on one tonight. Follow me!"

Opening the screen door, Sam stepped out onto the porch. With the moon still high, she hoped the hanging plants would block the view from the street as she pointed to her dirt bike at the bottom of the stairs. "As soon as I kick-start the engine, you hop on behind me. Keep your feet on the pegs and hang on tight. These people are on my turf now, and I'm about to give them a run for their money."

"I don't know, Samantha. Maybe this is what they're waiting for … to see if I'm really here."

"If you wanna hang around and find out that's fine by me, but I'm outta here. These guys aren't playing by the rules. They're acting like we're terrorists or something, and the soldiers headed this way are probably in my back yard by now. I'm telling you, this is no time to stand around trying to figure out what they want. Are you coming?"

Dana peered down at the little dirt bike. "Yeah … let's go!"

Flying down the steps, Sam straddled her bike. With a priming twist of the hand throttle, she raised up and came down hard on the kick starter. The engine coughed to life just as she felt the back of the motorcycle dip when Dana jumped on behind her.

"Do you have a helmet?" Dana asked.

"Really?" Sam twisted the throttle all the way back. The rear tire spun and the bike lurched forward, crashing through the little front gate and leaving a trail of splintered wood in their wake as Sam threw the bike into a slide and rocketed down the street.

Glancing back over her shoulder, she saw a sight that sent chills down her spine. The black sedan was rushing up behind them, and the soldiers in the dunes had completely surrounded her house. Dozens of red laser beams danced along her front porch, converging on the windows and painting the walls inside with bright red dots that made the house appear to glow red from within.

It was almost too late by the time she saw them. Blocking the north end of her street, two military Humvees switched on their bright lights, temporarily blinding her. Turning her head, Sam blinked to clear her vision.

"Hang on!" she shouted over her shoulder. Braking hard, she leaned sideways and gunned the bike between two parked cars, fishtailing in the soft sand as they sped through a row of pilings beneath one of the elevated beach houses on the opposite side of the street. Sam swerved just in time to miss a rusty barbeque pit and held her breath when they shot between a wooden stairway and a parked truck. The dirt bike's engine was screaming as they crossed the next street over, barely missing another military Humvee rushing to block their escape.

They raced from street to street under the elevated houses, weaving their way through a forest of pilings until they reached the last street and bounced over a shallow ditch into the tall grass of a darkened field. Sliding to a stop, Sam let the engine idle while she raised up and scanned the area around them. To the west, shining through the trees, she could see the lights of the marina on the other side of the field.

"You okay back there?" she shouted to Dana.

"Yeah. My knee hit something, but I'm alright. Are we stopping here?"

"No. They can see us out here in this moonlight even without their night-vision goggles. I think our best bet is the marina."

"The marina?" Dana looked up and squinted through the trees at the distant lights. "Then what?"

"I haven't figured that out yet," Sam said. "Hang on."

John Lyman

CHAPTER 9

Weaving her dirt bike through a scattering of live oaks and palm trees, Sam jumped another shallow drainage ditch at the far end of the field and bounced up onto a paved road before streaking for the marina. They were almost there when the black car pulled out from a side street and blocked the road ahead.

Behind her, the two Humvees were catching up, and to her right, the boozy glow of neon beer signs filled the windows of a local bar. With her options quickly running out, Sam whipped past a line of pickup trucks in the bar's parking lot and plowed into some tall weeds before gunning the bike around to the back of the weathered building.

"Get off!" she shouted to Dana.

"What?"

"We'll have to run from here." Sam laid her bike against the building and took off at a dead run with Dana right behind her. Jumping a chain link fence, they ran through a littered boatyard—dodging fifty-gallon oil drums and stacks of rotten wood filled with rusty nails. Stumbling through the maze of land-locked boats, they moved to the left until they came to a concrete bulkhead at the water's edge and stopped. A line of red and blue flashing lights was converging on the bar behind them from two directions, and they could hear men shouting in the distance.

With nowhere left to go, the two girls looked out over the harbor's light-streaked water and exchanged glances. Wrapping her arms around herself, Dana withdrew into the shadow of a leaning shrimp boat. "If you think I'm swimming in that dark water, you can forget it."

"No. That's what I want them to think. Just stay with me!" Looking off to her side, Sam kicked an empty oil drum into the water. As soon as she was sure it would float, she motioned to Dana and the two girls took off running toward the marina.

Scrambling over another chain-link fence, they jumped down onto the mossy, rock-strewn shoreline and struggled through the foul-smelling tidal mud before darting under the wooden deck of the marina's restaurant—closed for the night.

From their hiding place they peered out at the lighted boat yard and worked to catch their breath. A few soldiers had reached the bulkhead, and moments later, agents Preston and Redding came jogging up behind them. They were all watching the floating oil drum drift away.

"Good move," Dana whispered, gripping Sam by the arm. "They think we're swimming behind that drum. You think they'll shoot at it?"

"They don't want us dead. They could have easily made that happen if that's what they wanted."

Huddled in the mud under the deck, the two girls shivered from the adrenaline coursing through their bodies as they watched more soldiers arrive. The beams from their lights were crisscrossing the water, and two of the men had shed their gear and were swimming furiously toward the drifting barrel.

Sam bit her lower lip as she looked out over the yacht-encrusted marina and the rows of darkened boats gently tugging at their dock lines. "As soon as they discover we're not swimming behind that oil drum they'll move their search here."

"Great!" Dana stared back at her. "Now what are we supposed to do? Sit here in this smelly mud until they find us?"

Sam's eyes narrowed. "I'm working on the fly here, Dana! Can you swim?"

"I already told you, I'm not…"

"There's no other way. Believe me, swimming isn't at the top of my list of favorite things to do right now either, but you'll be fine … I promise. I've been swimming in this marina for years."

Without waiting for Dana to answer, Sam crawled between the pilings and slid down the sloping embankment beneath the deck to the water's edge. Glancing back toward the voices in the boatyard, she waded in until the bottom dropped away and she began swimming.

Against the tinkling melody played by the wind among the masts of the sailboats, a muffled cough in the water behind her made her smile. Looking back, she saw Dana's wide eyes peering just above the surface, shining in the moonlight as she breaststroked behind her like some following reptile. Together they kept swimming, glancing up through the spaces in the wooden dock, until finally Sam spotted the name she was looking for painted in gold script on the stern of a large sport-fishing boat.

Just in Time.

Heaving herself onto a small aft deck extending just above the waterline, she reached out to Dana and helped her out of the water. For awhile they just sat there, watching and listening with their legs dangling in the water. The boat yard had grown quiet, which meant the soldiers were probably moving into the marina. They were still being hunted.

"Are we going to duck under the water if they come down the dock?" Dana whispered.

"You can if you want." Sam pulled a set of keys from her front pocket. "I'm going inside and lock the door."

"You have a key to this boat?"

"The owner is a friend of mine. I stock all his bait. I have keys to most of the fishing boats around here, but this is one of the largest with more places to hide."

"You think they'll search the boats?"

"I doubt they'll search the ones that are locked," Sam said. "They aren't going to go around and start breaking into all the boats around here. It would take them all night, not to mention it would start a riot with the fishermen."

Opening a sea locker behind her, Sam reached in and pulled out a towel. "Here, dry off before we climb over the transom and walk across the back deck. We don't want to leave any wet footprints behind."

Dana managed a weak grin. "Sounds like you've done this before."

"Maybe a little, but mostly when I was a teenager. We didn't go parking on some back road to play kissy-face like kids in most other places do. It was much more comfortable to hang out on a boat. We had AC, and there was usually beer on board. It was a lot safer than parking in the middle of nowhere. Most of the time we would just lay out on the deck and look up at the stars, but we learned to wipe away our wet footprints just in case any grownups showed up." Sam jangled the keys in front of Dana. "Come on. Let's get inside."

John Lyman

CHAPTER 10

Inside the black motor home parked on the beach, Admiral Nathan Bourdon pounded his fist against the table. "Hell, Preston! Are you trying to tell me that you and a shit-load of some of our best men were just outsmarted by two girls on a dirt bike!?"

Gil Preston stared back at the admiral with unblinking eyes. As a former Special Ops guy himself, he had endured more than one dressing down by a superior officer in his long career, and he knew the best defense in these kinds of situations was to play dead so that the big bear sitting across the table would tire of chewing on his backside and eventually turn his attention to someone else. Showing any signs of life at this point in the ass-chewing would be the worst thing he could do right now. He had to wait and choose his next words carefully.

"Haven't you got anything to say for yourself?" Bourdon continued. The admiral had known this officer for years, and both men knew the game well.

Preston looked out at the beached ship and exhaled. "We'll find them, Admiral. After all, this is an island, and there are only three ways off. The ferry, the beach road, or one of the boats in the marina … and we've got them all covered. You kinda have to hand it to those girls, though. They were on to us right away, and the one we interviewed knows this island a lot better than we do."

Bourdon stood and began pacing, a sign the big bear was thinking of different prey. "Well, at least this confirms our original suspicions. Now that this so-called local girl has hooked up with Dinning's assistant, it's pretty obvious the two of them have been working together. She wasn't sailing around out there in the Gulf with a storm coming just for the fun of it. Maybe the collision between her boat and the ship was an accident, only it wasn't part of the plan. If she was out there to meet him, how the hell did Dinning get off … and where is he now?" The admiral thought for a minute. "Has anyone talked to her Coast Guard boyfriend?"

"Yes, sir," Preston replied. "He seemed genuinely upset. He has no idea what's going on. He said she doesn't even know anyone named Dana in Austin."

His mind riddled with unanswered questions, the admiral walked to the front of the motorhome and stared out at the sea through the big front window. "We have to find those two girls, Gil, and it has to be soon … for all our sakes."

CHAPTER 11

The sun was still thirty minutes away from painting the horizon when Randy Monroe stepped onto the deck of the *Just in Time* with a box of wrapped sandwiches for the day's fishing trip. The inspiration for the boat's name had originated during one of the island's biggest fishing tournaments, when Randy had made it back to the dock with only seconds to spare before the 4 PM gun went off. He really had made it back just in time, because he had the winning sailfish on board. A few seconds later and the fish would have been disqualified, along with the bragging rights and prize money that went with it. After enduring months of teasing by his fellow captains, he had finally retaliated by having the name *Just in Time* painted in big gold script on the stern of his new boat.

Balancing the box on his shoulder, he unlocked the cabin door and stepped inside. Sam and a girl with spiky black hair were staring back at him. Dropping the sandwiches, he stumbled back, uttering a few choice words that sent a couple of roosting seagulls screeching from the deck outside. "Sam … what the hell?"

"Sorry, Randy." Samantha reached down and started picking sandwiches off the floor. "I didn't have any way of contacting you, and this was the only place I could think of to go."

Looking back over his shoulder, Randy closed the door. "You scared the hell out of me. Your pictures were on the news when I turned on the TV this morning. They said you ran from the police last night after they tried to stop you for speeding."

"They weren't the police, Randy. They were military, and I was sitting in my house when they arrived … not speeding. We don't know why they're chasing us, but it has something to do with that ship."

Randy cast an accusing eye at Dana. "Who's this?"

"A friend. It's a long story. She knew someone on the ship and wanted to see it."

"That's true," Dana shot back. "He was my boss. There's nothing else I can tell the people chasing us, because I have no idea what went on over in Africa."

"Why don't you just tell that to the police?" Randy kept peering through the small window in the door, expecting a SWAT team any minute. "Running away only makes you look guilty of something."

"They came to my house, Randy," Sam said. "I was expecting the FBI, but these guys were from the Pentagon. Have you seen the beach around that ship?"

"No. They still have all the roads blocked. Why?"

"It looks like D-Day down there. Something big is going on, and they aren't exactly handing out leaflets telling us what's really happening. They told me it was classified."

"Classified! How do you know what they were doing on the beach?"

"I snuck through the dunes and looked. That's how I met Dana."

Randy leaned against the cabin door. He was looking a little pale for a tanned boat captain. "And what was she doing out there?"

"I already told you. She wanted to see it. We both did. Those bodies didn't just end up in the freezers all by themselves, and there's no way that ship made it all the way back over here from Africa without someone alive on board to run it. I think we all deserve to know what really happened."

Randy took a quick look outside again. "Look, Sam … I don't mean to sound like a jerk, but I have a fishing charter in an hour. These government people could confiscate my boat if they find you two hiding here. We need to think this through."

"Relax, Randy. We just needed a place to hang for the night. We'll leave."

Randy's stern expression slowly melted. "You're not going anywhere until I'm sure you're safe. When's the last time you two had something to eat?"

Both girls shrugged their shoulders.

"That's what I thought." Randy tossed them a couple of sandwiches and watched silently while they ate.

"Did you see any military vehicles parked out front when you drove up?" Sam asked between mouthfuls.

"Yeah, as a matter of fact, I did. Two Humvees and about a half-dozen soldiers."

"Did they say anything to you about us?"

"No. They just looked at me when I walked by."

Sam exchanged glances with Dana. "Don't you find that a little strange?"

"What do you mean?"

"Why didn't they show you our pictures or tell you to be on the lookout for us?"

"How should I know? It's not like you're wanted for murder or anything."

"I believe there's a different reason. They know we're probably still around here somewhere, which means they can't allow any of the boats to leave without searching them. But they have to be careful how they go about looking for us. I mean, they can't just go around and start breaking into million-dollar yachts. That would start a riot among the fishermen … and the rest of the town wouldn't be too happy about it either. So instead, they're keeping a low profile while they watch every captain walk to his boat this morning. If I'm right, they'll be here any minute with a polite request to search the cabin."

Before Randy could respond, the boat rocked slightly, followed by the sound of boots clomping around on the deck outside. Reaching down, Randy pulled up a small hatch in the floor and pointed to a storage area below. "Down there … and don't even think about coughing or sneezing."

As soon as Sam and Dana had scrambled below, he closed the hatch and opened the door. A soldier was just about to knock when Randy looked back at him with a pair of lazy brown eyes. "Are you the guys who chartered my boat?"

The young soldier standing in front of him started to say something but Randy prattled on. "I think it's great you military guys are getting some time off to go fishing while you're here. This is one of the finest deep sea fishing ports in the world, and you've just stepped onto the best boat here. Come on in and get settled while I check on the bait." Randy paused to look at their guns and uniforms. "Ya'll might want to get out of that heavy gear and change into something more comfortable before we leave, and the weapons will have to stay behind. Coast Guard finds any weapons on board and my ass is grass."

A smiling corporal stepped forward. "We're sorry to bother you, Captain, but we're not here to fish."

71

"Not here to fish?"

"No, sir. We're helping the police look for a couple of girls who ran from them last night, and we need to search your boat to make sure they aren't hiding somewhere on board."

"Two girls, you say?" Randy stepped out on deck, blocking the door. "Well, they're not here. My boat was still locked when I got here this morning, and there's no sign of a break-in. I always check."

"Just the same sir, we have orders to search every ..."

"Orders? Orders from who? What did these two girls do?"

"Speeding," a private chirped in.

"Speeding! You've got to be kidding. Are you seriously telling me the U.S. military is looking for a couple of girls for speeding on a civilian road?"

The soldiers exchanged a few sheepish looks but maintained their positions. "Yes, sir. It sounded a little strange to us too, but orders are orders."

"They sure are ... for you. But I've got a charter party on the way, and I can tell you right now that no one but me was on this boat before you showed up. Like I said, the cabin door was locked and ..."

Randy paused as if he had been struck by a sudden idea. "Maybe we should check the engine room," he said to the corporal, adding a conspiratorial wink for effect. "There's no lock on the access doors. That's the only place they could have gotten into without a key."

"Can you show us where it is?" the corporal asked.

"You're standing on it." Pushing his way past the soldiers onto the back deck, Randy lifted the two large hatches covering the engines and stepped back. "Help yourselves, but you can see pretty much everything from here." Peering down, Randy spotted a puddle of oil under one of the engines. "Damn it to hell. There goes my charter. Looks like I've got a major oil leak. You boys might as well take all the time you need to look around now, because I'm not going anywhere today." He looked up to study the soldiers' faces. "I've got some stuff that will get most of the grease stains out of your uniforms if you need to poke around down there."

The soldiers traded looks. "Uh, I think we've taken up enough of your time, sir." The corporal held a hand to his radio earpiece. "Some of the other captains are showing up and we need to check their boats. Thank you for your cooperation."

"No problem. I'm a veteran too, and if you guys ever do get some time off to go fishing, give me a call. We can work something out on the price."

"Sounds great, sir, but most of us are pulling out this afternoon."

"That so? You gonna open up the beach again?"

"Yes, sir, but I'm afraid you're going to be stuck with that ship out there for awhile until the engineers can find an ocean-going tug powerful enough to pull it off the beach."

"That'll be fun to watch." Randy smiled. "Y'all have a good day."

Without answering, the soldiers headed back up the dock. As soon as they were out of sight, Randy entered the cabin and helped the two girls from their tight hiding place.

"What time is your charter party supposed to show up?" Sam asked, stretching to restore her circulation.

"They're not. I'm going up to the marina office right now and tell Dorothy to cancel my trip today. She can always find another boat for my fishing party. In the mean time, you two wait here … and stay away from the windows."

"Do you really have an oil leak? We heard what you told the soldiers."

"Yeah, but it's just a gasket. Shouldn't take more than a half hour to fix, but I'll make it look like an all-day job. As soon as it gets dark, I'll get you two off the island. I was thinking about Conn Brown harbor in Aransas Pass. You two stowaways think about it."

Randy started to leave but stopped. Looking straight into Sam's eyes, his face grew serious. "What in the hell have you gotten yourself into, Samantha?"

73

John Lyman

74

CHAPTER 12

B y mid-morning the cabin had grown stiflingly hot, and Randy had stretched a power cord to the dock to run the AC for the two girls inside while he sweated out on deck. He was making a real show of working on his engine while keeping a wary eye out for strangers. For a moment he thought of walking up to the marina store for a six-pack, but he quickly shook off the idea.

Staying sharp for their nighttime departure was a no-brainer.

It wasn't that unusual for a boat to be making a run after dark, but if anyone asked, he would simply tell them he was testing his repair job before venturing out into the Gulf the next morning.

In one of the forward staterooms, Sam and Dana lay across from each other on a pair of built-in, single bunks. For awhile they both tried to sleep but ended up staring at the ceiling as each rock of the boat sending their nerves on edge.

"Why did you reach out to me?" Sam asked.

Dana turned on her side. "What?"

"In the dunes. Why did you trust me enough to warn me about the soldier? You could have let me keep going to see what he would do."

"You mean use you as bait?"

Sam smiled. "Something like that."

"I guess I never thought of that. I was just reacting on instinct. It was like watching someone cross a frozen lake and I knew the ice was too thin. I had to stop you."

"I'm glad you did." Sam looked back at her. "You talk a lot differently from what I imagined a scientist would talk like. More creative, if that's the right word."

Dana yawned. "I'd like to think I was creative, because science and creativity are so intertwined. Without any creative, out-of-the-box ideas, we wouldn't have anything to aim for. Some of the best scientists are also

75

some of the best daydreamers. Don't tell me. You majored in English and the scientific world turns you off. Am I close?"

"You're getting warm, but it's not that science turns me off. I was just never really any good at it. I grew up by the sea and my house is only a few blocks from one of the top marine science labs in the country, but I never look at the ocean like it's something to be studied. I mean, I'm curious, but that's not the problem. I like to know about all the little creatures that live in the water, and it helps me in my bait-catching business, but my thoughts tend to drift when things start to get too scientific. I like to take in the beauty of my surroundings ... to see the deep blue of the ocean and feel the wind on my skin and not care that it's mostly nitrogen. Put me in a lab or in front of a computer all day and you might as well pull the trigger. My mother's health and problems with money weren't the only reasons I dropped out of college."

"You've probably got more field time than most marine biologists," Dana said. "You just don't realize it. While you've been taking in all that natural beauty along the shore you've also been mentally filing away the behavior of the fish you catch for bait. You could probably teach a course on it. I've watched you. You see everything."

"Yeah, except for that soldier hiding in the dunes."

Dana smiled and stared back up at the ceiling. "Yes, and I guess now would be a good time to tell you there's another reason I came here ... something I probably should have told you about before."

Sam blinked back at her. "Go ahead ... I'm listening."

"It has to do with the marine lab you mentioned. That lab was an integral part of the project we were working on, and no one besides Peter and I knew that we backed-up all of the computer data from the research ship there. After I erased all of our DNA analysis from the mainframe in Austin, it finally dawned on me what my boss was up to. We still have all of our data, but now it's hidden away here at the marine lab in an encrypted file no one would recognize. If I could get to one of their computers and access our analysis, I might be able to find out why these people are so intent on getting to us."

"Don't you think the military already knows about the connection with the lab here?" Sam asked.

"I doubt it. When I walked past the institute yesterday there weren't any military vehicles parked out front. If they had made the connection the place would have been crawling with them. Obviously, we can't just walk through the front door and ask the staff there if we could use their computers for a few minutes, but I was thinking that maybe your captain friend could drop us off somewhere close by after it gets dark. If we can get inside and I can access Peter's last data uplink ..."

"You mean break in ... right?"

"I don't see any other option. Do you?"

Sam rolled on her side and stared across at Dana. "Not really. We're already fugitives for some reason, and if we don't find out why before those DIA guys discover there's a connection between the lab and that ship out there, we'll probably never know. My mother used to say the best defense is a strong offense. She was the strongest person I've ever known. It's time to go on the offensive, because I'm tired of feeling like a criminal just because my boat happened to be in the way of an out-of-control ship."

"I don't think it was out of control." Dana's eyes narrowed. "You and I both know there had to be someone on board that ship ... someone who could guide it back here from Africa to a beach that's only a mile away from the same lab where all the backup data for the expedition is stored."

Sam wondered if she should tell Dana what Brian had told her about the autopilot before finally deciding she should keep that piece of information to herself a little longer. "Are you sure you're telling me everything you know, Dana?"

Dana seemed unfazed by the question. "Actually, no, I haven't told you everything. But I can assure you we weren't working on anything secret if that's what you're thinking. It was just science, pure and simple. I realize I haven't had time to discuss any of the details of our DNA research with you. I can try if you want me to, but frankly it's an impossibly complex subject. Even the so-called experts are always disagreeing with one another. Everything I've told you has been true, Samantha. My life's also been turned upside down, and I want to know why we're being chased just as much as you do."

The drone of the air conditioning was slowly lulling them to sleep, but even with her eyes drifting shut, Sam's mind refused to surrender. "I still can't believe I'm hiding from the military because a ghost ship took out my new sailboat."

"Ghost ship," Dana mumbled in her sleep-deprived state. "Sometimes I wonder if there really are such things as ghosts."

"What?"

"Ghosts. I was just wondering. What if we do leave a little piece of ourselves behind after we die ... like a ghost or a spirit of some kind? I guess that's the big question everyone probably asks themselves when they're lying awake at night, thinking about their own mortality and wondering if there really is a heaven or hell. But how would something like that be possible? Just think about it for a moment. Even if we did leave a little piece of ourselves behind, the unseen world around us would be a very crowded place. I mean, everywhere we went, even when we were alone, we would be surrounded by those who had passed through the physical world before us. One can hardly imagine such a spirit-filled world ... where the invisible residue of all those long-departed souls continues to drift in the great karmic ocean of spiritual ectoplasm that supposedly envelops us all. I guess a physicist would have to answer that one."

Blinking back between the bunks, Sam shook her head. "That was pretty heavy, Dana. I don't think I could have come up with a thought like that in a thousand years. Now I can see why you chose to pursue a career in research. People like you see the world in a whole different way from the rest of us."

The muffled sound of soft breathing coming from Dana's bunk told Sam the frail-looking girl had finally drifted off to sleep. A few minutes later, Sam had followed her pale new friend into the land of dreams, where both girls remained until Randy banged on the door.

Rubbing the sleep from her eyes, Sam looked up to see his backlit form standing in the doorway. It was almost dark outside, and she could hear the comforting sounds of captains and deckhands on nearby boats—laughing and enjoying a few beers while they washed the salt spray from their decks before heading home for the night.

Holding a folded bundle of clothes, Randy dumped the pile on Sam's bunk. "Here ... Julie thought you two could use some clean clothes."

Lifting her head from her pillow, Dana's large eyes blinked up at him. "Who's Julie?"

"My wife."

"You called her on your cell!"

"Of course not. I watch TV. I know they can listen in. She was on her way to the store and saw that our boat was still at the dock. She knows my poker face too well. I had to tell her what was going on."

Sam stretched. "When did all of this happen?"

"Right after you two fell asleep. She's really worried about you, Sam. She drove home and brought back some clean clothes when she heard the two of you were sleeping in the same ones you went swimming in last night."

"What about the soldiers around the marina?"

"Pulled out a few hours ago, but I'm pretty sure they're still watching." Randy paused. "This is the part where I'm supposed to tell you that you're only making things worse by running, but that would be a lie. To tell you the truth, I don't much trust these government people, especially since you haven't done anything wrong. Julie and I talked, and you're right. None of this adds up. Have you decided where you'd like to go yet?"

Sam traded looks with Dana. "We need to get something from the marine institute before we leave. We thought maybe you could drop us off at their dock."

"The institute?" Randy looked surprised. "Probably not a good idea right now, Sam. Their dock extends into the channel near the end of the jetties, and the number of night fishermen on the jetties has tripled since the pier was closed. Someone is bound to spot me dropping you off there … but I guess I could …"

"Could what?"

"I was just thinking I might be able to slip into their little marina next door. Why don't you two grab your showers while I'm still hooked up to the water on the dock." Randy hesitated. "What about Brian?"

"I can't let him get involved in any of this," she said, picking out a pair of jeans and a T-shirt from the stack of clothes. "Helping me right now would probably be a career killer for him."

"I had a feeling you'd say that. I need to run up to the marina store and grab a few things. Need anything while I'm at it?"

Sam reached up and gave his perpetually sun-burned face a quick peck. "You're a good friend, Randy Monroe. Tell Julie I said thanks for the clothes."

"I'll tell her." Thirty minutes later, Randy released the lines to the dock and climbed the ladder to the flying bridge above the cabin before starting the engines. Looking around the marina, the docks appeared deserted as he gently pushed throttles forward and edged out into the harbor. Increasing his speed, the boat evaporated into the twilight gloom that hovered over the rougher water of the channel beyond.

The wave-slapping ride to the marine institute lasted all of ten minutes before Randy pulled back on the throttles and glided through the tight opening into a much smaller private marina. The entire west side was taken up by a large condominium complex and a single row of boat-filled docks, while the east side by the institute had a concrete boat ramp that descended into the water by the marina's office.

Idling the big boat, Randy's eyes were immediately drawn to an unlit concrete dock that ran along the side of the boat ramp. He inched the throttles a tad forward, motoring past the protruding bows of several older-looking boats before swinging the stern around in a slow arc so that the back of the boat was almost flush with the deserted dock.

A few seconds later, he saw both girls bolt from the cabin below and leap for the dock, barely making it before he was forced to shove the throttles forward to keep the stern from crashing into the unyielding concrete. Peering back over his shoulder he raised his hand to wave, but Sam and Dana had already disappeared into the shadows.

CHAPTER 13

The throaty roar from the *Just in Time's* twin engines faded in the channel, leaving the two girls huddled on the sloping boat ramp next to the eastern bulkhead of the marina. Peering over the edge, Sam pointed to a two-story brick building on the opposite side of a lighted parking lot. "That's the institute's administration building."

Glancing back, Sam noticed for the first time that Dana's thin forearms were hanging from the sleeves of a T-shirt that extended past her elbows, and she was struggling to hold up a pair of jeans that were way too large. "Wow ... looks like someone was in a hurry when they got dressed."

"Nothing fit." Dana sighed as she squinted over the bulkhead at the institutional-looking, two-story building with a thin line of narrow windows running along the tops of both floors. "Doesn't look anything like the campus buildings in Austin."

"Let me guess. The science building at the university was a big square block of glass with floor-to-ceiling windows."

"Something like that. Why?"

"Wouldn't work here on the island," Sam said. "These buildings were built to withstand a hurricane. The lab is on the other side of that administration building, and there's a student dorm beyond that. From what I've seen, they're all connected."

"You mean there are people inside?"

"Yep, so you'd better hold on to those big-girl jeans and try to keep up once we start running."

Dana frowned at the back of Sam's head as the two girls began crawling up over the edge of the bulkhead. A flash of headlights rounding the corner of the admin building forced them back down as a little security pickup truck drove past.

"Great! They have a roving security patrol. We'll never be able to get in there now."

"Oh, we're getting in alright." Sam's eyes narrowed as she peered across the parking lot. "I'm more worried about getting out. You ready?"

Dana cinched up her pants. "I'm right behind you."

Taking a final look around, Sam jumped up onto a grass strip next to the ramp and sprinted across the parking lot before running up a short set of steps to an unmarked metal door. Standing beneath a yellow light fixture that had been permanently dimmed by the remains of hundreds of dead insects, she glanced over her shoulder to make sure Dana was right behind her and reached for the door. It was locked.

Dana's once spiky hair was now hanging in her eyes as she blinked back at Sam. "Forget it. Administration buildings are always locked. We need to go straight to the lab. Absent-minded researchers are notorious for leaving doors unlocked."

"I thought we were looking for a computer area," Sam said. "Wouldn't that be in here?"

"Probably, but I'd rather go for one of the computers in the lab itself. Researchers are also notorious for leaving their computers on without logging out, and I seriously doubt my password works anymore."

Together the two girls walked around the side of the building fronted by a wide lawn, moving through the shadows behind a line of palm trees that blocked most of the street light. Peering around the back corner, they saw a narrow service road running between the lab and the admin building, and crossing above it, a sky bridge made from heavy steel beams and thick panels of glass connected the upper floors of the two buildings.

In the distance, the guard in the security pickup could be seen shining his spotlight around the perimeter. "That security guard sure loves his job," Dana remarked.

Sam frowned. "He'll be coming back around this way any second now." She looked across the service road toward the lab and noticed a pair of glass doors at the top of a short ramp extending from a little garden alcove directly under the sky bridge. "You stay here while I try the lab doors. If they're locked, I can probably make it back here before the security guard shows up."

Without waiting for Dana to answer, Sam took off at a dead run. As soon as she reached the top of the ramp, she made a grab for one of the door handles. The unlocked door swung open so easily she almost fell over backwards, but her surprise was short-lived when she caught the reflection of the security truck's headlights turning onto the service road behind her.

Diving through the open door, Sam slid across a polished lobby floor and hit the base of a wooden reception counter with her knees. She held her breath.

There was no way he had missed seeing her lunge into the building!

But the truck kept going, painting the walls with its searchlight as it continued up the service road. Lifting herself to her feet, she was rubbing her knees when Dana came rushing through the doors.

"That was close!"

"I know. I didn't really expect to find the doors unlocked." Still massaging her knees, Sam looked past a metal stairway into a darkened hallway. "Where to now?"

Dana walked toward a lighted red exit sign at the end of the hall and stopped when she saw the nameplates on the doors. "Looks like most of the faculty offices are down here on the first floor. The lab is probably upstairs."

Glancing back over their shoulders, the two ascended the stairs and pushed through a pair of swinging white doors. Moonlight was streaming through the small windows set high along the walls, revealing a typical-looking college lab with a center aisle separating two rows of tall work tables filled with trays of shiny instruments. To their right, along one side of the open space, they noticed several office-like cubicles, and in the back, the filtered light reflected against a wall of stainless steel doors.

While Sam maintained a watch, Dana took off down the center aisle looking for a computer terminal, but the only computers she saw were closed laptops lying on the tables. As soon as she reached the back wall, she opened one of the stainless doors and was met by a blast of cold air that smelled of formaldehyde, confirming her suspicions that this was where they stored their prime specimens. This was definitely the main lab. Closing the door, a flickering glow in the nearest side cubicle caught her eye. The cartoon-like image of a dancing dolphin was scrolling across a computer screen.

Bingo! A screensaver! Someone had left their laptop on without logging out. She bent down and tapped the keypad. Instantly the screen came to life with a welcoming blue glow. Taking a seat, she dove into the menu.

For the next several minutes she scrolled through a seemingly endless list of files looking for a familiar name, but the bar on the right side of the screen had barely moved.

This could take all night!

With their options quickly fading, she kept scrolling. Faster and faster the file names flew by in a random blur, until finally ... there!

Conrad!

Dinning had named their secret file after the author of *Heart of Darkness*, and judging by the last entry date, nothing else had been entered after all communications had been broken off. Quickly she clicked on the file name. The screen went black and a white block appeared in the center.

Password protected!

Dana held her breath and typed in her password.

Password invalid! Contact system administrator.

Dana swore under her breath. *She had to think!*

She typed in her first name.

Password invalid! Computer will be locked after next invalid entry!

Dana could feel the perspiration forming on her forehead.

One more chance!

"Why don't you try *Musa*," suggested a disconnected voice in the darkness behind her.

Looking back over her shoulder, Dana screamed when Dr. Peter Dinning stepped into the light.

CHAPTER 14

Bolting from the lab doors, Sam grabbed a razor-sharp dissection knife from one of the work tables and ran toward the back of the lab. As soon as she reached the cubicle, she froze when she saw Dana staring up at an older-looking man with sun-scorched skin and a scraggly beard—his filthy clothes in tatters.

"Get away from her!"

Glancing down at the knife in Sam's hand, Dinning took a step back and held up his hands.

"It's okay, Sam!" Dana jumped to her feet. "It's Peter." She threw her arms around Dinning and started to cry. "I thought you were dead!"

Holding her in a fatherly embrace, he stroked her short hair. "So did I … for awhile."

The two stood there, holding on to one another like a couple of dazed tornado survivors that had just discovered they were both still alive. Gently, he took her by the shoulders and stepped back to peer into her watery eyes. "You don't know how relieved I am to see you … to see you're alright!"

"What happened over there Peter!"

"They killed everyone else on the ship while I hid and listened to the screams."

"My God, Peter. I'm so sorry. But why … who!?"

"That's what I'm here to find out." Looking past Dana, Peter's eyes narrowed at the angry-looking girl who had come running to her aid. "Who's your friend?"

"Oh … this is Sam … Samantha. She's been helping me." Dana was still sniffling and using the sleeves of her T-shirt to wipe the tears from her eyes. "Sam, I'd like you to meet Dr. Peter Dinning."

Sam remained transfixed, unable to speak as she stared back at the man whose ship had sunk her boat—the man who supposedly held all the answers to their questions. "So you're the missing part of the puzzle."

Studying the coiled girl with a knife, Dinning wasn't sure if he should smile or run, so he chose to smile. "If you're asking if I was on that ship out there on the beach, then the answer is yes." He hesitated, looking to Dana. "How much does she know?"

"I know that a ship full of bodies ran over my sailboat, and that I almost drowned," Sam shot back before Dana could answer. "Oh, and the military is chasing us and we have no idea why."

Dinning leaned against a work table, his voice trembling from exhaustion. "I'm sorry. I don't know anything about the ship colliding with another boat, but I can tell you that the bodies you're referring to are the remains of some very close friends of mine who were slaughtered by white soldiers."

"It doesn't make any sense," Dana said. "Why would they do something so horrible?"

"I have no idea. I still can't wrap my head around what happened. I overheard one of them talking about our computer data. That's why I erased it and emailed you before I hid. The only explanation I've been able to come up with is that we must have stumbled onto something over there. If that's the case, it's still hidden somewhere in the massive amount of data we compiled over the past six months. I was worried the same people might show up at the lab in Austin looking for it. That's the reason I told you to run and stay out of sight."

Dana looked to Sam. "Sounds like I was right. All of this does revolve around something in the data."

"It has to!" Dinning continued.

"So you brought the ship back here because this is the last place in the world where that data still exists."

"That's part of it. I also wanted to bring the bodies of our friends back home."

For a moment they remained silent, looking at one another, until the sound of voices in the hallway outside sent them scurrying into the cubicle.

"I'll just be a minute," they heard a man say. The double doors at the end of the lab swung open as a tanned young man with a beard entered and switched on the lights. The three huddled in the cubicle, praying that the computer they were using wasn't the reason for his visit. Glancing around, the man grabbed some papers off the end of one of the work tables and switched off the light before leaving. They heard voices again, then silence.

Dinning stood, keeping his eyes glued on the double doors at the far end of the room. "Probably one of the students from the dorm. That's the way I came in."

"How long have you been here, Peter?" Dana asked.

"I walked in here just before you did."

"No, I meant how long have you been on the island?" Dana shifted nervously. "The *Searcher* has been on the beach for almost three days now. How did you get off the ship without being seen ... and where have you been staying?"

"I wasn't on the ship when it hit the beach. I ..."

"I already know," Sam interrupted. "You programmed the GPS coordinates for Port Aransas into the ship's autopilot before you got off."

Dinning stared back at her. "How do you know that?"

"Yeah ... how do you know about that?" Dana chimed in.

"My boyfriend told me. One of his Coast Guard buddies noticed it when he entered the bridge after the ship ran aground."

"She's right," Dinning said.

"But why did you decide to bring a ship that size all the way back across the Atlantic by yourself?" Dana asked. "There are easier ways to cross the ocean."

"Six months of work was on that ship, not to mention the bodies of some very good people. I couldn't bring myself to leave them behind, and I couldn't exactly stay in *Matadi* either. Our days of shining promise had just been turned into a surreal nightmare, and I wasn't about to hang around and wait for something else to happen."

"But the local authorities," Dana continued. "Why didn't they hold the ship in port for some kind of investigation?"

"They probably would have if I hadn't gotten the *Searcher* out of there. I couldn't risk having the ship and all of our specimens confiscated. It's not like it is here in the states, Dana. We're talking about the Congo ... a place that's remained pretty much unchanged compared to the rest of the world. There's a fine line between the good guys and the bad guys over there, and I had no idea what was going on. There are about thirty known militias operating in Central Africa, and no one really knows if they're rebels or terrorists or just plain thugs trying to profit from the climate of instability in the region. All I can tell you is that they are capable of committing unimaginable atrocities with sudden, unprovoked violence, and we had been told by the locals that the army and the police weren't much better.

"When the government troops showed up on the dock, the last thing I wanted to see was another soldier with a gun boarding the ship. I shouted down over the side that we were all okay, but that a bunch of white guys wearing camos had tried to steal the ship. That really piqued their interest. I heard one of their officers speaking in French about foreign mercenaries being spotted in the area, so they took off in hot pursuit."

"But how were you able to maneuver a ship that size out to sea by yourself?"

"I had some help from a Russian cargo vessel that was docked in front of us. They witnessed the attack, and their engineer and a couple of crewmembers ran over to see if they could help after the troops left. The engineer got the engines started and called for a tug to help move the ship out of the harbor. Luckily, the *Searcher* was already fueled for our impending departure, and I've spent a lot of time on ships over the past few years. I knew how to keep her on course, but the Russians showed me how to set the alarms on the radar to wake me up in case my course crossed the path of another ship while I was sleeping."

"I think you missed one," Sam said. "Your ship snapped my little boat in two like it was a twig."

Dinning could feel his patience wearing thin. "Like I said, I don't know anything about a collision with another boat. If you were sailing within five miles of the coast, I was off the ship by then."

"And just how did you manage that?"

"It was pretty easy, actually. After I set the autopilot, I lowered one of our inflatable Zodiac boats over the side. I wanted to make sure the ship made it to shore, but I knew I had to get off before it hit the beach."

Sam didn't hold back. "Kinda irresponsible, don't you think, Professor? A few hundred yards to the left and that ship would have struck a pier full of people."

"I thought it would run aground farther to the north away from any populated area … on Saint Joseph's Island. I don't know what happened. Maybe the storm threw it off course … who knows?"

"Where have you been staying?" Dana asked.

"Across the channel … on Saint Joe's. When I arrived offshore in the Zodiac and saw that the ship had already run aground on the wrong beach, I made for Saint Joe's and camped in the dunes behind the lighthouse. At that point I knew the beach over here was probably swarming with police, and I couldn't risk being detained. I had one goal in mind, and that was to find out what in the hell was going on and who was behind it. I couldn't do that from a jail cell. The next morning, I crossed the channel in the Zodiac and saw that the military was already here in force, so I hightailed it back across. I decided to wait a few more days for things to calm down before trying to make it back here to the lab."

"So you still have the Zodiac?" Sam asked.

"It's tied up in the little marina across the street."

Dana's gaze drifted to the moonlight filtering in through the high windows. "Did the Russians help you with the bodies, Peter, or did you have to do it by yourself?"

"There wasn't enough time in port." Dinning's expression collapsed. "That was left to me after I was already out at sea. I wrapped them all up the best I could and put them in the freezers." His eyes glazed over with the memory. "I'd rather not talk about that right now … if you don't mind."

"Of course." Dana glanced at Samantha. "I'm sorry, Peter. The past few weeks must have been hell for you."

"It still is." Dinning paused when he noticed Dana holding up her pants. "Why are you wearing those big clothes?"

"Someone is after us too. We had to swim … it's a long story."

"Sounds like the past few weeks haven't been too easy on you either. This entire business is crazy, which is why we need the data on those files. Unless we can find out what triggered the attack, we'll be hiding in the shadows like this for a very long time."

"But the database is huge, Peter! I have no idea how we're going to download the entire thing." Dana glanced back at the laptop. "We're going to need something with lots of memory."

Sam's face came alive with an idea. "Don't the students in the dormitory have flash drives for their laptops? I mean, they probably have …"

"Unless they're carrying around the kind with a terabyte of memory, which I seriously doubt, we're out of luck," Dinning stated. "What kind of laptop is that?"

"It's one of the new scientific ones UT has been loaning out to grad students," Dana said. "They supposedly have a ton of memory."

"It still probably won't be enough, but it's the best we can do for now. Start downloading as much as you can from the mainframe. Begin with the most recent data first and work back. We'll take the laptop with us when you're done."

Looking at the soft blue glow from the computer screen, the three were jolted when the walls of the lab suddenly came alive with the pulsating reflections from dozens of flashing red and blue strobe lights outside the windows.

"Better hurry with that download," Dinning said with a measured calm that belied the fear in his eyes. "I'm afraid our time here has come to an end."

CHAPTER 15

D riving from a meeting at the Corpus Christi Naval Air Station, Admiral Nathan Bourdon and Commander Steve Brooks decided to stop in the small town of Aransas Pass to grab a bite to eat before continuing on to Port Aransas. Because of the similarity in the names of the two towns, people unfamiliar with the Texas coast always got them mixed up. Port Aransas was on the island, while the sleepy town of Aransas Pass sat on the mainland overlooking Redfish Bay.

The town was the last jumping off point before one crossed the bridge over the Intracoastal Waterway and continued across the seven-mile-long elevated causeway that spanned a watery world variously referred to as the tidal flats, or mud flats, or just *the flats*. The causeway ended at the ship channel. From there, anyone wishing to cross over to Mustang Island would have to board the ferry for the short hop across the fast-moving water to the island.

Aransas Pass had a rustic feel to it; a short trip back in time to the simpler days before the internet and terrorists and the spreading global community that was rapidly changing all the things we had cherished about an America that only existed in our memories. The storefronts along Main Street still retained the welcoming look of another era, while the briny, humidity-laced air permeated the night, creating rings around the street lights and dampening the haunting cries of sea gulls circling overhead. It was as though someone had placed a warm blanket over the town to hide it from the greedy eyes of those who would try to change it.

Slowing their car, the two men spotted the only restaurant open and parked nose-in, the way they still did it in most small towns. Like many of the other landmark restaurants that still dotted the rural landscape—the sign outside proclaimed it had been open since 1929—it was an eclectic time-warp of a place. Tables faded from thousands of cleanings filled the space between an old-style lunch counter and a row of booths lining a wood-paneled wall.

Sliding into one of the booths, they picked up their menus and listened to the muted chatter of the locals, talking mostly about fishing and all the things going on in a world that seemed very far away.

Within seconds of their arrival, a smiling waitress brought two red plastic glasses filled to the brim with ice cold water and set them down with an expert touch next to a napkin dispenser. Right away both men knew they had stepped into one of those rare places that aren't supposed to exist in the real world anymore, and the smells coming from the kitchen told them they were about to taste the kind of homemade food most people only wrote about with mournful, past-tense longing.

"What can I get for you boys this evening?" the waitress asked, her steady brown eyes smiling down at her two fit-looking customers.

"What's good?" Bourdon asked.

"Everything on our menu is good," she said, her pencil poised over her order pad. "You like chicken-fried steak?"

Brooks looked up from his menu. "Chicken steaks?"

Her smile broadened into a grin. "I had a feeling you two weren't from around here. I've seen a lot of strange faces since that ship showed up out there on the island. If you like beef steak battered and fried and smothered in cream gravy, you won't be disappointed."

"We'll have two," Bourdon said quickly. "And a couple of iced teas."

"Comin' right up." Taking the menus, she disappeared into the kitchen.

"I love small towns," Bourdon said, leaning back. "I spent most of my high school years in one … before I went off to the Naval Academy."

"I didn't know that, sir. I was raised in Chicago, but whenever I drive through a small town I always get the feeling I missed something growing up."

"You did. Not to say it's not exciting to live in a big city, but whenever I go back it's like opening the page of a book right where I left off. There's a continuity there that always draws me back … even in my dreams."

"You've never struck me as being the sentimental type, Admiral."

The admiral's far off look quickly evaporated. "I guess it comes with age, but if you ever repeat what I just said to anyone, I'll promote you."

92

A look of horror crossed Brooks' face as he held up his hands in mock surrender. "No thanks, sir. No desk job for me. The day they pull me out of the field is the day this Navy SEAL takes early retirement."

The two men laughed, and soon the waitress was back with two heaping platters dripping with gravy. They dug right in, and amid the clatter of tableware mixed with the din of voices echoing off the walls of this little treasure from the past, they hardly drew a second glance from the other customers who had no way of knowing that the two men who had just driven into their little part of the world belonged to the most lethal military unit in America.

Brooks' cell phone vibrated on the table. "Brooks here."

"Are you with the admiral, Steve?"

Brooks immediately recognized the voice of his best friend and fellow Navy SEAL, Bill Parker. "Yeah. He's sitting across from me right now eating steak fried like chicken. What's up?"

"You two need to get to Port Aransas ASAP. The police received a report from a security guard at the Marine Science Institute. He told them a female student saw a man with a beard dressed in ragged, wet clothes walking through the dorm entrance. Because of the way he looked, she thought he was probably just one of the researchers taking a shortcut to the lab after checking on a nearby wetland experiment. But the more she thought about it, the more she wondered why he had been out there after dark, so she called security just to be safe. When the DIA guys heard the call, they beat it over there to take a look at the images from the dorm's security camera. The man who entered the dorm was Dr. Peter Dinning, and they have the building surrounded."

John Lyman

94

CHAPTER 16

Inside the marine institute, Peter and the two girls were running. As soon as they burst through the swinging doors of the lab, the sound of their footsteps echoed off the tiled hallway until they hit the carpeted sky bridge and streaked across into the administration building. Clutching the stolen laptop under one arm, Dinning paused at the end of the bridge just long enough to look down through the glass at the service road below. A police car and military Humvee were already pulling up in front of the alcove that framed the lab entrance, and in the distance, they could see a line of red and blue flashing lights snaking their way along a two-lane road that twisted through the dunes.

Squinting in the faint light, they looked to see if anyone had seen them cross over. For now all eyes seemed focused on the lab, so they continued on into the darkened administration building.

"Where to now?" Dana asked, pulling her jeans up past her waistline.

"First floor," Dinning said. "They'll be swarming all the buildings in a matter of minutes. Our only hope now is to slip out an unguarded exit while we still have a chance."

Taking off together, the trio ran down a dark hallway, looking for a stairway to the first floor as the flashing lights outside pierced the windows in an oppressive lightshow of force. An even darker hallway branched off to their right, running the entire length of the building.

Exchanging glances, they took off running again until they came to a stairwell at the end of the hall and flew down the stairs. As soon as they hit the first floor, Peter opened the stairwell door and stepped out. Red beams of light were shooting down the hall.

Backing into the girls, he held his finger to his lips and herded them into the stairwell before peeking back out. Several soldiers were headed their way—their laser sights painting the walls with red dots as they advanced from the opposite end of the hall.

"We're screwed!" Dana cried, still gripping her pants. "There's nowhere else to go."

Looking around for another doorway, Sam pointed to a sunken space beneath the stairs. "What about that?"

Dinning looked back to see a three-foot-deep concrete pit in the floor beneath the stairs. "What is that?"

Sam inched closer and peered over the edge. "There's a little metal door down here."

"Do these buildings have basements?" Dinning whispered.

"No. None of the buildings on the island have them. The water table is too high. But that little door has to go somewhere." Jumping down into the pit, she lifted the latch. The rusty hinges squeaked when she pulled it open and peered inside. "There's a lot of pipes down here!"

Jumping down beside her, Dinning's eyes followed a dozen multicolored pipes stretching into the darkness along the side of the tunnel-like space. "I should have thought of this sooner when I saw stairs leading up to all the entrances. Without basements, the first floors of these building were built above ground level to create a crawl space for the plumbing."

"Where do you think it leads?" Dana asked.

"No idea, but right now this is our only option. Anyone have a light?"

Both girls shook their heads. The voices of the soldiers outside were growing closer as Dinning crawled inside. Dana was next, and when Sam closed the little door behind them, everything went pitch black.

Wrapped in total darkness, their sense of hearing took over as they felt their way forward. The sound of the soldiers' boots on the concrete floor above their heads seemed amplified, filling them with the fear that any second now the little door behind them would come swinging open. Their pursuers' lights would reflect in their eyes, making them look like a family of opossums surprised by the headlights of a car traveling down a dark country road. They stepped up their pace.

After several minutes of crawling, their knees were already calling out in pain from the constant pounding against the concrete. They felt the tunnel make a turn to the right. They followed, moving at an angle, listening and feeling their way as it became hotter and more humid. The tunnel took another turn. It was becoming even warmer when the echo of their heavy breathing and the rub of the concrete wall brushing against their right shoulders told them that the space they were crawling through had suddenly narrowed.

Feeling trapped in the total darkness of the tight space, Sam stopped to relieve the pressure on her knees and wipe the sweat from her eyes. "Where the hell are we? And why is it so hot all of a sudden?"

Up ahead, they could hear Dinning's labored breathing. "I believe we might be in a shallow service tunnel that leads to another building ... listen." The sound of the soldiers' boots was gone, replaced instead by total silence. "We might even be somewhere outside the walls."

Sam squinted ahead into the blackness. "Outside the walls?"

"Judging by the distance we've covered, we must be. All of these pipes have to be leading to some kind of service building. I noticed steam coming from a big brick building at the southern end of the campus when I was walking to the dorm. Come on ... we have to keep moving."

In the thick humidity of the narrow passage, sweat was dripping in their eyes as they started off again, breathing in dank air heavy with the smell of wet soil and dead insects.

Drenched in sweat and coughing in the fetid, claustrophobic space, the exhausted trio continued on until Dinning stopped again to peer ahead. A pin-point of light was shining in the distance. For several agonizing minutes they crawled toward the light, until finally, they emerged in a large, industrial-looking machine room. Inhaling the fresh air, they collapsed on their backs beneath a single bare light bulb.

Dana raised her head to look around. "Where are we?"

Taking in a few more deep breaths, Dinning sat up and studied the way the pipes branched off to connect with two rows of shadowy machinery that hissed in the dim light. "This has to be the physical plant I saw earlier. If I'm right, the little marina is about a hundred yards from here. If we can make it to my Zodiac without being seen, we can zip back across the channel to my camp on Saint Joe's."

Sam raised up on an elbow. "Your camp? Who said anything about going to your camp?"

A look of incomprehension crossed Dinning's face. "Unless you have a better idea, I don't see any alternative. We have to get off this island tonight. The longer we stay here, the more likely it is we'll all end up in handcuffs before the sun comes up tomorrow."

"But I live here!" Sam exclaimed. "I haven't done anything wrong. I can't just leave my home and all my friends. Brian is probably freaking out by now. This is crazy!" She paused, her eyes darting back and forth like a trapped animal. "I'm turning myself in."

"I wouldn't do that if I were you," Peter shot back. "No one is asking you to abandon everything you love, but the people who are after us are pulling out all the stops to find out what we know. They're obviously afraid of something ... something they don't want the rest of the world to know about." Dinning held up the laptop he had been carrying. "Whatever they're looking for is in here. We're holding their secret in our hands ... and people who stumble onto secrets have a way of disappearing when someone very powerful is trying to prevent those secrets from being revealed."

Sam blinked in the dim light. "By saying someone very powerful ... are you talking about a government?"

"Could be. Feels like it. Unfortunately for the rest of us, all governments are usually controlled by powerful people who work behind the scenes. We could be dealing with any number of people who have a stake in protecting whatever it is they think we've uncovered."

Dana's eye grew wide. "That's even scarier than running from the police."

"Yes it is. At least they have some kind of judicial oversight, but. after what I witnessed in Africa, I believe the people looking for us now are playing by a whole different set of rules. Something has stirred up a hornet's nest, and I intend to find out what the hornets are so pissed about. I owe it to the people who died in Africa."

For a while they were silent, just breathing in the fresh air. Sam was the first to raise herself off the grease-stained floor. A dented metal door in the cinder block wall obviously led outside. Inching it open, she peered through the crack. A hundred yards to the north, the marine institute was surrounded by the flashing lights of dozens of military and police vehicles. "Looks like the police to me," she said to Dinning.

"A lot of them probably are," he replied, "but if we're captured we'll be turned over to the guys in the black cars. You can count on it. Our only way back is to expose their secret before they find us, and they know it."

Sam peered back outside, weighing her options as she watched the flashing lights and thought of what Dinning had just said. If he was right, turning herself in to the authorities could be the biggest mistake of her life. All she really wanted to do was go back home. She wanted to wake up in the morning and drink a cup of coffee with the sun streaming through her salt-fogged windows again—to be free to cast her net on the rippled water and joke with the fishermen on the pier. But most of all she wanted to see Brian's red motorcycle speeding toward her down the shell road and hear his laughter.

Closing the door, she turned around to face the two people staring back at her. "Are you positive the people chasing us are the bad guys?"

Dinning hesitated before answering. "I think we're operating in a gray area right now, because there's no way to tell who the bad guys are until we find out what they're trying to protect. Until we know that, we can't trust anyone … no matter how friendly or harmless they appear."

"What about our friends?"

"Anyone we associate with is probably being watched right now. It's the easiest way to find someone on the run."

Sam leaned her back against the door. "I guess that's what we are right now … people on the run. Okay, Professor. I'll stick with you and Dana for now. What's your plan?"

"To get away from here as quickly as possible." Moving next to Sam, Dinning cracked the door open again to peer outside. "I can see the marina through the trees of a little park across the street."

"What about all the cops and soldiers?" Dana asked.

"A few are standing around next to their vehicles, but it looks like most of them are still inside looking for us. The whole place is lit up like a Christmas tree."

"Well, we can't stay here," said Sam. "That's for sure. What about just taking off into the dunes behind this building?"

"We'd still be trapped on the island," Dana answered for Dinning. "Our best shot is to make it to the Zodiac and cross the channel before we're spotted."

"We'll go through the park," Dinning said. "The Zodiac is tied up on the other side of the boat ramp behind the marina office." Slowly, he opened the door and stepped outside into an obvious work yard filled with a jumble of rusty lawn-care equipment and a couple of newer-looking pickups. Moving behind the trucks, the two girls followed him to the edge of the building and stared into the dark park across the street.

"I'll go first," Dinning said. "If they see me, take off for the dunes and don't look back."

Dinning made a final check of the area. The soldiers around the administration building were still watching the exits with their backs turned. Taking in a lungful of air, he took off running across the street and disappeared among the twisting trees. When none of the soldiers reacted, Sam and Dana sprinted behind him.

Blending in with twisted shapes of the trees, they all looked toward the marina office and the nearby administration building. The entire area was ablaze in light, and what seemed iffy at best now looked impossible. They would be heading back into the teeth of the tiger, and it was waiting to pounce as soon as they stepped from the peaceful quiet of the park.

Sam flopped back against a tree and slid down to stare up at the stars through the leafy branches. "There's no way we're going to make it back to that marina without being seen."

Suddenly, Dinning pointed. A man in a blue jumpsuit was walking through the park, and he was headed straight for them. Together they all flattened against the grass. He was almost on top of them when Sam leapt to her feet and wrapped her arms around his neck. "Brian! How did you find us?"

"You can thank Randy."

Looking back over her shoulder, Sam saw Peter and Dana still clinging to the grass. "It's okay, you guys. This is Brian ... my boyfriend. You can trust him ... I promise."

The two raised statue-like off the ground as Brian looked them up and down. "Randy told me about the girl, but who's the guy?"

"Dr. Peter Dinning. He was on the ship."

"What!"

"It's a long story."

"I'll bet. He's got a lot of questions to answer."

"He's not one of the bad guys, Brian." Sam nodded toward the flashing lights. "They are, and we've got to get away from here!"

"She's right," Dinning said, clutching the laptop to his chest. "None of us knows why we're suddenly the focus of a manhunt, including your girlfriend, and we really do have to go."

For a few adrenalin-charged seconds, Brian studied the bearded man in dirty clothes before heaving a sigh of resignation. "I have a car parked behind the condos next to the marina. We need to move to the other end of the park and cross the street there."

Sam nudged him with her shoulder. "We're right behind you."

Keeping to the shadows, they wove through the trees to the west, trying to put as much distance between them and the institute as possible before their pursuers spotted them.

Now that there were four of them, they decided to cross the street as a group when they exited the park so that anyone watching from a distance would assume they were just looking at two couples out for an evening stroll. As soon as they were across, they walked through a crowded parking lot behind a three-story condo built in the mimicking architecture of a New England seaport.

Finally away from the searching eyes around the institute, they could afford to breathe a little easier now. A cough and some quiet laughter came from one of the balconies overhead, lending an air of normalcy to the scene—but Sam was feeling anything but normal. There had been nothing normal about her life since the day she had taken her little boat out for its last sail. For all she knew, Peter and Dana might be bad guys. She could be running from the very people who could help, and now she had involved two of the people closest to her—Brian and Randy.

"The car is just up ahead," Brian said, pulling his keys from his pocket. He glanced sideways at Sam and pointed to a new Ford Mustang.

"Where's your Camaro?" Sam asked.

"I'll explain on the way. Why don't you two girls hop in the back and let Dr. Dinning ride up front with me?"

Sam caught on instantly. Brian was evening out the odds by driving a different car and not allowing both strangers to sit behind him. It was one of the things she loved about him. *He was always thinking.*

As soon as the car started, the low steady rumble from the Mustang's high-performance engine shattered the stillness of the night as Brian edged out of the parking lot and drove slowly for a block before turning onto a side street and heading south.

Peering out at all the trucks and dune buggies parked along the sandy shoulder, Dinning asked the expected question. "Where are you taking us?"

"Sam's favorite fishing spot on the bay side of the island."

"Why there?" Sam asked.

"Because that's where Randy will be waiting for us. He's anchored just offshore."

"Randy?" Sam grabbed the back of Brian's seat and pulled herself close. "What's going on, Brian?"

"You might as well know. I've been talking to Randy since this morning."

"But he promised he wouldn't tell anyone where we were. Great! Bee Hastings probably even knows by now, and she has one of the biggest mouths in town."

"Don't go blaming Randy, Sam ... and it was Bee who told me you were in trouble."

"Bee?"

"Yeah. I got off duty at ten last night and drove over to your house. There was a black car and a couple of Humvees parked out front, and all the neighbors were out in their yards. Bee told me what happened and how you went tearing off down the street on your dirt bike with another girl on the back. She saw all the soldiers surrounding your house, and they wouldn't answer her questions. You know Bee. That made her mad, and no one had to tell her you were in trouble."

"So how did that lead to Randy?"

"I drove around for awhile ... looking for you, but the military and police had thrown roadblocks up all over town. I had to show my ID every couple of blocks, so I finally went back to my apartment and caught a few hours sleep. When I woke up I turned on the TV. You were all over the news again like you were when your boat went missing, but this time they were saying you had been involved in some kind of chase after the police tried to stop you for speeding. They were urging people to call 911 if they saw you. I knew right away something wasn't right. You're not exactly the kind of person who would run from the police unless you had a really good reason, and there was a big difference in the story Bee told me and the one they were broadcasting on TV. I couldn't understand why the police were lying, and I couldn't just sit there, so I went looking again. That's when I drove by that bar next to the marina and saw them loading your dirt bike into the back of a military truck."

"My dirt bike?"

"I stopped and showed the officer in charge my Coast Guard ID, and you know what he said?"

"What?"

102

"He said he couldn't discuss it with anyone, especially me because I was your boyfriend. He just turned his back and walked away like I was some kind of ... civilian."

Sam glanced over at Dana and smiled. "That's like a dirty word in the Coast Guard."

"Yeah, they definitely weren't acting too friendly," Brian continued. "It was like the whole thing was a big secret ... a military secret, and I was being kept out of the loop because I couldn't be trusted. For awhile I just sat there, looking out at all the boats in the harbor. That's when it occurred to me that you had been trying to make it to the marina for some reason. I mean, why else would you leave your bike behind the bar next door."

"You knew we were hiding on one of the boats?"

"It seemed likely, but I still wasn't sure. The military and state police still have roadblocks by the ferry landing and on the road leading south, so I knew you were probably still on the island. After I parked my car at the marina and started walking up and down the docks, I saw Randy working on his engine and stopped to ask if he had seen you. You should have seen the look on his face. He started stuttering and wouldn't look me in the eye. That's when I knew you were hiding on his boat."

Sam leaned back in her seat and gazed out the window. "I wanted to tell you ... to get word to you somehow. I knew you'd be worried, but I didn't want to risk ruining your career by getting you involved. What did Randy tell you?"

"Everything he knew. As soon as I told him I knew you were hiding on his boat he spilled. Said the same thing you did about ruining my career if I became involved, but he was also afraid for you. He was freaked out about me being there by the boat, so he told me to come back at dusk and meet him in the restaurant. We hatched our plan while you were taking your showers."

"What plan is that?"

"Once he told me you wanted to go to the marine institute, we thought it might be a good idea if you had some backup in the area. I was sitting here in the park when he dropped you off with ... "

"Dana," Sam reminded him.

"Yeah ... Dana. Anyway, I saw you and Dana trying doors before you ran around the side of the building. After that I lost sight of you, so I just stood behind a tree and waited for you to come back out. That's when all hell broke loose. A line of at least twenty police cars and military vehicles raced past the park and surrounded the building."

"Why didn't you leave?" Dinning asked. "I mean, there wasn't much you could do at that point."

Brian grinned as he steered the car out onto the highway. "I can see you don't know Sam very well yet. I knew she would make it out of there if anyone could. I mean, we're talking about a girl who swam all night in heavy seas without a life jacket after her boat got run over by a ship. No man in his right mind would leave a woman like that behind."

Sam blinked back at him with a sudden realization. Brian was obviously madly in love with her, and she had just gained some points among the Coast Guard crowd too.

"Are you sure you weren't followed?" Dana asked, looking back through the rear window. I mean, they always watch the people closest to the ones they're looking for ... right?"

"If they're following my car they're halfway to Corpus Christi by now," Brian said. "I asked my partner Larry to trade cars with me back at the Coast Guard station. We both walked out at the same time with our hats pulled down low. We trust each other every day with our lives, so he didn't ask why and I didn't tell him."

Looking out as the town faded behind them, Dinning shifted uneasily in his seat as he tried to get his bearings. "Are you sure we're going the right way?"

Before Brian could answer, Sam squinted through the windshield at a line of flashing lights blocking the highway up ahead. "Uh, Brian ... where are you going?"

"I'm getting you and your friends out of here tonight." Spinning the steering wheel with the palm of one hand, he veered off the highway onto a familiar white-shell road and headed for the bay.

CHAPTER 17

A thickening film of fine white dust coated the Mustang's windshield as they rumbled along the shell road to the water's edge. As soon as they stopped, Brian's eyes followed the particle-filled beams from their headlights shining out over the dark water of Corpus Christi Bay. "Randy should have been here by now."

Sam peered at the glowing city across the water, its tall bridge arching across the entrance to the harbor. "Maybe he's just running late."

"Maybe." Reaching for the ignition, Brian killed the engine and switched off the lights.

Alarmed, both girls twisted to look back through the rear window to see if any cars were turning off the highway behind them.

"Now what?" Sam asked.

"I don't know. We weren't even sure if I would be able to help you … but he was supposed to be waiting here just in case."

"Can you call him on your cell?"

Brian caught her reflection in the rearview mirror and shook his head. "I even took the battery out."

"Oh, right. I keep forgetting those damn things are like locator beacons." Sam rolled her window down and breathed in the salty air. "I can't sit here anymore. I've got to get out."

The four exited and stood around the car. They were surrounded by reedy wetlands filled with the sounds of chirping crickets and croaking frogs, and a musty breeze drifted off the water. It filled their nostrils with the fresh smell of the ocean mixed with the mustiness of the nearby mud flats as they looked toward the empty ship channel for signs of an approaching boat.

Boosting herself up on the hood of the car, Sam leaned her head against Brian's shoulder and squeezed his arm. "I can just see you stalking around that park in the dark, waiting for me. I'm so sorry I

105

disappeared on you like I did. I should have called you as soon as I got back from the dunes with Dana, but the DIA guys showed up so quickly that …"

Brian reached up and patted her hand. "It's okay, Sam. It doesn't sound like you had a whole lot of control over the situation. I really wish I knew what those army bastards are up to."

"Wow. I don't think I've ever heard you talk about the military that way."

"These guys aren't your typical military types. I could tell. They're different somehow."

"What makes you say that?"

"Just something about the way they act … the nervousness. They're wound a little too tightly if you know what I mean. I don't think I saw any of them joking around like most soldiers do, especially in a beach town where there are a lot of girls in bikinis walking around."

Sam pinched his side. "So, you notice all the girls in bikinis?"

Brian grinned as he cocked his head to one side and listened. The gurgling throb of an approaching boat with no lights showing drew everyone's attention to the water. They strained to see, but nothing appeared to be moving in the darkness until the sleek silhouette of a tall sport fishing boat passed in front of the distant lights from the city and turned toward the shore.

"Thank God," Sam heard Dinning say, walking up beside them. "It looks like your friend came through."

"Our friends always come through, Professor," Sam said, leaping off the hood. She grabbed Brian by the neck and pulled his face close to hers, kissing him slowly before looking up into his eyes. "Thank you."

"Take care of yourself, Sam. I'll be waiting for you. Hurry back after you find whatever it is you guys are looking for. I'm only a phone call away if you need me."

"Remember to put your battery back in your phone," she said. With tears streaming down her face, she turned away and walked to the water's edge with Peter and Dana.

Up on the flying bridge of the *Just in Time*, Captain Randy Monroe was inching the throttles back and forth, feeling for the soft sand bottom with the boat's thick fiberglass bow. It was almost as though the boat had become an extension of his own body—a blending of man and machine that came from years of experience navigating the coastal backwaters. He could actually feel the hull kiss the bottom as he held it in position only a few feet from the shoreline and waited for his passengers to wade out and scramble up onto the main deck.

"Everyone on board?" he shouted down.

Three moonlit faces glanced up at him and nodded. "All except for Brian," answered Sam.

"Who's the guy?"

"He's with us. I'll explain later."

Randy frowned. Shoving the throttles into reverse, he backed the boat into deeper water while Sam watched the shoreline recede. Brian was already growing smaller, and she could feel the tug of separation as she watched him leaning against the car, waving to the fading outline of the boat.

As soon as he felt the boat rocking in the fast-moving current, Randy switched the navigation lights back on and pushed the throttles all the way forward. Slowly the bow lifted and the boat gained speed as the big twin engines pushed them into the nighttime mist that sometimes formed over the warmer water of the channel after the sun went down and the air began to cool.

"You guys need to get below before we pass the ferry landing," he shouted over the roar of the engines to the deck below. "The place is crawling with cops and soldiers, and you can bet they'll be taking a good look at us when we go by."

Nodding to one another, the three entered the main cabin and pulled the curtains shut before sitting at the table across from a small galley. Laying the laptop down, Dinning stared at it while Dana rested her chin in the palms of her hands; her eyes suspended in perpetual thought.

"Anyone care for a drink?" Sam asked.

Dinning lifted his head and smiled. "Any beer in the fridge?"

"Uh, knowing Randy, that would be a yes."

"Good, but I should probably wait until I get back from Saint Joe's."

"Saint Joe's?"

"Yes. I left something at my camp … something very important."

"I'd like to help you out, Professor, but we don't have time to stop. Besides, poking around Saint Joe's right now might draw some unwanted attention."

"Then you might as well leave me there, because I can't leave without it. It's just as vital as this laptop is to us right now."

107

Sam bit her lower lip. "I have to go up and talk to Randy. He's a good friend and it wouldn't be right if I didn't tell him who you are. I'll ask him about Saint Joe's while I'm at it, but I can already tell you he's not going to be real thrilled when he hears about all of this."

Without waiting for a reply, Sam opened the door and stepped out onto the back deck. Bracing herself against the roll of the boat, she tried shouting up to Randy. Against the throbbing engines her words were carried off with the wind. She would have to climb the ladder to the flying bridge perched high above the main cabin.

Grabbing onto the ladder, she took one rung at a time—an old sea-going mantra playing over and over in her head. *One hand for yourself, and one for the ship.*

With the boat running at full speed, the rushing wind was blowing her hair straight back as she heaved herself up over the edge and inched her way along a handrail until she reached the captain's chair.

"The sea mist is really thick out here tonight," she said.

"Hey ... I thought I told you to stay out of sight! We're almost to the ferry landing."

"I'll duck down, but I had to talk to you. Is Conn-Brown harbor in Aransas Pass still part of the plan?"

"Yeah, I think that's our best bet for getting you and your friends to the mainland. Right now the town is still relatively calm. There's no military presence like there is on the island ... just the usual city cops doing their thing."

"What about the locals?"

"We'll probably see some of the usual, die-hard fishermen looking for flounder out on the flats, but the harbor there is pretty deserted this time of night." Reaching into his pocket, he handed Sam a key. "We keep a pickup truck parked by the abandoned shrimp processing plant for when we need to go into town for supplies. It's a crew cab. You can use is as long as you need it."

"Thanks. There's something else I wanted to talk to you about."

"Does it have something to do with my extra passenger?"

"Yes."

"He was on that ship, wasn't he?"

Sam started to open her mouth but was too surprised to speak.

"I thought so," Randy continued. "Everyone knows there had to be someone alive on that ghost ship full of bodies. There's a lot of rumors spreading around that whoever it was is still hiding somewhere on the island." Randy's knuckles were white as he gripped the wheel and stared straight ahead. "Is there any reason you can think of why I shouldn't stop at the ferry landing and turn his ass in, Sam?"

"I'm sorry, Randy ... really, but that man is as innocent as I am. He's just a university researcher, not some crazed killer like the feds want everyone to believe. Those bodies on that ship were his friends. He was bringing them home after they were killed by soldiers in Africa."

"Wow ... so the rumors are true. Why is the military so interested in him?"

"We don't know, and neither does he. I can steer this boat. Go talk to him. The man needs our help, and we need his. Something is going on ... something the government doesn't want us to know about, and they're trying to turn him into a scapegoat."

"So you're putting your trust in a complete stranger? I don't like it, Sam. I don't like it one bit."

"Look, Randy, I had my doubts at first too, but then I started thinking. If he had anything to do with the deaths of all those people on that boat, why bring it back to the states? I mean, why not just stay in Africa? You should have seen him at the institute. He's desperate to find out what's really going on, and so am I. If you want us off your boat I'll understand. All I can tell you for sure is that the military is making up lies about me, which means they're probably making up lies about him as well. The only question is, why? Whatever it is can't be good, because there's no telling what those government assholes are trying to hide."

Sam had finally struck a chord, because like a lot of fishermen, most of Randy Monroe's run-ins with the government had been on the unpleasant side.

"Okay, Sam. I'll get you to the mainland, but after that you're on your own."

"Um, there's one more thing."

Randy stared back at her with a *what now* look.

Sam crossed her fingers. "We need to make a quick stop around the back side of Saint Joe's."

The first hint of a smile showed on Randy's face. "I can read you like a book, Sam. I knew you had something else on your mind."

"It's important."

"Relax, sweet cheeks. I was already planning to stop back there for a few minutes to make sure we weren't being followed before we head for the mainland."

Sam slumped with relief as she patted him on the arm. For awhile they both stared silently into the mist, until a halo of lights told them they were approaching the well-lit ferry landing. Sam ducked down as they glided by. The entire area was lined with state police cars and military Humvees, and soldiers along the shore could be seen looking through their binoculars and night vision goggles at every boat that passed.

As the lights of the ferry landing faded behind them, Randy steered his boat into Aransas Bay on the backside of Saint Joe's island. Together they looked out over the unpopulated land mass that lay between the bay and the Gulf, where only the dark silhouette of the old lighthouse stood out among the glowing dunes in the moonlight.

Coming back off the throttles, Randy held the boat in position a few yards from shore. "I'll wait here … and tell your friend to hurry."

Sam was already descending the ladder. "I'll tell him."

A minute later, Dinning emerged from the cabin and promptly jumped over the side. He disappeared below the surface for a moment before splashing back up and spitting out a mouthful of seawater.

"Sorry about that, sir," Randy said, peering over the side. "The shoreline here is too rocky for me to bring my boat any closer. I'm afraid we're still in the channel."

"I can see that," Dinning sputtered. "I'll be right back." Stroking for the shore, he scrambled up over some rocks and took off in the direction of the lighthouse. On the back deck, Sam motioned for Dana to follow her back up to the bridge to watch his progress.

Leaning back in his captain's chair, Randy looked toward the dim lights across the channel for any boats headed their way. "That guy seems pretty cool under pressure. He just jumped into unfamiliar water over his head and swam to shore without missing a beat."

"I guess living in the Congo for six months does that to a man," Dana said. "Peter's been through much worse in places a lot tougher than this."

"So I've heard," Randy said, looking over at the thin girl holding her jeans up with one hand. "What are your plans once I drop you off on the mainland?"

Dana looked out at the hundred-year-old lighthouse, the moonlight reflecting in her oversized eyes. "That will be up to the professor."

In the ultimate quiet of an ocean backwater, the sound of heavy breathing and footsteps plodding through the sand drew their attention to the shore.

"I'm back!" Dinning shouted. He was clutching a small wooden box as he stumbled over the rocky shoreline. "I'm swimming out."

A few seconds later, a splash was followed by a pair of hands reaching over the side of the boat as Dinning climbed aboard and flopped onto the deck.

"You okay down there, Professor?" Randy shouted down from the flying bridge.

"I'm good, Captain. Thank you."

Swiveling in his big padded chair, Randy made a final check of the area before motoring away from the island. As soon as he reached the center of the ship channel, he could feel the current's tug as he gunned the engines and turned into a narrow side channel dredged from the mud flats years before. The smaller channel was the quickest route to the mainland and Conn-Brown harbor, but it was also a precarious one. For the next seven miles he would be trapped. Unlike the open water of a bay, where his boat would be nothing more than a shadow on a starry horizon, he would be unable to disappear into the vastness of a large body of dark water.

To his left, the lighted causeway paralleled the channel all the way from the ferry landing to the mainland town of Aransas Pass, and to his right, miles and miles of mud flats stretched beneath knee-deep salt water as far as the eye could see. Veering only a few feet from the center of the old channel could bring a large, V-hulled boat like the *Just in Time* crunching to a sudden stop, so for the next seven miles Randy would have to thread the needle between the highway and the mud.

Rubbing his eyes, he turned on his depth finder and peered ahead as Sam and Dana climbed back down the ladder to the cabin. Shuffling inside, Sam reached into the fridge and pulled out three beers before they joined the still-dripping professor, toweling his hair dry at the table.

"You know I have to ask you," Sam said to Dana. "How could something as microscopically small as a piece of DNA send the most powerful military in the world into a panic?"

111

Dana looked at Dinning with the expression of a person caught between two bad choices. "I'm not trying to hide anything from you, Samantha … really. It's just that I'm not sure you'd understand even if I told you. No offense."

"No offense taken." Sam held Dana in her gaze. "Why don't you try me? You said yourself that I probably had more field experience than most marine biologists."

"That's true, but we're talking about something that's about as far from the field as you can get, and we still have tons of unrelated data to sort through. Hopefully it won't take too long, because we're going to start with the last specimen they collected and work our way back to the first."

"So you believe all of this is connected to something they discovered during the last few weeks of the expedition?"

"Could be. The last DNA sample I received from him contained something none of us has ever seen before. I checked all the genetic databases and did a computer search of all the scientific literature. There's nothing on file that even remotely resembles what I saw. It's possible it could be some kind of natural aberration, but only Peter will be able to tell for sure. It might even be something he's already familiar with, but we won't know until he sees it with his own eyes."

Dinning sipped his beer with a teacher's patient smile. "To answer your earlier question about the military, it's quite possible they are in a panic about something at the molecular level. The military is always looking to science for the next leap in battlefield superiority. Maybe they're looking to genetics for the answer to a problem. Who knows? They've certainly come up with stranger ideas. All I can tell you at this point is that we'll know it when we see it if it's in the data. The people chasing us seem to think it is. Like Dana said, for all we know it might be some kind of natural aberration."

"Or something people are willing to kill for," Sam said, taking a long sip of beer.

CHAPTER 18

Sometime after midnight, Randy spotted the lighted Seaman's Memorial at the entrance to Conn-Brown harbor. Backing off the power, he watched the bow of the *Just in Time* cut through moonlit ribbons of oil-streaked water as they glided past a line of docked pleasure boats and a closed seafood restaurant.

Drifting lines of stagnant foam floated along the sides of the hull as Sam climbed up to the bridge and watched silently as they continued on to the industrial end of the harbor and Randy edged the gleaming boat up to a leaning, barnacle-encrusted dock.

"I know this sounds cliché, Randy," she said, giving him a hug from behind, "but I don't know what we would have done without you."

"Just take care of yourself, Sam. You don't really know these people. I just did an internet search on my phone and found a very interesting article on Dr. Peter Dinning."

"You Googled him on your cell?!"

"Don't worry. Everyone is Googling him now. They just put his picture up on the news. Like you said, he's highly respected in his field, but no one seems to know what his latest research project was all about. Apparently, he's always been an enigma to his colleagues, and anything that's been written about his expedition to Africa seems to have fallen into a black hole. All of the internet sites about it have been taken down."

"Wow. Sounds like they're already trying to erase anything he was working on. Someone's definitely trying to hide something."

"You could be right. I'm not one of those conspiracy guys, but I also don't believe everything our government tells us. It's beginning to look like the people chasing you are becoming desperate, which makes them even more dangerous. To tell you the truth, Samantha, I'm even more worried about you now than I was before."

"I'll be fine, Randy. To quote Brian, I'll be sure to stay *frosty*."

Randy frowned back. "You know where to find us if you need us. I'll bring the cavalry … even if they are a little past their prime and have pot bellies now."

Sam felt herself fighting back the tears as she turned away from a man who had become like a brother to her over the years. They were both products of the same, sea-scented pocket of isolation they called home, and they would always be close, even when they were distant. Just like a family.

Jumping onto the dock, she stood back and watched him move the throttles into reverse as he fixed Dinning with his best guard-dog stare. Seconds later the *Just in Time* was roaring off though the oil-slicked water, leaving behind a cloud of fine, wake-induced mist that swirled over an aged wooden shrimp boat that lay on its rotted side, illuminated by a lonely harbor light.

The sudden silence made the deserted waterfront seem even more forlorn as the three made their way to the end of the dock and climbed a chalky embankment to look for the old pickup. In the moonlight, they could see an abandoned shrimp processing plant looming above them— its corrugated metal siding warped by the sun and pitted by the salty breeze that blew off the shallow bay, wrapping the structure in a corrosive haze.

Skirting piles of broken concrete and a rusting ice-making machine as they made their way toward the building, the crumbling infrastructure around the old plant was a sad reminder that Aransas Pass had once been called the shrimp capital of the world. Over three hundred shrimp boats had graced its docks until the industry had collapsed back in the 1970's— a message from the natural world that the fortunes of man and the bounty of the sea could change in an instant.

Walking around to the street side of the building, they spotted the old pickup parked in the shadows.

"At least it has a back seat," Dinning observed, looking at Sam as he poked his finger through a rusty patch of metal.

"It might look rough, but Randy babies the engines of his machines. It should get us where we're going. Want me to drive?"

"Please." Dinning slid onto the front passenger seat while Dana climbed in back. As soon as they were all settled in, Sam gripped the wheel and looked ahead. "This might be a good time to tell me where we're going, Professor."

Dinning looked out at the dark shapes of broken machines lying in the grass along the empty road next to the sea wall. "Head north."

"Austin?"

"No. San Marcos. It's a small college town south of the city."

"I know where it is. It's one of my favorite places. I love all the clear springs. Why there?"

"I own a little house outside of town."

"Don't you think that's a little risky? I mean, they're bound to be watching it."

"It's not in my name … never has been."

"Is anyone there?"

Dinning looked out his window. "Not anymore."

The engine started on the second try, and soon the rusty truck was creaking and groaning up the old road that topped the sea wall before descending into the fog-shrouded coastal flatlands. A few minutes later the sleeping town of Aransas Pass faded in their rearview mirrors as they headed north.

John Lyman

CHAPTER 19

The morning sun warmed the truck's windows as they followed the concrete ribbon of Interstate 37 north toward San Antonio. Through the hypnotic, flickering blur created by miles and miles of uninterrupted fence posts along the sides of the highway, Sam looked out over a rolling vista of plowed farms and mesquite-covered ranches joined together in a patchwork of sameness broken only by the occasional small town with a grain silo or large metal building surrounded by rows of new tractors.

Looking around at her silent passengers, she smiled when she saw their heads rolling from side to side—lulled to sleep by the rhythmic hum of the big V-8 as they sped over the interstate. A couple of wires hanging from an empty slot in the dash told her the truck's radio had long since disappeared, so she tried humming to herself against the sound of the tires thumping over the maddeningly regular seams in the concrete roadway, providing a kind of background beat to her solitary concert.

For the next hour the truck passed through an endless expanse of furrowed fields that stretched wave-like across the land as far as the eye could see. The stark emptiness seemed to trigger something inside Sam, and her thoughts returned to that night alone on a dark ocean. The scene played over and over on a recurring loop that filled her with an unreasoning fear, making her close her eyes for just a second in an attempt to push the thoughts back down to that place where they rested but would never leave.

Why couldn't she just put it behind her?

Was it the sight of open spaces that triggered her fear? Or was it the cadenced bumps in the road that came at her like the spaced waves at sea—jarring her memory of being cast alone on a great void. Sam tried to think of something else as she glanced down at the fuel gauge. The big engine was guzzling gas, and they were already down to half a tank as the interstate dipped into a lush valley and passed over a trickling stream.

Vestiges of old wooden structures lay collapsing in the thick green underbrush along the highway, making her think of her mother and that day long ago when they had taken off into the unknown on their great adventure.

She remembered her mother guiding their big Chevy off the interstate onto an aged, two-lane road with weeds growing all the way up to the edges. They had driven past weathered signs with the writing faded beyond comprehension, and off to the side, there had also been tumbled-down wooden structures like the ones she was passing now. They had frightened her for some reason. It was as if the old buildings were looking back at her from another era, whispering about the lives once lived within their leaning walls—lives that were now gone forever, leaving behind only the essence of their passing.

Sam's memories of that time seemed almost sepia-tinted—like looking through an old photo album. She remembered the old combination grocery store and gas station, where they had walked past a sleepy dog lying in the shade and through a torn screen door with a faded metal sign that read *Wonder Bread*. The worn wooden floor had creaked beneath their feet when they passed shelves with canned stew and boxes of cereal across from another aisle that contained things like tools and hinges and nails—practical things for the people who lived away from the city.

It had been less than twenty years since they had stopped at that old store—a store that even then was beginning to fade away like all the other crumbling buildings along the interstate. She felt its loss and longed to walk back through its squeaky doors again—to be welcomed by the old man with the smiling eyes and red bow tie standing behind the counter.

The road curved and the sun's glare filtered through the pickup's side windows as it followed the interstate up a hill, leaving the lush valley behind and passing through flat farmland dotted with pockets of trees and white-framed houses. Her return to the present from a nostalgic past seemed jarring, especially now that she was looking at the world through the eyes of an adult again. The memories had left her with that empty feeling that came when one realized they were a product of simpler times. The world was changing; moving away from quiet evenings spent watching fire flies from the front porch into something else.

If a time traveler from the 1950's had landed in today's America, he would have thought he had landed in some Technicolor nightmare vision of a future that couldn't possibly exist in a country that had just watched the live broadcast of opening day at Disneyland. He would have shoved his time machine in reverse as quickly as his fingers could throw the switch without ever looking back—praying that what he had just seen wasn't real.

Sam leaned back and looked over at Dinning's face pressed flat against the window while he slept. With an overwhelming feeling of fatigue setting in, she rolled her window down and inhaled the aroma of freshly plowed earth warmed by the sun. She blinked in the sunlight and shook her head before opening her eyes wide just as the black and white blur of a state trooper's car came swooping by to catch up with a speeding motorist ahead.

At least this truck wasn't on anyone's radar yet, she thought to herself, now fully awake.

In the back seat, Dana stirred. "Where are we?"

"About twenty miles from the loop around San Antonio."

"So about another hour to San Marcos?"

"Sounds about right. Should we wake the professor up?"

"No, let him sleep. I have a feeling he'll be awake all night after he sees the images I captured using our new scanning electron microscope."

John Lyman

CHAPTER 20

Five miles outside San Marcos, Dinning was wide awake as Samantha steered the truck off the interstate onto a winding, two-lane road that twisted through the cedar-scrub hills that had given the Texas Hill Country its name. They drove another five miles, crossing over a narrow bridge that spanned a turquoise stream glinting in the sunlight, until finally Dinning pointed to a yellow fence post next to a dirt road up ahead. "That's it ... that's the road. Turn in there."

Sam glanced in the rearview mirror. No cars. As soon as she made the turn the tires kicked up a swirling cloud of dry, chalky dust that billowed behind the truck, marking their progress through a forest of bent live oaks to a distant ranch house half-hidden behind a massive pecan tree.

Climbing from the pickup, they stretched and looked around. The ticking of the hot engine and the occasional buzzing insect were the only things that broke the stillness of the scene, but the sudden switch from the frantic activity of the past two days to the antique stillness of a place removed from time was almost disorienting, especially for three people on the run who had depleted their adrenalin reserves.

Walking toward the house, Dinning seemed to be looking for someone peering back at them from behind the large plate-glass window set back under the covered front porch.

There had been someone looking back at him the last time he had been here.

Carefully, almost reverently, he retrieved a key he hadn't used in years from beneath a painted rock and unlocked the front door. Pushing it open, he stepped inside. Beneath a fine coating of dust, everything was just as he had left it. His desk, his old typewriter ... papers yellowed with time. He ran his fingers over the scarred edges of the desk, lingering for a moment until his eyes began to moisten and he forced himself to look away.

Squinting through the picture window, he looked past the large pecan tree at an old barn in the distance. Ethereal beams of sunlight pierced the gaps in the sun-bleached wood, and next to it, a pile of split logs that had once been a corral lay at the base of a gigantic gray boulder that blocked the view of the ranch house from the road. He was home. He had finally come home—to a place he had sworn to himself he would never return unless the world went to hell in a hand basket and he was forced to retreat back to the only sanctuary he had ever known.

"What is this place?" Dana asked.

Dinning turned to see the two girls hanging back by the open door like a pair of feral cats afraid to step across the threshold. "I used to live here ... a long, long time ago."

"But I thought you said your name wasn't associated with this place!" Dana said, her voice rising. "They could be watching us right now!"

"Relax, Dana," Peter said calmly. "It belonged to a woman ... a woman I loved ... still love. She taught English at the university. We lived in a small condo in Austin when classes were in session, but we spent our best times here. She died almost seven years ago, and I've never been back."

Dana glanced sideways at Sam, both girls trying to look at him and away from him at the same time, not knowing what to say until Dana finally spoke up. "I'm sorry, Peter. I never knew about her."

"Not many people do. We never married ... I wish we had. The last time I saw her I was leaving to make a run into town to buy a bottle of wine. We were cooking outside that night. I remember waving goodbye to her through that big picture window before I left, and when I got back she was gone."

Dana laid a comforting hand on his shoulder. "You don't have to talk about it."

"It's okay. I've been wanting to talk to someone about her, but it didn't seem right until now for some reason. Her name was Angela. She had been sick for a long time ... cancer. She had just finished with chemo, and we were enjoying the fall weather out here. It was our favorite time of the year. I guess I had never really considered the fact that a person I loved so much could leave my life so suddenly. I thought we had more time, but she had been through so much that her heart gave out before the cancer took her. She was lying on the couch looking like she was just taking a nap when I returned."

As the dust particles swirled around them in the soft afternoon light, both girls remained locked in silence. Closing the front door, Sam crossed the room and set the laptop gently on the desk. "Here, Professor. You left it in the truck."

Like a man who had just awakened from a dream, Dinning had a blank look in his eyes as he stared down at it for a moment. "I completely forgot about it when I saw the house again."

"I think the battery is almost dead." Sam reached over and tried the desk lamp. Nothing happened. "That's what I thought. No power."

"The bulb in that lamp burned out the night Angela died," Dinning said. "Try the overhead."

Sam hit the switch on the wall and the entryway light blazed. "Wow! We do have power. How is that possible?"

"You mean who pays the light bill?"

"Well, yes. If you don't own this place, who does?"

"A trust. Angela set up a trust to pay for things like utilities and taxes after her death because I was always going off on expeditions. After she got sick, I told her I couldn't stand the thought of living here after she was gone, but she told me this was our place. She had a feeling I would return one day, so she stipulated in her will that I was the only one allowed on the property until my time came. After I'm gone this ranch will be turned into a wildlife sanctuary for abandoned and abused animals."

Sam felt her legs grow weak. "Which means your name is still associated with this property through the trust."

"Only if you're looking through thick stacks of papers tucked away in a lawyer's office," Dinning replied. "None of this has ever been entered into any computer database. I know that for a fact, because the attorney for the estate and I have been friends for years. Someone would have to dig pretty deep to discover the connection. No one knows we're here."

"I hope you're right, Professor, because the people chasing us are spooky. I'm talking military and CIA kind of spooky, and they can find out anything about anyone."

"She's right, Peter," Dana added. "This might not be the best place to be right now."

123

"Maybe not, but I checked the road when we were driving in. No tire marks. That tells me no one's been poking around here since the last rain, and this area is in a drought right now." Dinning pulled a roll of cash from his pocket and handed a couple of hundred-dollar-bills to Sam. "Here, take this. We'll need some groceries, and coffee, lots of coffee … and sugar too. There's a little store up the road, but the lady who runs it is really nosy so try not to get sucked into her web of questions."

"You want me to go to the store?"

"You're the best choice. If I'm seen around here word will spread like wildfire, but they don't know you. I doubt they have a security camera at that little store, but be sure to wear your baseball cap and sunglasses just in case someone there has seen your picture on TV."

"Where did you get all of that money?"

"I grabbed it from the ship's safe before I went over the side. We always carried cash for emergencies when we were in Africa."

"At least we have money," Sam said, stuffing the bills into a back pocket of her jeans. "The gas gauge on the truck is almost on empty."

"You can fill it up at the store. Park it in the old barn when you get back. In the meantime, Dana and I can start cleaning up around here before we eat and start work."

"How long do you think we'll be here?"

"Hours … days … maybe weeks. I have no idea." Dinning stared at the laptop again. "This is the largest amount of data I've ever collected on a single expedition."

Sam jangled the keys as she headed for the door. "Okay … I'm off for the store. Any last requests? Slim Jims? Pork rinds?"

Dana visibly paled. "Really? Maybe I should go. I only bought the beef jerky as survival food."

"I'm kidding, Dana. I was raised on granola, trail mix, and fish. Back in a few."

Through the big window, Peter and Dana watched the trailing cloud of dust behind the pickup until Sam turned onto the paved road. Looking back inside, they surveyed the debris of time.

"I guess we should open the windows and find something to wear over our noses when we start dusting," Dinning suggested. He noticed she was still holding up her jeans. "You know, Dana, I was thinking you might find some jeans in the bedroom closet that would fit you a whole lot better."

"Angela's jeans?"

"Yes ... they were hers. But I can tell you right now that she'd be the first one to offer them to you if she was here now, and she'd expect me to do the same."

Dana looked past the fireplace to a cedar hallway lined with tall windows running along the back side of the house. "Which room?"

"End of the hall."

As soon as she was gone, Dinning opened the desk drawer and pulled out a worn brown bandana—a gift from Angela. He wrapped it bandit-like across his nose, but when he inhaled, the room began to spin. After all this time he could still smell her scent imbedded in the cloth. He closed his eyes and inhaled once more before folding it back up and gently returning it to the drawer.

He had always known it would be like this if he ever returned. Everywhere he looked there was something to remind him of the countless tender moments they had spent together—moments that clung to his heart, scar-like, embedded somewhere deep within his soul. The memories flooded his thoughts like they did every night, when they came at him like stray wisps of steam just before he drifted off to sleep.

Looking through the front window, he thought about walking outside to avoid stumbling into another emotional landmine. But the painful reminders were all around; tender memories lying in wait—even outside under the big pecan tree.

The past was the past, and this was the present. He could hear Angela's voice telling him to live his life until the time came when they would be together again.

He needed to start cleaning. Anything to take his mind off the past. Crossing into the kitchen, he turned on the tap to flush the pipes while he began opening cupboards to look for cleaning supplies. Starting with the desk, he began wiping away literally years of webbed insect history before moving on to the sofa. He grabbed an armful of red cushions and walked outside to beat them together, coughing in the cloud of dust that turned orange as it rose through the slanting rays of the setting sun.

Craning his neck, he suddenly found himself thinking about Hantavirus as he watched it drift away. If any infected mice had found their way into the house, their dried droppings were surely mixed with

125

the orange cloud now disappearing in the direction of the barn—and he was a dead man.

Good! He thought to himself. He was starting to think like a scientist again. He had a job to do, and if he did it right he would be able to come back here one day. It was finally time to make peace with his past, and the next time he returned it would be to stay. Walking back to the porch, he sat on the dusty swing and just looked out over the quiet hills.

He could hear Dana in the kitchen now, washing dishes, but he couldn't bring himself to look back. He wanted to see someone else standing there with a dish rag in her hand. He sat there for what seemed like a long time, until he saw the pickup turn in from the highway and pull up under the shade of the big tree. Right away Sam hopped out and began hefting bags of groceries from the back.

"You were right about that woman at the store," she said, shoving two bags into Dinning's outstretched hands. "She's a human question machine."

"She also remembers everything she sees," Dinning replied. "Any cameras?"

"Not that I could tell. I kept my hat pulled low when I pumped the gas and paid for the food. There's hardly any traffic on the road."

"At least that hasn't changed. When I first moved to Austin thirty years ago it was still a relatively small town and easy to get around in, but now it's a traffic nightmare."

"You're starting to get *old guy* syndrome, Professor."

"You mean because I sound like I long for a past that can never be regained?"

"Something like that. I hear that kind of talk on the island sometimes, but it's worse on the mainland. I guess that's because the island will always be the island ... like this place. It's still just like it was the last time you saw it. At least that's something to be grateful for."

Dinning looked back at Sam, puzzled. She had sensed his pain and was trying to steer him back on course with her disarming, ponytailed, Texas charm. For the first time in days, Dr. Peter Dinning grinned.

The screen door slammed behind them and they turned to see Dana standing on the front porch with her feet planted apart and her hands on her hips. She was wearing a pair of jeans that fit her perfectly around the waist, but they were almost six inches too short.

"I can't win here!" she cried out.

Dinning lowered his head so she couldn't see his grin, but nothing could stifle Sam's laughter. "At least pedal pushers are coming back in style."

"Very funny, Sam. I've had problems finding clothes that fit my whole life, so believe it or not, this isn't exactly a new experience for me."

A smiling Samantha turned around and reached into the bed of the pickup to retrieve a case of Lone Star beer.

Dinning's eyes brightened. "Beer?"

"That's right, Professor. It was part of my well-crafted cover story. I told the woman back at the store I was headed for a party at the river. I mean, I couldn't exactly leave without beer could I? Besides, you could stand a little loosening up … we all could. Can someone grab the ice chest?"

* * *

Staring out across the ship channel, Admiral Nathan Bourdon was fuming. "How the hell did they get off the island?"

"We don't know, sir," an older-looking Navy SEAL answered. "That local girl had a lot of friends with boats, and the DIA guys only get blank stares when they start asking questions around the marina. This is a pretty tight-knit community. These people all grew up together."

"Where's Commander Brooks?"

"He mentioned something earlier about having to get back to his own team on the ship. Do you want me to call him?"

"No, we'll keep him and his team in reserve off the coast in case things change, but it might be a good idea to have some of our people on the ground start moving toward the Austin area."

"Austin, sir?"

"He could be trying to make his way back to his lab."

"Do you want the team here on the island to handle it?"

"You mean like they handled that fiasco at the marine institute?"

"There are only so many of us, Admiral. We were the only ones qualified to be the entry team. The police and a few regular army troops had the perimeter."

The admiral continued to gaze across the water. "I know, Chief. Let's go. I need to start calling in some favors from my friends in the CIA who haven't resigned yet. It's time to start stacking the deck in our favor for a change."

CHAPTER 21

With the sun dipping below the hills across the road, a chorus of chirping crickets filtered through the open windows, drowning out the sound of Dana stirring something in the kitchen that smelled like chili. Ensconced on the sofa in the warm glow from a pair of table lamps, Dinning felt refreshed from his shower and shave. He was relieved to see that a sense of normalcy had returned to their lives, if only for a little while. Just like the lamps—left in darkness for years but now shining brightly again—some kind of cosmic sleight-of-hand had returned him to that comfortable space where he and Angela had once sat enjoying the simple act of just staring at the woven Navajo rug over the fireplace without giving any thought to the passage of time.

But now, time was something very much on Peter Dinning's mind as he reclined and opened the laptop. The beer tasted good as he waited for the computer to power up.

"I forgot to buy matches," Sam said, walking through the front door with a bundle of firewood. "Got any?"

"Yeah, in the desk drawer." Dinning ran his hands over his scalp as he stared at the screen. "You know," he said to Dana, "whatever we discovered could have been found anytime during the expedition. Personally, I'm becoming more worried we might have stumbled onto some new kind of virus out there. That would explain a lot of things."

"If it was viral they wouldn't be chasing us," Dana said. "I still say we should start with the most recent samples first, which brings us back to the most interesting specimen to date ... the fish from the river. It's the most fascinating genetic puzzle I've ever seen."

"What did you see?"

"I'm not sure." She walked into the living room with a tray containing three steaming bowls of chili and set them on the knotty pine coffee table. "That's why you need to see it for yourself."

129

Wolfing down his chili, Dinning squished back into the sofa with the computer on his lap and clicked the file marked *Yangambi Library Specimen*. The first picture that flashed up on the screen showed the remains of the blind fish lying in the wooden box Musa had given him. He was looking at the bones of a creature chased from its dark world by something that had frightened it, and the same poignant emotion he had felt when he had extracted a sample of its DNA in the ship's lab came rushing back to him. For some reason he had been unable to return it to the freezer with the others, so he had stashed the box in his desk drawer to keep it close to him, even though it made him feel sad.

On his solitary journey back across the Atlantic, he had felt compelled to open the box every day to look at the fish. It comforted him somehow, and there was a connection he couldn't explain. It was the last thing he had grabbed before he had gone over the side and the first thing he had hidden when he reached Saint Joe's Island. Now, after bringing it across thousands of miles of ocean, the little wooden box was still with him—sitting on the coffee table—never far away.

Moving his fingers over the keyboard, he scrolled down through pages of seemingly endless columns of numbers until he came to a set of pictures that had been taken using a new system designed to capture ultra sharp images of biomolecules using special fluorescent proteins that could paint structures less than 10 nanometers apart—the size of an antibody. Using the new technology, they could now study the classic double-helix structures they wanted to explore in stunning 3D color—the twisting strands of DNA fluorescing, making them appear almost otherworldly, like the luminous images of distant galaxies captured by an orbiting telescope.

He continued to scroll, stopping for a moment to study each image before moving on to the next, his eyes searching, until finally he came to the image he was looking for. A single strand of DNA with an unusual morphology.

Dr. Peter Dinning had seen numerous aberrations throughout his career. Through bloodshot eyes he had studied them for uncounted hours, comparing them to others, and as aberrations went, this one was right up there at the top of the list. Unlike the other protein-tagged strands of DNA that appeared cobalt blue, this one gave off a phosphorescent glow that was almost sun-like. Rays of golden light seemed to spin off its surface, lighting up nanometers of space in the micro world that surrounded it. He looked closer.

What was that?

Something else—small dots, glowing green, circling within. Dinning could feel the hair rising on the back of his neck with the sudden realization that he was looking at the fingerprint of genetic manipulation—a fingerprint left behind when the genome of an organism had been modified by introducing lines of genetic code from the DNA of another species. It was the hallmark of genetic engineering.

This strand of DNA had been engineered!

Dinning was stunned. He was looking at what's known as a transgene, but how did an engineered gene find its way into a species of blind fish that had evolved at the bottom of an African river seven hundred feet from the surface?

Removing his feet from the coffee table, he sat bolt upright and glanced at Dana. "Are these the images you sent me?"

"They should be. I attached them to the email I sent you."

"Would you mind looking again?"

Reluctantly, Dana stopped ladling her second helping of chili and joined him on the couch. Turning the screen toward her, Dinning nodded to the glowing spiral.

"Yes ... that's what I've been talking about all this time. That was taken from the DNA you extracted from the fish bones. It was the last sample I received from you."

"You're positive?"

Dana glanced at the time stamp with her initials in the corner. "Yeah, I'm sure. I numbered it right away and logged it in our database like I always do so it wouldn't get mixed up with another sample. Why?"

"Because this is the first chance I've had to see these pictures, and without a complete sequencing report, I have to be absolutely sure this DNA came from that fish and nowhere else."

They both paused to stare at an object that drew them in, holding their gaze in a hypnotic embrace.

"You see the way it's glowing?" Dinning continued.

"Yes, it's beautiful."

"Now, look closer ... in the middle. You see those little green dots that are also glowing?"

131

"Yeah, we all did, but none of us had ever seen anything like that before."

"That's because none of the grad students currently working in my lab have had any experience working with transgenic organisms. You're looking at a strand of DNA that's been engineered, or more specifically, a transgene ... a segment of DNA containing a gene sequence that's been isolated from one organism and microscopically introduced into a different organism to alter its genetic code."

Dana gasped. "You mean this came out of Africa?"

"Yes, from the same fish in that box on the table ... the one that evolved in total darkness and has lived its entire life at the bottom of the Congo River."

"But that's impossible," Dana responded. "Only a world-class lab would be able to genetically modify a section of DNA like that and successfully insert it into a living creature, and we couldn't find a record of anything like this in any genetic library, natural or otherwise. I know ... I checked."

"Which begs the question of how an engineered gene ended up in a blind fish that lives seven hundred feet underwater and has never been seen before. According to Musa, not one of these fish has ever been caught, which means they never venture too close to the surface."

Dinning glanced up at Sam blinking back at them from the breakfast bar. *This must be really hard for her*, he thought. A few days ago she was just living her life, catching bait fish for a living, and now she was running from the military with two virtual strangers—trapped in the nightmare of a scientific enigma that had them running from ... from who? Who was really chasing them? And why? Could an engineered string of DNA found in a species of African fish really be the reason they had suddenly become the object of so much attention? It seemed a little farfetched, but if it were true, it still didn't answer the biggest question of all. What was it about this particular genetic puzzle that made someone feel justified in taking out a ship full of scientists just to keep its existence a secret?

Setting the laptop aside, he slipped on his shoes and walked outside to sit under the big pecan tree. He had often gone there in the past to think—to look up at the stars and ponder his place in the universe like most people did when they stared at the nighttime sky. Lowering his gaze, his eyes followed a faint line of bluish light outlining the hills to the north against an indigo sky. The light from Austin had grown brighter since the last time he had been here.

Leaning against the tree, he closed his eyes and listened. Aside from the low voices of the two girls talking inside, he was enveloped in silence. Even the crickets had stopped chirping for some reason.

And then he heard it.

It was barely audible at first, like a distant buzzing insect, and it was coming closer. Sitting up, his eyes strained in the darkness as he peered in the direction of the sound.

And then he saw it.

It passed right by him—a small buzzing machine not much bigger than a bird. He watched, fascinated, as it flew toward the house and came to a hover in front of the big picture window.

A drone!

Dinning flattened himself against the tree, his breath coming in short, shallow gasps. Somehow the people chasing them had discovered his little sanctuary, and they were using a drone to scout the area.

But was this its first visit? Could this be the reason they hadn't seen any tire tracks on the dirt road leading up to the house when they first arrived?

Holding his breath, he moved in a crouch away from the tree, never taking his eyes off the drone as it hovered outside the window. Like an aerial paparazzi, it was probably sending back real-time images of the two girls inside to whoever had sent it.

He had to stop it!

Looking around, he grabbed a rock the size of a fist off the dark ground and took off running as fast as he could directly toward the drone. A red light on the little machine blinked, and he could hear a mechanical click as it sensed his presence and started to spin around. But the warning had come too late. Before the thing could complete its turn Dinning brought the rock down as hard as he could and smashed it down onto the porch. For a few moments it whirred and clattered until, like the dying mechanical thing that it was, it finally stopped moving.

Carefully, he picked it up by a dangling piece of broken plastic. The camera was obviously shattered, as was the power source. Alerted by the crash, the two girls came stumbling out onto the front porch with firewood sticks in their hands.

"You okay out here, Professor?" Sam asked.

133

Dinning held up the crushed drone. "I was having a little fight with this."

"Eww!" Dana yelped. "What is that … a bat?"

"A drone. Somehow they've found us. I'm afraid we don't have much time." Dinning whirled around, half expecting to see soldiers advancing through the mesquite and live oak forest surrounding the ranch. "Where's the truck?"

"I parked it in the barn like you told me," Sam said.

"Good. That means the drone didn't see it. I'll grab the laptop while you two get the truck. We have to move quickly! I have a feeling they'll be here any minute."

The two girls took off running while Dinning headed for the house. His heart was pounding when he crossed the living room and peered through the back windows. Nothing seemed to be moving. Scooping the laptop from the couch, he ran back out through the front door and sprinted toward the barn. He could hear the truck's engine revving inside as he ran through the open doors and dove into the front seat. Sam stepped on the gas and the truck lurched out into the cool night air. Looking off to his right, Dinning saw the light from the house reflecting up into the shimmering leaves of the pecan tree.

"Stop!"

"What!" Sam shouted back.

Dinning could see the fear in her eyes. "I forgot something. We can't leave without it."

Slamming on the brakes, she brought the truck to a stop while Dinning took off running toward the house and burst into the living room. In one frantic motion he grabbed the wooden box off the coffee table and made it to the front door before he stopped. Slowly he turned and looked back into the room, pausing for a moment to let his eyes take in the protective radiance of a place that had once been his safe haven from the world for so many years. His fingers reached for the light switch, but his hand began to tremble and he moved it away. He couldn't bear to turn the lights off—to leave the little house in darkness again when it had just returned to life. With tears in his eyes, he fled.

As soon as he reached the truck, Sam gunned the engine and spun the tires. They shot past the pecan tree and flew down the dirt road, leaving behind a spinning cloud of dust that drifted over the field. It blotted out the view of the little house behind them as they pulled out onto the dark highway and headed for the bright lights of the city.

John Lyman

CHAPTER 22

"They killed the drone," Redding said, staring at the blank picture on the screen in the back of the DIA's mobile command center.

"But that was one of the same kind of drones we use to sneak up on SEAL teams during field exercises, and they almost never spot it," Gil Preston shot back. "How the hell did that happen?"

"I have no idea, sir, but apparently the drone's infrared sensors missed someone outside when it approached the house. We believe Dinning was the one who destroyed it, because the drone sent back images of the two girls inside before it was brought down."

"Do we have a rapid response team in the area?"

"Not yet. We only received the coordinates for that location from the admiral's CIA friends an hour ago. To be honest, it sounded like a long shot because they didn't see Dinning's name on the property deed when they searched the lawyer's office. That's why we sent in the drone first to see if anyone was home."

"Technology," Preston huffed. "Most of the time it works really well, but there's no substitute for boots on the ground. We'd have them now if we'd sent in a ground team."

"Most of our teams are already stretched to the limit, Gil. Half of them are currently deployed in the Middle East, and the few that we were able to pull from the standby roster weren't too happy about having to chase a middle-aged college professor and a couple of girls all over Texas."

Preston glared back. "I don't give a damn how happy they are. Do you have any idea what will happen if those three people discover what they have and word leaks out to the world?"

"I understand, sir, but personally I don't think many people will believe it. We have a group of spin doctors with scientific backgrounds standing by to debunk any of their claims. Once our people in the press get hold of this, anything Dinning and the two girls say will sink to the level of an urban legend in a matter of days."

"We can't afford to take that chance, especially if Dinning figures out what he's discovered. Flood the Austin area with every available asset we have. If he's already discovered our little genetic friend, he's probably headed for his lab. It's the only place within a hundred miles that has the kind of equipment he'll need to break down the structure so he can determine how it was created."

"I guess at this point anything's possible, sir," Redding said. "But as far as we know, all he has are some digital images. Our people entered his Austin lab the morning after his ship was attacked and saw that his sequencing machine was still being reprogrammed when they destroyed the DNA sample from the fish."

"All of it?"

"We believe so."

"You believe? Do you really want to hinge the security of this entire project on a *belief?* This man has been one step ahead of us since all of this started, and I don't expect things to change anytime soon unless we catch a lucky break. He's a brilliant scientist. We could use a man like that."

"He'll never agree to work with us, especially when the immensity of what he's discovered hits him."

Preston leaned against a recessed gun rack and lit a cigarette. "In that case he becomes expendable and we press on without him."

Redding's eyes grew wide. "What about the two girls?"

"Collateral damage."

"None of the teams here will stand for something that."

"I know. We have other people for that."

CHAPTER 23

As soon as they reached the frontage road, Sam let the truck idle behind a stop sign while Dinning looked out at the moving river of lights on the interstate. To their left, Austin, and to the right, San Antonio. "Which way, Doc?" she asked.

"Take a right and keep going until we hit I-10."

"I-10?"

"It's the quickest way to Houston."

Dana's head popped up from the back seat. "Houston?"

"Yes. Now that we know the DNA from the fish was engineered, we have to find out what kind of genetic material they used to create it so we can determine its function."

"Which means you're looking for a very specialized genetics lab, right?"

"Exactly. Returning to our lab in Austin is out of the question, but I have another idea. Before I left for Africa last year I did some consulting work for HBG ... the Houston Biotech Group. It's a new start-up company that was looking to begin work on gene-targeted cancer research."

Dinning paused, a mental picture forming in his head. "The last time I was there they had just finished construction on their new, state-of-the-art facility. But you'd never guess what they were doing in there by looking at it from the outside. The lab is located in a windowless, concrete building set back from the highway to Galveston on a soggy piece of land. It looks more like a big warehouse than a high-tech lab, and the only signs are the ones that say *keep out*."

"But why would they want to hide such a cutting edge research facility?"

"Probably because they don't want to advertise what they're doing," Dinning replied. "The potential financial rewards for gene-based therapy are huge, and industrial espionage in the field has become rampant over the past few years. The fact that they've kept it off the radar makes it perfect for us."

Dana glanced out the window as a deer bounced across the road right in front of their stopped truck. "Why not use one of the UT labs at the Health Science Center instead? The molecular genetics department there is world class."

"And so is their security. By now our pictures are all over the internet, and the guy in charge of security for the Houston campus is a former FBI agent."

"He's right," Sam agreed. "They're probably watching every UT lab in the state." She arched her back to stretch her spine, and Dinning could hear the bones in her neck crack as she snapped her head from side to side.

"Why don't you let me drive for awhile," he said. "Dana and I napped on the way to the ranch, but you haven't slept at all. I'll wake you up when we get to Houston."

"Deal." Sam glanced over her shoulder into the back seat. "Wanna trade seats, Dana?"

"Sure."

While the two girls traded places, Dinning slid behind the wheel and steered the truck from the frontage road onto the interstate. It was cooler now, and the earthy Texas breeze rattled the leaves in the shadowed woods along the side of the highway as Sam leaned her head against the glass and peered outside. Every now and then she would see a pair of glowing eyes from one of the creatures that lived in the woods as they stared out at the river of speeding lights moving through their world. It reminded her of the ecosystem on her own little island, where the fish watched every move she made as she waded through the water—ready to dart to safety if she turned and headed their way.

The world was an endless eating machine. *Predators and prey.*

But where did we fit in on the food chain? Sam wondered. It was a question most people would laugh at because the answer seemed so obvious, but after listening to Peter and Dana, she was beginning to believe that it was the microscopic world that stood at the top of the heap. The invisible world had been here long before us, and it would almost certainly be here long after we were gone.

Peering through the window of a speeding truck at night in her sleep-deprived state was almost like dreaming. Her questions took on a tactile quality, hovering in front of her open eyes.

Were the little things winning? Is that what all this was about?

She remembered Doc Roberts sewing up a cut on her hand while telling her that a million-man army of bacteria could be marching across her face and she'd never even know they were there. It had been his subtle way of explaining the need to keep her wound clean. There was power in smallness—in the ability to remain hidden. Like the creatures who peered from the shadowed woods waiting to cross the road, the tiny things were waiting too. But none of us would ever see them coming. Slowly, her eyes drifted shut and she was fast asleep.

As the truck hurtled toward Houston, Peter slid the little wooden box across the seat next to him … never far away.

John Lyman

CHAPTER 24

A big city is an impersonal thing. Like a symbiotic organism, it doesn't care if you're hungry or full, happy or sad, or even if you're dead or alive. It seeks only to grow—to feed on the energy of those drawn to its egocentric aloofness by the nectar of motion, light, and sound that was almost disorienting to new arrivals—especially the three new arrivals who still had no clear idea why they were being hunted.

Driving through the western fringes of the city just after midnight, the truck carrying Dinning and the two girls sped through islands of halogen light that painted the Katy Freeway with faint, orangey circles. With traffic still heavy, they were forced to slow when they passed a cluster of tall buildings off to their right that defined the Houston Energy Corridor—center of the universe to many of the biggest oil and chemical companies in the world. Surrounded by the largest swath of urban parkland in the country, high-end homes and bike trails mingled with glass towers that housed such corporate icons as BP America, ConocoPhillips, Dow Chemical, Shell Oil and ExxonMobil—an oily version of Silicon Valley.

They continued on, but as soon as they topped the next overpass, Dinning's heart skipped a beat. A line of flares was steering traffic into the far right lane ahead of a mass of flashing red and blue police lights.

Dana jumped in her seat and leaned forward against the dash. "Oh my God! Is that a roadblock?"

"Looks like it," Dinning said. He could feel the sickening grip of fear working its way up from his stomach as they inched toward a line of police officers. Dana pointed. A car was lying upside down next to the inner guard rail, and one of Houston's finest was waving them around the accident site.

Taking a few deep breaths to calm his nerves, he gripped the wheel and merged into the southbound lane. They skirted the downtown

143

skyline, snaking between the second and third wards to intersect with the Gulf Freeway, where they could see the belching, fiery glow from the Pasadena refineries lighting up the odorous night sky in that part of the city. Continuing on past the Johnson Space Center, the lights from Houston faded behind them as the freeway to Galveston cut through miles of flat land too swampy to build on.

Dinning could feel it now. They were getting close. The air was becoming more humid by the second when he finally spotted the turnoff he was looking for and exited the freeway next to a lighted cluster of outlet stores. He peered ahead, searching the darkened area off to their right before making a sudden turn onto a muddy road that followed a drainage canal.

"Better wake her up," he said to Dana. "We're almost to the lab."

"Out here?"

Dinning nodded as the truck splashed through the water-filled ruts in the road.

"God I hate dark water." Leaning over the front seat, she looked back at Sam. "Time to wake up, Sam. We're almost there."

Smoothing her hair back, Sam sat up and peered out into the murk. "Where's Houston?"

"Behind us."

"Behind us? Where are we?"

"We're on a muddy road next to a canal," Dana said. "Sorry, but Dr. Paranoid here wouldn't stop to buy coffee."

"That's hard core, Doc," Sam said, pulling herself up against the back of the front seat.

Dinning seemed not to be listening as he peered into the stark blackness beyond the reach of their headlights. To their left, the narrow canal was filled with still, muddy water, and all around them low, wet fields glistened in the moonlight. "Ah … there it is!"

Dana held her face close to the windshield. "I'm not seeing anything, Peter."

"A single light … up ahead on the left. See it?"

Both girls strained until Sam finally pointed. "There! I see it now."

On the opposite side of the canal, they all saw an immense structure rising from a waterlogged field. "That's the lab," Dinning said.

Dana eyed the canal on their left and the steep drop off into an area of glistening reeds on the opposite side of the road. "You sure, Peter?"

"Positive. There should be a small bridge up ahead."

As soon as the words were out of his mouth, the truck's headlights reflected off a sign pointing to a low, flat bridge. Crossing over, the dirt road suddenly turned to pavement as Dinning drove toward a warehouse-sized building built on high ground that sloped down around the sides.

"See those huge brown pipes that slant from the side of the building into the ground?" he asked.

"Yeah. What are those?"

"They're fake. They built them like that so people would think this was some kind of pumping station. This entire area used to be a swamp."

"Still looks like one," Dana said.

Driving through the empty parking lot, Dinning pulled into a space close to the building and stopped. Through the windshield, they stared out at the immense structure with a single recessed light illuminating the only door they could see.

"Now what?" Dana asked.

Dinning's expression remained flat. "I'll get out first and walk over to that door while you two wait here. This place might look deserted, but I can guarantee you we're being watched right now."

"What about security guards?"

"There's no on-site security here. They're too paranoid to let anyone inside. Industrial espionage spies know all the tricks, including having their own people get hired as security guards or cleaning people. The man who owns this lab has his own security team monitoring everything by camera from an offsite location. He loved showing me all of their security precautions when I was here. They have at least a dozen cameras covering this area alone, and that's what I'm counting on."

Dana eye's zeroed in on the single door. "What are you going to do, Peter?"

"There's a phone by that door for visitors to call into the lab. Right now the people watching us don't know if I'm a potential thief or one of the drunken frog hunters that prowl these fields every night. I'm hoping that will keep them from sounding the alarm until I can make it to that phone so we can have a friendly little chat."

"A chat!" Sam practically shouted. "What are you gonna say? *Hi. I'm Dr. Peter Dinning, and I'd like to use your lab for awhile.*"

145

"Something like that." Dinning's eyes narrowed. "I'm going to tell them I need to speak to the owner. Once he hears who's standing outside his lab, I'm pretty sure he'll take the call."

"What could you possibly say that would make him want to let you into his secret little world behind that door?"

"The truth ... or at least part of it. I'm going to tell him that I need to use his lab to work on something I'd rather not discuss on the phone. He's a very astute business man with the instincts of a gold prospector, which means he's obsessed with secrecy ... especially when it concerns the new genetic frontier. He'll understand."

"What about the cops, Peter?" Dana asked. "Our pictures are all over the internet now, and even though you may think this guy is your buddy, what makes you think he won't just call the police after he hangs up?"

"That's a distinct possibility of course, but I'm betting he'll be so curious about my urgent need to use his lab in the middle of the night that he won't do that. We got to know each other pretty well when I was here last year helping him get things set up. His name is Ian Hamilton. He's not a scientist, but he's extremely bright and has dreams of becoming a billionaire in the biotech industry someday. If he thinks I'm on to something that could help him achieve that dream, he'll be more than willing to help."

"Even if he knows the military and about a dozen other government agencies are looking for you?"

"Especially if he knows the government is interested. That fact alone will make him even more curious, and curiosity and motivation go hand-in-hand."

"So you're going to tell him about the transgene?" she asked.

"I'll have to. Once we start work, anything we do will be logged into his computer database. Not only that, but he'll probably jump in his car and drive over here as soon as we're finished talking. That means he'll also see our little golden friend revolving on the screen in glowing Technicolor."

"But what if he tries to replicate it?" Dana looked like she was starting to panic. "I mean, he'll have all of our data, and if the military is trying to keep it a secret, there's no telling what it does. I don't like this at all. You're giving away the keys to the kingdom, Peter, and we don't know if it's a good kingdom or a bad kingdom. You're placing something we know very little about in the hands of a man who's already stated that his main goal in life is making money … a lot of money. You can't trust someone like that with something like this."

In a moment of pensive indecision, Dinning ran his hands through his hair and looked back out at the lab. "I realize it's a risk, but this could be our only chance to discover how that gene was created. Maybe we can find a way to delete the data after we're finished … I don't know, but right now we have to find out everything we can about that gene. A lot of our friends died because it exists, and I intend to find out why."

In the silence that remained in the wake of a final decision, Sam squinted at the silent building. "Better get going, Professor. I have a feeling the clock is ticking on us here."

CHAPTER 25

The squeak of rusty hinges was muffled by the thick muggy air as Dinning stepped from the truck with the laptop. Swatting at the first mosquito to sense his presence, he looked up at the cameras on the roof and headed straight for the building with the knowledge that whoever was watching him was already beginning to feel the hair rise on the back of their necks.

He definitely didn't look like a drunken frog hunter.

The men who hunted the wet fields at night usually parked their pickups in the parking lot away from the lighted entrance, and none of them had ever approached the building before. They were just good-old-boys out for a night of beer-drinking with friends. The frog legs they brought home with them were mostly just a tasty bonus and something to appease their wives—a guaranteed free pass to the sofa, where they could sleep it off without a lecture.

As Dinning continued toward the entrance, the three men staring at their screens in a darkened room at HBG corporate headquarters were sitting straight up in their chairs. What had been a mind-numbing night in a mind-numbing job had suddenly become interesting. Tonight something was happening. They could see the two girls waiting in the truck, and none of them had ever seen anyone take off and walk straight toward the building like that. He was even looking up at the cameras!

The men were frozen in their seats. By now there was no doubt in any of their minds that this was no frog hunter, but none of them wanted to be the first to jump the gun and call the cops. They were only authorized to call the police if an actual break-in was in progress, because cops asked questions—questions none of them wanted to answer because that violated rule number one. Never, ever reveal the fact that the building they were watching contained a biotech lab, or your career at HBG would be over.

But then there was rule number two. Never, ever allow anyone to break into the lab.

And then there was rule number three. Never, ever wake up Ian Hamilton in the middle of the night unless it was a dire emergency.

The men continued to stare. Dinning was almost to the entrance, and he kept looking up at the camera. Unable to wait any longer, one of the security men reached for his phone, but the senior man sitting next to him held up his hand. "What are you doing?"

"I'm calling the boss. We need to dispatch a mobile unit and find out what that guy is up to."

The senior man brought his face closer to the screen. Dinning had just walked up the short set of steps to the door and was looking at the phone. "Let's give it a few more minutes and see what he does before we hit the panic button. That outside door isn't the only barrier he'll have to get through to reach the lab, so there's no need to rush things."

A white phone buzzed on the console in front of him. "Crap! It's the boss!" Reaching for the phone, the man straightened in his seat. "Good evening, sir."

"Are you watching that man at the door?"

"Yes, sir. He's just standing there."

"I'll take it from here. I know him."

"Is everything okay, sir?"

"Yes ,… everything's fine. Just make sure no one knows he's at the lab. Is that clear?"

"Crystal, sir." The call ended abruptly. "The boss said he knows the guy." The security man paused, his eyes narrowing. "What in the hell is going on out there?"

A few seconds later his question was answered when the camera captured the outside door to the lab slide open. The tall, backlit figure of Ian Hamilton stood in the entrance, his blond hair caught in the light streaming from behind, making it appear to glow.

* * *

Peter Dinning took an involuntary step backward. "Ian?"

"Hello, Peter." Hamilton smiled. "I had a feeling I'd be seeing you soon."

"You were waiting for us?"

"Actually, I was working late, but I was hoping you'd turn up." A buzzing mosquito flashed into oblivion when it came in contact with a purple fluorescent light mounted above the open door. "Why don't you and your two friends join me inside for some coffee."

"Your special blend from Jamaica?"

"Where else?

They waited for Sam and Dana to join them before filing through the entrance. As soon as the automatic steel door slid shut behind them they felt the welcome kiss of dry, cool air. With the glow from another purple light painting their faces, they saw that they were standing in a pale blue room the size of a tall, walk-in closet, and the reflective walls looked like they were made from plastic.

"We still have to pass through another area before we enter the lab," Hamilton explained, walking over to another steel door. Leaning forward, he peered into a retinal scanner mounted on the wall. The second door slid open, allowing them to pass into a large, white-tiled space.

"It looks like you've made some changes since the last time I was here," Dinning remarked, looking across the room at a stainless vault door with a little round window. "This looks more like the entrance to a level-4 biohazard facility."

"Yeah," Dana added. "Only in reverse."

Hamilton looked impressed. "Very good, Ms. Wilkins. As you've already noticed, we're trying to keep contaminants out instead of in." He glanced at Dinning. "You were right about her, Peter ... she does pick up on everything. Any chance I can steal her away from you?"

Before Dinning could answer, Dana shot their host a look. "How did you know my last name?"

"Peter told me who you were when I toured your lab in Austin last year, but we never had a chance to meet. I tried to steal you away then too." Hamilton smiled charmingly as he glanced down at his smart phone. "Before we enter the lab, I'm afraid I'll have to ask all of you to shed your clothes and shower."

"Shower?" Sam blurted out.

"Yes." Hamilton pointed to a pair of tiled entrances marked *male* and *female* on opposite sides of the room. "At least fifteen minutes. We use the standard decontamination protocol here."

Once again, Sam found herself swimming in uncharted waters. "Decontamination protocol?"

"Come on, Sam." Dana took her by the arm. "I'll show you what to do."

As the two men headed for their showers, Dana led Sam into a small locker room. "We can hang our clothes in these lockers. When we're through showering we'll have to put on bunny suits. There's a stack of them inside that glass case over there."

"Bunny suits?"

"Hooded biohazard suits with bunny feet. You'll look ridiculous, but don't worry … we all will."

Opening a pair of lockers, both girls undressed and padded barefoot into a large, green-tiled, communal shower. Walking under an oversized shower head, Sam turned the water on and tilted her chin, feeling the warmth of the cascading stream against her face. "God this water feels good." She pulled her head back and squeezed the water from the ends of her hair. "What do you think of this Hamilton guy?"

"I don't know yet. Peter's never mentioned him before, but he seems to trust him." Dana retrieved two sealed packs marked *antimicrobial body scrub* from a dispenser on the wall and handed one to Sam. "There's a scrubbing sponge inside with a little plastic pick for cleaning under your fingernails. Use the sponge and start with your head first, then work your way down. Scrub every inch of exposed skin without reaching back up and touching the areas you've already washed. And don't get that brown soap in your eyes. It's got iodine in it."

"Fifteen minutes?"

"Yep. There's even a clock on the wall with a countdown timer that started as soon as we turned the water on."

Opening the scrub pack, Sam grinned at the sight of Dana furiously washing her short black hair. It was like being in gym class with the nerdiest girl in school, but there was also a sense of awe attached to her. She was obviously driven, but there was something else—something sad in her eyes that reminded Sam of her mother.

When they were done, they toweled dry and slipped on their bunny suits. "You're right," Sam said, looking in the only mirror. "I do feel ridiculous."

Dana managed a rare grin. "You'll get used to it ... but you do look funny."

Joining the men in the center room, they all looked toward the big round door with the little round window at eye level. Hamilton repeated his retinal scan and the click of massive door locks sliding open reverberated around the space as the vault-like door began swinging inward, revealing the fact that the steel was at least a foot thick. Stepping through the opening, they could feel the cool air rushing past their protective suits, and their ears popped from the change in pressure.

"I hope this doesn't make any of you uncomfortable," Hamilton said, "It takes some getting used to, but we have to keep the air in the lab pressurized slightly higher than the atmosphere outside. Keeps any unwanted critters out."

Looking around, Sam saw that they had entered an immense space that consisted mostly of glass rooms interspaced with rows of cubicles containing some of the largest computer screens and wildest-looking screen savers she had ever seen.

"What's in the little plastic bag, Peter?" Hamilton asked without emotion.

Dinning froze as both girls swiveled their heads in his direction. "You mean the one I taped inside my bunny suit?"

"Yes."

"Bones."

"Bones?"

"Yes, Ian. Fish bones, to be exact."

"From the little brown box you brought in and left in the locker with your laptop?"

"How did you ..."

"The first room you entered is really a concealed whole-body scanner. No one comes in or out of this facility without a thorough screening. I saw the box when I checked the images on my phone."

Dinning's shoulders slumped. "Okay. Now what?"

"Now we take a look at those bones and find out why every cop, the FBI, DIA, CIA, plus a large contingent of Navy SEALs ... is turning over every rock in the state to find you and that little brown box."

Sam was livid. "You mean you've known about us all this time!"

"Of course. Anyone who watches TV knows your face." Hamilton looked amused. "You're the girl who got run over by Peter's ship. I'll bet your first meeting was a little awkward."

"She had a knife in her hand as I recall," Dinning said flatly.

A moment of uncomfortable silence was broken when Hamilton extended his hand to Sam. "I'm afraid I've been very rude, Samantha. My name is Ian Hamilton, and I'm the owner of this place. Please accept my apology."

Sam hesitated for a moment before shaking his hand. "Apology accepted."

"Good. Ready to see my lab?"

CHAPTER 26

Moving into the gigantic lab, they followed Hamilton under a metal-beamed ceiling that rose at least three stories above their heads. They continued on, passing through a wide passageway draped in blue plastic that flowed out into an octagonal cluster of large glass rooms spaced around an open central hub with a rubber-coated floor.

Their footsteps were dampened as they crossed to a glass door with a red sign—*DNA Extraction.* Hamilton paused to enter his code on a keypad. A clear pneumatic door hissed open and they entered an air lock. After donning masks and gloves, another glass door hissed open and they stepped into an area known universally to researchers as a clean room.

Standing inside the silent enclosure, Dinning looked more like a surgeon than a molecular explorer as he ran his gloved hands over some of the genetic tools of his trade. Mounted on stainless steel work tables, most of the instruments they would need for their work were covered in clear plastic, and standing guard in the center of the room, the towering steel cylinder of a scanning electron microscope rose next to a curved computer station dominated by an enormous computer screen. To Sam, it looked more like a piece of steampunk art thrown in to add some aesthetic texture to the space.

On the far side of the room, they noticed another enclosed area—a smaller glass room that contained a separate work space covered by a stainless hood for venting toxic fumes and other contaminants to the outside.

Moving to one of the tables, the two men locked eyes. Hamilton's face glowed with expectation behind his mask, while Dinning's sagged with exhaustion as they listened to the hum from the big microscope's vacuum pump against the soft hiss of purified air cycling through the sealed room.

"This is just a wild guess on my part, Peter, but I assume a little DNA extraction is on your agenda." Hamilton looked around at the three faces staring back at him. "But before we start, don't you think this would be a good time to tell me just what in the hell is going on?"

"We don't know."

"You don't know?" Hamilton's eyes revealed his surprise. "So you're telling me the three of you are being hunted like a bunch of crazed terrorists, and you don't know why?"

"That's exactly what I'm saying. I might as well tell you now because you'll see it soon enough." Dinning glanced at Dana. "We may have stumbled onto something in Africa, Ian ... a gene ... a transgene to be exact."

"An engineered gene!" Hamilton practically shouted. "In Africa?"

"I'm having a hard time believing it myself."

"And you found it in a fish?"

"Yes. A blind fish that evolved at the bottom of the Congo River. But how a transgene managed to find its way into the genome of a species that probably hasn't seen the light of day for centuries is something that's left us all scratching our heads."

"What did the sequencing report say?"

"That's part of the problem. We haven't been able to sequence a sample of the DNA yet. Our machine in Austin was down for reprogramming the day our ship was attacked, and Dana and I haven't stepped foot in a lab since. That's why we had to come here. I've seen the images, but without sequencing the genetic code we have no idea what we're looking at. I'm dying to know what kind of genetic material they used to make that thing."

"And I'm dying to see what it does." Hamilton's eyes gleamed. "We'll find out what makes that little sucker tick, Peter. Mi casa es su casa, my friend. If there's a genetic ground zero in there somewhere, we'll find it."

Nodding back, Dinning slowly removed the plastic bag containing the brittle fragments of a genetic puzzle and gently shook them into a sterile tray.

For the next several hours, Sam watched as Peter and Dana went about the methodical task of grinding up a few of the precious bones before moving the powdery mixture under a vented hood, where a cocktail of toxic chemicals was used to disrupt the cell membranes, giving them access to the genetic material inside.

Once that was done, the samples were moved into another sealed cubicle for *sonication*, a process that used ultrasonic waves to shear the DNA molecules into even smaller fragments—the final step in separating out the individual lines of code in the genes that looked engineered. From there they would sequence their results, crossing their fingers that they would be able to find a match that would identify the unique genetic fingerprint in the engineered strand of DNA.

Thirty minutes later, Dana removed her gloves. "Looks like we're all ready to go here. The sequencing is complete. Now it's up to the computer to compare the results with the genetic database for a match with any other known species."

Dinning's expression showed his relief. "Good. Let's just hope the source of the genetic material they used is even in the database. If it is, we'll be a step closer to knowing what the designers were trying to achieve when they introduced that transgene into the genome of the fish."

Hamilton's eyes darted around the room. "I'll monitor the results. I may not have your training, Peter, but I know how to run every piece of equipment in here. I'll let you know when the computer finishes the comparative analysis."

While the others worked, Sam wandered around the lab, peering over her mask with her hands behind her back, afraid to touch anything. Finally, out of bored desperation, she plopped down in a chair next to Dana and watched her working the controls of the electron microscope while the computer-generated image of the glowing strand of DNA rotated on the screen before them. "Why are you all so concerned about that sequencing stuff?"

"Function," Dana answered without looking up. "Once we find out what kind of genetic material they used to create the transgene, we'll know what species the designers obtained their DNA from."

"But how does that determine its function?"

"The original DNA they used from another organism will tell us a lot about what they were trying to create. In other words, why start with the impossible job of starting from scratch if you can use the DNA of a species that already has the qualities you're looking for. After that you can begin playing with the code to achieve your specific objective. It's kind of like genetically modified food … like some of the new GMO corn that's resistant to certain kinds of bugs … you splice in a line of code from something the bugs don't like. That's the function of the genetically engineered variety.".

"You mean like molecular cloning?"

Dana looked up from the hypnotic image on the screen. "Not exactly. How do you know about something like that?"

"I read. Last year some scientist was talking about cloning redfish on CNN. Everyone on the island thought it was a bad idea because they were afraid something bad would happen to the natural fish population if they were exposed to the cloned ones, so I started reading up on the different cloning methods. To be honest, I don't get it. I mean, I understand the whole disease resistance thing, but something like a redfish is pretty darn perfect just the way it is. Why try to change something God's already given us into something that might screw up our ecosystem even more than it already is?"

Dana paused, her eyes searching Sam's face. "Are you speaking from a religious standpoint, Samantha?"

"I guess that depends on what you mean by religious. I wouldn't exactly call myself religious in the traditional sense of the word, but I still consider myself to be a spiritual person."

"What does that mean?"

"It means I'm not really into organized religion. To me our walk with God is a solitary journey, and I've always thought of the ocean as my church. I feel much closer to God when I'm out on the water and looking up at the clouds than I do in some stuffy building listening to someone else's interpretation of what the Bible is really trying to tell us."

"Makes sense to me. That's the same kind of feeling I get when I'm looking through an electron microscope at an invisible world most people will never see. When I look at things at the molecular level it's like I'm looking at some grand design, and to have a grand design, you have to have a grand designer. The framework of our world fits together in ways that didn't just happen by accident, and many of the other scientists I know feel the same way. Maybe that's the reason I've never been very interested in working with transgenic organisms, because personally, I think we're playing with fire."

"Holy shit!" Hamilton shouted out across the lab.

Everyone stopped what they were doing while Hamilton remained hunched in front of a computer screen, furiously scribbling notes as lines of code from the genetic database began to align.

Exchanging glances with the girls, Dinning walked over and stood behind him so he could see the screen. "Did you come up with a match?"

"Hang on a second, Peter. This can't be right."

Dinning continued peering over Hamilton's shoulder. "What can't be right? Something just elicited a *holy shit* from you."

"These sequenced lines of code!" Hamilton swiveled his chair and looked up at Dinning. "You're not going to believe this, but according to the database, someone used genetic material from three different species to create this engineered strand of DNA."

"Three species! But that's impossible. Check it again."

"I just did ... for the third time. I even checked the computer's comparative analysis program to make sure it was comparing the different genomes from the genetic library without mixing them up. There are three separate genomes here ... four if you count the host fish. But that's not all."

Dinning's eyes grew wide. "You mean you think there might be more?"

"No, just the three, but they were taken from three of the deadliest and most aggressive species on the planet.

John Lyman

CHAPTER 27

"Aggressive and deadly?" Dinning was stunned. "Are you saying someone was trying to turn a shy, docile creature into something deadly?"

"It certainly looks that way," Hamilton replied. "Actually, it kind of mirrors your own research on some of the more aggressive species found in Africa."

In the chilled air of the lab, Dinning's hands felt like ice when he picked up the comparative analysis printouts and scanned the pages. "I'll admit there's a startling correlation between the two, but something like this doesn't even begin to reflect what we were doing. My team was only compiling a genetic database for clues that might point to the origin of aggression, but in this case, it looks like someone was actually trying to create it. The only question is …why? And why did they choose this specific fish?"

Dinning was having a hard time sitting still. He began pacing— wringing his hands and muttering to himself like a bored commuter, until finally he stopped when he found himself standing in front of the electron microscope with Sam and Dana peering up at him.

Looking past them, he stared at the glowing image of the strange-looking strand of DNA, revolving slowly on the microscope's screen. "It looks so benign. It's almost angelic-looking."

"Or angry," Dana added, watching the golden light spin fire-like from its surface. "Maybe what we're looking at is the exact opposite of angelic."

"But why would anyone in their right mind create something like that?" Dinning straightened to look out through the thick glass walls. "And why would they let it out into the natural world? Why not keep it in the controlled environment of a lab? Whoever did this certainly had access to one, because what they've done is brilliant."

161

"It might be brilliant," Dana countered, "but it's also irresponsible and potentially very dangerous. We're looking at a transgenic organism that could be the genetic equivalent of a nuclear bomb if it replicates into a hyper-aggressive new life form with the potential for passing its genes on to other organisms."

"I'm afraid that horse has left the barn, Dana. It's probably already replicated, but whether or not it's had time to affect any other organisms on a genetic level remains to be seen. Who knows when it was created, or even how long it's been interacting with the natural environment!" Dinning turned back to stare at the screen again. "How in the hell could someone who's bright enough to create something like this be so pathologically careless at the same time? What three species did they use?"

"The computer came up with three matches," Hamilton said from across the room. "A bull shark, a black mamba snake, and a salt water crocodile."

"Good God! This is a nightmare."

"What's a black mamba?" Dana asked.

"The deadliest snake in the world … and the fastest. One bite has enough venom to kill fifteen men, and they're practically invulnerable from attacks by other animals. At least they usually run from people unless cornered, but a bull shark and salt water croc will come after you. Someone has created quite a cocktail."

In the silence following this latest revelation, Sam hesitated to mention her own pressing problem. "Sorry to interrupt, but where's the bathroom around here?"

"Bathroom?" Hamilton repeated.

"Yes. My bladder is reaching the point of no return."

Hamilton hesitated, looking through the glass walls. "I'm afraid there aren't any bathrooms in this section of the lab. Too much potential for contamination. They're all located on the other side of that thick steel door in the shower area, and once you go out you can't come back in until you take another decontamination shower and put on a new bunny suit."

"You're kidding, right?"

"No, I'm not. That's the reason I was saving my coffee offer for later."

"Fine!" Sam hopped up from her chair. "I'll take another shower and dress like a bunny again, but I have to go."

Hamilton's voice grated. "There's a big red button on the wall that will open the door, but once you go out you can't get back in without a retinal scan. You'll have to wait until one of us can come get you."

Sam took a deep breath. She was tired, she wanted coffee, and she had to pee. "Fair enough ... I'll ring the doorbell." The hiss of compressed air greeted their ears as the door to the clean room slid open and Sam stepped out onto the rubber-coated floor of the central hub. Looking up at the high ceiling, she noticed for the first time that there was a catwalk two stories up that circled the entire lab.

This place is really strange, she thought. Continuing on through the blue-draped area, she spotted the big red button by the entrance door straight ahead. By now she was squirming, and all she could think of was getting through that big thick door with the little round window so she could pee. Like a runner headed for first base, she practically lunged for the red button, but at the last second she saw something move on the other side of the door.

Was she seeing things, or had someone just peeked through the little round window?

Samantha instantly pulled her hand away from the red button and flung herself against the wall. With her back flattened against solid concrete, she could feel her heart pounding and tried to slow her breathing. She had definitely seen an eye, but there was something else ... something *green*.

Someone was in there with them ... someone who had made it through the other two steel doors that sealed the lab off from the outside world.

Samantha held her breath and moved closer to the window.

She had to know!

From her position, nothing appeared to be moving. No shadows—nothing green—no *eye*! She inched closer, and in one quick motion, she swung around and looked through the glass. A man with a green-painted face was staring back at her. Backpedaling away from the little window, Sam felt a warm trickle run down her legs just as the door swung open and a tight group of soldiers swarmed into the lab. They were moving as one with their heads on a swivel and their weapons pointing in all directions.

"Down on the floor!" The green-faced man was looming over her. "Do it ... now!"

Sam dropped to the floor and lay face down while two men quickly tied her hands behind her back with a plastic band before lifting her back up to her feet with surprising gentleness.

The green-faced man moved his face close to hers. Sam recoiled, twisting her head away.

They all had green faces!

She turned back. The man with his face close to hers was the same man she had seen staring back at her though the window. He was obviously some kind of soldier, with the requisite square jaw and the gray eyes highlighted by camouflage paint, but his gun was pointed toward the ceiling instead of at her—always a good sign.

"I hope we weren't too rough with you." The gray-eyed man's voice was husky to the point of being hoarse.

"Not at all." Sam's fear was simmering into something else, and she had to fight the urge to bring her knee up to his groin. "In fact, they were very gentle ... but you made me pee on myself!"

The man fought to contain a grin. "Sorry about that. We seem to have that effect on people sometimes ... and we're not soldiers. We're sailors."

"Sailors? What the hell's going on?"

"My name is Commander Steve Brooks. We're Navy SEALs, and we're not here to hurt you. Where are your friends?"

"Are you the ones who were chasing us in Port Aransas?"

"Yes. Some of us."

"But why?" Sam's anger was making her voice quiver. "Don't you think we deserve some kind of explanation?"

"Orders."

"That's it? That's your explanation ... orders! I'm not telling you anything until I find out why you people are chasing us."

"We don't have time for this," Brooks said to a SEAL standing next to him. "Gag her."

Before Sam had a chance to respond, she felt a piece of duct tape pressing against her mouth as Brooks turned away. Leaving her with two men guarding the door, Brooks and the rest of the SEALs moved into the lab, silently inching their way through the blue passageway.

In the clean room, Dinning was standing by the electron microscope, rotating still images of the strange transgene on the screen so he could study it from different angles. He looked closer. A red dot was moving across the screen. Glancing up, he saw that the glass walls were dancing with red dots.

Dana screamed. A dozen soldiers wearing floppy, olive-colored hats were advancing on the room—the red laser beams from their weapons crisscrossing the space. Even the floor was dancing with red dots, and when she looked up, she saw more soldiers in floppy hats moving along the crosswalk above, their rifles pointed down into the glass enclosure.

"What the hell!" Dinning shouted. "I thought ..."

"Those men out there are going to open the door to this room whether we like it or not," Hamilton said. Slowly, almost casually, he walked over and hit the switch. The clear door slid open.

Brooks raised his weapon and shouted to the group. "Out here ... move ... now! We don't give warning shots!"

Exchanging glances, Dinning and Dana stepped out into the hub.

"On the ground!" a younger SEAL shouted. "Don't even think of running."

Facing each other, Peter and Dana felt their hands being bound behind their backs as they lay on the rubber tiles. Dana's wide eyes had narrowed to slits of fury, and she kept nodding to Dinning. Turning his head to the side, he saw Hamilton. He was still standing in the doorway behind them.

"Why aren't you down here, Ian?" Dinning shouted up.

"Sorry, Peter. I didn't have a choice."

Dinning struggled on the floor, the realization of Hamilton's betrayal hitting him full force. "You bastard! You're a part of this, aren't you?"

"Only in a very peripheral way, Peter. What we've just discovered is fantastic! I always knew that someday we'd see a transgenic organism created from multiple species, but I had no idea someone had already done it."

"So, you think a gene that's been engineered with hyper-aggressive traits is a cause for celebration?"

"Of course. It's a giant leap forward in the field of genetic research ... one that will reap huge financial rewards in the future. I can't thank you enough for bringing it to me. Once all this Africa business gets straightened out, I'm hoping we can share in that future together."

165

"Okay, gentlemen," Brooks interrupted. "We're on kind of strict time schedule here." The SEAL commander's eyes narrowed as he walked toward the open doorway of the glass room.

"What are you doing?" Hamilton cried, blocking his way. "Our agreement was that you people wouldn't contaminate this area."

"I'm afraid we're going to do a little more than contaminate it, sir." With one swift motion, Brooks pulled Hamilton away from the door and tossed a grenade inside. "Time to go."

CHAPTER 28

Hamilton screamed at the two muscled SEALs who were dragging him by the arms behind the others. His feet were barely touching the floor as they ran with him through the blue passageway just as the explosion ripped through the glass room behind them, sending shards of glass flying through the air like thousands of tiny arrows. Fearing the worst, Sam watched in horror as a column of thick black smoke rose toward the ceiling, followed by a second, much larger explosion that took out the entire hub and all the lab modules around it.

The shockwave from the second explosion blurred her vision and almost knocked her off her feet, and when her vision cleared, she saw the SEALs on the catwalks rappelling down to the floor below. By now the smoke was growing unbearably thick as they all rushed from different directions through the open exit while Brooks counted heads. As soon as he was sure that everyone was out, he slammed his fist against the red button and jumped through the opening before the big steel door closed behind him.

Standing in the locker room, Hamilton shook with rage as he glared at Brooks. "You just blew up something that was potentially worth billions of dollars! I was told I could keep anything Dinning brought with him if he showed up at my lab ... that was the deal!"

"Cuff him," Brooks said without emotion. Two SEALs instantly took Hamilton to the floor and bound his hands as the commander leaned down close. "Any deals you made didn't include me or my men."

Hamilton's face was almost purple. "You idiot. I know people ... powerful people."

"We know some pretty powerful people ourselves, Mr. Hamilton, and if I were you I'd keep real quiet for awhile." Brooks looked back over his shoulder. "What's the fire doing?"

167

A SEAL standing by the door peered through the little round window. "Looks like it's beginning to spread, sir. We deactivated the halon fire suppression system when we cut the cameras and the alarm to the fire department."

"Good. That should take care of things." Brooks looked back at the four people in white bunny suits. "Move them outside."

"Wait!" Dinning shouted. "I need something. It's in the locker with my clothes."

"You mean these?" Brooks reached into an olive backpack and pulled out the little brown box and the laptop.

Dinning was stunned. "Yes. Please ... we can't leave them behind."

Brooks held the box up to his ear like a kid listening for the sound of the ocean in a seashell. "If I open this up, what will I find inside?"

"Fish bones."

"Fish bones ... from Africa?"

"Yes. I brought them back myself."

Cowering behind the same two SEALs that had dragged him through the lab, Hamilton's head jerked up. "Are you saying there's still another sample?"

"Of course, Ian." Dinning smiled back. "Apparently, you never learned one of the most basic rules of handling rare research samples. Never put all of your eggs in one basket. I only brought a fraction of the bones into the lab. The rest are in that box."

"This must be what they were looking for on the ship," Brooks said, turning the box over in his hands. "Is it dangerous to me or my men?"

"Not in its current state, but if you destroy that box you will be eliminating the only means we have of finding out why someone is releasing a potentially deadly new life form into our biosphere. You're holding a genetic puzzle in your hands that could affect the entire world one day ... and not in a good way. We could be looking at an extinction event the likes of which we've never seen before if the person who created it isn't stopped, and the contents of that box could lead us right to them."

"You're insane, Dinning," Hamilton quipped. "Do you really think these cretins are going to help you?"

"That's exactly what we're going to do," Brooks said, stuffing the box and laptop back into the backpack. "Cretins like us are always trying to save the world. You might say that's kind of our job description." He looked back at a grinning SEAL and nodded toward Hamilton. "Take the tape off the girl's mouth and gag him with it. Let's move out."

As soon as the tape was off her mouth, Sam started talking. "How long do we have to stay in these bunny suits? I peed in mine, remember?"

"One more word and the tape goes back on," Brooks said.

A chastened Sam exchanged glances with Peter and Dana as the SEALs hustled them outside, flanking them on both sides while moving past the old pickup and into the darkness at the edge of the parking lot. Dipping down into a reedy field covered in several inches of standing water, a symphony of croaking frogs and buzzing mosquitoes filled the humidity-laced air, while behind them, thick black smoke poured from the lab to mix with the night sky, blotting out the stars.

They moved in a line through the shallow water, no one talking, until they came to the end of the field and climbed to the top of a dirt embankment. Below, three black-hulled rubber boats with oversized outboard motors blended with the dark water of the canal.

Standing next to Brooks, one of the SEALs pointed to a line of headlights turning off the frontage road. "We got company, Commander."

"Yeah, they got here quicker than I expected."

"Where do you want to put these people?"

"Keep them separated for now." Brooks nodded toward Samantha. "Put her in the lead boat with me. Dinning and the other girl can go in the second boat."

"What about Hamilton?"

"Last boat. We'll let that little bunny enjoy the spray from the boats in front for awhile." Stepping down into the first boat, Brooks waited until all three boats were loaded before signaling the drivers. Without a word they shoved the throttles forward, sending the black boats shooting down the canal toward a slice of open backwater that separated the mainland from Galveston Island to the east.

Behind them, a line of black SUVs squealed into the lab's parking lot, their occupants tumbling out with guns drawn, but there was nothing they could do but stand and stare at the burning building. By now flames were leaping from the entrance, and as the orange glow reflected against the rising column of black smoke, the sound of approaching sirens filled the still nighttime air, drowning out the songs of hundreds of reptilian spectators peering up at the strange sight through eyes that barely broke the surface of the water.

CHAPTER 29

The black boats sped into open water, surprising a couple of night fishermen who stared open-mouthed at the green-faced men when they flashed by. Heading into deeper water, they swooped under a long causeway bridge and disappeared into the vast blackness of Galveston Bay.

In the lead boat, Samantha sat next to Brooks with the salty wind blowing her hair straight back. To her left, the lights from a Texas City refinery painted a dark horizon, and to her right, the Gulf of Mexico—where the only lights came from ships out at sea. None of the SEALs were talking, which made her even more nervous, but there was something about the man with the gray eyes sitting beside her—something different from what she had expected.

"Can you swim?" Brooks shouted above the wind.

"Of course I can swim," Sam shouted back. "I was raised on an island."

"Good." Using his knife, he leaned behind her and cut the plastic band around her wrist.

"What are you doing!" Sam instinctively glanced out at the dark water. "Are you throwing me overboard?!"

"So much for gratitude." Brooks smiled as he slipped his knife back into its sheath. "I just thought you might like having your hands free in case we hit something and you actually do go overboard." He pulled a black life jacket from under the seat and handed it to her. "Here, put this on."

In the brisk wind, the extra warmth provided by the jacket felt good as she looked back at him and massaged her wrists. "Thank you."

"You're welcome."

"Where are you taking us?"

Brooks pointed into the darkness ahead. Sam squinted. A looming dark shape was blotting out the lights from the distant shoreline, and as she strained to see, a gas flare from one of the refineries along the ship channel lit up the night sky, revealing the wedge-shaped outline of a ghostly apparition floating on the water.

"What is that thing?" she asked.

"A ship ... a very special ship." Brooks paused to listen to someone speaking in his earphone, then cupped his hand over his thin boom microphone and shouted into the wind. "No. Leave his hands tied. Put a life jacket on him."

Sam leaned close. "You don't like him much, do you?"

"Who?"

"Hamilton. You were just talking about him on the radio, weren't you?"

The SEAL commander smiled back without answering as the black boats approached the slanted gray hull of a very strange-looking ship. The first thing Sam noticed was the bow. Unlike conventional ships, where the bow angled from the pointed tip back down into the water, the bow of this ship angled forward—like a giant sword designed to cut through the waves instead of riding over them. Her eyes followed a featureless deck without railings to the center, where a seemingly windowless, trapezoid-shaped superstructure loomed six stories above their heads.

"Looks more like a giant sub than a ship," she said to Brooks.

"Yeah, kinda does."

Sam's eyes crinkled at the edges. "We're looking at a military secret, aren't we?"

"Yes ... yes we are. We'll talk about that later."

On the deck above, sailors in blue jumpsuits watched the boats head for the back of the ship as the drivers gunned their engines and shot up a ramp into a small boat hanger below decks. A few moments later, a large hydraulic door closed behind them like the mouth of a giant whale.

The SEALs wasted no time in leading the group from the tight confines of the boat hanger through a watertight door, where Brooks' raspy voice echoed off the steel walls of a long white corridor that ran the length of the ship. "Put Hamilton in the brig for now."

Nodding back, two SEALs hustled off with a wide-eyed Ian Hamilton looking back over his shoulder, his expression a mask of fear as he was dragged along.

"What about us?" Dinning asked. "Brig?"

"No, sir. You'll be assigned a bunk in officer's country. The girls will bunk with the girls. I apologize for the way we had to handle this situation, but we didn't have a lot of time for explanations. The good news is that you're out of harm's way and you're not prisoners. The bad news is that you're not exactly free to go either, so as long as you're here, all we ask is that you please follow our rules and we'll try to make you as comfortable as possible." Brooks paused to look at the drained faces staring back at him. "I might as well start off with rule number one. You may not, under any circumstances, go anywhere on this ship without an escort."

"What's rule number two?" Sam asked.

"You'll get the rest of the rules in your security briefing." Brooks stopped when he noticed all three were shivering in their thin bunny suits. "You all look pretty silly in those things. As soon as we get you to your assigned quarters you'll be able to take hot showers and change into some dry clothes."

Turning away from Samantha's venomous gaze, Brooks led them through the corridor to a surprisingly wide, carpeted hallway with rich wood paneling. Dozens of colorful military plaques lined the walls.

"What kind of ship is this?" Dinning finally asked.

"Zumwalt-class destroyer," Brooks responded without hesitation.

"I know a little about naval vessels, Commander, but I've never seen a destroyer like this before."

"She's a stealth ship, sir ... the only one of her kind. Cost three-and-a-half billion dollars. The stealth design of this thing gives us the radar signature of a row boat. We can get real close to some pretty unfriendly countries without them knowing we were ever there."

"I thought you said this was a military secret," Sam said.

Brooks turned down another corridor. "It is and it isn't. Pictures of it are already springing up on the internet ... we expected that, but very few people know what's inside. The technology on this ship rivals anything in the space program, and most of it is still highly classified. That's why rule number one makes it clear that civilians aren't allowed to wander around outside their quarters without an escort. Break that rule and you'll find yourself in the brig playing long games of chess with Mr. Hamilton."

The three exchanged glances, almost tripping over each other when Brooks stopped and banged on a steel door below a sign that marked it as the entrance to the women's living quarters. A few moments later the door swung open and a diminutive, red-haired girl wearing camo pants and an olive T-shirt looked up at them. "Good morning, Commander," she said. "What brings you to our neck of the woods? Looking to explore your feminine side?"

"Very funny, Rita. We have a couple of ladies here that could probably use a little looking after."

Major Rita Trent looked Sam and Dana up and down. "Where did they come from?"

"They were in the lab."

"That explains the bunny suits. Hamilton's people?"

"No, they're with Dr. Dinning here."

Stepping into the corridor, Trent reached out to shake Dinning's hand. "Pleased to meet you, Professor Dinning. I've read some of your papers."

Dinning's eyes betrayed his surprise. "You're familiar with my work?"

"I should be. I'm a physician, and genetics is the wave of the new medical frontier." Smiling, she waved Sam and Dana through the door. "Come on, you two. Showers are down the hall." Glancing back at Brooks, she grinned. "See you at breakfast, Commander."

Before Brooks could answer, the door slammed in his face.

"So much for military protocol, huh, Commander," Dinning mumbled.

"She's the ship's doctor. Medical people don't seem to care much for things like protocol and rank, and they're not the only ones. We have some very independent thinkers on board, and we've had to make some adjustments."

"Are you talking about scientists?"

"Engineers and computer experts, mostly. Many of them are reserve officers who seem to be in their own little world half the time. Trying to get people like that to follow military etiquette is like trying to herd cats, but we couldn't run this ship without them."

"Is Major Trent the only Navy doctor on board?"

174

"She isn't Navy … she's Air Force. There are no majors in the Navy. This is a JSOC ship."

"A JSOC ship?"

"Joint Special Operations Command. We're a unified force of Special Forces operators that come from every branch of the military. The primary mission of this ship is to move our best trained fighters around the world and provide them with a base of operations in hostile territory. Warfare as we once knew it is gone forever. We're the tip of the spear now, Professor, and you're standing inside the biggest spear in the world."

Brooks motioned to Dinning and continued down the corridor, descending a ladder-like set of stairs to the deck below. Another steel corridor stretched before them as they made their way toward the front of the ship through a series of *knee-knocks*—watertight doorways that sailors everywhere were forced to step through when passing from bow to stern.

Stopping in front of a door stenciled, *Officers Quarters*, Dinning followed Brooks into a quadrangle of two-man rooms connected to a central day room. Looking around a space the size of a standard living room, Dinning noticed it was comfortably furnished with a pair of black leather couches and several recliners facing a wide-screen TV.

"You'll be bunking in my cabin with me, Professor. It's the blue door with the big number four painted on it." Brooks nodded in another direction. "The head is through that door over there if you need to grab a shower before breakfast. Towels are in the cabinet."

With that, the big SEAL commander heaved his large frame into one of the recliners and grabbed the remote. The sound of baseball filled the room as he removed his boots, wiggled his toes, and leaned back. "I recorded this game last night so I could watch it today. You go ahead and grab that shower, Professor. I'll be right here."

Dinning hesitated. "When are you going to tell me what's going on, Commander? Why did you bring us here?"

"We'll talk about that later. All I can say is that you and your friends are in the safest place you could be right now."

An exasperated Dinning stared at the back of Brooks' head for a moment before heading for the showers. Practically everything was stainless, and when he was done, he wrapped a towel around his waist and stepped back out into the day room. A half-dozen SEALs watching the game turned their heads in unison.

"Uh, excuse me, Commander," Dinning said, his face turning red. "I believe you said something about clean clothes."

"A man from supply just put them on your bunk," Brooks said, jerking his thumb toward the blue door. The men cheered at the screen when the batter sent a grounder between second and third bases, but their cheers quickly turned to groans when the shortstop's lunge fell short and the ball continued rolling toward the far wall between center and left field. "What the hell!" an older SEAL shouted. "He was right there! My ten-year-old could have stopped that ball!"

Relieved by the distraction, Dinning padded into the commander's cabin and grabbed a set of military camos from the top bunk. Dressing quickly, he paused to look in the full length mirror on the back of the door—a feature he had noticed in the living quarters of almost every military base he had ever been on. He heaved his chest out and posed full front, then to the side. Stepping back, he sighed with the realization that no matter how hard he tried, he would never again look like one of the fit young men watching baseball in the room outside. Dinning opened the door and allowed his posture to sag again as he stepped out—but he kept his chest puffed up just a little more than usual.

"Ah, Professor," Brooks said, looking back over his shoulder. "Ready for some coffee?"

CHAPTER 30

S tepping from the shower stall, Samantha felt the deck rumble beneath her feet. She braced when the boat tilted, dropping her towel as she tried to slip into of a pair of black and gray camo trousers, but the boat tilted again and she ended up hopping into the women's day room with one leg in and one leg out. "What gives?"

"We just got underway," Trent said. "We only move in close to land at night, and the ship has to be back out at sea before the sun comes up."

Sam blinked back at her. "Where are we going?"

"I'm afraid that's classified, sweetie. They usually don't tell us until we get there."

"Great," Sam muttered under her breath. As soon as she finished dressing, Trent led her and Dana out into the corridor and up another set of ladder-like metal stairs. Making a quick left, they entered the mess deck. Unlike the subdued atmosphere they had noticed in the rest of the ship, the huge space was a brightly-lit blur filled with the din of a hundred voices and the clink of plates against metal trays, making normal conversation almost impossible.

Heading straight for a tall stainless urn, Samantha poured a steaming cup of coffee and took a luxurious first sip. It tasted so good she almost felt like crying. Grabbing a warm plate, she picked out some crisp bacon and piled her plate with eggs and toast before finding a spot on a bench seat at a long metal table next to Rita and Dana.

"I think this is the best coffee I've ever tasted," she sighed.

Dinning plopped his tray down beside her. "I see you finally got your shower."

Sam tried not to smile at the sight of Dinning in military camos. "You look pretty spiffy yourself, Professor. What's on the agenda?"

"I believe Commander Brooks is going to tell us why we're here after he finishes loading half the hash browns in the kitchen on his plate."

"Those Special Forces guys can really pack it away," Rita added. "And we're sitting with the cream of the crop. The Special Forces officers eat with their men on this ship."

Dana looked up from her plate. "I see a lot of different uniforms at the tables."

"Yeah … the gang's all here. This room is full of some of the best SMUs in the country."

"SMUs?"

"Special mission units. They all fall under the command of JSOC. You got your Delta Force guys over there … basically Army Green Berets on steroids. Then you have your SEALs sitting at the next table. They're from DEVGRU, the Navy's Special Warfare Development Group. You probably know them as SEAL Team Six … the guys who took out Bin Laden."

Sam stared openly. "Those are the men who took out Bin Laden?"

"Same unit, different men." Trent pointed with her fork. "And those guys sitting off in the corner over there are Air Force pukes like me, but I wouldn't call them that to their faces. They're from the 24th Special Tactics Squadron. Adrenaline junkies. They like to get in close so they can paint targets with their lasers for the fighters and bombers. They're usually the first boots on the ground if we're mounting an air offensive. A lot of former Green Berets and SEALS have transferred to that unit."

Rita continued scanning the room. "Oh, and those men standing in the chow line are Marine Recon. Some of the best snipers in the world are in that unit. A pair of those eagle-eyes can pin down an entire battalion from a mile away."

"What about the ones walking out the door?"

"Army Rangers. They're always the first in the chow line after morning calisthenics on the flight deck out back."

Samantha watched them leave. "Can we go outside too?"

"I don't see why not. I'll ask Brooks to clear it with the captain after breakfast."

"Thanks. Some fresh air would be great." Sam looked around at all the giant pictures of outdoor scenes on the walls. "Seems a little claustrophobic in here without windows."

178

"Windows and stealth design aren't real compatible," Trent said. "But we do have a few. They had to install some kind of special glass in the front part of the superstructure in case the computers got knocked out and they had to steer the boat the old fashioned way."

"Old fashioned way?"

"I keep forgetting," Trent said. "You guys haven't had your tour of the boat yet. This ship is steered by computer. In fact, just about everything on board is run by computer from a massive control room in the center of the superstructure. That's where you'll usually find the captain."

"Giving away all our secrets again, Doctor?" Brooks chided, sliding his tray onto the table.

"Only our most secret ones, Commander," Trent replied, chewing on a piece of toast. "I'll be giving them a demonstration on how to sink this floating money pit after breakfast."

"Good for you. It's about time you showed some initiative."

From the side, Dana watched, fascinated by the way Rita's pupils dilated when she looked at him. There was definitely some chemistry there—a chemistry that seemed to be missing from her life for some reason.

"While we're on the subject," Trent continued, "who's giving them their security briefing?"

"Williams," Brooks answered, looking away.

"The captain? You're kidding, right?"

"Nope. He told the security officer he'd do it himself."

Trent stood and glanced around the table. "You guys must be VIPs. All I can say is that you're in for a real treat." She turned and walked away, slinging her tray on a growing pile in the scullery window on her way out the door.

"What got into her all of a sudden?" Sam wondered out loud.

"I wouldn't take it personally," Brooks explained. "She has a lot on her mind right now. Single mom with a sick kid she had to leave behind with her ex-husband, and none of us knows when we'll be back."

Sam pounced. "Back from where, Commander?"

"You should probably save that question for the captain. He's a real sharing guy."

Sam glanced around Brooks' wide shoulders. The SEALs at the next table were all looking back at her ... and they were grinning.

179

* * *

The man in charge of the *USS Zumwalt* was sitting at his computer console when Brooks escorted Dinning and the two girls up to a glass-enclosed loft overlooking the ship's cavernous command center.

"Here they are, sir."

Captain Robert Williams swiveled in his chair to study the trio. "Thank you, Commander. I just finished reading your action report." The captain paused to massage his temples. "So ... let me get this straight. Did you and your men actually make one of these poor girls piss themselves when you entered Hamilton's lab?"

Sam felt her face flush as Brooks cast a quick sideways glance in her direction.

"Her?" Williams laughed out loud. "I would have guessed it was the skinny one."

Absorbed by all the streaming live satellite pictures and incoming data displayed on the gigantic flat screens in the control center below, Dana's only response was a passive sigh, but Dinning was livid at the insensitivity of the captain's remark. "Excuse me, Captain ... I'm Dr. Peter Dinning, and these two women are my friends. I would appreciate it if you would show them a little more respect."

The captain smiled. "Okay, Professor ... deal. But just so you know, any respect on this ship has to be earned. In my defense, I sometimes forget that I'm talking to civilians ... especially in here where most outsiders aren't allowed. We're a tight-knit bunch, and our military sense of humor can sometimes seem offensive to those who don't know us very well. Also, you needn't bother introducing yourselves. I already know who you are. No one steps on board my ship without a thorough background check ... and I mean no one. I have copies of the DIA's dossiers on all three of you in my cabin."

Williams stood. His six-foot-six frame towered over everyone else in the room. Even Brooks, who was six-foot-three, looked a little less impressive standing next to this giant. Like many of the other men on board, the captain also shaved his head, and his quick blue eyes divulged a sharp mind.

Looking up at him, Sam noticed the gleaming gold trident of a Navy SEAL pinned over the left chest of his tan uniform shirt.

"Come on, you three," Williams said. "Let's get this over with. The next few days will decide if we're all going to be heroes or if Brooks and I will be spending our golden years writing our memoirs from a cell in Leavenworth."

Dinning's face visibly paled. "Leavenworth!"

"Yes … prison. We're rolling the dice for you, Professor. We believe the attack on your ship in Africa is somehow connected to some of the people who were swarming all over it after it washed up on the beach in Port Aransas. In case you haven't figured it out yet, we're the good guys. This mission is totally off the books, because we're trying to find out what the bad guys are up to."

"I believe you're forgetting that some of the men who were chasing us on the island are on this ship right now." Dinning nodded toward Brooks. "If he's one of the good guys, what was he doing in Port Aransas … and why did he and his men raid Ian Hamilton's lab?"

"The commander and his men were just following orders," Williams shot back, "but they were also looking out for you. We were sailing just off the coast preparing to extract you from that little Texas island down the coast, but you and your two friends here outsmarted everyone."

"I'm afraid you have me at a total loss, Captain. Just what in the hell is going on?"

"Someone is up to something, Professor … something in Africa, and people are dying because of it."

"I already know that."

"I'm sure you do, but what you don't know is that the person responsible is probably someone inside JSOC." The captain's glowering presence seemed to fill the room. "Listen carefully, Professor Dinning, because I'm about to tell you something that could get me thrown into the brig. We think one of our own operators is involved, and whoever it is, they've slipped beneath the waves of secrecy for reasons that aren't clear to us yet."

"Are you telling me you believe one of your own commandos has gone rogue?"

"It's a little more complicated than that. There's some kind of dark cover operation going on over there, and no one else in the closed world of Special Ops has heard anything about a secret mission unfolding in that part of Africa. That's highly unusual in our line of work. Commander Brooks first became suspicious a few months ago when he kept getting reports of encrypted satellite communications coming from the jungle near Yangambi. It was routed though an intelligence satellite dedicated for JSOC use only, but what really got our attention was the fact that no one could break the new encrypted code."

"Did you say the signals came from Yangambi?"

Williams paused when he saw something blinking on one of the big screens in the room below. "Yes ... specifically the old Yangambi Research Station. I believe you're familiar with it."

Dinning stared back with his mouth hanging open, dumbfounded.

"I had a feeling that bit of information would leave you speechless, Professor. It also appears that the same library you got those fish bones from has been receiving some new visitors."

"You know about the bones?"

"Of course we know about the bones, and apparently so does someone else ... a man who visited the library. We received his picture from a source in Yangambi who's been working with us. After we ran it through Interpol, we discovered we were looking at the NATO expert on germ warfare who supposedly disappeared a year ago."

"Germ warfare?"

"Yeah. Sent chills down my spine too. Personally, I'd rather have bullets flying at me. Our source in Yangambi has been keeping his eye on the jungle surrounding the ruins of the old station. He and his friends have been finding military boot prints on some of the paths in the area, especially down by the river. But the real kicker came when he told us an American soldier in full combat gear walked into a Yangambi bar and proceeded to get drunk as a skunk. According to the other people in the bar, he got real hostile and aggressive. Before the police arrived, he beat the hell out of two local men before fleeing into the jungle."

"And you think this NATO scientist had something to do with that?"

"I'll get to his involvement with the soldiers in a minute," Williams said. "But a white soldier in Yangambi wearing an American uniform got our full attention. Something very strange is going on over there, and if there are American boots on the ground, JSOC hasn't been informed about it. That's a direct violation of our operational security protocol. It's our job to know the location of any American forces operating in foreign countries, and according to a four-star friend of mine at the Pentagon, there are no American forces in that part of Africa."

The captain paused, looking back down at one of the big screens again before turning his attention back to Dinning. "Did you happen to notice any kind of unit patches on the uniforms of the men that attacked your ship in Matadi?"

"I'm afraid all I saw were men in camos carrying big guns. But they were definitely white and spoke English with an American accent."

"If they were Americans, they have to be stopped," said Williams. "We have rules, and we would never take out a ship full of unarmed scientists ... especially American scientists."

Dinning thought for a moment. "Is there any reason why someone higher up the chain of command would want to keep JSOC out of the loop about an American operation?"

"We've been wondering the same thing. That's the kind of scenario that keeps me awake at night. The admiral is looking into it, but even the head of the military's Joint Special Operations Command has to tread lightly when he starts asking questions ... especially if he's been left out of the loop for some reason. If someone is doing something that's sanctioned from above, it doesn't stop at the Joint Chiefs. If they wanted boots on the ground in the Congo we'd be the first to know, and they don't have the authority to green light an attack on an American vessel. An order like that would have to come from the White House, which is just the kind of conspiracy nonsense I was hoping to avoid."

"So you and your people are going it alone because you're not sure who you can trust at the top?"

"You're getting there, Professor. We're caught between the proverbial rock and a hard place. I have a real bad feeling about all of this."

Dinning studied the captain's face. "Are you sure you're not the one going rogue, Captain?"

"I always go rogue, Professor." The captain grinned. "That's how I roll. Unless someone lets us in on what's happening over there, we have to assume the worst and proceed on our own. That's why I mentioned the possibility of Leavenworth earlier, because that will be my new home if I'm wrong."

"And if you're right?"

"If I'm right … well, this is where you come in, Professor. Our man over there tells us you've been collecting samples from the jungle around the old station for years, and apparently, this so-called missing NATO scientist has been doing the same thing. When he found out you had taken the old fish bones from the library, our source told us he freaked."

Dinning exchanged glances with Sam and Dana. "Actually, all of this is starting to make a little more sense now. I also have a connection in the old library. It's just possible we may have stumbled onto something that may provide us with a window into what this scientist might be up to. Somehow, fate may have brought our two worlds together."

"Enlighten me, Professor."

"I'll start with the fish bones. To put it simply, someone was messing around with the DNA of that fish."

"What exactly does that mean?"

"It means that someone introduced engineered genetic material into the genome of a living organism that lives at the bottom of the deepest river in the world." Dinning adopted a wistful expression. "And I believe they've returned to do a little fishing."

"What are you getting at, Professor?"

"I believe this scientist may be involved somehow. The transgene we …"

"The what?"

"The transgene … a segment of DNA containing a gene sequence that has been isolated from one organism and introduced into a different organism."

"Okay. Go on."

"The transgene we discovered was elegantly designed and beautiful to look at, and it was created using the DNA from three different species. Something like that could only have been created in a world-class lab staffed by equally world-class scientists."

"You mean like a group of Belgian scientists that just got off a plane in Yangambi a few days ago and disappeared into the jungle with a group of men dressed like soldiers?"

"Belgian scientists … in Yangambi again … with soldiers! Good God … what in the hell are they up to over there?" Dinning looked around the room. "Has anyone spotted them since? I mean, they must have some kind of camp nearby."

"That's one of the weirder parts." The captain pulled an unlit cigar from his pocket and clamped it between his teeth. "No one's been able to locate any camp. In fact, there's no evidence that anyone has camped in the area for years, yet these people disappeared into …"

"The deep green."

"The what?"

"The deep green." Dinning's eyes glazed for a moment, his mind locked on a distant image. "It's what I call the jungle. Most people prefer the term *rainforest* nowadays."

"The deep green, huh? Sounds kind of poetic, but you can call that humid green crap anything you like, Professor, because we need your expertise." The captain leaned close. "Tell me more about this artificial gene."

"Engineered," Dinning corrected.

"Right … engineered. I can tell you right now that JSOC isn't involved in any kind of biological warfare program … at least not that I'm aware of. If they were, none of us would have anything to do with it."

"I seriously doubt someone is working on a biological weapon, Captain. We're not talking about viruses or bacteria here. I believe we're looking at something entirely different."

"Different? How?" The captain's eyes narrowed. "Just what do you think those people are up to out there in the *deep green* if it doesn't involve germ warfare?"

Dinning was silent for a moment. "I'm afraid it could be much worse. All we know for sure right now is that someone altered the genome of a living creature in the wild with an engineered strand of DNA that can replicate, and we don't know what it does. Until I know more, anything I say beyond that would be pure speculation."

"And that's exactly why we need you. You're our expert. Not only that, but you're the only other scientist we know of who's actually been to that exact location."

"But I need more time to study the genetic material … and a lab."

"You'll get your chance to study that thing again, Professor … I promise."

"What did you have in mind?"

"A little trip."

"You can't be serious!"

"Oh, but I am." Williams grinned around his cigar. "You're going back to Africa, Professor, and we're coming with you."

CHAPTER 31

To say that the *USS Zumwalt* was a giant leap in ship design would have been a gross understatement. After conferring with a junior officer, the captain led the group downstairs into the cavernous mission control center.

Manned by some of the best-trained men and women in the navy, five curved rows of computer stations faced a thirty-foot-high wall lined with six enormous flat-screens. "Have any of you ever been on a destroyer before?"

"Not like this," Dinning replied. "This looks more like the inside of a space station."

"Took me awhile to get used to it too," Williams said. "A lot of the stuff on this ship has been taken over by computers, which means it takes half as many sailors to run it. The man who captained her during her initial sea trials actually had two PhDs. One in computer programming and the other in electrical engineering ... which makes perfect sense, considering this is basically a computerized electric boat."

"Electric? You mean like a sub?"

"Similar. We're as quiet in the water as one of the Los Angeles class attack subs ... which is pretty damn quiet for a surface ship."

"So what's your power source ... nuclear?"

"Rolls-Royce ... two gas turbines. They're based on the same jet engines you see hanging from the wings of a Boeing 777."

"Doesn't sound too quiet to me."

"Our turbines purr like kittens. Come on. Let's take a walk outside." The captain turned to Brooks. "Keep an eye on those two radar returns that keep flashing on the center screen, Steve. They're riding low in the water on an intercept course, and you know how I feel about unidentified radar blips on an intercept course." Williams winked. "I'll be on the back deck showing our guests around."

"Aye aye, sir."

Williams led Dinning and the two girls through the wood-paneled hallway and down a narrow stairwell to a steel corridor that ran to the back of the ship. Opening the watertight door at the end, they stepped out into an obvious aircraft hangar. Two black helicopters sat facing a pair of open, garage-like doors.

"This is the hangar deck," Williams explained. "As you can see, we have just enough room in here for two Sea Hawk helicopters and a drone." Continuing on through the space, they walked out onto a large, paved landing pad covering the entire back deck. Beyond that, the sea.

The captain seemed just as happy as they were to be outside. For a few luxurious minutes they all squinted in the reflected sunlight and inhaled the fresh sea breeze.

Holding her arms out, Samantha lifted her face to the sun. "I could stay out here all day long."

"Be my guest," the captain chided. "We have a lot of experience treating sunburn in the navy."

Dinning watched Sam winding up for a comeback and stepped between them. "How far are we from the coast, Captain?"

"We're about fifty miles out of Galveston right now. As you've probably already noticed, we're doing a little zigzagging to avoid being spotted by other ships as we make our way across the Gulf."

Walking close to the edge, Dinning was fascinated by the way the hull parted the thick rolling swells without the usual pitching and rolling experienced on other ships. "Strange hull shape," he said. "The way the sides angle out away from the deck instead of curving back in reminds me of the hulls on the old WWI battleships."

"It's called a tumblehome hull, Professor. Narrow at the top and wider at the waterline … the exact opposite of a modern ship. Same with our extended, wave-piercing bow. Tumblehome hulls were used on warships for centuries because of all the heavy cannons they carried on their upper decks. Naval architects stopped designing them like that almost a hundred years ago in favor of newer hull shapes that provided greater speed and stability. But like a lot of things, what was once old is now new again after the stealth guys discovered that the angle of the old hulls drastically reduced a ship's radar signature, making it much harder to see. Overall, this destroyer's angular shape makes it fifty times harder to spot than an ordinary destroyer."

"What about guns?"

"Up front, but you can't see them right now."

"Classified?"

"No, I mean you really can't see them now. They retract into watertight compartments below decks next to the Tomahawk missile tubes. The computers only raise them if we're preparing to shoot. Like almost everything else on board, the guns are a new design too. They're pretty amazing, actually." The captain instinctively puffed out his chest and lit his cigar. "They fire 155mm rocket projectiles at a rate of ten a minute, and they can hit a target the size of a soccer ball sixty-three miles away."

Sam leaned in close to Dana and whispered. "Where's the margarita machine? In the spa?" Both girls laughed out loud, drawing a look from the captain as he puffed on his cigar.

Dinning was thinking of another ship as he looked around. "I have to say, this is a pretty amazing piece of technology, Captain. I'll bet Congress choked when they got the bill for it."

Williams looked down, the blue smoke from his cigar trailing up one side of his face as he kicked at the tarry surface of the landing pad. "They did more than choke. They killed the project."

"They what?"

"They scrapped it." Williams stared up at the composite superstructure. "This ship is the only Zumwalt class destroyer ever built. The navy wanted thirty-two of these state-of-the-art marvels to replace the older destroyers in the fleet, but cost overruns doomed the project."

"But that's crazy!" Dinning said. "This is just the kind of cutting edge technology that's made us the world's leading superpower."

"Tell that to Congress. They're cutting everywhere now, and with a price tag of three and a half billion dollars each, this was one of the first places they started cutting." Williams sniffed the wind like an old hunting dog. "But bad news for the fleet turned out to be good news for us. For ten years now the Pentagon has been looking for a combat ship specially designed for Special Forces missions. This ship fit the bill perfectly ... so they gave it to us so we could be the tip of the arrow in the war against terrorism."

"I was wondering about that, Captain. I couldn't help but notice you're also a SEAL."

Williams laughed out loud. "Yeah, this is pretty much SEAL heaven. We don't mind catching rides on other ships, but it's about time the navy gave us one of our own." The captain stopped to gaze across the flight deck at the white horizon in the east. "Most ships usually take a week or more to make the crossing from Galveston to West Africa, but this baby will get us there in three days. Once we arrive off the coast, we'll be going in dark and fast, so I want you and those two girls to pay close attention to the battle station drills."

Looking around the high-tech marvel, Dinning wondered. "I almost hate to ask, Captain, but you wouldn't happen to have a lab on board, would you?"

"Sure, but it's not the kind you need. We checked. Dr. Trent has a medical lab, but it doesn't come with an electron microscope or anything else on the checklist we pulled up for genetic labs."

Dinning felt slightly amazed by the thoroughness of this man, but he could also feel his frustration level rising. "But what about Hamilton's lab? Your men could have grabbed some of the best lab equipment in the world."

"Not enough time. It would have been logistically awkward, and our primary mission was to get you out of there before the others arrived."

"Others?"

"Yes. You don't just drive a ship full of bodies up on a Texas beach and disappear without becoming one of the most wanted men in America, Professor Dinning. I admit I had my doubts too until we saw the pathologist's report in the DIA file. Apparently, the people on your ship all died from multiple gunshot wounds from different weapons firing from different directions. We knew right then that you didn't kill them … that you were an innocent man on the run for some reason. I'm surprised all the agencies looking for you didn't connect the dots like we did."

"What dots?"

"The dots that led us straight to you. After the drone spotted you and the girls at that little house in the hill country, everyone figured you were trying to get to your lab in Austin. But a guy like you doesn't reach the top of the heap in a profession like yours by being stupid. Brooks and I knew that you were probably headed somewhere else. We drank a lot of coffee and started going over your history for the past five years."

"My history? Seriously?"

"Yeah. The FBI, DIA, CIA … those histories. Their field officers were literally bumping into each other trying to piece together your life story. Hunting you down had become a top priority for some reason. They gladly gave us everything we asked for. But we were only interested in the past five years … places you had traveled to and people you had been working with. Stuff like that. That's when we discovered you had been doing some consulting work last year for Hamilton's new biotech company in Houston. Also, his lab was isolated, and as you've already pointed out, he had some of the finest equipment in the world that you could use to study your little gene friend."

"So, basically, you guys were waiting for us."

"Yeah."

"But Hamilton knew you were coming."

"Yeah."

John Lyman

CHAPTER 32

Commander Steve Brooks walked out onto the back deck and stood between Williams and Dinning to scan the empty-looking horizon.

"Is our mysterious blip still on an intercept course, Steve?" Williams asked.

"Yes, sir. Looks like a couple of our friends from south of the border. We should be able to see them off our starboard side in the next couple of minutes. Do you want me to sound general quarters?"

"Are you sure of the targets?"

"Yes, sir. We have them on satellite now."

"Good. No need for general quarters, but raise the guns just in case."

Brooks relayed the order to a seaman standing behind him, and a few seconds later a pair of phalanx guns rose from the deck. Called R2D2s by the crew because they resembled the little robot in the Star Wars movies, they were basically a pair of radar-guided Vulcan Gatling guns that fired over four thousand rounds of 20mm armor-piercing shells a minute, and their six revolving barrels were now zeroed in on a pair of fast-moving targets approaching over the horizon.

Looking through a pair of binoculars, the captain spotted the spray from two fifty-foot speedboats leaping over the waves a mile off the *Zumwalt's* starboard side before suddenly making a radical 180 degree turn away from the ship and speeding back in the opposite direction.

Lowering his binoculars, the captain chuckled. "I think I could see the surprised looks on their faces from here."

"Who were they?" Samantha asked.

"Drug runners," Brooks said. "We see them all the time in this part of the Gulf."

"So what's the use in having a three-and-a-half billion dollar stealth ship if a bunch of drug runners can spot you?"

"They have radar too," Brooks explained. "They were probably making a run for the Texas coast from somewhere down south and thought we were just a shrimp boat because we look a lot smaller on radar. It's actually kind of funny watching them haul ass, wondering what the hell they just saw."

"But they still saw us."

Brooks smiled patiently. "Like I said, we only looked smaller to them on radar. Being stealthy doesn't make us invisible. Anyone with a pair of eyeballs can see us once they get close enough, which is one of the reasons we only operate near shore at night."

The captain snuffed out his cigar. "Playtime's over. We need to get to work. Dr. Dinning, I'd like you and your assistant to begin working on a plan of action from a scientific point of view."

Dinning stared back at him. "A plan of action, Captain? And just how exactly are we supposed to come up with a plan of action? Action against what? We still don't know what that transgene was engineered to do, or why … and no one seems to have a clue what those Belgian scientists are really up to out there."

"It's kind of like stealth, Professor. Sometimes you don't know what you're looking at until it comes into view. I want you to put your heads together and look back over all your data to see if you can come up with anything that might be useful to us before we hit the coast of Africa a few nights from now."

"Yes," Brooks chimed in. "We'd like you to start thinking of the invisible threats. We'll take care of the visible ones."

"What about Hamilton?"

"What about him?" Williams asked.

"I'm still waiting to hear how he knew your men were on their way to his lab."

"Feeling betrayed, Professor?"

"Yes, Captain … wouldn't you be if someone you trusted lured you into a trap?"

"Hamilton isn't who he appears to be, Professor. Let's just leave it at that."

"No, I won't leave it like that. I worked with the man practically every day for six months. We became friends … at least I thought we were. The first clue I had that something wasn't right was when he told us he had been working late in his lab. The man hated working late."

"So what convinced you to help him with his new biotech start-up venture?"

"He was very persistent, and to be frank, I needed the money. When I first began working with him he said he was looking for the genetic Holy Grail in the fight against cancer. As time went on, I discovered that he was also fascinated with things that seemed more like science fiction ... things like life extension and creating new intelligent life forms. Some of his ideas were really out there, but he seemed to know a lot about molecular biology ... especially for a businessman. I even found myself forgetting he wasn't a scientist when we were discussing some very complex scientific issues. I guess you could say I had come to think of him as one of those entrepreneurial geniuses ... one of the new breed of visionaries who had the money to back up their dreams ... and he had a lot of them."

The captain's scowl deepened. "Yes, he's a dreamer alright. And he had all the money he needed to fund those dreams, because the U.S. Treasury was his bank. Hamilton was working for someone in the government, Dr. Dinning, and just so you're not too enamored by his intellectual capacity, the man really is a scientist."

"A scientist? Are you sure?"

"Positive."

"What's his field?"

"Virology. He's an expert in viruses, Professor."

Dinning's eyes fluttered with a sudden realization. "He was working with viruses! Did he ever mention anything about engineered genes ... or use the word, transgenes?"

"Sorry, Doc, but I didn't really know the guy. What are you thinking?"

"I'm thinking we have an interesting scenario here, Captain, and it might be a good idea to start breaking it down. First, you have a missing NATO expert in germ warfare and some white troops showing up in Yangambi. Then this scientist goes ballistic when he finds out I took the fish bones containing genetic evidence of a transgene ... a transgene that could only have been created and inserted into a living organism by people who knew what they were doing. And then there's Hamilton ... a man who claims to be a businessman when he's really a virologist working for someone in our own government."

"Meaning?"

195

"Meaning that we now have a man who's an expert with viruses and another who undoubtedly knows a lot about bacteria. Viruses and bacteria are both things that can be used as gene carriers, Captain. One of the primary ways of introducing an engineered gene into a living organism is by letting it hitch a ride on a modified virus into a cell, and you need a highly qualified virologist and a very specialized lab to make something like that happen. Same thing with bacteria."

The two men felt the breeze stiffen behind them as they walked toward the watertight door at the back of the hangar.

"It sounds like you're starting to fit some of the pieces together, Professor." The captain watched the blue smoke curl from his cigar. "I knew snatching you back at that lab was the right move. Any ideas on why they would be fooling around with fish in the Congo River? I mean, what would be the point in doing something like that?"

"That's what we have to find out. It's pretty obvious someone is trying to create a transgenic organism. The next thing I need to know is what it does. Just knowing that alone might tell us what they're up to. Now that I know Hamilton is a virologist, he might be able to help us connect the dots."

"Then why don't we march down to the brig and simply ask him what the gene does?"

"Because he doesn't know."

"What do you mean he doesn't know? He has to be involved somehow."

"Yes, but he told us himself that it was only in a very peripheral way. A lot of scientific research is compartmentalized by farming out pieces of work to other scientists, especially in genetics research. You might say it keeps all the mice from knowing what the cat is up to when it comes to proprietary claims. I believe Hamilton was only contracted to modify a virus for gene transfer. His lab was just a small piece of a very well-guarded puzzle." Dinning stopped to mop the sweat from his brow. "Are you positive he was working for the government?"

"Not *the* government, Professor. Someone *in* the government. When we discovered the money was coming from the same account that funds black operations, that really fueled our paranoid fire. I have a feeling that once Hamilton found out he was working for someone in the government who wanted to remain in the shadows, his sphincter muscle really started to twitch. That also explains his weird security set-up."

196

"That still doesn't tell me how he knew the SEALs were coming."

"We think he was probably given a number to call if you contacted him. We accessed his cell phone records. The last call he made was routed through the main switchboard at the Pentagon. After that we have no way of knowing who he spoke to, but twenty minutes after he made the call we received orders to stand down because you and the girls had been spotted at his lab. Apparently, another military team was closer and was already on the way."

"I thought you were the closest team to the lab?"

The captain smiled. "We were, but no one knew that. We were supposed to be cruising twenty miles off the coast of Port Aransas, but like I said before, we had already gambled on the fact that you were headed for the Houston lab, so we took the *Zumwalt* into Galveston Bay. Whoever is calling the shots wasn't aware that we were in the area, which is exactly what we wanted. We didn't know who was coming for you, but Brooks and I had a feeling that if we didn't get to you first, there was a good chance no one would ever hear from you again. From that moment on it was a race to extract you and the girls before they got there. Hamilton too. I'd be willing to bet the SUVs speeding toward the lab were carrying a lot more than just a bunch of high-paid security guards."

"So Brooks blew up the building to make them think we all died in a lab explosion?"

"That was part of it. The whole Africa thing had us really spooked. We didn't know what the hell they were making in there, so we decided to err on the side of caution and burn it. It won't be long until they discover there aren't any bodies, and when that happens all bets are off. I can't predict what their next move will be. As far as we know no one is aware that we were ever there, and that might be our ace in the hole."

"What do you mean?"

"That means we can still fly under the radar, and what better way to fly under the radar than on a stealth ship, Professor."

CHAPTER 33

It was dark outside, but it was hard to tell from inside a ship without windows. After the destroyer had slipped through the Caribbean and out into the Atlantic, the sword-like bow of the *Zumwalt* had sliced through the building waves of a fast-moving storm front for two days, until finally the eastern Atlantic swell softened and Sam felt the ship shudder to a stop.

Lying on her bunk, reading, she hung her head over the side and peered down at Dana in the bunk below. "Africa?"

"I'd say we stopped for something." Dana swung her bare feet out onto the floor and looked up. "Are you nervous?"

"In case you haven't noticed, I'm always nervous. How do you do it, Dana? I mean, you always seem to be so in control. Sometimes I even forget you're in the room, but then I see you … hanging back, just listening and watching."

Dana looked down, blinking as she studied her flaking toenail polish. "I suppose it's a learned response."

"A learned response?"

"Yeah. It probably comes from living most of my life on my own. I was only nine when my parents died in a car accident. The only other living relative was my mother's alcoholic sister, so they put me in a foster home. There were other kids there too … mean kids, so I stayed to myself as much as possible. I hated school because all the other kids knew I was living in a foster home. I guess I kind of shut down, because they labeled me as being slow and sent me to a special school."

"A special school? Why didn't you tell me any of this before?"

"Because it sounds like a *poor me* story, and I hate talking about it. The past is past, and there's no point in dragging it out so everybody can feel sorry for me."

Sam hesitated, but her Texas curiosity had her by the throat. "What happened at the special school, Dana?"

"That was even worse than foster care. There wasn't anything special about it. It was just a place to send hopeless cases … the children who had no one to speak for them. It was like a prison, and I withdrew even more."

"But you're so smart! I mean, you have a degree from one of the best universities in the country."

"I got lucky. When the school was inspected by the state, I told one of the inspectors that there was nothing wrong with me … that I just didn't like talking to the people around me. So she had my I.Q. tested. They tested me twice more before they were finally forced to admit my I.Q. was over 140 and sent me off to another school … one for gifted children. By then I was eleven … and things were way better at the new school. I started feeling normal again and ended up getting a scholarship to UT when I was sixteen. I've never looked back since, but I still have trouble trusting people."

"Sorry, Dana. I didn't …"

"Nothing to be sorry about, Samantha." Dana managed a funny little smile. "We're both in the same boat."

"Ha … very funny. Is humor part of that defensive armor of yours too?"

"You mean like a tragic comedian?"

Sam winced. "Well, when you put it like that."

Dana continued staring at her toes. "At least now you know why I don't talk much about my past."

"Actually, I think I understand you a lot better now." Sam laid her book down and slid from her bunk. "You hungry?"

"Great. Now you're starting to mother me."

"BFFs?"

Dana smiled. "That would be a first. I think I'll just hang here and read for awhile."

"Suit yourself, but just in case you change your mind I heard they're serving shrimp tonight."

Slipping into her camos, Sam walked out into the day room to call for an escort just as Rita burst through the door. "Have you heard?"

"Heard what?"

"We're here … Africa! I was just up in the control room and they're using all their night vision stuff to study the coastline."

"Are we going up the river?"

"Captain Williams won't risk taking a ship like this up an African river. We wouldn't make it past the falls at Kinshasa anyway."

"So where exactly are we?"

"Five miles off the West African coast and the Conkouati Nature Reserve. There's nothing but beach and jungle out there. It's one of the largest areas of biodiversity in the world. The nearest city is Pointe-Noire … about sixty miles to the south, which means there shouldn't be too many human eyes looking out to sea when the teams start going ashore."

"I can't wait to see the river."

"If you're talking about the Congo River, that's about a hundred and fifty miles south of here … near the port of Matadi. That's where the professor's ship was attacked. We're not going anywhere near that area." Rita reached into a tiny metal closet and pulled out a leather jacket to cover her olive T-shirt. "They're getting ready to launch the drone if you two would like to go watch. Brooks told me we should get some interesting infrared pictures of the area from the air."

"What about Yangambi?" Sam prodded.

Rita thought for a moment. "Let me put things in perspective for you. The Congo is about three times the size of Texas. The straight line distance from the coast to Yangambi is nine hundred miles."

"Nine hundred miles! But if the ship can't go upriver, how are we supposed to get there?"

"You're not … and neither am I. Our place is on the ship, honey, because Commander Brooks likes to keep his teams small and fast, and from what I'm hearing, Dinning is the only civilian going ashore with them."

"But if it wasn't for me and my friends, the professor wouldn't even be here now," Sam shot back. "I'm as fit as anyone on this ship. They have to let me go."

"You can always ask Dinning to put you on the essential personnel list. But good luck convincing Brooks."

"Damn!" Sam folded her arms and gritted her teeth. "I can't believe I'm this close to Africa and I can't even set foot on it." Sam paused, thinking. "When are they going to send the drone to Yangambi? If I can't go at least I can look at the live pictures."

201

Rita laid a sympathetic hand on Sam's shoulder. "Sorry, girlfriend … too far away for our drone. Only the big Reaper drones have that kind of range, and you need an aircraft carrier to launch one of those babies."

"Reaper drones?"

"Big turboprop jobs armed with hellfire missiles. They have a range of a thousand miles and can loiter over a target for days. Our drone just takes pictures. It's a lot smaller, but it can take off and land vertically, which is perfect for this kind of ship."

"What about satellite pictures?"

"We don't want to communicate with the intelligence satellites right now." Rita paused. "I guess I really am getting into that gray area of classified information. Don't repeat what I just said, especially to Brooks. He'd kill me." Rita zipped up her jacket. "Where's Dana?"

"She's in her rack, reading."

"Maybe she would like to watch the drone launch too. That girl needs to get out more."

Sam nodded and opened the door to their room.

"I heard," Dana said, buttoning her shirt. "I'm coming."

Walking out into the corridor, the three women made their way up to the flight deck and stood off to the side in the hangar while three navy technicians busied themselves making a pre-flight inspection of a gangly-looking, black drone. To Sam, the Prius-sized flying machine looked just like a large version of one of the much-publicized hobby drones—the kind with all the little propellers that lifted them into the air like a helicopter.

Sam and Dana moved closer to the open hangar door and peered outside. The night was clear but the coast was invisible as they stared up at a sky full of stars. Sam cast a wary glance over her shoulder and stepped beyond the door, running right into Brooks.

"Good evening, Miss Adams. Here to watch the launch?"

"Yes. I thought I'd get some unfiltered air for a few minutes."

"Feels good out here, doesn't it? Can you smell it?"

"Smell what?"

"The jungle … or the deep green, as the professor likes to call it."

Sam sniffed at a steady breeze that resonated like a giant beast sleeping in the darkness. And then she smelled it. It was the smell of wet earth tinged with the aroma of smoke from wood fires. And there were other smells mixed in—spice-like smells that awakened her senses to the fact that she was in a place so far removed from her sphere of reference that it sent an uncontrolled shiver down her spine. She had never even been outside of Texas before. Yet here she was—on the other side of the world—inhaling the scent of an invisible dark continent that had seemed more fable than real to her until now.

"We're ready to move her out," a technician shouted to Brooks.

"Good ... let her fly. We only have a few hours of darkness left before we have to move away from the coast."

The technicians shoved and the drone rolled out across the black deck into a big white X painted in the center of the landing pad. From a virtual cockpit station inside the *Zumwalt's* windowless control room, a naval aviator took over. The drone's six props began to spin, and as the pilot increased power, the strange-looking craft lifted straight up. For a moment it hung in the air like a wobbly baby bird pushed from its nest—wondering what to do next. Focusing on his screen, the pilot edged his hand controller back and the little drone began climbing skyward, disappearing against the background of stars.

"That was quick," Sam said.

"Should be," Brooks said. "The drone guys practice launching that thing at least once a day, weather permitting."

Sam walked to the edge of the flight deck and peered out at the humid mist covering the sea.

"Just so you know, there aren't any railings on a stealth ship," he reminded her.

"You're about the tenth person to tell me that. I was hoping I could see Africa from here."

"We're still several miles offshore. You probably couldn't see it from this distance even in daylight. Sometimes the cool air from the sea mixes with the warm air from the jungle, creating a hazy fog along the coastline. Back in the days before radar, sailors heading to Africa sometimes found it the hard way. By the time they saw the coastline through the fog it was usually too late to turn away."

"I think I'm beginning to feel the same way ... too late to turn away. Do you ever feel drawn to a place, Commander?"

"Only if it has a neon beer sign in the window."

"Very funny."

"I was being serious."

203

Sam looked up at him, and in that single glance something changed. He reminded her of Brian. She looked away, wondering what he must be thinking right now back in Port Aransas. *He must be frantic!*

"Thinking of home?"

"Are all SEALs psychic too?"

"No, but I've seen that same look many times before, especially at sea. Even when you're surrounded by other people it can be a very lonely life out here, because the people who really matter are waiting for you back home."

"What made you join the navy in the first place, Commander?"

"The attack on New York. I was still in high school then, but I knew the minute I saw those towers coming down that I was going to be a Navy SEAL. I almost didn't make it."

"What ... a big guy like you?"

"You'd be surprised. A lot of men didn't make it through the first week of SEAL training. Some of the little wiry guys we all thought wouldn't even make it through the first day turned out to be some of the best SEALs in the bunch. You never really know how a person's going to perform until you see them under pressure. Everyone thinks we're a bunch of *Rambos*, but most of us are just regular guys who like to watch football and take the kids to the beach."

"You have kids?"

"Yes. A boy and a girl. They live with their mother."

"Oh, sorry."

"Comes with the territory." He looked out at the ship's phosphorescent wake. "Rita tells me you've been reading up on genetics. Thinking of a new career?"

"Not really, but I thought I should know a little more about it considering the fact that a microscopic piece of DNA seems to be responsible for all of this. It's a pretty fascinating subject, actually ... especially when you get into the way they engineer genes. It made me wonder why we don't hear more about it. I mean, some of the things they're doing now could affect us all one day, and there's still a lot they don't know about some of the stuff they're messing with."

"Just like us," said a voice off to the side. "We're probably messing with one of the greatest genetic puzzles of our time."

Sam turned to see Dana leaning against the superstructure—her pale skin glowing blue in the faint starlight.

204

"Have you talked to Peter today?" Samantha asked.

"No, why?"

"I want to go."

"Go where?" Dana asked. "Yangambi?"

"Yes. I want to see it ... I want to see it all. The deep green ... the old library."

"I'm afraid that's not the professor's decision to make," Brooks said. "We're about to go into an area that's probably a ten on the mission difficulty scale even for a fully trained team of Special Forces operators. Dinning and Hamilton will be the only civilians coming with us."

"Hamilton!" Sam was sure she had misheard him. "What are you talking about?"

"Dinning wants him involved for some reason. He just put him on the essential personnel list. Hamilton's out of the brig now under marine guard. I just saw him drinking coffee on the mess deck."

Without a word, Sam turned and headed for the back of the hangar. Brooks followed. "Hey, where do you think you're going?"

"To find Dinning. I want on that list too."

John Lyman

CHAPTER 34

The three had just entered the corridor behind the hangar when an ear-splitting alarm began clanging overhead and a booming southern drawl blared from all the speakers throughout the ship.

This is not a drill! This is not a drill! General quarters! General quarters! All hands man your battle stations! The bell-like alarm continued to clang. *General Quarters ... General Quarters! This is not a drill!*

Frozen in place, the two girls glanced back over their shoulders. They were alone in the corridor.

"Where did Brooks go!?" Samantha shouted.

"I don't know. He was right behind us!"

The two girls took off running back toward the hangar just as Brooks stepped through the watertight door and pulled it shut behind him. "Sorry ... I had to make sure they closed the big doors."

The bright fluorescent lights in the corridor suddenly went dark, replaced a few seconds later by the muted red of battle lighting.

"What's happening?" Sam shouted over another alarm.

"I don't know yet." Brooks jerked an intercom phone from the wall by the door. His muscles were taught and his eyes were alive. He was in that transitional state between inaction and action—that momentary pause that only seasoned military men and police officers experienced when they knew their next decision could be their last if they made the wrong one.

Should I act or react?

"This is Commander Brooks," he said into the phone. "I need to speak to the captain." He waited; his already dark features deepened by the red battle lighting. "Captain, why are we at general quarters?" He listened. "Aye aye, sir." Brooks slammed the phone back into its holder and looked back at the two girls. "Follow me."

Passing through the watertight door into the hangar, they saw that the big doors were open again and one of the helicopters was already on the landing pad outside. Glancing back at Sam and Dana, Brooks herded them into a corner. "I'm going up in the chopper. The drone spotted some men that looked like soldiers in the jungle."

The ship lurched, throwing Sam and Dana against the wall as it made a tight turn into the wind. "You'll be safe here until one of the men can escort you back to your quarters. Don't move until someone comes for you … is that clear?"

Dana and Sam nodded back as two SEALs ran up to Brooks and handed him his weapon and a lifejacket. "Let's go, Commander. The drone just picked up a bunch of heat signatures in the trees next to the beach."

Brooks turned and sprinted toward the chopper. Through the open doors, Sam and Dana could see that the rotors were already spinning as a bright flash lit up the sky over the coast.

"Holy shit!" one of the sailors shouted. "They just took out the drone!"

By now the ship had moved closer to shore and the SEALs could see the flaming debris from the drone falling into the jungle. Tossing in a few extra boxes of ammo, Brooks and the other two men jumped through the chopper's open doors. The men on deck moved back through the dancing gray whirlwinds that spun through the mist as the rotor spun faster and the helicopter lifted into the darkness before banking away toward the coast.

With their backs against the hangar wall, Sam and Dana could hear the sound of bullets hitting the superstructure. A series of loud booms was coming from the big guns at the front of the ship—their tracer fire zipping across the water as they began pounding the shoreline. The ship lurched again, and when Sam looked back out through the dark haze, she saw it. The deep green—illuminated against a black sky by a line of fiery explosions that followed the curving shoreline.

Mesmerized by the sight, Samantha edged closer to the doors. But in a repeat of their first meeting in the dunes, Dana's thin hand grabbed her shirt from behind. "Don't go any farther, Sam! Remember what Brooks said."

"Look, Dana … look. The jungle!"

Dana stared out in awe but quickly moved back when the rounded domes of the Phalanx guns rose from the deck with their revolving barrels pointed toward the shore. Flickering patterns of firelight painted the water between the dark ship and the glowing beach, and they could see the chopper flying low over the trees. A stream of fire was coming from the mini-gun in the open doorway, chewing up the edge of the jungle—the shredded green leaves falling all around—Nature's confetti celebrating its own demise.

In the control center, the captain had just given the order to bring the ship in even closer to shore. They were now running parallel to the coast as he tried to absorb the impossible amount of information cascading on the giant screens overhead. The ship's sonar was pinging the sea floor all around them—the underwater rock formations appearing as color-coded peaks and troughs on the helmsman's screen.

Williams cursed under his breath, wishing he was standing on the bridge of a more conventional ship so he could view the action through real windows. As much as he appreciated all the new technological toys the navy had entrusted to his care, it had been his experience that nothing beat the human eye when it came to sizing up an evolving battlefield situation. Sometimes the most lethal threats came from the periphery of the action. It could be something as simple as a puff of smoke or a subtle movement in the trees, and it took the very real eyes of a skilled warrior to spot the vague shadows that could warn them of things to come.

Smoke from the guns drifted back over the ship, making it harder to see the chopper as it strafed the jungle one final time before angling away over the surface of the water.

"Chopper's coming back aboard, Skipper," a junior officer said to the hulking figure of the captain looming behind his console in the control center.

"Good. Set a course away from the coast as soon as they land."

Back out on the stern deck, the flight officer switched on the infrared circle of lights embedded in the deck. Invisible to the naked eye, they were a shining beacon to the chopper pilots peering through their night vision goggles as they crabbed into the wind and aimed for the landing pad.

The light and heat sensors on the ship picked it up first—a brilliant yellow flash deep in the jungle, followed by an arc of yellow fire that leveled out before streaking arrow-like toward the ship.

Sometimes the most lethal threats came from the periphery of the action.

The landing helicopter was still a hundred feet above the moving deck when the radar-guided phalanx went off. The word phalanx came from the ancient Greek. Roughly translated, it meant *wall of shields*. And that's just what a phalanx gun was—a wall of impenetrable firepower that destroyed anything headed toward the ship.

A hundred yards out the rocket streaking toward the ship was shredded, exploding in a massive fireball over the water. But throwing up a wall of 20mm armor piercing shells at a rate of over four thousand rounds per minute was not without its risks. In a world filled with unintended consequences, a red-hot piece of the exploded rocket made it through.

Spinning through the air at almost 500 miles per hour, a jagged piece of metal tore through the tail rotor of the helicopter hovering above the landing pad. With the small rotor virtually gone, the chopper began to spiral out of control. Coming back off the power, the pilot watched the spinning deck below and tried to aim his damaged bird for the water. *Better to go for a swim*, he thought, than to be tangled up in the wreckage of a burning helicopter on the deck of a destroyer.

They almost made it.

Out of control, the helicopter tilted on its side. Men and equipment spilled through the open doors into the sea before the rotor blades struck the edge of the deck, hurling the chopper into the side of the hangar, where it exploded in flames. The force of the explosion sucked the air from Dana's lungs and sent her skittering across the hangar floor. Gulping for air, she looked up through the smoke and saw that both hangar doors were now gone.

An intense, fuel-driven fire was raging from the helicopter's twisted wreckage as Dana staggered to her feet. Coughing in the thick smoke, she began making her way back across the hangar to the spot where she had last seen Sam. She wasn't there.

Feeling disoriented, Dana backtracked. She thought maybe Sam had been thrown in the same direction she had, but in the melee of sailors donning fire suits and pulling hoses, Sam was nowhere to be seen.

A feeling of dread grabbed at Dana's stomach as she turned in a circle, her eyes searching through the smoke. No Samantha. With her head spinning, she stumbled back to the wall. It was hotter there now, and when she stepped closer, she saw it. A gaping hole in the hangar's composite outer wall. It was right where Sam had been standing when the chopper had crashed.

A faint cry escaped her lips. Afraid of what she might see, she crept toward the dying flames beyond the shattered doorway. The smoke seemed thinner, and she felt a throbbing pain in her head. More men now ... more hoses. She stopped and looked out over the debris-strewn deck, her thin arms hanging at her sides. No Sam. She was gone. Whatever had just taken out a chunk of the hangar wall had also taken Sam with it.

Dana began to sob as her vision blurred. Two sailors were by her side. They were laying her on a stretcher. She touched the side of her head and her hand came away red. Her hand was red and Sam was gone. Dana's eyes fluttered, and then everything went black.

CHAPTER 35

This can't be happening again, Samantha thought. She must be dreaming. No one ended up all alone on a dark ocean at night—treading water without a life jacket while they watched the stern of a large ship disappear into the mist—twice!

This must be one of her flashback nightmares!

But the cold tug of an offshore current told her she wasn't dreaming, and when she breathed in, she could smell the deep green blowing from the distant shoreline.

She remembered the ship's guns pounding the shore, the helicopter trying to land … a yellow streak across the water, and then the crash. She had just taken a step beyond the open hangar doors when the helicopter struck the edge of the ship, spraying the deck with jagged pieces of metal as the fuselage came spinning straight at her. If she hadn't jumped overboard when she did she'd be dead by now. But with the memory of her last terrifying swim alone on a dark ocean still fresh in her mind, she wondered if her desperate leap into the sea had only served to delay the inevitable. She might have cheated death the last time, but tempting the gods of the sea twice was never a good idea. Especially in foreign waters.

"Damn it to hell!" she screamed, pounding her fists on the water. "I can't do this again!"

"I wouldn't beat the water like that if I were you," said a voice from the darkness. "It draws sharks."

Spinning around, Sam saw Brooks and another SEAL swimming toward her. "You're alive?"

"Yeah," Brooks answered, "but I think I'm bleeding … another thing that draws sharks."

Like a lost child, Sam reached out and began sobbing as Brooks took her in his arms.

"Are you hurt?" he asked.

213

Unable to answer, she could only shake her head while she clung to his life vest. Treading water beside them, the other SEAL looked to the east. "We should probably try to make it to shore before the sun comes up, Commander."

Brooks followed his gaze through the mist. "Shouldn't be too much of a swim. The captain brought the ship in pretty close this time." Gently, he pushed Samantha away so he could give her his life jacket, but her eyes opened wide and she grabbed at him, terrified by the thought of any separation. "It's okay, Sam. I'm just putting my life jacket on you. I swim better without it anyway."

Without a word Sam slowly began to relax, but her eyes seemed fixed, staring straight ahead as he cinched the jacket around her waist. The two SEALs exchanged glances. Her distant gaze had spooked them, because they had seen that look before. It was the look of shock, which sometimes preceded surrender.

With Sam floating on her back between them, the SEALs began swimming toward the beach. On the eastern horizon, a thin pink line announced the coming of the dawn, and through the mist, they could see the smoke and dying fires in the trees farther up the coast. For the next hour they continued swimming, taking long, even strokes. A well-trained Navy SEAL could swim all day, and the day was fast approaching as the first orange rays of early morning sunlight painted the dark green jungle with streaks of yellow haze.

With the sun's rise, they could see the color of the water change from deep blue to turquoise, and when the next big swell lifted them up, Brooks strained to see where the current was taking them. Straight ahead, beyond the breaking surf, he saw a sloping white beach lined with overhanging palm trees.

"Did you catch any movement on shore, Skipper?" the other SEAL asked.

"Just a few fishermen hauling nets and a small crowd of natives gathered a half mile to our north around the scene of the firefight. The current's been pushing us south … toward Pointe-Noire."

Sam stirred and rolled over on her stomach. "When did it get light?"

"About half an hour ago. We're almost to the beach."

In the growing daylight, Brooks noticed Sam rubbing her left shoulder. "I thought you said you were okay."

"I am," she replied in a sleepy voice. "It's just sore. I landed on the same shoulder I hurt when Dinning's ship ran over my sailboat."

Brooks reached out to feel along the bones. "It's a little swollen, but it doesn't look broken. At least you didn't hit your head."

The other SEAL nodded. "She would have been fish food for sure if that had happened."

"Who's he?" Sam asked.

"That's Dawson," Brooks said. "Master Chief Frank Dawson. He used to be a surfer. Now he's a SEAL."

Brooks continued staring into her eyes.

"What?" She squinted up at him. "Why are you looking at me like that?"

"You didn't stay inside the hangar like I told you to … did you?"

Sam covered her eyes against the light. "I'm sorry, but I had to look outside. I've never seen a real battle before. It looked like you were mowing the jungle with fire from that gun in the chopper."

"We took out a few of them, but mostly we were just trying to keep their heads down while the ship moved away. You really have to listen to me, Samantha. Will you promise to do that for me from now on?"

Sam nodded just as another blue swell lifted them up before breaking. They could see the smooth sandy bottom now through the clear swirling water, and a few minutes later they were walking up onto the sloping beach. Sam started to sit, but Brooks held her arm and pointed to the jungle. "In there."

Together they pushed through a tangle of oversized leaves and hanging vines to a little clearing while Dawson erased their footprints in the sand with a palm frond. Feeling the ground beneath her feet again, Sam felt a numb sense of relief as she propped herself against a tree and looked up through the branches. Two little brown monkeys were staring back down at her. "Monkeys." She smiled. "I guess we really are in Africa. What else do you think is in here with us?"

"I could tell you," Brooks said, "but you're probably better off not knowing."

Dawson looked at his watch. "Should we contact the ship on the tactical frequency now, Skipper?"

"Might as well. They already have our coordinates, but we need to let them know we have the girl with us."

Sam pushed away from the tree. "You mean they know where we are?"

"We have GPS trackers in our vests," Dawson said.

"Then why didn't they send someone to pick us up?"

"My decision," Brooks said. "The most technologically advanced destroyer in the world just sailed into a hornet's nest full of some very smart and very well-trained hornets, and they were waiting for us. Right now the ship is our entire world, especially over here. Our number one priority is to protect the *Zumwalt* and the people on her. Whoever attacked us had long-range, heavy weapons, and I wasn't about to risk our last chopper or a boat full of SEALs in some rescue attempt when we were so close to shore. We're SEALs. We swim in the ocean. It's what we do. We didn't need rescuing."

Sam gazed through the giant green leaves at the penetrating shafts of reflected sunlight bouncing off the white sand beyond their hiding place. The beach and water here reminded her of home, and she wondered what she would catch in these strange African waters with her little throw net.

Looking back at Brooks, she knew there really wasn't much she could say. It was obvious he was in his element and knew what he was doing. Her shoulder was throbbing, but worse than that, she kept thinking about the people who had just attacked a US Navy destroyer without batting an eye. They were probably still out there somewhere right now—somewhere in the deep green.

Who in the hell were these guys?

CHAPTER 36

In the Zumwalt's control room, the captain stood next to the communications officer and stared up at the massive center screen. "Anything?"

"We have the coordinates from their GPS trackers, sir. It looks like Brooks and Dawson made it to the beach."

"Good. Any report on their condition?"

"Hang on, sir. We're receiving a burst transmission from Dawson." All eyes rotated toward the communications console. "They're in the jungle just south of the area where the firefight occurred, and that girl who went missing when the chopper crashed is with them."

"She survived? And Brooks and Dawson found her!"

"Apparently so, sir."

"Damn. That's one tough girl. Maybe we should recruit her. Where's her friend?"

"Still in sick bay, sir."

"Any chatter from the Congolese military?"

"Not a word, Captain. They seem totally unaware of any military action in the area."

"Hmm. Sounds like independent operators." The captain flopped down in a chair next to the communications officer. "How in the hell did they know we were coming ... and how were they able to spot us so quickly?"

The room grew quiet, because no one knew the answer to his question.

"Okay. It's pretty obvious we're going to have to alter our original plan of sending the teams through the jungle to Loubomo. Has that C-130 touched down there yet?"

"Yes, sir. They're on the ground refueling."

"Tell them to hold their position." The captain stood and began pacing. "And put that satellite picture of the area between Pointe-Noire and the nature reserve back up on the center screen."

Seconds later an aerial view of the coast and the deep green flashed above their heads. Looking up, the captain placed a fresh, unlit cigar in his mouth and studied the screen—his eyes following the geographical triangle he had just created in his mind. Starting on the west African coast, at the port city of Pointe-Noire, he drew a mental line that followed the coast north for sixty miles to the Conkouati Nature Reserve. This was where the attack against his ship had come from and where Brooks and the other two had made it to shore. He then drew another line that ran inland from the nature reserve southeast to the inland town of Loubomo, and from Loubomo, he drew the last line of the triangle southwest back to Pointe-Noire on the coast. In the middle of the triangle, the only thing he could see was a thick green blob of jungle.

The captain grinned and clapped his hands. "That's where those bastards are waiting!"

The young communications officer looked around the room. "I beg your pardon, sir?"

"Somehow they knew exactly where our ship was going to be last night, which means we have to assume they also know we're headed to Yangambi. It would't take a military genius to figure out we have to go in by air, and Loubomo is the closest town with a nice long runway. I believe they're regrouping. They're just sitting out there in that green triangle waiting to ambush our teams on the way to the plane. Patch me through to the British Special Forces liaison for this area."

"The British, sir?"

"Yes. Keep using the Air Force satellite."

The officer typed in some commands on his keyboard and looked back up at the captain. "They're on the line now, sir."

Williams reached over and pulled a red phone from the console. "This is JSOC Captain Robert Williams. You have our ID codes. Put me through to the duty officer."

"Stand by for the Air Marshall, Captain," a female voice replied before switching the call.

"Smith speaking." The English accent dripped with the mustached image of a British Spitfire pilot.

"Would that be Air Marshal Terrance Smith?"

"Yes it would. How are you, Robert?"

"I just lost my drone and one of my choppers to hostile fire off the west coast of Africa."

"Africa, eh. I assume you're on the *Zumwalt*, even though our satellite telemetry has you in the Gulf of Mexico."

"We left a communications relay package on an abandoned oil rig. It's sending out false position data while routing any JSOC traffic for us through an Air Force weather satellite."

"Sounds like you've got yourself into a bit of a pickle down there. Any idea who the hostiles are?"

"Not yet, but I can tell you they weren't government forces. I need a favor."

"And you can't call home, right?"

"Right."

"What do you need, Robert?"

"I need one of your C-130's to land at Pointe-Noire tomorrow morning at 0400 hours local time to pick up four of our six-man teams."

"Twenty-four SEALs?"

"No ... mix and match. Some operators from the Army, Air Force and Marines will be joining us."

"And just where will our C-130 be flying them?"

"Yangambi."

"Yangambi! That's over nine hundred miles, old boy. What happened to the plane I assume you were going to use?"

"Also off the books. It belongs to a former SEAL pilot ... a friend of Brooks who went into business for himself last year. It's sitting on the ground in Loubomo now, but we believe the mission's been compromised. We think the bad guys know we were headed for the airport there. As long as that plane is sitting on the ground waiting for us, the attention will be on Loubomo while we throw them a curve ball and head for Pointe-Noire instead."

"Ah ... a diversion. Just what the bloody hell is going on down there, Robert?"

"We won't know until we get there, Terrance. To tell you the truth, we have no idea what we're walking into."

"This has something to do with the American research ship that was attacked in Matadi, doesn't it."

"Yes." Williams paused. He knew the effect his next words would have on his British friend. "There's something else I have to tell you, Terrance. We also believe there's a leak inside JSOC."

"Good God! I had a feeling it was something like that when you said you couldn't call home."

Williams' voice sounded strained. "Can we have the plane?"

"Of course. It's the least I can do for the man who saved my life."

"You and I both know I was just doing my job, Terrance."

"Tell that to my wife and kids. They love hearing me tell the story about the time I had to bail out over Kandahar when my jet flamed out. Especially the part after I hit the dirt—when the biggest SEAL I ever saw appeared from out of nowhere and told me to come with him before the Taliban showed up."

Williams laughed. "Yeah, good times."

"Indeed. I just thought of something, Robert. We have a 130 on the ground in Mali delivering some equipment to the French. I'll have them break off and fly down to Point-Noire tonight."

"Perfect. Thanks, Terrance. If I find out anything else I'll let you know."

"Please do. By the way, I also have a team in Kenya. They're there if you need them, old boy. Good hunting!"

The captain continued to pace after he hung up. "Get Commander Brooks on the horn."

"Yes, sir." The communications officer looked puzzled as he punched in the code for Brooks' radio. A few seconds later Brooks' gravelly voice filled the room. "Brooks here."

"Hello, Commander. See any bad guys yet?"

"No, sir. They seem to have disappeared."

"They're still there, Commander, only they've moved inland. These guys are weird, Steve … real weird, and they seem to be one step ahead of us. We believe they're waiting somewhere in the jungle between the coast and the airport in Loubomo, which means we're going to have to scrub our original plan. I want the three of you to head south along the beach toward Pointe-Noire instead. As soon as you find a good landing zone for the chopper, hole up there and ping us with your GPS tracker from that location. The chopper will pick you up there at midnight, so get some rest. You'll get a full briefing on our new plan after the chopper drops you off at the rendezvous point.

"Aye aye, sir. Will do."

As soon as Brooks was off the line the captain glanced back up at the center screen. "Send a coded message to the plane on the ground in Loubomo and tell them what's going on. We'll use them later for the extraction from Yangambi."

John Lyman

CHAPTER 37

Peter Dinning sat next to Dana's bed in the ship's hospital. He was drinking his third cup of coffee and watching the Andromeda Strain on DVD while she slept.

"Great movie, Doctor," Rita said, her dark brown eyes swooping around the room when she entered.

"Yes, it's one of my favorites. That could happen, you know. But I'm afraid that any deadly new pathogen that suddenly appears from out of nowhere will be of our own making—not something from outer space."

"You really think so?"

"I do. It's not a matter of *if*, but *when*. Back when I first entered the field of molecular biology, the study of genetics held so much promise. It still does. I mean, my God, just look at some of the advancements in medicine alone. Gene therapy and predictive medicine ... the entire field of genetic medicine is taking off with some pretty miraculous results that would have been impossible just ten years ago. But there's also a dark side."

"A dark side?"

"There's always the potential for unintended consequences with new discoveries, and the field of genetics is no exception. I keep thinking back to the first man-made nuclear chain reaction."

"The pile?"

"Yes ... the pile. It still amazes me that a man as brilliant as Enrico Fermi could build a crude reactor from a pile of bricks under an old football stadium in Chicago. It had no radiation shielding and no cooling system, and the man initiated a self-sustaining nuclear reaction inside the thing based purely on the assumption that his calculations were reliable enough to rule out a runaway chain reaction in one of the most densely populated areas of the country."

"But that was 1942, Professor, and we were at war. People tend to go to extremes in times of war."

"We're always at war. Today it's a bunch of bloodthirsty, religious nut jobs, and when this war is over we'll have another enemy to worry about. Who's going to build the next pile? Someday someone is going to conduct an equally dangerous experiment with something just as lethal as radiation, and their calculations might not be as accurate as Fermi's were."

Dinning grabbed the remote and turned off the TV. "Altering the genetic code of anything within our biosphere could be just as dangerous as splitting the atom, especially now that it's entered the commercial landscape. We still have no idea what the long term effects on the planet will be from things like GMO corn or genetically altered purple rabbits. The genie is out of the bottle, and the new genetic frontier is open to anyone with the money and expertise to explore it, no matter what their intentions are."

Rita folded her arms. "And I thought medical doctors were the only ones who scared people."

"You are." Dinning smiled. "I'm just getting even."

Moving to the bedside, Rita watched Dana breathe for a moment before she grabbed a light and lifted one of her thin patient's eyelids to check her pupils. Dana was instantly awake, her enormous eyes jerking around the room as if they were receiving pulsed electric signals. "Where am I?"

"You're in the ship's hospital, Dana," Rita said. "You hit your head and you've got some stitches. Feel like sitting up?"

"I thought I heard Peter talking. I guess I was dreaming."

"You weren't dreaming, sweetie. Peter is here ... and he has been talking."

Dana sat up and looked around. "How long have I been here?"

"Since early this morning when the chopper crashed. Do you remember that?"

"I didn't see the crash ... just the aftermath." Dana's eyes widened again as she sat up. "Samantha! What happened to her?"

"She ended up in the water, but Brooks and Dawson found her. The last we heard, the three of them were on the beach."

"Oh ... thank God!" Dana flopped back against her pillow.

"You think she can go, Doc?" Dinning asked. "I could really use her help when we get there."

"We'll give it a few more hours, but I think she'll be good to go by then."

Dana squinted at Dinning. "Go where?"

"The old research station at Yangambi. I have a feeling I'm going to need your help once we get there, so I added your name to the list of essential personnel. Hamilton too."

"I heard. Why are we dragging him along, Peter? Sam and I were on the way to ask you about that when the ship was attacked."

"Oh, I thought I told you. Hamilton is the only one who knows what kind of virus he used as a promoter to break the species barrier."

"Are you saying he was the one who introduced the transgene into the genome of that fish?"

"No, he only worked on the virus that gave the genetic material a ride. After it left his lab he had no idea what they did with it. But he won't tell us which virus he used unless he goes along, and we may need that information later."

"What about the marker genes?"

"He'll be able to point those out as well. We're going ashore with the SEALs at midnight."

John Lyman

CHAPTER 38

The rotating navigation beacons marking the channel to Pointe-Noire harbor slashed the water with intermittent streaks of red and green as the two black boats from the Zumwalt zipped past the entrance and headed north along the coastline for another half mile before rounding a pointy split of land.

Approaching the beach through the surf, the drivers held the boats just offshore while twenty-four Special Forces operators and three civilians slipped over the sides in the darkness and began wading up onto the sand. Struggling through the swirling water, Dinning looked back. Dana's eyes were extra wide as she tried to outrace a breaking wave; her thin legs propelling her stork-like all the way up to the beach. Hamilton was the last to reach the shore, coughing up sea water as two SEALs dragged him up onto the sand.

A young lieutenant signaled the boats, and with their mini guns still pointed at the jungle, the drivers slowly backed into the sea gloom and disappeared. It was just past midnight, and the twenty-seven souls on the beach had exactly three and a half hours to make it through the city to the airport without being spotted. But they would have to wait. They had orders to hold in place until Brooks arrived.

In the Zumwalt's control room, the captain leaned back in his chair and sipped his coffee. "Where's the chopper?"

"He should be approaching the commander's position now, sir."

* * *

With the moon obscured by a thin line of dark clouds, the only light came from the stars. But even starlight was enough to make the grains of crystalline white sand glow softly against the phosphorescent waves breaking in the distance as Brooks pushed from their hiding place in the deep green and looked out across a hundred yards of flat beach between the jungle and the sea.

A perfect landing zone for the chopper.

Moving more like a breeze than a solid presence, Dawson appeared off to his left. "Nothing to the south for a quarter of a mile, Skipper."

"What kind of night eyes are you using?"

"L-3s."

"I need to borrow them for a minute … and Chief, get the girl. The chopper's almost here."

Looking out toward the water, Brooks strapped on the strange-looking night vision goggles—the kind with four lenses spaced around the front, making him look like a big camo insect as he walked out onto the beach and turned to scan the jungle. With the larger field of view provided by the new generation L-3s, he swept the jungle in all directions.

Nothing.

He switched to thermal mode and swept again, picking up the heat signatures of a few animals along with the moving images of Dawson and Samantha walking from the edge of the jungle. Removing his night eyes, Brooks faced the sea just as the black helicopter materialized over the surf, coming in low.

Dawson and Sam sprinted out onto the beach beside him, shielding their eyes from the swirling sand. As soon as the chopper touched down the three ran beneath the spinning blades and flew through the open doors.

Looking back over his shoulder, the pilot powered back up and yanked on the controls, swooping around before shooting back out over the water at top speed.

CHAPTER 39

Curled up in the bottom of a rusty cage, Musa Longolo looked up at one of his captors and waited for what would come next.

"Look at the monkey in the cage," the hefty sergeant taunted. His once-spotless uniform was in tatters, his teeth yellowed, and a strange light radiated from the irises of his bright green eyes. "I think all you people belong in cages." He kicked the bars, causing Musa to jump. Laughing, he tossed a piece of bread stained with his dirty fingerprints into the filthy cage. "Enjoy your dinner, my little monkey friend."

"That's enough of that!"

The sergeant gazed back over his shoulder to see a white-haired man standing in the open doorway of the moldy room. "Sorry about that, sir. I was just getting ready to tell our *guest* here that his friends arrived off the coast last night just like you said they would." The sergeant turned back to Musa. "But the men we sent kicked their asses and sent them running back home to their mamas."

Musa looked up. His face sagged around hollowed eyes, and his damp, filthy clothes clung to a thin frame that was becoming thinner by the day. Slowly, he picked up the bread and threw it out onto the floor.

Yellow tooth grinned. "Suit yourself."

"When did he stop eating?" the white-haired man asked.

"Couple of days ago ... when we offered him some fish."

"Why didn't anyone tell me?"

"Didn't think it was important, sir. Besides, this old guy won't last much longer. Why don't we juice him up and see what happens?"

"That will be all, Sergeant. Leave us."

The man cast a final, bullying glance at Musa before walking from the room and slamming the door behind him.

Pulling up a chair, the white-haired man sat next to the cage. "I'm sorry for that, Mr. Longolo, but you have to eat. I admit the sergeant's a crude brute, but I'm afraid I need him just as much as I need you right now." The man lowered his head to peer back at Musa through the bars. "You knew what you were doing when you gave those fish bones to Dinning, didn't you?"

Musa maintained his silence, his moist eyes searching the man's face.

"That's okay." The man sat back up and stretched. "I already know the answer to that question. You've never really understood what I've been trying to achieve out here, have you?"

"I know you bring evil men with you." The sound of Musa's dry, scratchy voice startled the man. "And evil begets evil."

In one swift motion that belied his age, the man stood, kicking the chair out from beneath him. "Maybe the sergeant's right about you. Maybe your kind only understands brutality. But you and I both know you're still hiding something, and unless you want that reeking excuse for a human being to be your permanent guard, you'd better start talking."

The man paused to look around the dank room. "Tell you what. I know you have another specimen hidden in the jungle somewhere, and since all of the other transgenic fish have apparently disappeared, you're the only one here in this miserable place who can tell us where we can find it. All you have to do is tell me where it is and you'll be out of this cage today … free to return to your precious library."

Musa twisted his back in an attempt to straighten his crippled leg, stirring the pungent smell of old urine that forced the man back. "Evil begets evil," Musa repeated, coughing. "The thing you seek will be here soon enough."

"What … you think your ticket to freedom lies in some stupid riddle?" The man's eyes narrowed. "What in the hell are you talking about?"

"Death." Musa blinked. "The thing you seek is death, and I can promise you that it will be here soon."

CHAPTER 40

On the narrow strip of beach just north of Pointe-Noire harbor, the prone figures from the *Zumwalt* looked like shadows on the sand. The surf behind them was growing heavier with a force that shook the beach—the rhythmic pounding filling the air with anxious expectation as they peered at the edge of the jungle across a shallow lagoon.

Edging up to a young SEAL lieutenant, Dinning breathed in the exotic mixture of watery plant and animal life blowing across the lagoon. "You won't find that smell anywhere else on earth, Lieutenant. Is this your first time in Africa?"

"Yes, sir. All my other deployments have been in the Middle East."

Dinning looked back with a smile of resignation. "Of course … the ancient wound that never heals. Why do you think that is, Lieutenant?"

"I don't know, sir. The level of religious fanaticism and intolerance in that part of the world is a big part of it, and some of their tribal feuds have been going on for centuries. But now they seem really pissed off at the rest of us for some reason. The radicals keep nipping at our heels like a pack of wild dogs, and it's beginning to change the way we live our lives. The admiral said that we'd better be prepared for a real war over there someday soon, because the rest of the world is tired of their crap."

"The admiral?"

"Admiral Bourdon … the head of JSOC. He gave a speech a few months back on the spread of radical Islam. He made it sound like World War III."

"He may have a point. These new terror groups have attracted thousands of psychopaths who seem to be culturally hard-wired for violence based on a flawed belief system. Jihad has become almost like a sport to them. And your admiral is right, Lieutenant. The world is tired of their crap."

231

The unmistakable chop of an approaching helicopter made both men glance off to the north. The dragonfly-like outline was blotting out the stars as it skimmed over the beach and circled around before touching down on the sand. Brooks was the first one off, followed by Dawson and Samantha. As soon as they were clear, the chopper lifted off.

"What the hell?" Brooks shouted, looking back at Sam. "She was supposed to stay on the chopper. I wanted her back on the ship."

Dawson shrugged his shoulders. "No one said anything to me, sir."

"Well, I'm here now, Commander," Sam said, finding a spot on the sand next to Dana.

"Do you want me to call the chopper back, sir?" Dawson asked.

"No, they're probably running low on fuel as it is." Brooks looked back at Sam like a father unable to control his excited child in a crowded mall. "You two stay together. Understood?"

Sam and Dana nodded, but as soon as he turned his back they hoisted their arms in a high-five.

"I thought you were dead for sure, Samantha!" Dana exclaimed.

Sam grinned. "So did I until Mr. Personality showed up. I don't think I would have made it without him. I think we have a love-hate thing going on."

Walking over to the lieutenant, Brooks checked the beach in both directions. "If anyone was waiting for us they know we're here now. Have you seen any movement out there, Lieutenant?"

"No, sir … nothing."

"Where's Dinning and Hamilton?"

The lieutenant pointed to the pair lying on the sand in the middle of a group of SEALs.

"Okay. Bring me up to speed on the captain's plan, and make sure someone keeps an eye on that Hamilton guy."

"Yes, sir. We're flying out of Pointe-Noire to Yangambi on a British C-130."

"A British C-130? What happened to our plane at Loubomo?"

"They're holding their position as a diversion."

"Do they know they're being used as a diversion?"

"Yes, sir. The captain sent them a coded heads-up. They'll be extracting us from Yangambi when the time comes."

"Pointe-Noire, huh? Can't say I like the thought of going into a big city. That's why we chose Loubomo."

"We were running out of options, sir."

"Adapt and adjust. That's what we do, and I trust the captain's instincts on this one. The man has a lot of mission time under his belt, and he's got thirty years worth of military contacts in his little black book. He even called the Russians once to help us … and they did."

Brooks looked back at the shadows on the sand. "What about the airport? Did the captain happen to mention how we're supposed to make it there through the city without being seen?"

The lieutenant smiled. "We're taking the bus."

Brooks did a double-take. "The what?"

"The Royal Marines are coming to the party, Commander. Whoever the captain talked to about sending a British plane for us also figured we probably needed a ride to the airport. The marines from the British Embassy will be picking us up in an unmarked embassy bus. The airport is about seven miles from our current position, and from the pictures I've seen, Pointe-Noir doesn't look like one of those mud-hut towns I was expecting. It's big, with wide boulevards and new high-rise buildings. Our British friends warned us not to underestimate the police here."

"Good to know," Brooks said. "Where are we supposed to catch this bus?"

"There's a road just beyond that thin strip of jungle on the other side of the lagoon. The Royal Marines will pick us up there."

"Anything else?"

"No, sir. It's a pretty basic plan."

"Sometimes the basic plans are the ones that work the best, Lieutenant. Let's move out."

One by one, thirty figures dressed in green jungle camouflage peeled off the beach and waded across the knee-deep water of the small lagoon before pushing through the jungle to the edge of the thick greenery bordering the highway. Looking out at a dark, empty road, they waited. A single car passed and disappeared around a curve. Brooks looked at his watch. A few minutes later a large red bus rounded the curve and flashed its lights. An army ranger signaled back with a laser and the bus pulled to the side of the road. Thirty figures ran from the jungle. As soon as everyone was on board, the Royal Marine posing as a driver hit the gas and headed for the airport.

Inside the bus, the darkened windows hid the green faces of the men as they passed the harbor and peered out at a line of gigantic white cranes towering over several big container ships. The entire waterfront was ablaze with light, making it easy to see a couple of security guards with dogs patrolling the fence line across the placid, light-streaked water.

Glancing back at Brooks, the driver tried to stifle a yawn. "Sorry, Commander. They woke us up out of a dead sleep. In case you haven't already noticed, we armed a couple of our men with RPGs and stationed them in the back of the bus to keep an eye on the road behind us. I would ask you what you and your men are up to, sir, but I know you probably can't tell us."

"To tell you the truth, Corporal, we're not real sure ourselves what we're heading into. Where are you dropping us off?"

"The embassy hangar, sir. It's closed now, and we don't want to light it up for obvious reasons. You might want to deploy your people along the dark side of the building until the plane arrives."

"Got it," Brooks said. "We definitely owe you one."

The marine winked back before turning onto *Boulevard Felix Tchikaya*. For another three miles the bus drove past shuttered businesses, dodging an old woman walking in the street as the airport lights came into view. A few blocks from the terminal, they took a side road and rolled to a stop in front of a tall, unmarked metal hangar. The first men off the bus held their guns at the ready, but only a sleepy dog wagged its tail at the fearsome-looking group flowing through the doors.

Glancing back at the Royal Marine behind the wheel, Brooks saluted before disappearing around the corner to crouch in the weeds along the side of the hangar with the others. In almost every Special Forces operation, waiting was a big part of the job. Some of the men spent their time searching an empty sky, looking for landing lights, while others re-checked their weapons or just gazed out across the blue lights dotting the field.

Twenty minutes later, an Air Force sniper pointed silently to the south from his perch fifty yards away. The bright landing lights of a large transport plane could be seen descending on a steep glide path to the end of the runway.

As soon as the aircraft touched down, the pilots took the first runway exit and killed their lights before taxiing straight for the hangar. With the four turboprops still whining, the large cargo door at the back of the aircraft was already coming down as the big plane spun around on the tarmac. Before the door had even touched the ground, the teams poured through the opening and began strapping in. Five minutes later, the big gray airplane with a Union Jack painted on its tail was streaking down the runway.

Lifting into a humid sky, they banked to the east, climbing through the wet air as the lights from Pointe-Noire blinked out behind them. For the next several hours, those peering down at the world below would see no lights, for they were flying over the deep green and the dark river that snaked through it. They were on their way to Yangambi.

John Lyman

CHAPTER 41

Walking up to the cockpit, Brooks and Dinning sat behind the pilots and leaned forward to peer through the C-130's panoramic windows. Those who had been to this part of Africa before knew that the interior of the Congo was much hotter than it was on the coast, and with the sun rising over the nose of the aircraft, they could already see wisps of steam rising from the jungle through breaks in the clouds below.

"Can we circle the old research station before we land?" Dinning asked Brooks.

"Sorry, Professor, but this is an RAF plane, and these guys are Special Forces pilots. The only time they fly around and announce their presence is at air shows. You'd better tighten your seatbelt, because they're going to come in high and fast using the clouds for cover. Just tell your stomach you're on a roller coaster. Works for me."

The co-pilot moved his left hand to the flap selector switch and set the wing flaps at fifty degrees. They could feel it in the pits of their stomachs when the aerodynamic shape of the wings changed, curving downward at the back to decrease speed while increasing the angle of descent on their plunge through the clouds. Grayness exploded against the windows, and when they finally broke through into the clear, the red dirt runway was right below them.

The pilots kept the aircraft at an impossible forty-five degree angle all the way down, flaring the nose just before the tires squished into the red mud at the approach end of the runway. With no traction, they began sliding. The co-pilot shoved the power handles all the way forward, throwing the four screaming turboprops into full reverse.

Hurtling down the jungle strip, the pilots looked maddeningly calm to Dinning. Their decision point to add power and go around for another attempt was coming up, but with a steady calm born from years of landing in places that looked suicidal to most pilots, they kept the turboprops spinning in reverse and plunged ahead. They were now committed to bringing the plane to a stop before it collided with the trees at the far end of the runway.

The hard-packed earth looked drier ahead. As soon as the wheels bounced from the slippery mud onto more solid ground, the pilots pumped the brakes and the aircraft finally began to slow. By the time they had reached the end of the strip, the men up front were talking about a favorite pub in Scotland while they spun the plane around and rumbled back over the uneven terrain toward the old rusty hangar.

Looking out at a green world through the cockpit windows, a lump formed in Dinning's throat when he saw the old hangar. The memory of Allison waiting for him under its tin roof the last time he was here was still painful for him. The young researcher had been cut down in the prime of her life along with the others on the ship, and she had been the first one he had tearfully wrapped in plastic before placing her in one of the freezers for the trip back home.

The rain had stopped just before they landed, and the sky was growing lighter as the crew chief lowered the big ramp door. Once again, thirty figures dressed in green camos flowed from the back of the aircraft and sprinted across the field past the old hangar before quickly disappearing into the jungle.

The only witness to the sight had been an old man who had been sweeping the draining red mud from a blue-painted arch framing the entrance to the old, Art-Deco terminal building. He paused only long enough to watch the lumbering gray plane make its take-off run before banking away over the jungle canopy. Shrugging his shoulders, he returned to his work. Nothing he had just seen seemed odd or out of the ordinary to him. After all, this was the Congo—and he had seen much, much stranger things.

* * *

For anyone who had ever stepped from a cool, dry aircraft into the rising steam of an equatorial jungle, the transition was instant. Slammed by an invisible wall of heat and humidity, Samantha's first instinct was to peel off her outer camo shirt in favor of the olive-colored T-shirt beneath, but she had already been warned against doing just that by some of the more experienced men on the plane.

There are things out there you can't even see ... biting things, so keep your arms covered.

Pushing into the jungle, a broad green leaf slapped her in the face when she looked up from the muddy path. The Army Ranger walking in front of her was even wearing gloves, and his torso was wrapped in a layer of body armor.

He must be baking, she thought. The soldiers all had their heads on a swivel, looking up into the trees as well as to the sides as they trekked silently up a hill away from the airport. The foliage on either side of the path was so thick that a man standing only a couple of feet away would have been virtually invisible, and Sam heard one of the men behind her grumbling about their tactical situation all the way up the hill until the jungle finally opened up.

Standing with their backs to a wall of green behind them, they stopped for a moment at the top of the hillside to look down through the wavering brown grass at the wide river below. It was the biggest river Sam had ever seen, and when she walked up beside Dinning, she could tell by the look on his face that he was totally captivated by this wild and unforgiving place.

"Are we close to the old research station?" she asked.

"You're looking at part of it."

"Where?"

"Down there, in the grass. I'm afraid only foundations remain in this area. The main campus is down by the river, but you can't see it from here."

"The library?"

"Yes. A lot of the old buildings are still standing, and there are acres and acres of abandoned homes that are slowly being reclaimed by the jungle." Dinning's eyes gleamed with anticipation. "Some of the ruins are quite spectacular ... you'll see."

Sam blew a wisp of stray hair out of her eyes as she studied the grassy hillside. "It doesn't make any sense."

"What doesn't make sense?"

"I was just thinking. If this place was really as beautiful as you say, why didn't the native people move in after the Belgians left? Why leave it to rot in the jungle like some old ghost town?"

239

"I've never really understood that myself," Dinning said. "What you just said about it being a ghost town might have something to do with it. Superstition has always been synonymous with African culture, but I've always had a feeling there's a deeper reason."

"Okay, people," Brooks announced. "Let's keep moving. We're too exposed here."

"What about the research station?" Dinning asked.

"We're not going to the station, Professor."

"But I thought ..."

"Too dangerous. Until we find out what in the hell is going on around here, no one is going anywhere near that place. We're going to circle it and set up camp a few miles to the west."

"The west? But the only thing in that direction is a few hundred square miles of rainforest."

"Exactly." Caught by the hypnotic lure of the river, Brooks' eyes lingered on the churning brown water for a moment before he signaled the two marine snipers at the top of the hill and they all pushed back into the vast green world that lay beyond.

For the next two hours they moved at a downward angle through the jungle. The constant screeches from the birds and monkeys in the leafy canopy above their heads was the only sound that broke the stillness as they followed in the footsteps of a two-man recon team Brooks had sent ahead to scout the area on the other side of the old station.

By noon the sun was directly overhead and everyone was drenched in sweat. The sound of rushing water off to their left told them they were moving parallel to the river as they threaded the deep green and pushed through some overhanging vines into a clearing where the air felt still and lifeless. Even the screeches from the trees had stopped, and Sam felt a sudden chill as the group moved cautiously beneath a dark green canopy that filtered the sun's rays into smoky shafts of gray light that dappled the fern-covered ground around them.

Walking ahead, the sun was in her eyes when she looked up at a rocky outcropping through the steamy haze and froze. She could hear herself screaming before she could stop it.

Rushing forward, Brooks and the other men squinted through the shafts of light at the spread-eagled, backlit figure of a man tied between two trees twenty feet off the blood-splattered ground.

Cautiously, they inched closer until they could make out his features. "Oh my God!" Dinning exclaimed.

Brooks cursed, his nostrils flaring and his jaw tightening as he looked up at the body of one of the scouts he had sent ahead. The man's throat had obviously been slit, and both eyes had been removed. It was a macabre message to the solemn group of Special Forces operators that one of the men they had sent ahead to be their eyes was now sightless. Instantly, the other men spread out to form a heavily-armed circle around the clearing while two Rangers climbed up and cut the body down.

Brooks was seething as he stared down at the gruesome sight on the moist ground. "There's lots of boot prints around here … and we still have another man out there somewhere. Let's see if we can find him."

"We just did, Commander," Dawson said. "He's over there. Looks like they were trying to drag him off through the jungle when they heard us coming."

The young lieutenant avoided looking at the body lying in the ferns. "Who the hell is out here with us, and why would they do something like this? They have to know this will only piss us off … and this is definitely the wrong group of guys to piss off."

"Whoever did this wants us pissed off, Lieutenant," Brooks said. "I've seen this type of thing before. First they attack your emotions and cloud your judgment by killing one of your men and leaving his mutilated body behind for you to find. Then they drag another man off and leave a trail for you to follow, and anyone who's angry or stupid enough to follow it will be walking right into a trap. Whoever is out here with us definitely knows how to play the terror game, but so do we. We'll camp here tonight."

"Here, sir?"

"It's time for us to start screwing with their heads for a change, Lieutenant. The people who did this won't be expecting us to stay in an area where two of our men were just killed, but this is actually a very defensible position. That's probably why they chose it to ambush our scouts."

"But they'll know where we are, sir."

"Look around, Lieutenant. It's pretty obvious they already know where we are, but they're smart enough to know that a full-on firefight with us wouldn't exactly be a walk in the park. They're moving through the jungle like ghosts so they can chip away at us one or two at a time until we're all dead or forced to leave. Whoever's calling the shots knows our tactics, and you better believe they'll be using that knowledge against us."

Without speaking, Dawson and some of the other men moved off to check the outer perimeter.

CHAPTER 42

At the base of the rocky outcropping, Samantha and Dana sat huddled on the ground, Dinning by their side. "I'm sorry you had to see that," he said. "Can I get either of you anything?"

"No thanks," Sam said. "I doubt they carry what I need right now in their backpacks."

Dinning winked. "Back in a moment."

After talking to a group of Rangers, he was back a few minutes later with a handful of airline-sized bottles of whiskey. "Sorry ... nothing to mix them with."

Sam kissed Dinning on the forehead and downed half a bottle with one swallow. Using both hands, Dana took small, slow sips as she stared into the jungle. Dinning didn't like it. She had taken on that look of detachment some people get after they've seen something so horrible all they wanted to do was curl up into a ball and forget. It was as if a switch had been thrown, shutting them down while one half of their brain tried to process what they had just seen and the other half tried to erase it.

Standing off to the side, Hamilton was starting to look more freaked out by the minute. "You know, whoever killed those men don't seem to be too concerned about keeping a low profile."

"I was thinking the same thing," Dinning said. "It's almost like they're taunting us. We're missing something here ... I can feel it."

"Me too." Hamilton's eyes were drawn to their stash of small whiskey bottles. "Mind if I have one of those?"

Without answering, Dinning picked one up and tossed it to him.

"Thank you, Peter." Hamilton sat and twisted the top off before downing every last drop. "It wasn't personal, you know."

"It was for me, Ian. How long have you been involved in this?"

"Ever since they recruited me straight out of graduate school."

"Who? The CIA ... the military?"

243

Hamilton glanced at Sam and Dana. Both girls were staring holes through him. "To be honest, Peter, I didn't have a clue who I was working for at first, but it really didn't matter. All I cared about then was the funding. You know how difficult it can be. Most new PhDs spend upwards of twenty years trying to build the kind of reputation needed to attract enough funding for their research. And there I was … fresh out of school, and someone wanted to hand me millions of dollars."

"You mean you never spoke to them?"

"Only the man who contacted me at first. He said he represented a pharmaceutical company, but he wasn't allowed to tell me which one. After that, all of our correspondence was through courier. At first it was great, but then I started worrying the money might be coming from a foreign government. So I stuck a note in the courier's pouch demanding proof that I wasn't involved in anything illegal. For several weeks I never heard back from them. Then one night two men from the DIA showed up on my doorstep and shoved a non-disclosure statement in my hands. They told me my research was vital to national defense and that if I wanted to continue receiving the money I had to sign it. On their way out the door, they let me know that if I ever told anyone I was working for the government I'd be spending the next thirty years in prison."

A vision of the two DIA men who had stood on her own front porch played in the back of Sam's mind. "One of those DIA men didn't happen to be a guy named Preston, did it?"

Hamilton looked back at her, stunned. "Yes, Gil Preston. How did you know?"

"He paid us a visit too … right after the professor's ship washed up on the beach."

Dinning capped his half-full bottle. "Have you told any of this to Brooks, Ian?"

"No. I haven't had a chance yet. Besides, the man obviously hates me for some reason."

"I seriously doubt he hates you, Ian. He's just one of those people who sees the world in black and white, and right now he's not sure if you're one of the good guys or the bad guys." Dinning paused. "Are you, Ian? Are you one of the bad guys?"

"Of course not, Peter. I never laid eyes on that transgene until you brought it to my lab. I was only contracted to provide the viral promoter they used to transfer their genetically engineered material."

244

"And you never asked what they were creating?"

"No, because I knew they'd never tell me. I was only responsible for a piece of the puzzle. They were obviously using different scientists in different locations to create a single transgene, when it would have been much more efficient to do all of it in one place. It's like the ship we were just on. Most of the parts were probably made in different locations by different people. That's how they keep things secret."

Dinning kicked at the ground and stared out across the clearing before looking back at Hamilton. "What's the first thing that popped into your mind the moment you first laid eyes on the transgene, Ian?"

"The truth? I thought it was beautiful."

"So did I. But I also wanted to know what it did and why it was created. Our primary job as scientists is to answer those two questions … that's the only reason we're here. Granted, someone is trying really hard to scare us away, but we have to stay focused on the science. No matter what happens, I'm not leaving until I find out what that thing does."

Dana stood and tossed her empty bottle on the ground. "Whatever it does, we're paying the price for stumbling onto a military secret. Doesn't anyone find it strange that the old Belgian research station is sitting right square in the middle of the same jungle where HIV and Ebola evolved, and now someone in the exact same area is creating transgenes using genetic material obtained from three of the most aggressive species on the planet. I mean, WTF?"

"WTF is right," Dinning shot back. "I'd love to know more about this NATO expert on germ warfare who disappeared a year ago before suddenly turning up in Yangambi. Dana's right … no one really knows what kind of experimentation has been going on here since the 1930's. The Belgian scientists who originally built the old station chose to build it in this part of the world for a reason. They had an entire ecosystem covering hundreds-of-thousands of square miles at their disposal, and they were about as far away from any official prying eyes as they could get."

"And now a new generation of researchers has returned. Is that what you're saying, Peter?"

"Why not? It makes perfect sense. We're on the same continent where humans evolved, and this is still the center of the universe for endemism."

Sam blinked her eyes. "Center of what?"

"Endemism," Dinning repeated. "Epicenters for species found nowhere else in the world. We're standing in the middle of the richest one of all. For a molecular biologist this is DNA heaven. That's why I targeted this area to collect samples, and the people who engineered that transgene undoubtedly chose it for the same reason."

"At least you were seeking knowledge instead of profit," Sam said, casting a withering look in Hamilton's direction.

"Hey, I don't blame any of you for doubting my motives," Hamilton said, "I'll be the first to admit I was in it for the money, but I always poured everything back into my research. I live in a one-bedroom apartment and drive a five-year-old pickup for God's sake. I'm no Lamborghini Cowboy ... I'm a scientist, and I swear to you I've told you everything I know."

"If it makes you feel any better, Ian, I believe you," Dinning said. "That's why I put your name on the essential personnel list, because if we ever do locate the people who created that gene, we're going to need all the expertise we can get. Most people think we know all there is to know about the role genetics plays in our lives, when in truth we've barely scratched the surface. Now is not the time to start playing around with the genomes of living creatures in an uncontrolled free-for-all, no matter how insignificant those creatures may appear to us.

"We're moving into uncharted waters, and to think that someone has engineered a gene with so much lethal potential and released it into the wild makes chills run down my spine. This has always been the nightmare scenario all molecular biologists talk about when we get together at conferences. If I find out that this thing does what I think it does, we have to stop these people here and now."

Hamilton tilted his head toward Dinning. "This NATO scientist you've been talking about ... I think I may have met him!"

"At your lab?"

"No. You just reminded me when you mentioned conferences. I believe he's the one I spoke to at a conference in the Netherlands a couple of years back."

The others were suddenly hyper-alert. "Would you recognize him if you saw him again?" Dinning asked.

"Probably. He was in his mid-sixty's. Wore a bow tie, and he's got snow-white hair."

Sam's expression was still simmering. "Why were you there?"

246

"Like I said, I was at a conference … a microbiology conference. Bacteriologists and virologists from around the world were there to discuss new ways of using bacteria and viruses to transport genetically engineered material into cells. The two fields have a lot in common … we all learn from each other."

"And what did you learn from him?"

"Not much, really. He was talking about sourdough bread."

Sam traded looks with the others. "Bread?"

"Yeah. As a bacteriologist, he was fascinated by the fact that there's a microbe in sourdough starter that's never been found anywhere else. They've been trying to unravel the mystery through DNA sequencing, but so far they've come away scratching their heads. No one knows where it comes from. It doesn't come from the wheat or the water or our bodies … but it has to come from somewhere."

"Did anyone at the conference bother to quote the famous microbiology saying?" Dinning asked.

"What saying is that?"

"*Everything is everywhere, but the environment selects.*"

John Lyman

CHAPTER 43

Throughout the night the men took turns sleeping and standing guard duty, their automatic weapons pointed out at the deep green while they used their night vision and thermal imaging goggles to look for anything moving. With the first rays of sunlight, Brooks allowed small fires for coffee. The aroma drifted through the camp, and soon Dinning and the other civilians had joined the SEALs for a dubious breakfast of MREs.

Looking around the camp, Dinning walked over to the young lieutenant. "Where's Commander Brooks?"

"Down by the river, sir."

"The river?"

"Yes, sir. He and Chief Dawson scouted a trail down to the river last night. They wanted to lay a trap for anyone approaching from that direction."

"Can we go down there?"

"He said you'd ask that. A couple of the Air Force tactical guys are going down there in a few minutes. You can go with them."

"Thank God!" Dana exclaimed. "I don't like it here. This clearing is starting to feel like the Alamo. It's creepy."

"Then you'll be glad to know we're pulling out, ma'am. The commander is taking us to the old research station."

"The old research station!" Hamilton exclaimed. "Are you serious? After what happened here!"

"No point in avoiding it now, sir. We've obviously lost the element of surprise, and they seem to know our every move. Besides, the men are itching for a firefight with the people who killed our guys, and the old station is probably where we'll meet up with them."

Dana looked up from her brown package of cold food. "You sound just like an old-west sheriff when you talk like that. Where are you from, Lieutenant?"

"Seattle, ma'am."

"Really? What's your human name?"

The young lieutenant smiled. "Chris … Chris Seaborne."

"Seaborne," Dana repeated. "Kind of a cool name for a SEAL."

Dinning and Sam exchanged glances. Neither of them had ever seen Dana initiate a social conversation before, and they weren't exactly sitting in the kind of place singles usually meet.

"Still trying to get a date with the skinny one, Lieutenant?" Brooks said, walking up behind him.

The lieutenant turned bright red. "No, sir! Just telling them about our plan to move out, sir."

"Relax, Lieutenant. You could do worse. She's cute and smart."

Dana almost choked on whatever it was she was eating, but Brooks kept walking—always scanning the tree line.

From the trail leading up from the river, they all heard shouting. "We got one of the bastards!" Instantly, Brooks and the lieutenant took off running toward the edge of the clearing just as a two-man marine sniper team burst from the trail with a bleeding soldier. His hands were tied behind his back with a plastic band, and as they pushed him ahead into the clearing, he did a face-plant on the ground.

"Son-of-a-bitch walked right past us!" one of the marines said.

Everyone who wasn't on the perimeter gathered around to look down at the filthy young man in tattered camos. Raising his head in defiance, he glared up at them. The irises of his eyes radiated with a fluorescing, emerald-like ring of light that any budding rock star would have killed for.

The otherworldly sight made Dawson take a step back. "What the hell's wrong with his eyes?"

One of the marines prodded the man with the barrel of his weapon. "Kind of freaked us out too, but this guy isn't talking." The marine leaned down. "Were you one of the psychos who killed our …" The marine stopped in mid-sentence when he noticed the edge of a black and yellow patch on the man's uniform. Brushing away the grime, he saw the embroidered outline of a skull wearing a green beret. "I'll be damned! This guy is wearing a Special Forces *Ghost Recon* patch!"

"Where did you come from?" Brooks asked the soldier.

The man spit, barely missing Brooks as the marine slammed the butt of his rifle into the man's stomach.

"Get away from him!" Dinning shouted.

Dawson held out his hand. "Better stay out of this, Professor."

"No, I mean stay away from him ... don't touch him. Something's not right. We need to isolate him until we find out what it is."

Brooks and the marines looked back at Dinning with blank expressions.

"Look at his eyes! Does that look natural to any of you?"

"Not really," Brooks said. "You think he has something contagious?"

"It's possible, especially in this area of the world."

Walking up behind the soldier, the medic quickly slipped a mask over his nose and mouth so he couldn't spit at them again.

Dawson seemed unable to take his eyes off the man's shoulder patch. "You think this guy really is *Ghost Recon*, Skipper?"

"If he is, he's gone off the reservation. We need to start gathering some intel from him, but he doesn't look too cooperative. Get the kit."

The medic reached into his backpack and pulled out a little red plastic box that held a pre-filled syringe.

"Give it to him, and don't get any of his blood on you."

The medic nodded and jabbed the needle into the soldier's bicep straight through his sleeve. A few minutes later the soldier's eyes had become glassy, and he was drooling.

"What's your name, soldier?" Brooks asked.

The man's eyes rolled, still glowing with the eerie green light. "O'Brian," he responded, slurring his words. "First Sergeant."

"What outfit are you with, Sarge?"

"Company C ... 2nd Battalion ... Special Forces, sir."

Brooks felt a chill run down his spine as he glanced back at the medic. "Are you sure the stuff you gave him is working?"

"We've always had good results before, sir. It works a lot better than the old truth serums we used to use."

"Let's hope so, because if this man is telling the truth, we really are looking at a ghost. All the members of Company C died last year when their plane crashed in the Indian Ocean."

"We didn't crash," the man mumbled. "We were diverted."

"Diverted!" Brooks looked stunned. "Diverted where?"

"Africa." The man grunted. "Heart of darkness."

"Do you know where the orders came from?"

"JSOC, sir."

"Who at JSOC?"

"Huh?" The man's head lolled to one side.

"He probably doesn't know the answer to that question, Commander," the medic said.

The man lifted his head, his radiant, glassy eyes staring up at Brooks. "Something happened to us."

"What was that?"

"Something happened … "

"What happened?"

The soldier's head slumped forward, his drool creating a small puddle on the ground. He looked like he was starting to drift off to sleep. Brooks started shouting. "What happened to you … where did the other soldiers go … are they camped nearby?!"

"You have to ask one question at a time, sir," the medic said.

Brooks could feel his heart pounding. "Where are the other men now?"

"They're down in …" The soldier's eyes opened wide with a look of surprise. Suddenly, his back arched and he began to thrash about. Everyone backed away. His eyes were bulging, and he began to vomit, prompting the medic to jerk the mask off his face just as dark blood began gushing from his mouth. Still thrashing, blood was slinging through the air all around him as he twisted into a full-blown seizure.

The others looked on in horror, backing even farther away, until finally the soldier stopped seizing and his body went limp. His sightless eyes were now frozen on something no one else could see, the green light slowly fading, until nothing was left but a dull stare."

"What the hell just happened to him!" Dana screamed. "This place is a nightmare!"

Everyone stood there, staring at the man's body and wondering the same thing as Samantha wrapped an arm around Dana's shoulder.

"Yeah. What *did* just happen to him?" Brooks asked the medic. "Was it the shot?"

"I don't think so, sir. It's never done that before."

"Maybe he was allergic to it."

"Allergic reactions don't usually present that way. Your throat swells up and you stop breathing, but you don't start bleeding from the mouth and just die like that."

"You don't catch on fire, either," Hamilton said, pointing. A wisp of smoke was curling from a small flame that had just erupted around the collar of the soldier's shirt.

Instinctively, the medic reached out with a gloved hand to beat it out, but Dawson grabbed his arm. "Easy, boy. Back away. Unless we just witnessed a case of spontaneous combustion, I suggest we all stand back until we can get one of the Air Force EOD guys over here."

"Explosives disposal?" Brooks quizzed. "You think that man had a bomb inside his body, Chief?"

"That fire had to come from somewhere, sir. It wouldn't hurt to have our guy take a look first. This place is full of surprises."

"I'm right behind you, Chief." An Air Force Master Sergeant patted Dawson on the shoulder and nudged him away before pulling on a pair of gloves. Using a wound dressing from the medic's bag, he quickly smothered the flames before slowly peeling the soldier's shirt back. "Holy shit!"

The others leaned closer.

"Something just blew a hole through this guy's neck!" The sergeant pulled a pair of tweezers from his pocket and tugged at the blackened wound over the soldier's carotid artery. "Whatever it was, it blew outward with enough heat to ignite his collar. We'd need a full autopsy to find out what happened, because I don't see ..." The sergeant paused, thinking. "Whoa ... it couldn't be."

"It couldn't be what, Sarge?"

"Well, this is pretty far out there, Commander, but there was a case like this last year ... in England. A Russian dissident died the same way. Hang on a second, sir." The sergeant retrieved a pair of special magnifying glasses and began examining the soldier's neck before looking at the collar of his shirt. "I'll be damned!" Reaching for his tweezers, he pulled a tiny silver dot from the blood on the soldier's collar and held it up to the light. "Here's your bomb, Commander ... or at least the thing that triggered it."

"What is it?"

"It's a micro receiver. Whatever blew his artery out was remotely detonated."

"Brooks squinted at the object as the sergeant placed it on a piece of white gauze. "So you're saying someone actually did put a freaking bomb in his neck? You've got to be kidding me!"

"No, sir, I'm not. The Russians have been working on an explosive chemical that can be injected in a tiny capsule just beneath the skin next to a major artery, and you're looking at the micro receiver that just detonated it. It looks just like the one in the pictures attached to a CIA report I read. Whoever this guy was working for just gave him one hell of a severance package. They obviously knew he had been captured, and someone just made sure he wouldn't talk."

Brooks was still staring at the glinting silver dot on the piece of gauze. "That thing is practically microscopic. How in the hell did it get there?"

"Probably an injection. The forensics report stated that the most likely way it got into the Russian dissident in London was through a large bore needle."

"A shot in the neck?"

"Had to be, sir. Sounds weird, but the medical people are always giving us shots in different places. Maybe he was told it had to be given in the neck. Who's going to argue with a doctor? We never do. Especially if it's a military requirement for wherever they're sending us. This guy probably didn't ask any questions either."

Brooks shook his head. "That's the most diabolical thing I've ever heard of."

"It's only going to get worse, sir. Some of the new nanotechnology stuff they're working on is invisible to the naked eye. There's no telling what we'll be dealing with in the next few years."

"We're going to need blood and tissue samples from the body, Commander," Dinning said.

"Why? You still think he might have something contagious?"

"Not in the traditional sense. But until we know what we're dealing with, we need to take precautions. That strange green light in his eyes is a definite physical marker for some kind of change at the genetic level. If you ask me, that poor soldier has been undergoing a genetic conversion that none of us would ever want to experience in our worst nightmares. His human side has been at war with something else that's in there with him. In fact, it's probably safe to assume that Sergeant O'Brian here hasn't been Sergeant O'Brian for some time now."

"You just lost me, Professor. Something else is in there with him?"

"If he has been genetically altered, his genome now contains genetic lines of code from another species. Possibly three other species if this has anything to do with the transgene we discovered. And it looks like it's replicating. If this is linked to the same transgene, I think we're beginning to see some of what it does now. Of course I can't be positive unless I analyze a sample of his tissue, but it's high on my suspicion list. Something changed him, and not for the better."

Brooks looked completely flustered. "But why would they do something like this to one of their own people?"

Dinning glanced down at the soldier's body. "I have a few theories, but at this point that's all they are. We won't have the answer to that question until we're able to talk to the person who did this to him."

"You think it was the NATO scientist?"

"I'd say he's our number one suspect. The person responsible for this is obviously a very narcissistic individual. He's determined to prove his superiority to the world. He's also not thinking rationally. If he was, he never would have let this thing out of the lab."

"We really need to get this guy, Professor, and the fact that someone is trying really hard to keep us away tells me he's still around."

"The old station?"

"Could be."

"Then I'll leave finding him in your capable hands, Commander, because my job is to try to stop what I think he's done."

John Lyman

CHAPTER 44

They were forced to bury all three bodies at the base of the rocky outcropping, marking their graves with small crosses before leaving the clearing behind to follow the trail down to the river. Against the cacophony of screeching birds overhead, all of the other little jungle noises were drowned out as they walked beneath the towering green canopy. It made the Special Forces soldiers especially wary. With all the racket coming from the birds, they wouldn't be able to hear anything coming from the jungle.

Twenty minutes later, it was almost as if they had crossed an invisible boundary between night and day when they stepped from the deep green into the sunlight. Below them, the big brown river was flowing with a power that vibrated the ground beneath their feet. It seemed just as alive as any living creature—maybe more—and like the fitful beast that it was, it paid little heed to the tiny creatures walking beside it.

With the jungle to their left and the river on their right, they began heading east, moving upriver along a slick, muddy trail that snaked above the rushing water at the top of a sloping riverbank.

With every step they were mindful of the fact that they were only a slip away from becoming part of the flotsam they saw shooting past, and any chance of rescue was slim at best for anyone who fell into its fast-moving current. Even the SEALs looked somber when they gazed across its wide surface, watching the rushing water with a sense of awe.

"How far are we from the station?" Sam asked Dinning.

"I'd say it's about a mile-and-a-half up ahead. I've collected a lot of specimens from this area. The riverbank flattens out halfway between here and the old library."

Weaving her way around a couple of SEALs, Dana caught up to them on the trail. "Did you really mean what you said about that soldier, Peter?"

"What part?"

"The part where you said he'd been genetically altered."

"Yes." Dinning grew serious. "Whoever did that to him is a monster … a very smart monster."

"I know. Ever since I saw him I haven't been able to get his eyes out of my mind. What kind of genetic aberration would cause the irises of his eyes to take on a green fluorescent glow like that? It looked almost alien-like."

"It was alien to him. What we just saw reminded me of some transgenic experiments with lab animals that didn't go so well. If an engineered gene is responsible, we just got a glimpse of how it alters the human genome. His gums were red and swollen, his yellowed teeth were practically disintegrating, and the two marine snipers said he was so hyper-aggressive they considered shooting him until they finally got his hands tied."

"Yeah, and that smell. It was awful, and it wasn't just from him not bathing."

Dinning nodded. "It's certainly not the most pleasant transformation I've ever seen."

By mid-morning, the sun had done its work. Steam rising from the jungle was becoming almost fog-like as it drifted over the trail to mix with the cooler air by the river. No scouts had been sent ahead this time, but everyone knew that there were probably eyes watching them right now.

At the front of the line, the Army Ranger walking point suddenly stopped and held his hand up when he spotted a trip wire made from a clear piece of fishing line stretched across the trail. Following the line into the jungle, he froze when he saw a claymore anti-personnel mine aimed right at the trail—a stark reminder that they were being stalked by their own kind. Genetically altered or not, the men trying to prevent them from reaching the station were trained Special Forces operators, and they weren't called *Ghost Recon* for nothing. They were facing some of the best of the best—men who knew how to become invisible. Whoever had diverted them to the Congo had chosen wisely.

After disarming the mine, the ranger scrambled back up onto the muddy trail and paused for a moment to look across the river at something glinting in the sunlight. A split second later his head exploded in a red mist that splattered the soldiers behind him. Everyone flattened themselves against the ground as his body rolled down the embankment and splashed into the river. For a moment it floated among the reeds close to the riverbank before it drifted out and was sucked under by the current. No one had even heard a gunshot, which meant whoever was shooting at them was using a silencer.

Sniper. These guys knew what they were doing.

Right away Brooks knew the joint decision to take the trail had been a bad one. They were now in an exposed position pinned down by a sniper. On one side, the jungle. On the other, the river. Brooks stared into the jungle. If they were attacked now, it would come from there.

Looking back at the civilians, he motioned with his hand for them to stay down and crawled up to where Dawson had his M-60 machine gun pointed at the trees.

"Great minds think alike," Brooks said.

Dawson winked. "You got it, sir. If they come, it will be from the jungle. Any idea why the sniper stopped shooting? He has a clear field of fire from across the river."

"I don't know, Chief. I'm having a hard time figuring these guys out, and we're running out of options." Captain Williams' words came rushing back to him. *These guys are weird, Steve.*

By now the sun was slowly being erased by billowing walls of dark clouds flowing over the distant hilltops. Trapped by the varying air currents that rose and fell between the river and the land, they began piling up overhead, making it almost as dark out in the open as it had been under the thick jungle canopy. Minutes later, it began to rain.

Pushing the wet hair up out of her eyes, Sam looked back. Dana was holding her head down, afraid to look up, while Dinning and Hamilton hugged the ground. Neither appeared to be talking as they peered over the mud.

Sam felt the muscles in her legs tighten. She wanted to run.

Were they just going to lie there all day? Why not open up on them? They have to be in the jungle!

The thought shocked her, because Samantha suddenly realized she was thinking like a soldier. It was surreal. She was just a girl who caught bait for a living, and somehow she had taken that part of her and shoved it into the background in order to survive in a strange new reality. *Isn't that what soldiers did?*

Sam's eyes followed the narrow trail at the top of the sloping riverbank. The sniper was probably watching them right now from his nest across the river. Exposed as they were, they were easy targets from that direction, and by shooting the soldier walking point, the sniper had blocked them from going forward. No doubt he would do the same thing if they tried to go back the way they had come. The only place left to go was the jungle.

The rain was beginning to fall harder, and the skies were growing darker as twenty-seven souls clung to the top of the earthen bank and peered at the deep green through the downfall. Sam was the first to see them.

CHAPTER 45

Through the darkness and the rain, Samantha peered into the jungle and wiped her eyes. She looked again.

There! In the dark!

Between the leaves—little circles, floating—little green circles, glowing in the darkness.

They were there! Waiting!

The jungle was full of the green-eyed men, and behind her, she could almost feel herself in the crosshairs of the sniper across the river. Any minute now he would start picking people off. They would naturally run for the jungle, and the little green circles were waiting for them.

She had to tell Brooks!

Keeping low to the ground, she began to crawl, But it was too late. The sniper opened up, taking out one of the Air Force operators with a shot to the neck. With nowhere else to go, the men started to roll down the jungle side of the riverbank.

"Stop!" Sam shouted, making herself a target. "They're in the jungle! They're just waiting for us! I saw their eyes ... glowing green circles. They're there!"

Another silent slap as one of the SEALs took a hit in the arm.

"What do you wanna do, sir?" Dawson shouted. "We're getting hammered out here in the open. You think the girl really saw something in there?"

Brooks peered into the gloom once again. It was darker now, and he was finally able to see them too. Little green circles of light peering back out at them from the deep green.

"Maximum fire on the jungle!" Brooks shouted. "Open up with everything you've got! Now!"

Instantly, twenty-two Special Forces operators opened up, shredding the jungle in front of them with lines of tracer fire. The response was just as swift from the jungle as return fire erupted from the trees, spraying the riverbank and hitting some of Brooks' men. Both sides continued the steady stream of fire at close range as a swirling mix of mud and leaves filled the air.

The wounded were screaming out in pain, blood mixing with the rain as the gunfire dwindled and both sides reloaded. In a one-minute firefight, the number of Special Forces operators had fallen from twenty-two to eighteen. The sniper struck again. A marine. They were now down to seventeen.

The lull in the fighting gave Dawson a chance to crawl over next to Sam. She was watching the dying gasps of a wounded man that she had been talking to just moments before, and tears were streaming down her face.

"It would have been a lot worse if you hadn't warned us," Dawson said.

"We have to go into the river!" Sam shouted through the downpour.

Dawson's eyes widened. "The river ... are you crazy? We'd all drown in that current. I'll take my chances with the green-eyed freaks in the jungle."

"I've been watching it," Sam replied. "As long as we stay in the shallow water where those tall reeds are growing, the current shouldn't be a problem."

Another slap. A Ranger this time. Sam waited as Brooks and Dawson signaled each other. The marines began lobbing grenades into the jungle while Dawson opened up with a steady stream of fire from his machine gun. With the green eyes pinned down, Brooks and many of the other men advanced down the bank, shredding everything in front of them as they moved into the deep green.

The sniper struck again, hitting one of the men who had stood a little too high when he lifted up to follow Brooks. An enraged Dawson turned his big gun around and began peppering the tree line across the river with tracer fire until a final click signaled he was out of ammo. Reaching for the short automatic weapon slung over his shoulder, he waited. Another shot from across the river thudded into the mud next to his head. The sniper was letting them know he was still alive.

Making eye contact with the other three civilians, Sam pointed to the river before throwing herself down the embankment into the shallow, reedy water. Following Sam's lead as bullets pinged all around them,

Dinning and the other two dove down the side of the grassy bank and rolled into the river.

With the rain dimpling the still water along the river's edge, Dana and Sam peered at each other through the reeds. With only their heads protruding above the surface, Dana's lips were already turning blue and she was visibly shivering. "Now what, Samantha?"

"I'm thinking." Sam listened. The gunfire in the jungle had dwindled to a few occasional pops. "Where's Dawson?"

"Right behind you."

Sam turned to see his camouflaged face moving through the tall reeds. "How come you didn't go with Brooks?" she asked.

"He told me to stay with you."

Sam moved her arms back and forth through the water, planting her boots on the muddy bottom while she looked out at the rushing current beyond the reeds. With the heavy rain, the river appeared to be rising. "We can't stay here much longer," she told Dawson. "Dana's lips are already turning blue, and the rest of us are starting to shiver too."

Dawson looked around. "Maybe we can make it to the old station through these reeds. Think you can last a little longer?"

"Anything's better than staying here. I'm game."

"Good. We should be able to find someplace to hide there until the commander shows up."

"You mean *if* the commander shows up," Hamilton said, splashing up beside them. "Why can't we just go back the way we came?"

"Not an option. It's like those green-eyed bastards read our minds. You can bet the trail behind us is booby-trapped now just like it is ahead, and with a big wide river and a sniper off to our right, we were being driven into the jungle like a herd of cattle."

For a moment Sam was speechless. "But you guys are supposed to be the best soldiers in the world. How did you let something like this happen?"

Dawson's eyes never left the top of the river bank. "If those really are the missing *Ghost Recon* soldiers out there, we're facing off against some of the best Special Forces fighters in the world ... and they know this area a lot better than we do. Once Brooks and I saw that soldier's patch, we knew they owned the jungle. We decided to go around them and follow the river trail to the old station instead. It was a fifty-fifty coin toss. We lost. Come on, let's start moving upstream while it's still raining. At least that should keep the sniper off our butts."

Together the wet group waded through the thin shafts of river grass protruding high above the surface of the water. On a clear day, anyone watching could have easily followed their passage through the shallow water near the bank by watching the movement of the tall reeds, but in the tropical downpour, the stiff grass was whipping around in all directions, making it impossible to see anything moving through them.

After almost an hour of slow wading the rain stopped. The riverbank to their left had flattened, and up ahead, the jungle ended at the edge of a large swath of open land that ran from the river to the top of a distant hill. Sam looked closer. The wavering brown grass was filled with jutting ruins, and on the opposite side of the clearing, an immense, two-story Art Deco building faced a red dirt road that overlooked the river. In the fading light, Sam knew right away that she was looking at the old library.

"It had the same effect on me the first time I saw it," Dinning said, wading up behind her. "It's like looking into the past ... a past that's been left completely intact in this time warp of a place."

"It's beautiful!" Sam exclaimed. "It's just as I pictured it, Professor. Do you think we can ..."

"Hey ... a little help here."

Dinning and Sam turned to see Hamilton holding Dana up in the water. She was shaking violently.

"Shit!" Dawson exclaimed. "We have to get her out of the water ... now!" He dove through the reeds and took her in his arms before wading up onto the grassy bank with the others right behind him.

"You know this place better than anyone, Professor," Dawson said, rubbing Dana's thin arms. "We have to warm her up ... and we need to do it now."

Dinning popped his head up above the grass and peered across the road at the library. The front doors and all the windows were closed, but that was to be expected in the rain. He continued watching. The area looked deserted.

Had everyone stayed home because of the rain, or had they fled the area because of the soldiers in the jungle?

Either way, they had to get Dana inside. Standing erect, Dinning started walking across the red dirt road toward the building.

"What in the hell does he think he's doing?" Dawson said.

"He's going to check out the library," Sam answered. "I just hope that none of our little green-eyed friends are waiting for him."

John Lyman

CHAPTER 46

Pushing through the unlocked doors, Dinning walked into the silent lobby of the old Yangambi Library. The pungent smell of mildew hung in the air as he peered down a darkened hallway and listened for the sound of anyone opening the closed windows upstairs; something they always did in the tropics when the rain stopped. But there was only silence against the sound of dripping water outside.

Stepping back through the open front doors, he motioned to the others. Dawson made a quick check of the tree line before slinging Dana over his shoulder and sprinting for the building with Sam and Hamilton right behind him.

As soon as he entered the building, Dawson stopped to let his eyes follow the curving wooden staircase to the floor above. "Where should we take her?"

"There's a couch in one of the back offices," Dinning said. "I'll see if I can find some blankets." Looking down at Dana hanging motionless like an overtired child in Dawson's arms, he saw that her eyes were closed and her lips were still blue. Even though they were out of the water and the temperature outside hovered in the eighty's, she was still locked in the grip of full-blown hypothermia. They had to do something, and they had to do it fast. If they couldn't find some blankets they would have to build a fire—and that meant going back outside.

With their attention on Dana, the others ignored the fact that they were also shivering in their wet clothes and began tearing through the unlit building, pulling open drawers and peering into dark corners in a futile search for objects of warmth in an equatorial library. Returning to the lobby, Dinning and Hamilton stared at each other helplessly until they heard Sam shout and looked up to see her running down the stairs with an armful of curtains she had just yanked from a second-story window.

An hour later they were all gathered together in one of the back offices on the first floor, watching Dinning make tea on Musa's little propane burner. Wrapped in curtains, Dana's normal paleness had returned and she was sitting up taking sips of hot tea.

Peering from the edge of the window, Dawson looked for movement in the jungle as the others sat on the floor behind him, talking quietly.

"What do you think happened to Brooks and the others?" Hamilton asked Dinning.

"I wish I knew."

"We'll know soon enough," Sam added. "If they survived that firefight they'll probably show up here." She gazed past Dawson at the setting sun. "At least now that it's getting dark we'll be able to spot those glowing green eyes a lot easier."

"Then what?" Hamilton asked. "What if we do see them coming out of the jungle over there? Are we supposed to just hide in here and hope they go away?"

Dawson turned from the window. "You might have a point there. What about your African friend, Dr. Dinning?"

"Musa? He lives in a little house at the end of jungle path between here and the airport."

"Hmm. Might be a little safer. They wouldn't think of looking for us there."

"No. We can't put him and his family at risk like that."

"What about the airport itself?" Hamilton asked. "First plane that lands, we're on it."

Samantha stood and let her arms fall against her sides. "Well, while you guys figure out what we're going to do, I think someone should be upstairs watching the other side of the jungle. I'll go first." Without waiting for a reply, she walked out into the hallway and up the wooden stairs before passing into the darkened research area of the library. Choosing a tall window on the opposite side of the building, she settled in to begin her watch. The sun had finally dipped below the horizon, and a large crescent moon was rising over the deep green, turning the jungle blue.

The little chirps and calls coming from the trees seemed familiar to her now, and she could smell the wet jungle and the smoke drifting from fires burning miles away. Leaning from the open window, she inhaled the aroma again and glanced down at the ground. Two green circles were staring up at her.

She wanted to scream, but instead she pushed down her fear and slowly backed into the shadows.

How many were out there?

Sam's heart was racing as she took off running through the canyons of books and flew down the stairs into the hallway before flinging herself into the back office. The first thing she saw was Dawson. His eyes were wide open, and he was sitting on the floor with his feet straight out and his hands resting palms up on the floor. And there was blood—blood that looked black in the moonlight, running down the front of his body armor. With her heart still pounding, she inched closer. Dawson's throat had been slit.

Backing away, she felt someone behind her and swirled around. No one was there, and for the first time she realized the others were gone. She turned back to the dark room only to be met by Dawson's death stare again.

They were gone. Just like that. The green eyes had killed Dawson and taken her friends. Samantha Adams from Port Aransas, Texas was all alone in the deep green.

John Lyman

CHAPTER 47

Sam continued looking into the dark room with a feeling of total and utter helplessness. She had never felt this kind of emptiness before, even when she had been drifting alone at sea. At least the ocean was familiar to her, but this was something else. There was an intense sense of isolation in this place. It was omnipresent. She was in Africa. She was in the Congo. And she was alone.

She slid down the wall and looked across the room at Dawson. Big, strong, kind-hearted Dawson. He had been a good man, and they had killed him. For what? Some stupid gene! It was only a matter of time now, because she was all alone in a jungle full of green-eyed killers.

But why was she alone?

Something in Sam clicked. She felt angry. It was welling up inside her, yanking her back from the precipice of surrender. Instead of dwelling on defeat, she was beginning to think analytically again.

If they didn't get me ... that means they don't know I'm in here.

But what about the green eyes that had looked up at her from the darkness below the window? He must have seen her. Maybe he was still outside, just waiting for her to walk out. Or maybe old green-eyes himself was standing just a few feet away right now, beyond the open doorway.

She didn't care anymore. She had taken on the thousand-yard stare, and she was moving on instinct. Taking a deep breath, she braced herself and edged to the door before moving out into the hallway. No one was there. She peered into the musty gloom of the library. Nothing but shadows. She wanted out of there. She wanted to be down by the river away from the smell of mildew and blood. It seemed safer out there for some reason.

Glancing back into the office, she wondered what one of the Special Ops guys would do right now. She looked down at Dawson's body. His eyes were still open. Kneeling next to him, she gently closed them before

271

carefully removing his blood-stained body armor and taking his web belt and knife. Leaning forward, she kissed him on the forehead and started to back away, but something she saw stopped her. She was looking at the outline of Dawson's gun. It was protruding from beneath one of his outstretched legs—almost invisible, because the camouflage paint scheme matched the camo pattern of his uniform.

Retrieving the gun, Sam sat under the window with the moonlight streaming over her shoulder and turned the weapon over in her hands. The only military weapon she had ever fired was Brian's old, semi-automatic AR-15. He had taken her to an indoor shooting range one day, but she hadn't really enjoyed it. She had never seen the point in paying to shoot guns in a cinder-block building all morning when she could be out on her sailboat, watching the bow cleave through the blue water with the wind in her hair.

Running her hand over the weapon, she realized this was no AR-15. She had seen several of the SEALs carrying these short weapons with the long silencers, variously referring to them as *HKs* or *MP7s*. She had overheard Brooks telling Dinning back in the clearing that their short weapons were actually hybrid crossovers between assault rifles and sub machine guns—easy to use in close combat situations with lots of firepower.

Good, she thought. That meant the gun held lots of bullets, and she had seen some of the men firing them like machine guns when they had been advancing on the jungle back by the river.

Flipping it over, she found the selector switch. There were three settings. Safety, semi-auto, and full-auto. She flipped it to the semi-auto position so it would shoot like the AR-15 at the range. She couldn't afford to use up all her ammo in a single automatic burst against the green eyes. One shot at a time was all she needed for now.

Lifting up to peer over the window sill, she looked out over the jungle glowing blue in the moonlight. It was magical-looking. The outline of the trees against the moonlit sky, and the way the river glistened below. It looked more like a twinkling digital reproduction than something real.

She was just turning away when something in the jungle caught her eye. In the distance, on the other side of the old station's ruins, there was a shaft of red light reflecting against the bottom of the leafy canopy above. And there was something else—something dark rising in the light.

It was like looking through a gossamer screen at a shadow puppet show. Sam watched, transfixed, until slowly, the red light began squeezing out, becoming smaller until finally the area was wrapped in total darkness again.

What had she just seen?

It had to be the green eyes! This was their jungle, and they moved through it with impunity. Brooks and his men had walked right into a hornet's nest the minute they stepped off the plane, and they had probably paid the ultimate price while she and the others had escaped into the river. Dana had been right. They were living in a nightmare, and now the nightmare belonged to her alone.

Clutching Dawson's weapon, she moved out into the hallway and made her way to the back of the library. A back door was swinging open where the green eyes had probably left with her friends. She could feel them out there, watching the doors. Doubling back into the main section of the library, she walked past empty tables reserved for researchers to a window on the opposite side of the building. Standing off to the side, she waited.

It reminded her of the time she spent catching bait. You had to watch the water for signs that a school of tiny fish was moving toward you before you threw the net. It was the same with the jungle, only here she was looking for little circles of green light in the thick foliage, and the gun in her hands was her new net.

She stayed there for almost an hour, watching, but an inner voice kept telling her to leave. Finally, she opened the window and dropped to the ground outside. Clutching the short weapon in her hands, she moved along the side toward the front of the building, looking for moving shadows and glowing circles in the moonlight. Taking a deep breath, she stepped around the corner by the entrance and pointed her weapon at the front doors. No green eyes. Looking over her shoulder, she sprinted across the road into the waist-high grass.

Where were all the people that lived around the old station?

Had the green eyes done something to them too? Samantha's mind was filled with questions as she lay there, staring up at the stars. For a second she thought she heard voices, but the wind carried them off. Looking to her right, her fingers tightened on the trigger and she held her breath. Two green eyes were coming down the dirt road in front of the library. Their eyes were glowing even brighter in the moonlight as they walked right past her, stopping for a moment to sniff the air before turning up an overgrown street and heading off into the ruins.

Is that where they had taken her friends? There was no way she was leaving anyone behind with the green eyes. Even if they were all dead she had to make sure before she tried to make it to … to where? The airport?

Glancing toward the tree line across the ruins from the library, she felt lost and confused. She thought about the light in the jungle. What was it about that faint red light she had just seen? There was something odd about it. In fact, there was something odd about everything in this place.

She wasn't staying there any longer than she had to. Looking at the hill rising behind the old station, she decided to make it to the top and wait for daylight to see if she could spot her friends. After checking for more green eyes, she ran across the road into the ruins. She headed west, away from the library, weaving around the empty shells of crumbling buildings toward the tree line that ran up the hill on the opposite side of the ruin-filled clearing.

As soon as she reached the tree line, she began moving uphill in a crouch. By staying close to the trees, she hoped the jungle would swallow her moonlit outline. Off to her right, the ruins rising in the wavering brown grass looked even more ghostly in the moonlight as she stepped on something that slithered away.

The SEALs had warned her of puff adders in the area. How had she forgotten about that? This was Africa, after all, and there were other things in the deep green besides green-eyed men that could snatch her life away in an instant. She would have to be doubly cautious now.

Thinking of Brooks and the other men, she glanced back across the ruins to check the library one final time. A chill ran down her spine when she saw a pair of fluorescing green eyes peering from one of the upper windows.

How long had they been there?

These things didn't look or act human, and if they had been genetically altered, she had no idea what kind of new abilities they might possess. Maybe they could see in the dark, or maybe they could even smell her, like an animal. All she knew about them at this point was that they were expert killers, and they were everywhere. Taking a deep breath, Sam followed the rising terrain with her eyes. It would be a miracle if she made it to the top of the hill without being seen.

She began climbing again but stopped when she heard something moving in the jungle. She took another step. The jungle rustled. She stopped. It stopped. Whatever it was seemed to be pacing her. Slowly, she moved away from the tree line. The risk of being spotted out in the open was greater, but it was better than being stalked by some invisible creature that lived in the jungle. At least out here she had the old buildings for cover.

The top of the hill was at least a mile away, and the gradual incline through the ruins had provided most of the old buildings with an unobstructed view of the river below. The streets that crisscrossed the residential section of the old station were now only outlines on the ground. Years of rain and mud and wind had helped Nature reclaim that which had once been hers, and jungle vines twisted through the empty window frames of the once magnificent villas that dotted the landscape.

Sam noticed right away that many of the old homes were still relatively intact, while others had either been looted for building material or had burned to the ground. Avoiding the open streets, she stayed close to the buildings, moving along the outer walls. In the shadows next to one of the villas, she stopped for a moment to peer through a window. Surprisingly, there was still furniture inside. But everything was covered in mildew, including the pictures on the splotchy walls. She crept past the front steps, looking through the dark entryway before moving across the street to the next block.

Up ahead, she could see the outline of a much larger building … bigger than the library. She moved even more cautiously now with the short gun tucked under her arm, pointing forward so that all she had to do was pull the trigger if she turned and saw something she didn't like. The villas she was walking by now seemed older somehow as she made her way to the end of the block and peered through the front door of the last house.

Sam froze. A green-eyed soldier was sitting on the living room floor, playing with a child's toy. Sam slowly backed away and started running up the street as fast as she could away from the freak show behind her. She kept running until it felt like her lungs were going to explode, stopping only when she reached the base of what had once been a sloping lawn.

Looking up, she saw she was standing below the large building she had seen from a distance. It had obviously been built on an elevated rise so that it overlooked everything around it—the perfect place to look for

275

green eyes. Climbing over a fallen chain-link fence, she walked up the slight incline and stopped to look back out over the ruins. The outlines of the streets radiated outward from where she was standing. Whatever this place was, it had obviously been the focus of some kind of activity for the people who had lived here.

Continuing up the incline, she stopped again when she found herself teetering at the tiled edge of a large, rectangular hole in the ground. The sides looked smooth. They were almost white, and at the bottom, puddles of black water reflected in the moonlight. Puzzled, she looked around until her eyes fell on an obvious diving board on the opposite side. She was standing next to a swimming pool!

What the hell was this place?

Skirting the pool, Sam kept moving until she reached the large, peak-roofed building with a wide veranda overlooking the grounds of the old station. Outdoor tables warped by humidity lay on their sides, and shards of broken glass glistened in the moonlight where a wall of floor-to-ceiling windows had once provided those inside with an unobstructed view of the deep green and the river below.

Stepping through one of the tall metal window frames, she moved across a squishy carpet covered in green fuzz, passing an obvious bar into a room littered with broken furniture and an old wooden phone booth. A wide stairway across the room descended into total darkness, and to her right, moonlight was streaming through the open doorframe of what had once been the main entrance.

Feeling uncomfortable in the dark interior, Sam walked through the empty door frame and stood on the wide front veranda to take in a deep breath of humid air. She looked up at the hill rising to the north and checked the area off to her left. The edge of the jungle was only about twenty yards away.

Jungle or ruins. The jungle probably held things she didn't even want to think about, but the ruins were giving her the creeps. She was still searching for a decision when she heard the voices. They were coming from the edge of the jungle, and they were moving closer.

Backing up toward the entrance, she darted back inside just as a pair of green eyes stepped from the deep green and headed straight for the building. Inside the littered bar room, Sam's heart was racing. The green eyes would be coming through the open doorway any moment. She turned to run back out by the pool. Another green eye was just standing outside in the grass, looking down at the river.

Trying to blend into the shadows, Sam looked across the room to the stairway descending into darkness. She had to think! She didn't have a flashlight ... or did she? Glancing down, she saw a light attached to the stock of the gun.

But how to turn it on?

She would have to figure it out later, because time had run out. Taking a deep breath, Sam flew across the room and down the stairs. With one hand on the handrail, she hit the landing and continued down into total blackness. Inching forward, she was forced to hold her hands out in front of her until she touched something metallic and pushed. The door swung inward.

Passing into another area of total darkness, she began running her hands over the outside of the plastic stock next to the side-mounted light. She felt a button and pushed. A red laser beam pierced the darkness. She hit the button again and turned it off before moving her fingers to a tab at the back of the light. Flipping it up with her thumb she found another button and pushed.

A bright, white beam shot down a long strip of wooden flooring. Shining the light around, her mind finally grasped what she was looking at. She was standing in a bowling alley! Following the beam of light to the far end of a lane, she saw that the bowling pins were still standing. They had been waiting after all these years for the roll of the next ball—a ball that had never come.

She heard voices again.

Shit! They were coming down the stairs!

Shining the light behind her, she spotted a faded soda fountain and ducked behind it, turning off the light just before the green eyes walked in. She crouched low, wondering if they had seen her. Were they sniffing her out? Sam wanted to jump up and spray the room with bullets, but she held her position, listening to the distant hum of machinery. Suddenly, all the lights came on and she heard the green eyes open and close a door. The lights went back out again.

Sam was shaken. What in the hell were the green eyes doing, and where had they just gone? She had to get out of there. Flicking the light on, she bolted through the door at the bottom of the stairs and climbed back up to the floor above.

Dousing the light again, she moved along the walls. The green-eyed soldier who had been standing outside staring at the river was now gone, but it didn't matter. They seemed to be everywhere as she made her way outside through the front entrance and began running as fast as she could away from the building.

A bright white light flashed behind her. Sam froze. She could see her elongated shadow projected against the tall grass. Diving for the ground, she lay there with her heart pounding, knowing that she had just been fully illuminated. She heard voices again.

They were coming for her!

Samantha began crawling as fast as she could, pushing wet earth and leaves ahead of her as she wriggled up under a thick clump of bushes. Lifting her eyes, she could hear her own breathing as she looked back, but all she could see was a pair of jungle boots at the top of the veranda steps. Using her forearms, she pulled herself forward to see better.

And then she saw him. He was standing in the doorway. He was shorter than the others, but there was something different about him. Sam squinted. *His eyes weren't glowing green!*

Stepping into the moonlight, the man looked normal, but she could only see him in silhouette as he turned and pulled something from his pocket. Moments later he flicked a lighter, illuminating his snow-white hair as he lit the pipe in his mouth. For a few minutes he paced the veranda, smoking and looking out over the ruins, until two green eyes walked from the building and stood behind him.

Sam actually felt fear for the man, but after watching him interact with the two, it quickly became apparent that it was the green eyes who were afraid. They almost cowered in his presence, and she could hear the white-haired man shouting something to them about *Brooks* and the *SEALs* and *that girl*, until finally they walked back inside.

Silently, Sam inched back under the bushes. She couldn't believe her luck. The green eyes had been living in the ruins all along, and it appeared that she had just stumbled into their hiding place!

She had to tell Brooks!

Sam choked with the memory. There was no more Brooks—no more Dawson—no more anyone except for maybe her friends. She felt a tear run down her cheek as she rolled over on her back and stared up through the dark foliage. She was wondering if she should try to make a break for it when she noticed the leaves above her moving. She thought about the puff adder, and as she continued staring into the moving foliage, the branches parted right above her head. Squinting against the falling debris, she saw two pairs of glowing green eyes staring down at her!

Sam screamed.

John Lyman

CHAPTER 48

Sam felt the green eyes dragging her by her boots. Closing her eyes against the swirling debris, she clawed at the moist earth beneath the bushes, feeling for Dawson's weapon.

She could smell them before she could see them, and as soon as her head and shoulders were free, she opened her eyes to see the two green-eyed soldiers grinning down at her with yellowed teeth. With her hands still stretched over her head in the bushes, Sam yanked the weapon free and opened fire at point blank range. Blood splattered her face and clothes as their bodies thudded to the ground right beside her. Instantly, she was on her feet and running. She ran straight for the jungle and dove into the deep green just as dozens of green eyes erupted like ants from the long building.

As soon as Sam felt the jungle's moist embrace, she stopped and stood still—listening—looking for more green circles floating nearby. But there was nothing but darkness. She turned back. The sight that greeted her made her blood run cold. She could see green eyes running from the old library down by the river, and there were others racing down the hill to the north—the very hill she had been heading for. They were everywhere.

Sam took a few deep breaths and turned her attention back to the large building and the area around it. She had to stay focused on the immediate threats. She saw the white-haired man again, standing outside. She could see him clearly now in the moonlight, surrounded by green eyes. Holding his pipe, he walked over to the bodies of the two green eyes and stared down at them for a moment before looking out over the ruins. Slowly he turned, and like a man who had just found true north on his compass, he pointed to the jungle. A wall of green eyes began heading in her direction.

Sam was beyond panic when she raised her weapon and switched it to full-auto.

Come to mama you green-eyed bastards!

"Not yet," a voice whispered close to her ear.

Sam almost lost it. She had come to know that voice well. It was Brooks. As soon as she saw his face a deep sob rose in her throat, forcing her to bury her forehead against his chest.

"It's okay, Samantha. You're not alone anymore." He looked out at the bodies of the two green eyes on the ground. "But it looks like you were doing pretty well on your own before we showed up. We've been watching ... but so have they. They can see in the dark, and they can sense you if they get close enough."

"I knew it!" Sam lifted her head and looked back out at the wall of advancing green eyes. "Why don't we shoot?"

"Because there are more of them behind us. The lieutenant is watching our backs, but as long as we stay hidden and they don't get close enough to sense us, we should be okay. Otherwise, you'll get your chance to go full-auto."

"How did you know what I was about to do?"

"I heard the click."

"Where's everyone else?" she whispered.

"Gone." Brooks kept his eyes focused straight ahead. "Ten of us survived the initial firefight. They started taking us out one-by-one while we were making our way here through the jungle, until finally we figured out they could see in the dark. Seaborne and I are the only ones that made it."

Sam studied the commander's fatigued expression before checking the progress of the green eyes. They were making a slow, tactical advance toward the jungle off to their left.

"Looks like you spooked them," Brooks said. "Just so you know, we had our sights on those two green eyes but you beat us to the punch. Nice shooting."

"Aren't you going to ask me about Dawson?"

"I knew he was dead the moment I saw you with his MK7. He was a good man. What about the others?"

"I don't know ... the green eyes took them, but I think I just stumbled into their nest or whatever. Everyone's been looking in the jungle, but they've been hiding in the ruins this entire time."

Brooks peered into the fading moonlight. "That big building out there?"

Sam nodded. "I think it used to be some kind of recreation center. There's even a bowling alley in the basement. I saw an old guy with white hair too. He must be the NATO scientist you were talking about. His eyes are normal, and he tells the green eyes what to do."

"Did I hear you say you made it down into the basement of that place?"

"Yeah ... until a couple of green eyes showed up and all the lights came on. They went through a door and the lights went out again ... and I could hear noise beneath the floor. It sounded like a generator running. There must be another level down there. I went through the entire building and only saw two green-eyed soldiers, but they came pouring out of there like ants when I opened fire on their buddies."

Brooks leaned forward to get a better look. "They're definitely protecting that building for some reason. If there is another level beneath the basement, that could be where your friends are."

"What are we going to do?"

"We're going in to look for them."

"Good, because I wasn't leaving without them."

"Somehow I didn't think you would." Brooks signaled Seaborne, who jogged over from his hiding place. "See anything?"

"Nothing, sir."

"I forgot to mention I saw a weird red light in the jungle earlier," Sam added. "Was that you guys?"

"Wasn't us," Brooks said. "Must have been the green eyes. How much ammo do you have?"

"I'm not sure. I only fired a couple of shots."

Brooks checked the clip in Sam's weapon. "It's almost full." Reaching into his combat vest, he pulled out another. "Here, take this. There's forty more rounds in there."

"What are you thinking, Commander?" Sam asked.

"I'm thinking you fight just as well as any of the Special Forces operators I know ... maybe better. Can't have you running out of ammo now, can we?"

Sam gave him a tired smile and shoved the clip in a side pocket of her camo pants.

John Lyman

CHAPTER 49

For the next several hours, the three watched the green eyes coming and going from the strange building. They seemed to travel alone or in pairs, and with the moon fading over the distant hills, Lieutenant Chris Seaborne was getting restless. "We're never getting in there ... at least not tonight. The green eyes are still too stirred up after two of their own just got taken out on their front doorstep, and it will be getting light soon."

Brooks lifted his head and rubbed his eyes. "You're probably right, Lieutenant. They're waiting for us inside, and others are undoubtedly watching from some of the other buildings. We're going to have to find a place to hole up for awhile until things settle down." Brooks rolled over and offered Sam some water from his hydration backpack before taking a few sips. "Where did you say you saw that light?"

Sam pointed to the south. "It was in the jungle ... about half-way between here and the river."

"And it wasn't pointed at anything?"

"No ... it just sort of made the trees glow red for a few minutes. There was a shadow, and it didn't just go out all of a sudden like most lights do. It got smaller."

"Smaller?"

"Yeah, like it was slowly being covered."

"Hmm ... interesting. We might as well start moving that way since we obviously aren't going anywhere else at the moment."

"Wouldn't it be better if we made our way to higher ground, sir?" Seaborne asked.

"The green eyes are up there too," Sam said quickly. "They lit up like Christmas trees when the others started pouring out of the building."

Brooks nodded. "Occupying the high ground is one of the oldest military tactics in the book. They have an unobstructed view of the entire station from up there, which means we'll have to divert their attention before we make a run for that building. Until then, we stay in the jungle where we can hide. At least we have them on the defensive now, which will make it easier for us to move around out here while they stay a little closer to home."

Seaborne made a final check of the area behind them before they moved off through the underbrush, feeling their way downhill toward the river. Every few minutes Brooks would stop to judge their progress by moving close to the edge of the jungle to look out at the ruins. He spotted a few green eyes peering from some of the vacant window frames, but the others that had been swarming the area earlier had disappeared somewhere.

The three had almost made it to the half-way point when they saw it. The jungle canopy was glowing red straight ahead. Looking around for green eyes, they dove for the ground.

"What the hell is that, Skipper?" Seaborne whispered.

"You got me."

Lying on their stomachs, they watched a diffuse beam of smoky red light rising from the ground, painting the canopy above. They heard a hum and felt a rumble. A black satellite dish was rising through the eerie red light on a telescoping metal shaft. It continued to rise, piercing the canopy above before disappearing from sight.

"No way!" Seaborne whispered excitedly. "They're raising a satellite dish above the canopy so they can acquire a signal. They're communicating with someone, sir!"

They continued to watch as the projected red light began to narrow just as Sam had described—growing thinner until it disappeared completely.

"You two cover me while I find out where that thing is coming from." Brooks adjusted his night-vision goggles and scanned the area before he started crawling. He almost ran over it. Painted to match the fern-covered ground, he was staring down at a concrete slab that was almost flush with the jungle floor. Lifting up on his elbows, he noticed that the telescoping metal shaft extended from an opening in the center of a large circular cover. He gave it a light rap with his knuckles. It was metal.

Making a quick sweep of the area, Brooks crawled back. "Looks like some kind of communications bunker."

286

"So what's with that weird red light?" Sam asked.

"Looks like battle lighting … like on the bridge of a warship. It's harder to see and it protects your night vision. I can think of only one reason for that kind of lighting in a place like this. Someone is down there … someone who doesn't want to be noticed. I believe we're sitting on top of a much larger complex that extends out from under that large building, and we just found their Achilles heel."

Sam's eyes widened. "You think that's a way in?"

"Maybe. It's also possible the dish is being raised from an area that's sealed off from the main complex, but we won't know until we go down there."

"Crap!" Seaborne exclaimed. "What about motion detectors and infrared sensors? If that's another way in, they're bound to have this area wired."

"None of that stuff works too well in the jungle, Lieutenant. Too many creepy crawlies set off the alarms. Besides, whoever's running this show doesn't need to plant a lot of high-tech gadgets out here. He has a bunch of green-eyed zombies that can see in the dark and sense our presence instead. Except for the obvious side effects, they're perfect soldiers."

Seaborne remained thoughtful.

"What's on your mind, Lieutenant?" Brooks said. "Spit it out."

"I don't know, sir. This whole thing just seems wrong for some reason. Those men were just like us once. The human part of them is still in there somewhere."

Right away Brooks sensed the young officer's moral dilemma. "What's your primary mission, Seaborne?"

"To stay alive, sir."

"That's right. To stay alive. A dead SEAL can't fight. If you really think those things out there are still like us, then walk out of the jungle right now and say hello to one of them."

"You know what I mean, sir. I keep thinking that could be us out there even though all I want to do is kill every last one of them for what they did to our friends. It's just this place. It's weirding me out … that's all."

"Well you'd better get un-weirded real quick, Lieutenant. Because as soon as that metal cover slides back open to retrieve that dish, we're going inside."

CHAPTER 50

While Brooks and Seaborne kept watch, Sam crept to the edge of the jungle to look for green eyes approaching from the ruins, but the only thing moving was the wide river below, glistening in the moonlight. She looked back at the large building, dark and silent now. The green eyes had obviously retreated to their hiding places.

Lying flat on the ground, she felt a slight vibration. The leaves around her were turning red. She looked toward the canopy. The beam of light was back, and Brooks was waving frantically to her as he and Seaborne took off running. The cover was open again, and the dish was already coming back down.

Sam sprinted across the clearing just as Brooks and Seaborne disappeared through the wide opening. Dropping to her knees, she peered into the red gloom and saw both men climbing down some built-in steel rungs set into the wall of a concrete shaft. She looked up. The satellite dish was almost on top of her as she stepped through the opening and followed them down.

As soon as she reached the bottom she blinked in the red light. Brooks was wiping his knife on his pants, and one of the green eyes was lying dead on the floor by an overturned chair, a widening pool of blood spreading from the slash in his neck.

In the reddish gloom, she saw they were standing in a concrete room that contained the blended electronics from two vastly different eras. To her right, behind a black metal screen, she saw a stack of dusty radio equipment—the kind with black-and-white dials and old vacuum tubes. But sitting on a curved desk against the opposite wall, where the green-eyed soldier had been sitting, there were three computer screens glowing in the red light.

Above their heads, the two halves of the metal cover slid together with a metallic click. No one had to say that their way back out was now sealed, and that the dead soldier lying on the floor was the only one who knew how to open it again.

Walking over to the desk with the computer screens, Brooks used a blood-splattered mouse to scroll through the last message received. The screen was filled with hieroglyphic-like symbols.

"What is all that?" Sam asked.

"It's encrypted, but I can still tell where it was sent from." Brooks straightened and looked at Seaborne. "This was relayed through a JSOC satellite."

"JSOC! You're shitting me! Are you sure, sir?"

"Positive." Brooks chewed on his lower lip while he continued to stare at the screen. "What the hell is going on here?"

"I don't know, sir, but those things seem to know when one of their own has been killed. We need to move out of here … now. I'll take point."

The tight concrete space held a single metal door with rusty hinges, making it squeak when Seaborne cracked it open. They were at the end of a musty-smelling concrete passage that made a ninety degree turn to the right at the end.

Brooks looked back at Sam. "Stay close, and do what we do. If one of us shoots at something, the other two are responsible for the sides and the rear unless it's a full-on frontal engagement. Then we all open up."

Sam nodded back as they slipped into the passage. The two advancing SEALs were holding their weapons at eye level, so Sam followed suit as they made their way to the dead end and rounded the corner. Three short steps led up to another passage that continued on, but as soon as Seaborne took the first step he quickly backed around the corner when he saw one of the green eyes step from an open side door.

Using hand signals to tell Brooks there was a single hostile standing next to a doorway, he pulled a small mirror from his pocket and slowly extended it around the corner. The soldier was locking the door when his green eyes flashed and he tilted his head in their direction, sniffing the air. Seaborne readied his silenced weapon. Green eyes took a step toward them and stopped. He looked confused and sniffed the air once more, then turned away and walked through a door at the far end of the passage. As soon as he was gone, Seaborne stowed the mirror and waved them on.

The second passageway was shorter than the first, but Brooks stopped them when they came to the locked door. "I want to see what's in there before we go any farther."

"He locked it, sir."

"That's a good reason to look inside."

Without having to be told, Seaborne moved to the closed door at the end of the passage to cover Brooks while he picked the lock. As soon as he opened the door the smell hit them. The room was completely dark, so Brooks and Sam switched their gun lights on before moving inside. The rust-colored walls were covered with dark splotches of mold, and sitting in a cramped, foul-smelling cage, an old black man squinted up at them in the light.

Sam stopped. "Oh my God! What the hell is this?" She could feel the hair rising on the back of her neck as she and Brooks shined their lights around the room. Except for the single cage and a curled hose on the wall, it was empty.

Brooks knelt down next to the cage. The old man's eyes were normal, but they fluttered as he leaned his head against the bars. His clothes were wet and he was shivering, and for the first time Sam noticed the floor around them was also wet. The green-eyed soldier had obviously just finished hosing the filthy cage out and left the poor man to shiver in the darkness.

"Do you speak English?"Brooks asked.

The man tried to speak but the shivering was too intense.

"The hell with this!" Sam said too loudly. "Let's get him out of there!"

Looking back up at her, Brooks lifted the lock. It was still open. The old man was so weak the green eyes had stopped bothering to lock his cage. Reaching inside, they lifted him out onto the floor. Sam tried to help him straighten his legs while Brooks retrieved a small brown package from his backpack.

"What's that?"

"Space blanket. Folds up the size of a pack of cigarettes. Never leave home without one."

The old man gazed up at Sam as she and Brooks wrapped the foil-like Mylar blanket around him. "Musa," he said.

"What did you say?"

"My name ... Musa."

291

"Were taking you out of here, Musa."

"The lib … the library."

"The library? What about the library?"

"The bones." Musa seemed to fade, his head dropping down on his chest.

"He's not making any sense," Brooks snapped. "And you shouldn't have told him we were taking him with us."

"We can't just leave him here!"

Brooks looked back toward the passage outside. "Shit! I didn't count on rescuing anyone this soon. How do we know he doesn't work for the green eyes?"

"If he does he has one hell of a workman's comp case against them," Sam shot back. "I'm not leaving here without him. They're keeping him alive for a reason. That means Dinning and the others are probably down here somewhere too."

At the mention of Dinning's name, Musa lifted his head and gazed into her eyes. "Is Peter here?"

"You know the Professor?"

Musa nodded before his head dropped again.

"There you go," Sam said, lifting her face to Brooks. "I believe you guys call it intel, but I call it information. This man knows the Professor, and I think he's trying to tell us something."

Another wave of shivers coursed through Musa's body.

"Can you stand?" Sam asked.

Musa shook his head with a look of resignation.

"Unless you plan on carrying him, we can't take him with us," Brooks said. "We'll come back for him later … I promise."

"And I promise I'll be waiting here with him."

Brooks ran a hand over his face and through his hair before looking back at Sam with fire in his eyes. "Sometimes I wish I could threaten you with a court martial."

"Well you can't, so what's it going to be?" Sam waited. "Just think of him as a wounded SEAL."

With an arm the size of Sam's thigh, Brooks leaned down and picked Musa off the floor, slinging him over his shoulder with one swift motion. "Let's go."

"Thank you, Steve."

Brooks blinked back at her. It was the first time Samantha had ever called him by his first name. Together, they stepped out into the passageway.

Looking over his shoulder, Seaborne spotted Musa's head protruding from the open end of the reflective silver blanket draped over Brooks' shoulder. "Who's that?"

"An old man they were keeping locked in a cage. Still think the green eyes are like us, Lieutenant?"

Seaborne's eyes narrowed. "No, sir. The one we just saw was sniffing the air … like an animal. He was definitely sensing something. I just checked to see what's on the other side this door. There's a bare concrete hallway that bends to the left. I thought it was a culvert until I saw the linoleum floor."

"Another hallway? What a surprise," Sam said. "This place is starting to feel like a giant maze."

Musa wiggled beneath the blanket, trying to raise his head. "The lab …"

Sam leaned closer. "The what?"

Musa's weak voice was barely audible. "The lab … end of the hallway … be careful."

"Brooks and Seaborne exchanged glances. "Makes sense," Brooks said. "The professor told me he thought there had to be a lab somewhere close because of some of the genetic stuff they might be doing here. Now that I think of it, the green eyes had to be down here the whole time his team was collecting DNA samples from the jungle up above."

"But if that NATO guy was so worried Dinning and his team had discovered the gene, why didn't he just tell the green eyes to kill them right then and toss their bodies in the river?" Sam wondered aloud. "No one would have ever known."

"Because this would have been the last place anyone saw them," Brooks countered. "And any search for the missing researchers would have meant even more people snooping around. That's the last thing these people wanted."

"So you think they waited until all the teams were back on the ship in Matadi to attack them so nothing could be traced back here to the old station?"

"That's my theory anyway," Brooks said. "Come on, let's see if there really is a lab down here."

293

Moving off down the concrete hallway, Brooks stopped before they reached the bend ahead and gently laid Musa on the floor against the wall. After giving him a few more sips of water, he unwrapped an energy bar and placed it in the old man's hand. "Here you go. Try to eat some of that while we take a look around. We'll be back for you in a few minutes." Brooks locked eyes with the old man and stood.

Sam tapped him on the shoulder. "What are you doing?"

"Trying to keep your friend here alive. There's a good possibility we could end up in a firefight in the next few minutes. We have to be free to move quickly."

"Okay ... you win. What do you want me to do?"

"The same thing I told you to do when we first came down here. Stay behind us, do what we do, and cover my rear."

Sam couldn't resist smiling as they raised their weapons in unison and moved around the bend to the left. Following the streaked gray wall, they could see bright light ahead. They slowed their pace—inching forward until the concrete ended. Their jaws dropped. What lay beyond looked like something out of a sci-fi movie.

They were looking out into a massive cavern that had been laboriously hollowed out of solid rock beneath the old station. A grated metal walkway extended around the entire perimeter ten feet above a white-tiled floor, and sealed off from the outside world by thick glass walls, an enormous underground lab filled the space. Everything was white. It glowed with a whiteness that stunned the senses. The glass walls were at least thirty feet high, and even the top of the immense structure was made from glass, making it look like a giant, glowing cube filled with the tools of science.

Sam squinted in the bright light. The lab she was looking at now varied wildly from the one she had seen in Houston. In the very center of the glassed-in space, she saw what appeared to be some sort of control room with large, green-tinted windows that angled out around the top. The concrete structure reminded Sam of an airport control tower, except this one was only twenty feet tall, and it was sitting underground in the middle of a lab the size of a hockey rink.

But there was something else none of them had ever seen before. Suspended ten feet above the floor, a large, round Plexiglas tunnel ran from the metal walkway through the lab's sealed environment to the windowed control room in the center.

"Wow!" Sam whispered excitedly. "Looks like a giant hamster cage without the wheel."

"Yeah ... funny," Brooks gray eyes were already taking in details of the area they were about to go into. "This place has a really weird vibe to it."

"A *weird vibe?*"

The big SEAL shrugged. "What can I say. There's just something different about it ... that's all."

Sam couldn't resist. "Well ... thanks for that psychic heads up, Commander."

Brooks frowned. Seaborne grinned.

Using his binoculars, Brooks took a closer look at the inside of the lab. A few people in clean suits could be seen working at various stations throughout, but there was no sign of Hamilton or Dinning as he had hoped.

He swiveled to look through the windows of the central control room, zooming in on a lighted console inside. Scanning to the right, his eyes searched for anything that looked familiar, until a window frame blocked his view and he jerked the binoculars to the right. A pair of green eyes were staring back at him, their emerald radiance reaching through the lens.

Yanking the binoculars away, Brooks waited for the alarm and the sound of running boots, but the only thing he heard was the drift of muffled voices coming from the lab. Slowly, he lifted the binoculars back up and refocused. He could plainly see two green-eyed soldiers sitting in the control room next to a white-haired man with his back to him.

Brooks' mind was running a hundred miles an hour, wondering if he had just spotted the man who held the answers to all their questions. He wanted to scream at them. *What are you people doing down here ... hidden from the world beneath the deep green?* Suddenly, the white-haired man turned in his seat and peered down into the lab through the large, tinted windows.

Brooks froze. A wave of fear washed over him—then confusion. He let the binoculars slip from his fingers on their short tether and began backing away, pushing the other two behind him until they were out of sight. Looking back over his shoulder, he slid down the streaked concrete wall and stared straight ahead, breathing heavily—a thin bead of sweat trickling down the side of his face.

Brooks' vacant expression spooked Seaborne. Brooks wasn't acting like Brooks. Seaborne raised his weapon and kept it pointed toward the end of the hallway. "What is it, Commander? What did you see?"

The young lieutenant waited, his attention divided between Brooks and the exit. But the big SEAL commander kept his eyes focused straight ahead; the veins in his forehead bulging, his jaw muscles working overtime.

Like a man who had just awakened from a fuzzy daydream, Brooks wiped away the sweat and looked at Samantha. "That white-haired guy you saw in front of the old recreation building."

Sam waited. "What about him?"

"He's not the missing NATO scientist. "

"He's not?" Sam glanced sideways at Seaborne. "Then who the hell is he?"

"He's my boss ... Admiral Nathan Bourdon ... JSOC's commanding officer. He's here now ... in that control room ... hanging out with the green eyes."

CHAPTER 51

Except for the sound of muffled voices inside the lab, the massive complex was locked in subdued silence when the trio wormed their way back to the end of the concrete hallway and looked out at the giant, glowing lab. Seaborne peered through his binoculars. "That's the admiral alright. Guess that answers the question of how they knew we were coming. What do you want to do, sir?"

Brooks' eyes narrowed at the sight. "I need to have a little chat with him, but with all this glass, we'll be exposed the moment we step out onto that metal walkway."

"No kidding, sir." Seaborne nodded. "Talk about your glass houses. Any guess as to why there's a clear tunnel running through the lab to that control room?"

"Contamination," Sam replied. "You have to go through a lengthy decontamination procedure before you can enter a lab like this. My guess is that tunnel is part of a sealed system so people can move back and forth between the outer walkway and the control room without contaminating the interior of the lab."

"But what the hell would they be controlling from there?"

"Not a clue. I catch bait for a living ... remember? I've only been in a lab like this once before, and it didn't look like a hamster cage." Sam paused, trying to take in the details of what she was looking at. "You see that big round door at the far end of the lab ... the one in the middle of that concrete wall?"

Seaborne looked closer. "Yeah, that's the only wall that's not made from glass."

"That's the entrance to the lab, and there has to be a decontamination area behind that door. That's where you shower and put on one of those white clean suits before going in." Sam glanced over at Brooks. "It's also where you go if you have to pee."

Brooks ignored her reference to their first meeting. His gaze was locked on the control room. "That's our target," he said to Seaborne.

"The lab, sir?"

"No, just the control room."

Seaborne could tell by the look on Brooks' face that he had reached a decision. "What's your plan?"

"Full-on frontal assault ... right down that freaking glass tunnel."

"You can't be serious, sir. That's suicide."

"Not if we catch them by surprise. We get as close as we can before we open fire on the two green eyes inside. I want the admiral alive." Brooks turned to Sam. "Are you up for this?"

"Full-auto?"

"Yep, you finally get your chance."

"What about Musa?"

"If we live, he lives. Tighten up that body armor, and stay right by my side when we go in ... got it?"

"Got it ... sir."

Brooks winked back at her before crawling out onto the walkway's rough steel grating. Staying low, they moved off to the right, glancing into the lab on their left as they continued around a corner and headed for the big Plexiglas tunnel. By the time they reached the tunnel entrance, they could already smell the green eyes.

Peering down the big glass tube, Brooks noticed that it had a slight downward slope that ended at the control room's open steel door. The open door meant they wouldn't have to blow their way in, but it also meant the green eyes could see them coming.

Directly behind them, a small, rocky alcove sheltered a concrete stairway that ascended to the floor above. Brooks made a mental note. If they were forced to retreat, anything that led up would be their best escape route out of there.

Samantha had fire in her eyes when Brooks looked back at her. "Remember," he whispered. "Right by my side!"

On the count of three, they stood as a group and raised their weapons to eye level before advancing through the tunnel. They were half-way to the door when the first green eye saw them and reached for his weapon, but Brooks dropped him with a single silenced shot. The other green eye dove for the door, but Sam hit him with a full-auto burst, knocking him back against an angled steel wall.

Ignoring a pistol lying within his reach, the admiral froze in place when he saw Brooks standing in the doorway, looking down at him with a look he had hoped he would never see.

"Hello, Admiral." Brooks' voice was icy cold.

The admiral turned slowly in his seat. "Are you going to shoot, Steve, or do I have time to explain?"

Brooks' weapon was inches from Bourdon's face. "I haven't made up my mind yet, sir. I just lost twenty-four of our best men to your little green-eyed freaks."

Slamming the steel door shut, Seaborne didn't hesitate. He moved around the commander and shoved the admiral to the floor before binding his hands behind his back.

Brooks felt like he was dreaming, but the smell coming from the green eyes told him this was real. "Where are the others?"

"What others are you referring to, Commander?"

"You know damn well who I'm talking about, Admiral!"

"Upstairs … on the floor above us," Bourdon said quickly. "And I can assure you they're perfectly safe."

Sam swiveled her weapon in his direction. "They'd better be."

Surprisingly, Bourdon smiled. "Two SEALs and a girl. Sounds like a romantic comedy."

"She just killed one of your green eyes, Admiral," Brooks said. "And she's pretty unpredictable. I'd be careful of the way you talk to her if I were you. Gag him."

Bourdon's eyes grew wide as Seaborne taped his mouth shut and they lifted him up into a chair. "What now, sir?"

"They might have tripped an alarm. Keep your eyes peeled."

While the two SEALs kept watch, Sam noticed that Bourdon kept glancing at the control panel from the corner of his eye. He had just been captured by one of the few men in the world he feared, and his future was anything but certain. But for some unknown reason, he seemed more concerned about the damned panel.

Sam knew right away that if she asked a man like Bourdon why he was so interested in something he would only feign ignorance, but she had to know. Trying not to be obvious, she watched the admiral's eyes and began running her hands over the control panel in an almost playful manner. Bourdon seemed uncomfortable at first, but when her hand passed over a red button beneath a protective plastic cover, his eyes practically flew out of his head. Moving her hand around the button, she continued watching. The admiral was sweating, but his pupils had returned to normal.

"The coast looks clear," Brooks said. "Let's prop these two green eyes up in chairs like they're just sleeping and get the hell out of here. I don't want to be trapped in a place with no back door if more of them show up."

Pushing Bourdon ahead of them through the door, they made their way up to the end of the sloping Plexiglas tunnel and stopped. Bourdon nodded toward the stairs in the alcove. They moved off, climbing to the floor above with their weapons pointed up. As soon as they reached the top of the stairs, they saw that the stairway continued up to the floor above through a concrete stairwell on their left, and to their right, a hallway with a red linoleum floor stretched off to a dead end.

The admiral nodded toward the hallway. It smelled like paper—like they were walking through an office building that reeked of bound volumes behind closed doors. A fluorescent light flickered and buzzed over their heads as they continued, looking ahead and behind them, until the admiral came to a plain wooden door and stopped.

Brooks backed Bourdon up against the door and placed the admiral's cuffed hands on the doorknob before stepping off to the side with his back against the concrete wall. "Open it, Admiral."

Bourdon twisted and the door swung open. Flicking the selector switch to full-auto, the commander raised his weapon and pushed the admiral ahead. Sam and Seaborne were right behind them, and as soon as they were all through the door, they froze. The space they had just entered looked nothing like they had been expecting. Instead of a drab office or another concrete room, they were looking at an elegant, wood-paneled space that resembled a corporate boardroom. From their padded leather chairs on opposite sides of a long, inlaid table, Dinning, Hamilton, and Dana were staring back at them.

CHAPTER 52

Fearing a trap, Sam kept her back to the wall while Seaborne made a final check of the hallway outside and closed the door.

"Sam!" Dana exclaimed. She struggled to stand on her thin legs, but the shackles on her wrists and ankles kept her pinned to her chair.

Brooks ripped the tape from the admiral's mouth. "Where's the key?"

"In my pocket, and you shouldn't have propped those two up in the control room like they were sleeping."

"Why? As a sign of respect? They don't even look human anymore, Admiral."

"No, you idiot. They don't sleep."

Brooks blinked back at him. "Why are you telling me this?"

"I have a lot to tell you, Commander."

Brooks studied Bourdon's eyes while he removed the key from his pocket and sat him in a chair at the table before releasing the others. Dinning and Dana both embraced Sam as soon as they were free, but Hamilton remained seated, rubbing his ankles and staring down the table at the admiral.

"Musa!" Sam blurted out. "He's still out there!"

Instantly, Brooks and Seaborne were by the door. "Stay here with your friends," Brooks said, "and watch the admiral like a hawk."

Before anyone could object, they were gone.

The two SEALs headed for the stairwell, moving back-to-back, their eyes sweeping the area around them as they descended into the alcove and stepped out onto the metal walkway surrounding the lab. They moved to their left, looking for signs of green eyes as they crept along the walkway's metal grating to the musty hallway where they had left Musa. Inching along the streaked wall, their hearts beat faster with each step, until finally they rounded the bend ahead.

301

Musa was sitting up. Like the stigma of a flower, he was sitting in the middle of his silver wrapping, gnawing on a half-eaten energy bar.

"Thank God!" Seaborne whispered.

Bending down, Brooks lifted the frail old man off the floor and gently laid him across his shoulder before they took off running for the lab. They were almost to the end of the hallway when the sound of gunfire erupted behind them. A bullet tore through Seaborne's shoulder, spinning him around. Stunned, he was unable to lift his weapon as the next bullet caught him in the forehead, throwing him back in a spray of blood. He was only twenty-six years old, and Chris Seaborne's plans for having a wife and children and grandchildren someday had just come to a sudden, final end.

From the corner of his eye, Brooks had seen the lieutenant go down, but he couldn't stop or even look back. The metal walkway was just ahead. Sparks from the bullets hitting the concrete wall by his head made him wince as he ducked around the corner and flicked the selector switch to full-auto.

The two green eyes that had ambushed them made the fatal mistake of darting from the hallway without checking first. Brooks was waiting, and his MK7 was pointed right at them. He pulled the trigger. What was left of the two green eyes covered the walls as he took off running again, his boots pounding the metal grating until he entered the recessed alcove and flew up the stairs. Thudding down the red-tiled hallway, he bolted through the wooden door and slid a frightened-looking Musa onto the table.

"Someone lock that door," he said, breathing heavily.

"Where's Seaborne?" Sam asked. And then she saw the blood splatter on his uniform. Their eyes met. Sam turned away with a blank look on her face. She was getting used to this new reality, but when Brooks saw the abandoned look in her eyes, he began to wonder if she wasn't nearing her breaking point.

Turning back, Brooks could feel himself reaching some kind of point himself as he glared at the admiral. "He was one of our best officers, sir. He graduated from Annapolis near the top of his class. Same with BUDs training, and I can't even retrieve his body. I can't retrieve any of their bodies." Brooks' eyes grew dark. "So now, Admiral, you're going to tell us the truth about this place, or so help me God you'll be joining those blind fish at the bottom of the river before the day is out."

The admiral leaned back in his chair with a neutral look on his face and waited for the emotion in the room to ebb. One wrong word from him now would be the only excuse Brooks needed in his current state of mind.

Using her free arm, Sam helped Dinning move Musa into one of the chairs before sliding down into a seat next to Dana with her weapon pointed at the door.

"Where exactly are we?" Hamilton finally asked Bourdon. "We were blindfolded when the green eyes brought us in here."

"We're under the old recreation building ... below the bowling alley, to be precise." The admiral paused before turning to Dinning. "I'm surprised you haven't asked me anything yet, Professor."

Dinning's eyes were red from lack of sleep, and his arms looked thinner as he leaned forward on the table. "I was just wondering how you were able to build a modern lab underground here without anyone knowing about it."

"We didn't. This facility was constructed almost sixty years ago during the Cold War. Of course we had to have the old lab completely rebuilt to meet modern standards. We replaced the old generators and installed a new air conditioning system. There were no computers. I don't even want to think of all the problems we had installing the network we have now, but the facility itself has remained unaffected by the jungle above our heads all these years. My father said we'd be back someday, and his words have turned out to be strangely prophetic."

Brooks looked stunned. "Your father?"

"Yes. My father was a scientist here, and so was his brother ... my uncle. He and his family lived in the villa next to ours until the station closed and we were all forced to leave when I was a teenager."

"I don't understand. You mean you were raised here?"

"Africa is my birthplace, Commander." The admiral's eyes had taken on the far-away look of a distant memory, and his train of thought seemed to drift for a moment before he continued. "My father was Belgian, but my mother was American, so my parents chose to move to America when they left Africa. Dad always believed we would return to the Congo one day, but he died two years after we arrived in the states."

"So he didn't make it ... but you did. Is that what you're saying, Admiral?"

"That's right, Commander … I have returned. My father may be dead, but his legacy lives on."

"Legacy?" Brooks traded looks with Dinning. "What the hell is this place?"

"It's just what it looks like … a genetics lab. All of the other labs in the old station were built above ground. There were over a dozen of them. The scientists who were studying the river had a lab right by the water. That was probably my favorite. The botanists collecting samples from the jungle worked in another lab next to the herbarium at the top of the hill … where it was cooler. But the largest one was the medical research complex. Five separate labs all interconnected. My father was one of the first microbiologists to be called a virologist. He studied tropical viruses, and my uncle concentrated on developing vaccines for them in another building. Sadly, the entire medical complex was burned to the ground the day before we left to protect the native people here from getting sick from anything left behind."

Dinning looked confused. "So why build an underground lab here in secret?"

"It was only a secret from the outside world, Professor. Most of the scientists who worked here knew about it. In fact, many of them helped with the design and construction. Like my father, they planned on returning one day to continue their research." Bourdon paused to scan the faces around the table. "They believed something had been unleashed in the jungle … something deadly, and they wanted to stop it in its tracks before it reached the outside world. I suppose they thought they could put the genie back in the bottle … so to speak."

Dinning's eyes grew wide. "Something deadly had been unleashed?"

"Yes, I'm coming to that, Professor. But before I do, I need to reveal a little more about my family history first. When my family departed Africa for America, my uncle and his family returned to Belgium. My cousin went on to become a well-known bacteriologist and worked for the Belgian military as their expert in germ warfare. I believe some of you may have already heard of him."

"Bourdon!" Hamilton blurted out. "The name of the NATO scientist … the one who disappeared last year! It was Bourdon!"

"Very good, Dr. Hamilton. The NATO scientist everyone has been looking for is my cousin, Felix Bourdon. In today's world of computer databases, I've often wondered why no one has ever made the connection, especially considering our respective positions in the U.S. Military and NATO. I suppose people assumed that it was purely a coincidence that we shared the same last name."

"Where's your cousin now?" Dinning asked.

"We had a little disagreement. He's off looking for a specimen in the library."

"What kind of specimen?"

Bourdon was still sweating as he looked around the table. "Look, I can sit here all day and answer your individual questions, but everything would make a lot more sense if you heard the entire story first. I believe when I'm finished most of your questions will have been answered."

"Go ahead," Brooks said. "You've got five minutes. After that we're getting the hell out of here."

"You'd never make it, Commander, and anyone associated with you could be in danger after you were killed."

"We'll take our chances." Sam's eyes blazed. "If the commander doesn't make it out of here, neither will you."

"Let him talk, Sam," Brooks said. "I want to hear this."

Bourdon winced when he tried to turn in his seat with his hands still tied behind his back. "I believe we were discussing my cousin. He and I are roughly the same age. We played together in the streets of the old station, swam in the community pool, explored the jungle like most teen-aged boys do. We even bowled in the bowling alley in the basement above us. Naturally we stayed in touch when our families became separated after we left Africa. But over time the communications became less and less … until five years ago. I received a phone call from him. My aunt had passed away several years before, but my uncle had just died.

"My uncle had a medical degree, but he never saw a patient after graduating from medical school. Instead, he became a university researcher who specialized in tropical diseases. Some of his early research was even instrumental in developing a smallpox vaccine. But after he returned from Africa he became reclusive … working alone in his old lab at the University of Leuven.

"When my cousin called, he told me he had been in his father's library going through his effects when he found several unmarked boxes stuffed with old notebooks. Turns out they contained his father's notes detailing all of the solitary research he had been conducting ever since he had returned from Africa over fifty years ago. That's when we first found out."

"Found out what?"

"That he was learning how to engineer genes. He and my father had first learned of the emerging new field of DNA research when they were still in Africa. Actually, the existence of DNA was first observed in 1869, but no one knew what it did back then. It wasn't until the 1940's that researchers discovered its role in genetic inheritance. But the big moment came in 1953, when Watson and Crick announced to the world that the double-helix structure of DNA contained the recipes for life itself.

"My father even talked about it at the dinner table when we still lived here. Apparently, one of the new scientists in the medical complex had known Crick at Cambridge before coming to Africa. He told my father that Crick had actually walked into a pub and announced the discovery by telling a few slightly inebriated patrons that he and Watson had just discovered the secret of life. They had no idea he was telling the truth.

"To say that my father and uncle had become fascinated with the subject would be an understatement. They were obsessed with it. But over time, as they learned more, the reality of it all began to sink in. Humans had finally discovered the hidden file cabinet containing the recipes for life, but as we all know, recipes can always be changed if someone decides they don't like the way their last batch of chocolate chip cookies tasted. In other words, they saw the potential for catastrophe, because the consequences of such a discovery in the wrong hands could spell disaster for humanity one day. In one of his papers, my uncle likened his genetic research to the development of nuclear weapons. It's all here … on this floor. All of his research kept safe for future generations."

"Not all of it," Musa said.

"What are you talking about?" Bourdon responded. "We never involved you in our work here."

"The mutated fish. The specimen your cousin is looking for right now. He didn't want it contaminating the lab, so he put it in the library specimen room." Musa coughed. "But now it's hidden, just like the one I hid and gave to Peter."

"Is that why you locked him up in a cage in a dark room?" Dinning fired back at Bourdon.

"No, that was the soldiers … on my cousin's orders."

"And you did nothing to stop it?"

"I just arrived two days ago, Professor. My cousin runs this lab. I'm no scientist, but I've been supporting what he was trying to do … what his father had been trying to do. We're walking a fine line here with the soldiers you call green eyes. I told my cousin to release Musa the moment I found out he had been locked up, but once the TGs classify someone as a threat, there's no going back."

"TGs?"

"Our acronym for *transgenic humans*. It's what we call the green-eyed soldiers. Unfortunately, they became a failed experiment, but we're still learning from them."

"Human experimentation!" Dinning was on his feet. "That's outrageous!"

"It was an accident, Professor. The *Ghost Recon* soldiers were diverted here to protect the station from a local warlord who wasn't afraid of the old supernatural myths that had kept others away. They were never meant to be test subjects. It's also why we had to make up the story of the plane crash."

"Then what the hell happened to them? The engineered genes didn't just leap into their bodies and alter their genome all by themselves. And what about this mutated fish Musa just mentioned?"

The admiral squirmed in his chair, trying to find a more comfortable position. "Like I said before … I'm coming to that."

Brooks eyed his old boss. Despite the shock of seeing him here in Africa with the green eyes, he still felt a kinship with the man who had become almost like a father to him over the years. "Go ahead, Admiral … we're listening."

"Thank you, Commander. As I was saying before, as soon as our fathers realized the implications of Watson and Crick's discovery, they immediately began collecting specimens from the jungle so they could delve into their DNA … much like the professor here was doing, only on a much more primitive level. They wanted to get a jump on the research, because in order to guard against the misuse of a new scientific discovery, they knew they had to learn all they could about it first. I'll never forget my father's excitement the day they received their first electron microscope. But without modern computers and sequencing machines to help sort through all the various genomes they had pulled from the jungle, they had barely scratched the surface when the station closed in the mid-1960's."

The admiral slumped in his chair and looked at Brooks. "Could I please have some water?"

No one answered. Slowly, Musa reached out with a trembling hand and slid an unopened bottle of water across the table to Bourdon. Everyone in the room felt humbled by the old man's kindness, especially Brooks, who walked over and cut the plastic band from the admiral's wrists so he could drink.

"Thank you," Bourdon said. His gaze drifted across the table to Musa's yellowed, watching eyes. It seemed like the old man had always been watching.

"Now that I've explained my connection to the station, it's time I told you about something else that was going on here before the twisting double helix had captured our fathers' imaginations. As you are undoubtedly already aware, an emerging rash of deadly new diseases has been popping up here in equatorial Africa over the past century, and many of the researchers in the medical complex, including my uncle, had abandoned their other research to concentrate on developing new vaccines."

"Vaccines?" Dinning looked surprised. "So the mission of the station was changing from biological and agricultural research to the study of tropical diseases?"

"Not exactly. The things they were studying here were all pretty much interconnected, but it's the reason the medical lab grew to become the largest lab here. We're talking about extremely deadly diseases that had never been seen before ... diseases like HIV, and no one knew where these things were coming from or even if they were really new. According to my cousin, molecular dating placed the emergence of HIV sometime around 1908, but the first known cases didn't begin appearing until the 1920's ... right here in the Congo ... in Kinshasa to be exact.

"Then there were the emerging hemorrhagic viruses. Marburg was one of the first that we know of. It showed up right here along the Kinshasa highway in 1960 and left its victims swimming in pools of their own blood ... just like Ebola."

" But Ebola came later," Dinning observed. "It sprang from the jungle here in 1976 after the station had closed."

"That's true, but my point is that the scientists here at that time had been the first to realize that some of the most lethal diseases known to man were springing from the same jungle that surrounded this very station. They and their families were living in some kind of biological ground zero. That's what I was talking about earlier when I said they believed something deadly had been unleashed in the jungle. Now we have another new hemorrhagic virus rearing its ugly head here in the Congo. It's called *Bas-Congo*, and its related to rabies."

"Rabies?" Dinning was dumbstruck. This was the first time he had ever heard of this new virus— and he was hearing it from a military man instead of from another scientist. Alarm bells began going off in his head. "A virus like that could be a real game-changer for our species if it ever mutates and becomes airborne. It would be the most horrific pathogen the planet has ever seen."

"Yes, and there are undoubtedly more we are still unaware of, Professor."

"I think most of us here are well aware of the viral history of this place, Admiral. But what does any of this have to do with creating transgenes and the green eyes ... or TGs, as you call them?"

"You'll see, Professor ... you'll see. According to my uncle's notes, after he returned to Belgium he continued his research looking for some kind of genetic link between all of these emerging new viruses ... even Ebola, which he began studying the moment he could get his hands on a sample. He theorized—correctly as it turns out—that a lot of these new hemorrhagic viruses were passed to humans by eating bush meat from the jungle ... monkeys, bats ... things like that."

Brooks glanced at his watch. "We know what bush meat is, Admiral."

"Of course, but this is an important part of the story, Commander ... one Professor Dinning and Dr. Hamilton will find very interesting. I wish my cousin was here now, because he could explain it much better than I can."

"I wish your cousin was here now too," Sam said, wrapping the foil blanket back around Musa's shoulders.

The admiral adopted the look of a man who had just missed a golf shot as he stared back at her for a moment before continuing. "From everything I've read on the subject, viruses are barely considered life forms. They can't even reproduce on their own. They have to enter the cell of another life form to do that, but they do carry genetic material."

"That's why we use them to introduce transgenes," Hamilton added.

"Exactly, and after reading his father's notes, my cousin could see that this was what his father had been thinking about when he made what I would call a giant intellectual leap. Rather than spending years trying to develop a vaccine against a viral threat that could mutate if challenged, he decided on a novel new approach. He decided he was going to eliminate the virus from the genome of the host animals in the rainforest through the use of engineered genes."

Dinning exchanged glances with Hamilton. "And the fish was your original test subject?"

"Yes, Professor ... the fish. My cousin described it as the perfect reservoir for the transgene he was developing. One day, when we were still prepping the lab, a native fisherman brought a strange-looking fish to the station. It was blind and covered in bubbles. The fisherman said he had found it floating in the reeds along the bank of the river ... farther upstream close to where the water is at its deepest.

"My cousin was ecstatic. He had an underwater camera flown in and towed it along the bottom of that section of the river for weeks until they finally found them. Schools of blind fish were living in their own little ecosystem down there ... never venturing close to the surface. The only time one was ever seen was after it died and floated to the surface. But occasionally, one was chased to the surface by something ... like the ones we found covered in bubbles from rapid decompression."

"I don't get it," Hamilton said. "What was so special about that fish?"

"It fit our requirements. We were trying to be responsible. In order for the results to be accurate, we had to test our transgenic organism in a natural environment outside the lab without endangering that environment. There were all kinds of scenarios. If we introduced the gene into something like a wild chimpanzee ... say an adult male past breeding age, it was possible he could still pass it on somehow and the new transgene could end up replicating in the environment."

Dinning and Hamilton traded looks.

"The nightmare part of that scenario is the gene itself," Bourdon continued. "If we had engineered a transgene that was flawed, it could produce some unintended results. There's no telling what kind of

310

creature we'd end up with if something like that happened. Or even worse, what if the transgene killed its host … like a virus? We would have been responsible for creating a new man-made disease that had the potential to wipe out any number of species around the world. We couldn't take that chance."

Hamilton slapped the table. "So you chose a natural ecosystem that was virtually sealed off from the world above to observe your little golden monster at work, but something went wrong with your genetic Manhattan Project … is that it?"

"Something like that, but our goal of eradicating these emerging new diseases from the human race was a noble one. You know as well as I do that sometime in the not too distant future we'll all be facing an Armageddon virus that has gone airborne. It's not a matter of if, but when, and one day the work we've been doing here may be our only defense."

Dinning locked eyes with Bourdon. "But something stopped you and your cousin from continuing your altruistic work against disease out here in the deep green, didn't it, Admiral? The transgene we saw wasn't designed to eradicate any virus. What was it really designed for?"

"One of the things I learned in the military, Professor, is how to prioritize threats. The world we live in now is changing, and not for the better. With the growing rise in international terrorism, we're facing a fanatic, suicidal enemy that is literally seeking the destruction of western civilization. Their stated goal is to wipe us from the face of the Earth, and its already starting to erode our freedoms and affect the way we lead our daily lives. It didn't take a crystal ball for my cousin and I to see that we had to reprioritize our research goals to meet this imminent new threat, so we switched gears."

Brooks arched his eyebrows. "Switched gears?"

"We felt we had no other choice. I'm talking about a total, unchecked world war on the horizon. Ten years ago I would have scoffed at the idea, but now I'm almost certain of it. You should know better than most, Commander. At this point in our history, we should be more concerned about the jihadists who are beginning to spread just like a virus. An unlimited war against these people is inevitable. They're practically begging for it, but our current leaders can't see it coming for some reason. They've kept our military stretched to the limit, and nothing we've seen from Congress tells us it's going to get any better.

"With nobody on our side willing to step up to the plate and make the hard decisions, we felt compelled to start looking for a smarter way to defeat our enemies. And what better way than to use something we already knew a lot about. We had the means right here at our fingertips. We could engineer transgenes that could enhance our troops, while engineering others that would turn our enemies into sheep. Why even go to war if you can change the genome of your opponent."

Ignoring the fire in Dinning's eyes, Bourdon took a deep breath before continuing. "We actually engineered two new genes. One was designed to lessen the aggressiveness of a species, while the other was designed to amplify it."

"And the green eyes," Brooks said. "You still expect us to believe that was an accident?"

"It was an accident. We weren't ready for human trials yet. It happened because of our experiments with the fish. We had underwater cameras and special nets designed to bring them to the surface slowly so they could decompress before we took them to the lab and injected them with the transgene for aggressiveness. If it worked on a docile creature like that, we knew we were on to something. But unfortunately, Murphy's Law inevitably came into play. One of the recon soldiers saw the equipment by the river and cranked the net up to the surface. There were about a dozen transgenic fish in it, so he decided to have a fish fry for his buddies. Fourteen days later their eyes turned green and they stopped sleeping."

"Is that when they started killing people too?" Sam asked.

The admiral blinked back at her. "They don't go around killing people. They only kill other soldiers, and you and your friends here are living proof of that."

"But what about the people on the professor's ship? They weren't soldiers, and the green eyes killed them."

"I believe this would be the perfect time to explain what happened in Matadi. The men who attacked the ship were mercenaries hired by my cousin, and they went way beyond what they had been told to do. They were only tasked with bringing back a hard drive. We had to find out if anything in your data pointed to the discovery of our transgene. If it did, we had much more effective ways of stopping your research. There was no reason to kill those people."

The admiral leaned back in his chair for a moment and stared at the ceiling. "They may have been affected by the transgene too … I don't know."

Dinning looked stunned. "Who … the mercenaries?"

"Yes. They all shared a meal together with the TGs the night before they went off to plan the raid on the *Searcher*. The recon men didn't look like they do now. The only observable change then was their green eyes, which we explained by telling the mercenaries they were trying out some new tactical contact lenses. But their genome was already undergoing a drastic conversion, accelerating much faster than we anticipated to what you see now. At that stage they could have passed it on somehow, but we have no idea how it happened. They haven't affected us, but then again, we take precautions when we're around them. It's like finding genetically modified corn in a Mexican field a thousand miles away from where the nearest GMO crop was planted. I mean, how the hell did it get there?

"When the mercenaries returned to collect their money they still appeared normal, but when they encountered the recon men in the ruins, it was like watching two mortal enemies eyeing one another. At that point, the conversion in the recon soldiers had advanced to a new level. They saw something in the mercenaries that triggered their threat response. All hell broke loose. They decimated the mercenaries in a matter of minutes. We were witnessing the power of the gene firsthand. It was awe-inspiring to watch."

Bourdon paused when he saw the looks on the faces staring back at him. No one had to tell him that he had just unwittingly revealed his enthusiasm for what the transgene was capable of.

Clearing his throat, he drummed his fingers on the table for a moment before continuing. "In my defense, I swear to you I had no knowledge of the attack on the ship beforehand. I would never have approved of something like that. It was stupid. It had disaster written all over it!" Bourdon paused, looking toward the door. "The incident with the mercenaries also alerted us to the fact that the TGs were becoming hyper-aggressive, so we've been forced to take measures to protect ourselves from them in case they begin to see us as a threat."

"You mean in case they began to mutate into mindless killing machines, don't you, Admiral," Dinning corrected. "Natural mutation occurs all the time within every species, but somehow you and your cousin missed the fact that the viral components you used to introduce the transgene created an evolutionary mutation process that accelerates exponentially. That's why the later changes came on so suddenly."

The admiral looked back at Dinning with a newfound sense of respect. "I assume Dr. Hamilton has already briefed you on the type of virus he used."

"Yes, in the clearing, where Commander Brooks' first two men died." Dinning had the eyes of a prosecutor just winding up. "What about that mutated fish Musa mentioned a moment ago?"

The admiral leaned forward and massaged the back of his neck before returning his gaze to the people gathered around the table. "That's when we knew we had another problem."

"Another problem?"

"Yes. At the same time we were witnessing the changes in the soldiers, one of the Russian researches we hired for the lab informed us that the number of blind fish at the bottom of the river appeared to be dwindling. When we switched on the underwater lights and cameras, the only thing we saw was a sandy bottom and dark brown water. All of the blind, transgenic test fish were gone. And then we saw it. It swam right in front of the camera … a fish from a different species with fluorescing green eyes."

"What does all of this mean?" Brooks asked.

"It means the damn things have now passed the gene on to other species of fish in the river!" Dinning said. "The Admiral and his cousin have released an untested transgene into the natural environment outside the lab, and the results of such an irresponsible act could be catastrophic to our world!"

They all heard it at the same time. Someone had just inserted a key into the locked door, and the doorknob was turning.

CHAPTER 53

The man standing in the open doorway stopped when he saw Brooks and Sam pointing their weapons right at his head.

The admiral exhaled. "You can lower your weapons. This is my cousin, Felix Bourdon."

Both men looked strikingly similar, with tousled, snow-white hair and an intense gaze that made some people slightly uncomfortable. The admiral swept his hand toward the group. "Felix, I want you to meet ..."

"I'm afraid we don't have time for introductions, Nathan," Felix replied. "Something's going on with the TGs. They're acting differently. Something's triggered a new threat response in them. We have to leave ... now!"

Dana withered in her chair. "How many of them are out there?"

"I'm not sure, but they're beginning to mass." The cousin's building panic was evident as he walked over to the wall at the end of the room and punched a button. A large wooden panel slid back to reveal three, wide-screen TV monitors displaying live images from cameras all around the station.

"As you can see, several TGs are headed this way from the hill, and ..."

The muffled sound of gunfire echoed through the facility as Dana pointed to one of the screens and screamed. "They're killing the people in the lab!"

Felix Bourdon sank against the wall when he glanced back at the screen and saw several researchers lying in pools of their own blood as two green eyes walked out of the lab. "My God, Nathan ... what have we done?!"

"We did what we thought was right ... what I still believe is right. We now have the means to create the ultimate soldier while reducing our enemies into slobbering sheep."

315

The others in the room looked back at him with a mixture of denial and horror, while outside in the hallway, they heard the sound of running boots.

The admiral's cousin reached for the door. "I'll talk to them. They'll still listen to me."

Before the others could stop him, he was out the door. A single shot rang out and they could hear the thudding sound of a body hitting the floor outside.

"I believe they've just killed my cousin," Bourdon said without emotion.

"And we're next unless we can find another way out of here," Brooks added.

"There is no other way out, Commander."

Without blinking, Brooks handed two grenades to Sam and flipped the huge table over on its side. "Everyone ... behind the table."

As soon as the others crowded behind the thick tabletop, Brooks jerked the door open and shot the green-eyed soldier staring back at him. Crouching down, he rolled a grenade out into the hall and slammed the door before diving behind the table. A few seconds later the blast shook the room, knocking the door off its hinges.

Brooks was instantly up again with Sam right behind him. "We've got to make it up the stairwell at the end of this hall," he shouted back to her. "It's the only way out."

Exchanging looks, they moved out into the hallway, keeping low while trying to peer through the choking wall of smoke. A pair of green rings were fluorescing between them and the stairwell. They fired at the same time, dropping the green-eyed soldier standing in the smoke. Sam watched the light in his eyes fade into darkness as he looked out at a world that no longer existed for him.

Looking back, Brooks saw Dinning and the admiral supporting Musa, while Hamilton and Dana stared at the dripping gore on the wall from the grenade blast.

"The control room!" Bourdon shouted.

Slowly—dreamlike—another pair of shining green rings emerged from the smoke behind them. The green-eyed soldier fired and the admiral sank to the floor. With her back to the wall, Sam aimed and pulled the trigger, dropping the green eye with a single shot to the head.

The red floor beneath her boots was growing redder as she looked down at the admiral lying next to his cousin—the two Bourdons, curled in death, side-by-side in the land of their birth.

A burst of gunfire from below pinged against the steel railings on the concrete stairs. Brooks swung around the corner at the end of the hall and opened fire, dropping two more green eyes advancing up the stairwell from the alcove below. Slowly, he made his way down past their bodies to check for more.

With her wingman Brooks downstairs, Sam stood against the wall of the hallway and wondered how many more of them were waiting at the top of the stairs on the floor above. The area around the lab was quickly becoming a killing ground, and the stairwell was the only way to the surface.

But where would they go once they were out? More of them would probably be waiting in the ruins. *Was it daylight or was it dark now?* She had taken her watch off before leaving her little house to walk through the dunes—the night she and Dana had fled on her motorbike after being chased by other soldiers.

Why was she thinking about that now?

Sam shook her head. She had to stay focused. Her mind slowly began to clear as she crept to the stairwell and looked up with her weapon at eye level. Standing in the alcove below, Brooks marveled at the sight as she began to climb toward the floor above, feeling for the steps with her feet while she kept her eyes and weapon focused up. Sam had moved beyond the stage of having to be told what to do next.

They all heard it at the same time. It sounded like a child had dropped a metal toy, and it was bouncing down the stairs.

"Grenade!" Brooks shouted, diving out of the alcove. But those still in the hallway on the floor above him were trapped. They had no choice but to scramble back the way they had come.

Looking back down the hallway, Sam knew they would never make it to the paneled room. She reached out and checked the closest door. It opened. Mentally counting the seconds, she yanked Dana by the arm just as the grenade exploded.

The concussion was followed by a wave of heat that filled the room and the hallway outside. Bits of paper floated in the acrid smoke. Sam was instantly on her feet. To her, it was obvious that the grenade was just a prelude. In the next few minutes the green eyes would be coming from verwhelming numbers. They would be tossing more grenades rming down the stairwell, until Sam and her friends were just ; the innocent researchers now lying behind the blood-splattered glass of the lab below.

Dana stood behind Sam as the two girls peered through the drifting smoke in the hallway. Dinning, Hamilton, and Musa had thrown themselves down against the concrete wall and appeared to be unscathed. Watching them lift themselves off the floor, Sam gave Musa a thumbs-up. The adrenaline rush from the blast had apparently kicked him into overdrive, because he was now moving on his own.

Tears of rage stained Sam's dusty cheeks as she looked out at them. Their eyes were searching—but they had become lost in the jumbled fog of war. They had no idea what was coming next.

They weren't dying today! Sam repeated to herself. *None of them were dying today! Musa was standing on his own!* She checked her ammo.

Moving out into the hallway, Sam went on the offensive. Advancing through the haze, she encouraged the others behind her until they reached the end of the hallway by the smoke-filled stairwell. Nothing appeared to be moving.

She began to think about how much chance played a role in combat. If the green eyes hadn't dropped the grenade when they did, she probably would have been shot making her way up the stairwell. Life was a thread, and it was beginning to fray. There was nowhere left for Sam and the others to run. The green eyes were massing above them, and they were coming.

With her eyes stinging from the smoke, she peered down the stairs to the floor below. Brooks was back in the alcove, standing against the wall to guard against any attack from that direction. He waved. They had no choice but to go back down.

Keeping her head and weapon pointed up the stairwell where the green eyes would surely be coming from, she stood like a sentinel while the others moved around the corner behind her and fled down the stairs. Backing up, she turned and ran down behind them before glancing over her shoulder. She shuddered when she saw the walls of the stairwell glowing from all the fluorescing green eyes gazing down from the floor above.

Standing next to Brooks in the alcove, they looked up and down the steel walkway. Right away Brooks saw them. Two green eyes in the concrete hallway off to their left. He gave them a quick burst just to back them away.

Sam grabbed Brooks' sleeve. "They'll be coming any second. I can feel it. Which way?"

Hamilton gestured toward the mammoth glass cube surrounding the lab. "The lab!" he shouted. It was the first time he had seen it. "If we can make it to the decontamination area, the thick vault door will keep them out!"

Dana looked at all the bodies inside and took a step back. "I'm not going in there." It was the first time she and Dinning had seen it too.

"Forget it," Brooks said. "We'd never make it out again." He turned and peered down the long Plexiglas tunnel.

Sam followed his gaze. "You can't be serious! The control room?"

"The glass looks bulletproof ... and the admiral was trying to tell us something about it before he was shot. Maybe it's a way out."

"What about the way we came in?"

"There could be an entire squad of green eyes waiting for us back in there, and if they've jammed the opening we came down through, we'd be running into a dead end. A couple of grenades would finish us."

Sam nodded. "Looks like the control room then. At least it will buy us some time." She glanced back at the stairs. In her mind's eye she could see the green eyes pouring down on top of them.

"You go first!" Brooks shouted. "I'll cover you!" Stepping out onto the metal walkway, the big SEAL began laying down covering fire in the direction of the concrete hallway while Sam grabbed Musa by the hand and ran into the glass tunnel. "Follow me!" she shouted to the others.

Taking deep breaths, they stepped from the alcove just as Brooks heard his weapon click. He was out of ammo. A green eye heard it too and jumped from the hallway, letting loose with an automatic burst.

Brooks flattened himself against the wall and was reaching for another clip when a bullet struck him in the shoulder, knocking him down as his weapon clattered across the steel grating.

In the glass tunnel, Musa stopped and turned back to help him, but he was forced back when bullets began glancing off the metal walkway around the entrance.

Panicked and exposed, the others took off running down the walkway in the opposite direction—toward the decontamination area. Sam screamed at them to stop as she ran from the tunnel and hit the

319

green eyes advancing from the hallway with a full-auto burst. But this time they weren't retreating. They walked over their own dead and kept coming.

Dropping down, she reached out and grabbed Brooks' hand. He shook his head no, but she refused to let go. He finally started to inch forward just as two bullets struck his vest. Fully exposed with no covering fire, Sam stood and pulled as hard as she could, dragging the big SEAL into the tunnel before collapsing next to Musa.

Brooks looked up at her. His eyes looked glassy, and he was breathing heavily. Ripping off her vest, Sam tore off part of her shirt to use as a bandage and pressed down on his shoulder to staunch the flow of blood. "Can you hold this?" she asked Musa. The old man reached over and pressed with both hands while she strapped her vest back on. Looking toward the hallway, the green eyes were still coming when she reached out and grabbed Brooks' weapon off the walkway.

She heard Brooks' gruff voice growling behind her. "Run, Sam … run."

Looking back, she saw his eyes roll up in his head and shouted into his face. "Don't go to sleep! Where's your extra ammo?!"

Brooks winced, but his eyes looked focused again. "Pants pocket."

Feeling along his leg, she pulled out two clips. "Is this all?"

"That's it!"

Looking toward the stairs and off to her right, she slammed one clip into Brooks' weapon and shoved it into his hands while sliding the other into her waistband. "Let's go!"

Inch by inch she dragged Brooks farther into the tunnel while Musa crawled alongside, holding pressure on his shoulder wound. They were twenty feet from the control room door when the green eyes came pouring down the stairs and out of the concrete hallway off to their right. Sam said a prayer and took aim, opening fire on the first wave running from the alcove toward the tunnel entrance. The first three fell, momentarily blocking the advance of the others.

These guys fight like demons! Sam thought to herself. It was as though they were all connected by some invisible genetic thread, like a herd of wildebeests or gazelles that had suddenly sniffed out a predator—and the way they moved without having to communicate verbally was eerie to watch.

"Use one of the grenades I gave you," Brooks whispered up to her. "Count to three after you pull the pin and aim for the end of the tunnel where it connects to the metal walkway."

Sam nodded that she understood and grabbed one of the grenades clipped to her vest. As soon as she looked up she saw that the green eyes were watching her. Realizing what she was about to do, several of them raised their weapons and charged the tunnel. Sam didn't have time to count to three. She pulled the pin and threw the grenade. The green-eyed soldiers stopped and flung themselves backward just as the grenade hit the joint where the Plexiglas tunnel joined the walkway. For a moment it teetered before it started rolling back down into the tunnel.

"Shit!" Sam threw herself over Brooks and Musa just as it exploded. A red-hot piece of shrapnel grazed her leg, but she barely noticed the pain as she rolled over and aimed her weapon back through the smoke-filled tunnel.

It was cracking!

Like someone stepping on thin ice, little spider web cracks began running the length of the tunnel. Sam seemed transfixed by the sight until the loud shriek of tearing metal filled her ears. The entrance to the tunnel was breaking away from the metal walkway.

Unbelievably, Sam heard another cracking noise behind her. The other end of the tunnel was beginning to separate from the control room.

Stay and die … run and live!

Samantha ran … diving through the open steel door of the control room just as the entire tunnel broke away, crashing down onto the floor of the lab ten feet below with Brooks and Musa still inside. Sam jumped to her feet and looked down at them through the open doorway. They were moving, and Brooks was pointing up at several green eyes aiming their weapons at her from the walkway.

Jerking the door closed, Sam could hear the bullets pinging outside as she locked it and ran around to the big windows. Standing back, she watched the bullets hit, creating star-like splotches of white against the thick glass like wind-driven snowflakes against a car windshield.

Thank God Brooks was right about the windows!

She moved closer to the glass. The last time she had seen Dinning and the other two, they were running toward the decontamination area, but now they were nowhere to be seen. She looked to the side, back toward the stairs. The green eyes were flowing from the alcove, and they were joined by others who seemed to be coming from out of nowhere.

The metal walkway between the alcove and the decontamination area was filled with them, and when she looked up, she saw that there were literally dozens of green eyes just sitting on the top of the glass ceiling of the lab itself. There was something about the way they moved together, and it sent chills down her spine whenever they would stop in a group and turn their heads in unison to look back at her with a snake-like stare.

Dead eyes. It was the way Old Hank described the eyes of a shark.

Too bad he can't see these guys!

A few of the green eyes by the stairs were setting up some kind of large weapon aimed at the control room just as more of them began pouring from the concrete hallway where Seaborne had been shot. Brooks had been right. If they had tried to go back out the way they had come in, they'd be dead right now. She glanced back toward alcove. They were climbing down into the lab through the gaping hole left after the tunnel broke away!

They were everywhere!

Sam grew calm. It was a strange feeling … like drifting on the ocean.

She was going to die.

There was no doubt in her mind. There were too many of them, and they had been genetically engineered to be lethal weapons with no conscience. Sam gazed back out the windows. There were green eyes in the lab now, moving toward the control room. There was nothing she could do. Brooks and Musa would be the first ones they reached before moving on to her and the others.

Standing there—looking out, the strange sense of peace she was feeling suddenly startled her. It was the same kind of feeling she had experienced when she had been lost at sea—when she had been thinking of giving up—letting go as she drifted just beneath the surface of the water.

She saw the green eyes advancing toward Brooks and Musa below. It was a mental kick back to the surface, where she could take a nice long breath of fresh air. Her cheeks felt warm. She was gritting her teeth and the fire had returned to her eyes. She was angry—more angry than she had ever been in her twenty-two years.

Opening the steel door, she unloaded a full clip on the advancing green eyes before swinging it shut and locking it again.

At least that would give Brooks and Musa a few more minutes.

She turned away and let the weapon fall to the floor. It wouldn't be long now until they blew the door. She wanted to cry, but she was too drained even for that. Falling back into a chair, she stared at the control panel for a moment. Her eyes fell on the red button the admiral had seemed so concerned about. *The red button.* She had forgotten all about it, and now with the admiral dead, she would never know what the damned thing did.

Whatever it was, someone had put a protective plastic cover over it to keep people from accidently hitting it—like they probably did with nuclear weapons. Maybe it was some kind of self-destruct button meant to incinerate the lab and everything in it in case of some kind of lethal viral outbreak. Maybe that's why the admiral had looked so freaked out.

If it was something like that ... why not just go ahead and push it?

At least she would go out on her own terms, and she would take all the freaking green eyes with her when they came crashing through the door.

She heard Brooks firing his weapon below until it stopped. In the sudden silence, she reached the point of no return, because she couldn't live with what was about to happen to him next.

Slowly she stood and looked out over all the swarming green eyes staring back at her. For a moment she felt like a queen bee—as if this was her hive and they were her workers. The sight had a hypnotic effect on her. It was like they were all talking to her with one voice.

Come out. We are your children.

Sam shook her head and turned away. She had already decided she wasn't going out on their terms, whatever they were. Taking a deep breath, she flipped the protective cover up and placed her finger on the red button. She thought of her mother and Brian and the two men that had taught her to swim—of Bee's roses and her little island house. The tears rolled down her face as she recited a short prayer before closing her eyes. She pushed.

Suddenly everything became deathly quiet.

So that's what it's like to die, she thought. But when she opened her eyes, she was still standing there with the red button fully depressed. Looking through the windows, she couldn't believe what she was seeing.

All of the green eyes along the walkway had dropped where they had been standing. They were lying in heaps with blood running from their necks. Releasing the button, she pressed her face close to the windows by the door. The green eyes by the stairs were lying piled on top of each other, blood from their neck wounds dripping down the glass walls into the lab below.

Some were lying face down, while others were lying face up, their dark eyes staring off into space.

Their eyes!

They weren't green anymore! Sam rushed to the door and opened it. The smell from the green eyes was overpowering, but she could hear whooping coming from below. Peering down, she saw Brooks give her a thumbs up with his good arm while Musa smiled weakly.

From the end of the lab, she saw Dana and Dinning and Hamilton, running through the space, dodging the bodies of the green eyes as they made their way to the base of the control room.

"What happened to them?" Hamilton shouted.

Dinning was speechless, surveying the scene around them.

"Like that soldier in the clearing!" Dana shouted out. Looking around, she knelt down next to the body of one of the green eyes and pulled his collar back. Blood was oozing from the blackened, exploded wound in his neck. "Looks like they all had those things in their necks, and someone just activated them. Goodbye Mr. Green Eyes!"

Brooks moved out into the lab with Musa, poking some of the bodies with the end of his weapon to make sure they were really dead before looking up at Sam. "I guess now we know what that control room was controlling."

Sam could feel her legs shaking. She tried to speak, but words failed her as she sank to the floor of the control room and wept.

All around them, the green-eyed soldiers' camo shirts began to smolder from the chemical explosions in their necks. Some of their uniforms had already burst into flames, and a fire at the end of the lab had ignited something flammable in one of the cabinets. In less than a minute, black smoke was rolling across the glass ceiling.

"We've got to go ... now!" said Brooks.

Looking down at him, Sam wiped her eyes and scooted to the edge of the doorframe, lowering herself down by her hands before dropping to the floor below. Together they moved out of the lab through the decontamination area—literally climbing over the bodies of the green eyes as they made their way along the walkway and up the body-strewn stairwell into the basement with the bowling alley. There were more bodies there too, along with extra weapons and boxes of ammo.

"Grab some ammo just in case," Brooks said to Sam.

Moving on autopilot, she leaned down and picked up an ammo belt as they all climbed the wide stairs and walked outside through the doorless entrance. As the others filed by, she just stood there, looking out over the deep green. Her hair was hanging down one side of her smudged face, and she seemed oblivious to the smoke beginning to pour from the building behind her. Things seemed to be moving in slow motion now, and when she looked toward the bottom of the steps, she saw Brooks holding his wounded shoulder, looking up at her.

"What now?" she asked.

"The airport. I always leave a satellite phone hidden by the extraction point just in case. Musa needs a doctor, and the extraction team always has a doctor with them."

"No doctor for me," Musa said, limping up to the big man who had saved his life. "Doctor for you. I need only a few days rest and some of my wife's good cooking ... and tea ... lots and lots of hot tea."

Brooks looked down at the sores on Musa's frail arms. "Are you sure?"

Musa just smiled. "Thank you for rescuing me from that dark room. I will say a special prayer for you." The old man reached out and embraced the big SEAL before kissing Sam and Dana on their foreheads and grabbing Dinning by the shoulders. "See you again someday soon, Professor. If you want that other mutated fish I can show you where it's hidden."

"I think it's safer with you for now, old friend, but you never know."

"That's true ... you never know. Goodbye my friends. I think now I will go take a long, hot bath." Musa turned and moved off through the ruins while the others took one last look at the river. The sun was already arcing downward. Lines of clouds floated above the jungle, making the river glisten one moment and dull brown the next with each change in the late afternoon light. Slowly they turned away and began trudging uphill through the ruins toward the jungle road that led to the airport.

They caught a ride from a passing game warden, and twenty minutes later, Sam was holding her boots and walking barefoot across the wet grass around the airport. For awhile she sat on the blue painted wall by the old terminal building and stared out at the jungle. Somehow she knew she would never see it again, and she wanted to drink in the sight and smell all the smells before the plane arrived. Over the tops of the trees, she could see smoke rising from the vicinity of the old station. It had all been so strange, so totally foreign to her. The reality of what had happened in this place was already beginning to feel like a dream before she had even left.

By the corner of the rusty hangar, Dana found Brooks. He was leaning against the corrugated metal siding with tears pooling against his prominent cheekbones as he peered inside. Her small hand found his shoulder and she checked his wound. "Does it hurt much?"

Brooks just pointed. Somehow the native people had gathered the bodies of all the Special Forces soldiers that had flown with them into harm's way. They had been laid out in neat rows, covered with colorful swatches of material that had probably been precious to the people who had brought them here for their last flight. Not everyone had made it, but everyone was going home.

EPILOGUE

Samantha Adams was sitting on her front porch, drinking a long-neck beer and listening to the hum of the ocean. Curled up in a wicker chair across from her, Dana sipped a glass of wine and stared out at the dunes.

"Whatever happened to the ship?" she asked Sam.

"Towed off to some government ship yard."

"Probably scrap by now." She lifted her head and felt the breeze against her face. "Let's go to the beach."

"Can't. I've got bait to catch ... and we have dinner reservations at the Tarpon Inn. Brooks' plane is landing at the base, and Brian went to pick him up. We have to be ready to go when they get here."

Sam finished her beer and grinned at Dana. "You and Brooks. I can't believe I never saw it when we were in Africa. I mean, maybe I saw him looking at you kind of funny sometimes, but none of us knew there was ever anything between you two." Sam giggled. "What's he like?"

"Just like most men, I guess ... except maybe bigger." Both girls burst out laughing.

Dana's face reddened. "You know what I mean. I'm afraid the couch in my apartment is going to break one day when he sits on it. It's funny now that I think back on it, but I used to think he had his eye on you. You two certainly seemed to bond."

"I guess we did in a way. It was a little confusing at first, but it was never romantic. I always told him I thought we had a love-hate thing going on, but that wasn't really true. We were more like two soldiers ... bound together by what we had to do. Now I understand that look SEALs give to one another when they meet. It's because they've been through some kind of hell together in a far off place, and they both know they were lucky enough to make it back alive to the real world again."

327

"Yeah, it's funny. Steve and I never talk about it." Dana paused, watching a kite that had broken away lift into the sky. "What about you, Sam? Still against going back to school?"

"That's not my world, and I don't especially feel like spending the next twenty years paying off a student loan. I'm just happy catching bait again, and I don't like living in big cities. Brian and I are thinking of buying a charter boat." Sam glanced down at her trusty divers watch. "Damn! I need to get a move on if I'm going to net any bait fish for Mable this afternoon. I promised her. You wanna come along?"

"Sure, why not." Dana smiled. "It's almost like going to the beach."

Grabbing their cell phones and beach bags, they headed down the stairs and through the little gate where Sam's old green and white VW bus was parked. She loved the feel of climbing up into the tall seat and staring straight ahead through the flat windshield—her feet inches from the front bumper as she went through the manual gears using a long floor shifter. It made her feel like she was flying over the road instead of driving on it—probably why Brian loved riding his motorcycle so much, she thought.

Driving away from the house, Sam looked past the end of her street. She could just see the red brick corner of the Marine Research Institute. It made her think of Dinning and Hamilton. Dinning had retired after they had returned from Africa. He lived at the ranch now. She and Brian had visited him there, and they had all sat under the big pecan tree, listening to Willie Nelson and drinking beer late into the night. He seemed quite happy, and he was writing a book on the dangers of transgenes in a perilous world that was already at the tipping point.

Hamilton was still Hamilton. He was back in Houston, building a new lab with the insurance money from the fire. There had been an investigation, of course, but he had been smart enough not to tell anyone who had started it.

Driving through Port Aransas, they looked out at a gray-and-white painted restaurant with the best fried shrimp and French fries on the island. The sun barked against something in the distance, sending an orange glare across her windshield just as she made the turn onto the highway and headed south. Something big passed her going the opposite direction. She felt a chill, and when the glare cleared, whatever had passed her was gone with a swirl of sand along the highway.

Sam glanced in her rearview mirror. The back of a large, black motorhome was growing smaller on the highway behind her.

Sitting in the back of the motorhome, Gil Preston looked back at six other men and toasted their success. "Your country owes you all a debt of gratitude, gentlemen. Without your help, the admiral's work would have died with him. To new beginnings." The men clinked glasses as the motorhome headed into Port Aransas.

The sun was still blaring though the passenger side window when Sam spotted the remains of the old Seaside Inn protruding through the dunes on their left as they turned off onto the white shell road and drove to the bay side of the island.

It was fall now. The sticky heat of summer had given way to the cool air from the north, and the water in the bay was especially clear in the coastal shallows this time of year. The current that welled up from the deep ship channel and flowed over the white, sandy bottom along the shoreline had a definite chill to it, and Sam was still wearing her summer shorts when she waded out into the knee-high water.

Looking out over the rippled surface, she squinted in the afternoon sun. It was always better in the morning with the sun to her back. The afternoon shadows on the tidal flats made the little schools of tiny fish harder to spot, but she could still see them moving under a cloudless sky.

The water seemed colder than usual. Sam could feel goose bumps on her legs and a shiver ran up her back. She made a mental note to herself. It was time to start carrying her wetsuit in the bus again. Looking back at Dana, she saw her kneeling down by the shoreline, entranced by the way the flowing sea grass moved back and forth in the water—as if it was dancing to a tune only things in nature could hear.

From the corner of her eye, Sam caught a distant movement—a disturbance in the water—moving close to the shore. Holding her throw net, she stood perfectly still, watching the circular patch of darker water move closer. Her silent presence had made her part of their underwater world, and this was where she would wait for them to swim straight for her.

They were almost to her now—a mass of darting fish the size of a finger. She readied her net. And then she stopped. She began backing away. The fish were still swimming toward her when she threw the net down and splashed toward the shore, shouting to Dana.

The fish followed her until she ran up onto the sand and whirled around to stare back down into the clear water. She looked to Dana, searching for words, but there was nothing she could say as the two girls stood next to one another and watched the fish thrashing and circling— *their eyes fluorescing bright green!*

ALSO BY JOHN LYMAN

"THE GOD'S LIONS SERIES"

THE SECRET CHAPEL

HOUSE OF ACERBI

THE DARK RUIN

REALM OF EVIL

ABOUT THE AUTHOR

John Lyman's thrillers have captured the imaginations of hundreds of thousands of readers around the world, and each new release continues to amaze. His first novel, *God's Lions-The Secret Chapel*, rose quickly to the number one spot on the Kindle bestseller list in several genres and is currently in development for a major motion picture. *The Secret Chapel* was soon followed by three sequels: *House of Acerbi*, *The Dark Ruin*, and *Realm of Evil*, all of which made it to the number one spot in several genres. His much-anticipated new release, *The Deep Green*, is a genetic thriller that is bound to leave readers breathless.

You can contact the author through his website: johnlymanauthor.com